INTERNATIONAL PRAISE FOR
Fever of the Bone

"At a stroke, McDermid is alr_____ns. Hill and Jordan's 'will they, v_____gu- ing in the crime field. . . . M_____ac- celerating tension as authoritatively as she characte_____ ___ ___arge cast. McDermid is a first-rate writer as *Fever of the Bone* resound- ingly reminds us. . . . [McDermid is] at the peak of her profession."
—*The Express*

"About as good a psychological thriller as it is possible to get. . . . *Fever of the Bone* is everything a great detective novel should be: pacey, gripping, clever, and stylish, and, most of all, a fantastic read." —*Sunday Express*

"It takes great skill to handle so many narrative strands with clarity without sacrificing the suspense—but McDermid does so with ap- parent ease." —*Evening Standard*

"A brilliant succession of shocks and surprises. McDermid has never written better." —*The Times*

"Hill's own family crises and his 'will they, won't they' relationship with Jordan are expertly dovetailed into a wonderfully complex plot. McDermid is especially good at serving up a mix of hi-tech and old-fashioned coppering, as well as showing how proximity to extreme brutality can take its toll on even the toughest police officer." —*The Guardian*

"The reader is drawn into a tightly woven plot which keeps you guessing from the word go. If you're already a fan of McDermid, then this is a must-read. If you are new to her work, it is a fine introduction. Highly recommended." —*Sunday Sun*

About the Author

Scottish crime writer VAL MCDERMID is the author of twenty-three novels. Her books have won the Gold Dagger Award for Best Crime Novel of the Year and a Los Angeles Times Book Prize, have been selected for the *New York Times'* 100 Notable Books of the Year list, and have been nominated for the Edgar Award. She lives in the north of England.

FEVER OF THE
BONE

VAL McDERMID

HARPER

NEW YORK · LONDON · TORONTO · SYDNEY

HARPER

Extract from *Collected Poems 1909–1962* by T.S. Eliot (published by Faber and Faber Ltd) reproduced by permission of Faber and Faber Ltd.

First published in Great Britain in 2009 by Little, Brown.

FIRST U.S. EDITION

Library of Congress Cataloging-in-Publication Data is available upon request.

ISBN 978-0-06-198648-2

10 11 12 13 14 RRD 10 9 8 7 6 5 4 3 2 1

For the gallimaufry that is my family, both biological and logical. I may hate camping, but this is one big tent I'm proud to inhabit.

Acknowledgements

Dr Gillian Lockwood sparked the first idea for this book with a chance remark. Kelly Smith made a crucial connection on the beach that opened up all sorts of possibilities. Professor Sue Black was invaluable as ever on all things relating to pathology and identity. Thanks also to Brian and Sue from Huddersfield whose blog of their canal boat trips is the kind of site that makes me love the internet.

I want to thank everyone at Little, Brown who has made this new adventure so satisfying, particularly my unflappable editor, David Shelley. Anne O'Brien the Mistress Yoda of copyediting continues to be. Jane Gregory and her team at Gregory & Co have steered me through choppy waters to safe harbour.

And finally, thanks to Kelly and Cameron, who make me laugh.

No contact possible to flesh
Allayed the fever of the bone

Whispers of Immortality
T.S. Eliot

It all comes down to blood in the end. Some wrongs you can get past. File under lessons learned, dangers to avoid in future. But certain kinds of betrayal need to be answered. And sometimes only blood will do.

Not that you take any pleasure in the killing itself. That would be twisted. And you're not twisted. There's a reason for what you're doing. This is about healing your life. This is about you needing to do this so you can feel better.

People talk a lot about starting over. But not many of them actually do it. They think just moving house or switching jobs or changing lovers will make everything different. But you understand what it really means. Dealing with your list, it's a cleansing. It's like someone going into a monastery and burning their worldly goods, watching what holds them earthbound going up in flames. And once that history has turned to smoke, you can truly start over. A whole new set of aspirations and ambitions. An acceptance of what's possible and what's past.

And this is such perfectly balanced payback. Betrayal matching betrayal, life balancing life, loss corresponding to loss. It feels like liberation when the last breath fades and you can be about your work with the knives and scalpels. And as the blood oozes steadily, you feel like you're finally doing the right thing, the only logical thing you could do in the circumstances. Of course, not everybody will see it like that.

Some might say NOBODY will see it your way. But you know that's not true either. You know other people would applaud you for taking this line if they were ever to find out what you've done, what you're doing. People who've had their dreams trashed like you have. They'd totally get it. And they'd wish they had your resources so they could do the same thing.

If this gets out, you could start a trend.

CHAPTER 1

The vaulted ceiling acted as a giant amplifier for the conversation bouncing round the room. A jazz quartet was putting up a filigree fight, but the competition was too strident. The air was thick with a broth of smells; cooked food, alcohol, sweat, testosterone, cologne and the exhaled breath of a hundred or so people. Not so long ago, cigarette smoke would have deadened most of the human tang, but as publicans had discovered since the ban, people were a lot less fragrant en masse than they liked to think.

There were few women in the room and most of them were toting trays of canapés and drink. As would have happened at this stage of any police retirement do, ties had been loosened and faces had reddened. But the hands that might once have wandered were stilled by the presence of so many senior officers. Not for the first time, Dr Tony Hill wondered how on earth he'd ended up where he was. Probably not for the last time, either.

The woman making her way through the throng towards him was probably the only person in the room he actively wanted to spend any time with. It had been murder that had drawn them together, murder that had led them to their mutual understanding, murder that had taught them respect for each other's mind and morality. Nevertheless, for years now Detective Chief Inspector Carol Jordan had been the single colleague who had crossed the border into what he supposed he'd have to label friendship. Sometimes he conceded to himself that friendship wasn't an adequate word for the bond that held them fast in spite of their complicated history, but even with his years of experience as a clinical psychologist, he didn't think he could come up with an adequate definition. Especially not now, not here in a place he didn't want to be.

Carol was much better than him at avoiding things she didn't want to do. She was also very good at identifying what those were and acting accordingly. But she had actually chosen to be here tonight. For her, it held a significance that Tony couldn't buy into. Sure, John Brandon had been the first senior cop to take him seriously, to lift him out of the world of treatment and research and put him on the front line of live criminal profiling. But if it hadn't been him, it would have been someone else. Tony appreciated Brandon's championing of the value of profiling. But they'd never progressed further than a professional relationship. He would have avoided this evening if Carol hadn't insisted that people would find it odd if he didn't turn up. Tony knew he was odd. Still, he preferred other people not to realise quite how odd. So here he was, a thin smile in place whenever anyone caught his eye.

Carol, conversely, looked born to the breed, slipping easily through the crowd in a shiny dark blue dress that emphasised all the right curves, from shoulders through breasts to hips and calves. Her blonde hair seemed lighter, though Tony knew this was because of the increasing strands of silver among the gold rather than the ministrations of a hairdresser. As she moved through the room, greetings animated her face, lips smiling, eyebrows rising, eyes widening.

Finally she made it to his side, passing him a glass of wine. She took a swig from her own. 'You're drinking red,' Tony said.

'The white's unspeakable.'

He took a wary sip. 'And this is better?'

'Trust me.'

Given how much more she drank than him, it was tempting. 'Are there going to be speeches?'

'The Deputy Chief Constable's saying a few words.'

'A few? That'll be a first.'

'Quite. And as if that's not enough, they've exhumed God's Copper to present John with his gold watch.'

Tony reared back in horror that was only partly an act. 'Sir Derek Armthwaite? Isn't he dead?'

'Sadly not. Since he was the Chief Constable who promoted John up the ranks, they thought it would be a nice touch to invite him along.'

Tony shuddered. 'Remind me not to let your colleagues organise my leaving do.'

'You won't get one, you're not one of us,' Carol said,

smiling to take any sting out of her words. 'You'll just get me taking you out for the best curry in Bradfield.'

Before Tony could say more, a powerful PA blasted through the conversation, introducing the Deputy Chief Constable of Bradfield Metropolitan Police. Carol emptied her glass and slipped away into the crowd, intent on another drink and, he imagined, a little light networking. She'd been a chief inspector for a few years now, most recently running her own crack major incident team. He knew she was torn between using her skills at the sharp end and the desire to reach a level where she could influence policy. Tony wondered whether the choice would be taken from her now John Brandon was out of the picture.

His religion told him that every life held the same value, but Detective Inspector Stuart Patterson had never been able to keep faith with that tenet in his relations with the dead. Some skanky heroin addict knifed in a pointless turf war was never going to move him as much as this dead and mutilated child did. He stood to one side of the sheltering white tent that protected the crime scene from the steady drumbeat of the night's rain. Letting the specialists get on with it, trying to avoid the comparison between this dead girl and his own barely teenage daughter.

The girl who was the centre of attention here could have been one of his Lily's classmates but for the different school uniform. Despite the scatter of leaf mould the wind and rain had plastered over the clear polythene bag covering her face and hair, she looked clean and well cared for. Her mother had reported her missing just after nine, which spoke of a daughter more disciplined about time than Lily and a family that ran to a more regular timetable. It was theoretically possible that this wasn't Jennifer Maidment, since the body had been found before the missing person report had been filed and they didn't have a photograph of the missing girl at the crime scene yet. But DI Patterson didn't think it was likely that two girls from the same city-centre school would go missing on the same night. Not unless one was implicated in the death of the other. These days, you couldn't rule anything out.

The opening of the tent flapped wildly and a slab of a man shouldered his way inside. His shoulders were so broad he couldn't actually fasten the largest protective suit the West Mercia force provided for its officers. Drops of rain clung to a shaven skull the colour of strong tea and drizzled down a face that looked as if much of its misspent youth had happened inside a boxing ring. He clutched a sheet of paper enclosed in a transparent plastic envelope.

'I'm over here, Alvin,' Patterson said, his voice betraying a depth of melancholy hopelessness.

Detective Sergeant Alvin Ambrose picked his way across the prescribed path to his boss. 'Jennifer Maidment,' he said, holding up the envelope to reveal a digital photo printed out on plain paper. 'That her?'

Patterson studied the oval face framed by long brown hair and gave a glum nod. 'That's her.'

'Pretty,' Ambrose said.

'Not any more.' The killer had stolen her beauty as well

as her life. Although he was always careful not to jump to conclusions, Patterson thought it was safe to assume that the congested skin, the engorged tongue, the pop-eyes and the close cling of the polythene bag added up to death by asphyxiation. 'The bag was taped tight round her neck. Bloody awful way to go.'

'She must have been restrained somehow,' Ambrose said. 'Otherwise she'd have tried to claw her way free.'

'No sign of any restraints. We'll know more when they've got her back to the morgue.'

'Was she sexually assaulted?'

Patterson couldn't restrain a shiver. 'He took a knife to her. We didn't see it at first. Her skirt covered it up. Then the doc took a look.' He closed his eyes, giving in to the urge for a swift, silent prayer. 'Bastard butchered her. I don't know that I'd call it sexual assault, as such. Sexual obliteration, more like.' He turned away and moved towards the exit. He chose his words carefully, weighing Jennifer Maidment's body against others whose deaths he had investigated. 'Worst I've ever seen.'

Outside the tent, the weather was atrocious. What had started that afternoon as a flurry of stinging rain driven by blusters of wind had whipped itself up into a full-scale storm. On nights like this, the citizens of Worcester had learned to fear the rising swell of the Severn. Flooding was what they expected, not murder.

The body had been found on the verge of a pull-in that had been created when the main road had been straightened a few years before. The old, tight bend had assumed a new role as a stopping-off point for truckers and van drivers, attracted by the greasy-spoon van that supplied snacks during daylight hours. At night, it served as an unofficial lorry park, usually hosting four or five rigs whose drivers didn't mind roughing it to save a few quid. The Dutch trucker who had climbed out of his cab for a piss that evening had got a lot more than he'd bargained for.

The pull-in was hidden from passing vehicles by a thick copse of mature trees and heavy undergrowth. The gale howled through the trees, soaking Ambrose and Patterson as they jogged back to the Volvo. Once inside, Patterson ticked items off on his fingers as he spoke. 'Get on to Traffic. They've got a couple of number-plate recognition cameras on this road, but I'm not sure where. We need a full run-down on every vehicle that's been down this stretch of road tonight. Get on to Family Liaison. I need one of their officers to meet me at the family home. Get on to the school head. I want to know who her friends are, who her teachers are, and I want interviews set up with them first thing in the morning. Get whoever took the initial report to email me the details. Get on to the press office and brief them. We'll sit down with the hacks tomorrow morning, ten o'clock. OK? Anything I've forgotten?

Ambrose shook his head. 'I'll get on to it. I'll get one of the traffic boys to run me back. You going to the house yourself?'

Patterson sighed. 'I don't relish it. But their daughter's dead. They deserve an SIO. I'll see you back at the ranch.'

Ambrose climbed out and headed towards the police vehicles ranged across the entrance and exit to the pull-in. His boss watched him go. Nothing seemed to daunt Ambrose. He took the weight on his stolid shoulders and ploughed on through whatever their investigations threw at him. Whatever the price of that apparent imperviousness, Patterson would happily have paid it that night.

CHAPTER 2

Carol could tell John Brandon was winding up. His sad bloodhound face was more animated than she'd ever seen it in working hours, and his beloved Maggie was at his side, wearing the indulgent smile Carol had often seen at the family's dinner table when Brandon had been shaking a subject like a terrier with a rabbit. She swapped her empty glass for a full one from a passing waitress and started to head back to the alcove where she'd left Tony. His expression would have been better suited to a funeral, but she couldn't claim to have had higher expectations. She was aware he thought events like this were an empty waste of time and for him she supposed they might be. She knew that where she was concerned it was a different matter.

It wasn't catching criminals that made the world go round in modern policing. It was politics, just as it was in any big organisation. Once upon a time, a night like this would have been an excuse for a no-holds-barred piss-up, complete with strippers. These days, it was about contacts, connections, conversations that couldn't happen in the nick. She didn't like it any more than Tony, but she had a certain gift for it. If this was what it took to make sure she kept her place in the unofficial hierarchy, she'd grin and bear it.

A hand on her arm made her stop and turn. Detective Constable Paula McIntyre from her team inclined her head towards Carol's ear. 'He's just arrived,' she said.

Carol didn't have to ask who 'he' was. John Brandon's replacement was known by name and reputation, but because he came from the other end of the country, nobody in Bradfield had much first-hand information about him. There weren't many officers who transferred from Devon & Cornwall to Bradfield. Why would you want to swap a relatively quiet life in a pretty tourist area for the constant attrition that was policing in a post-industrial northern city with eye-watering rates of violent crime involving guns and knives? Unless of course you were an ambitious copper who thought it would be a good career move to run the country's fourth-largest police force. Carol imagined the word 'challenge' had featured more than once in James Blake's interview for Chief Constable. Her eyes scanned the room. 'Where?'

Paula looked over her shoulder. 'He was giving out to the ACC Crime a minute ago, but he's moved on. Sorry, chief.'

'Never mind. Thanks for the tip-off.' Carol raised her glass in a salute and carried on towards Tony. By the time she'd worked her way through the crowd, her glass was empty again. 'I need another drink,' she said, leaning against the wall beside him.

'That's your fourth glass,' he pointed out, not unkindly.

'Who's counting?'

'I am, obviously.'

'You're my friend, not my shrink.' Carol's voice was icy.

'That's why I'm suggesting you might be drinking too much. If I was your shrink, I wouldn't be nearly so judgemental. I'd be leaving it up to you.'

'Look, I'm fine, Tony. There was a time after . . . I admit there was a time when I was drinking too much. But I'm back in control again. OK?'

Tony held up his hands, palm out, placatory. 'Your choice.'

Carol sighed deeply and put her empty glass on the table next to his. He was maddening when he was this reasonable. It wasn't as if she was the only one who disliked having the fucked-up aspects of her life dragged out into the light of day. *See how he likes it.* She smiled sweetly. 'Shall we go outside for a breath of fresh air, then?'

His smile was puzzled. 'OK, if you want.'

'I've found out some stuff about your father. Let's go somewhere we can talk properly.' She watched his smile shift to a rueful grimace. The identity of Tony's father had only come to light after his death, thanks to his decision to leave his estate to the son he'd never known. Carol knew very well that Tony was at best ambivalent about Edmund Arthur Blythe. He was as keen to talk about his recently discovered father as she was to discuss her putative dependence on alcohol.

13

'Touché. Let me get you another drink.' As he picked up the glasses, his path was blocked by a man who emerged from the press of bodies and stood four square before them.

Carol gave him her routine assessing stare. Years ago, she'd developed the habit of forming mental descriptions of people who crossed her path, assembling a picture in words as if it was destined for a 'wanted' poster or a police artist. This man was short for a police officer, burly without being fat. He was neatly barbered, the white line of a side parting dividing the light brown hair. His skin was the ruddy pink and white of a foxhunter from the shires, hazel eyes nested in fine lines that indicated late forties or early fifties. A small bulb of a nose, full lips, and a chin like a ping-pong ball; he had an air of authority that wouldn't have seemed out of place in an ancient Tory grandee.

She was also well aware that she was coming under the same acute scrutiny. 'Detective Chief Inspector Jordan,' he said. A rich baritone with a faint race memory of West Country speech. 'I'm James Blake. Your new Chief Constable.' He thrust a hand out for Carol to shake. It was warm, broad and dry as paper.

Just like his smile. 'Pleased to meet you, sir,' Carol said. Blake's eyes never left her face, and she had to break away from his gaze to introduce Tony. 'This is Dr Tony Hill. He works with us from time to time.'

Blake glanced at Tony and inclined his chin in passing acknowledgement. 'I wanted to take this opportunity to break the ice. I'm very impressed with what I've heard of your work. I'm going to be making changes round here,

14

and your bailiwick is one of my priorities. I'd like to see you tomorrow morning at ten thirty in my office.'

'Of course,' Carol said. 'I look forward to it.'

'Good. That's settled, then. Till tomorrow, Chief Inspector.' He turned and shouldered his way back through the crowd.

'Extraordinary,' Tony said. It might have meant any of a dozen things, all of which would have been equally valid. And not all of them insulting.

'Did he really say "bailiwick"?'

'Bailiwick,' Tony said weakly.

'That drink? I really need it now. Let's get out of here. I've got a very nice bottle of Sancerre in the fridge.'

Tony stared after Blake. 'You know that cliché about being afraid, very afraid? I think this might be a good time to wheel it out.'

The Family Liaison Officer, Shami Patel, explained that she'd recently transferred from the neighbouring West Midlands force, which explained why Patterson didn't know her. He'd rather have had someone who was familiar with the way he worked. It was always tough to deal with the family of murder victims; their grief made them react in unpredictable and often hostile ways. This case would be doubly difficult. Partly because the sexual homicide of a teenager was an emotional horror in itself. But in this case, there was the added difficulty posed by the time frame.

They sheltered from the rain in Patterson's car while he briefed her. 'We've got more problems than usual with this case,' he said.

'Innocent victim,' Patel said succinctly.

'It goes beyond that.' He ran his fingers through his silver curls. 'Usually, there's a gap between somebody like this going missing and us finding the body. We've got time to get background from the family, information about the missing person's movements. People are desperate to help because they want to believe there's a chance of finding the kid.' He shook his head. 'Not this time.'

'I'm with you,' Patel said. 'They've not even got used to the idea of her being missing and we're walking in to tell them she's dead. They're going to be devastated.'

Patterson nodded. 'And please don't think I'm not sympathetic to that. But for me, the difficulty is that they're not going to be in a fit state to interview.' He sighed. 'The first twenty-four hours of a murder inquiry, that's when we need to make progress.'

'Have we got a note of what Mrs Maidment said when she reported Jennifer missing?'

It was a good question. Patterson extracted his Black-Berry from his inside pocket, found his reading glasses and pulled up the email Ambrose had forwarded from the duty officer who had taken Tania Maidment's phone call. 'She phoned it in rather than come down to the station,' he said, reading from the small screen. 'She didn't want to leave the house empty in case Jennifer came back and found herself locked out. Jennifer had a key but her mother didn't know whether she'd have it with her. Mother hadn't seen her since she left for school in the morning . . .' He scrolled down. 'She was supposed to be going to a friend's house for tea and homework, should have been back by eight, no problem because her and her

16

pal often did that at one house or the other. Mum cut her a bit of slack, rang the friend's house at quarter past. The friend hadn't seen her since the end of school, no arrangement for tea or homework. Jennifer hadn't said anything about any plans other than going to the Co-op then heading home. And that's when Mrs Maidment calls us.'

'I so hope we took her seriously,' Patel said.

'Thankfully, we did. DC Billings took a description and circulated it to all units. That's how we identified the body so quickly. Let's see . . . Age fourteen, 165 centimetres, slim build, shoulder-length brown hair, blue eyes, pierced ears with plain gold sleepers. Wearing Worcester Girls' High uniform – white blouse, bottle green cardigan, skirt and blazer. Black tights and boots. She had a black mac over her uniform.' To himself, he added, 'That's not at the crime scene.'

'Is she an only child?' Patel asked.

'No idea. No idea where Mr Maidment is either. Like I said, it's a bitch, this one.' He sent a quick text to Ambrose, instructing him to interview the friend Jennifer had claimed to be with, then closed down the BlackBerry and rolled his shoulders inside his coat. 'We ready?'

They braved the rain and walked up the path of the Maidments' family home, a three-storey Edwardian brick semi fronted by a well-tended garden. The lights were on inside, the curtains pulled wide open. The two cops could see the sort of living room and dining room that neither of them could afford, all gleaming surfaces, rich fabrics and the kind of pictures you didn't find in IKEA. Patterson's finger had barely hit the bell push when the door swung open.

The state of the woman on the doorstep would have provoked a reaction in any other circumstances. But Patterson had seen enough frantic mothers to be unsurprised by the wild hair, the smudged eye make-up, the bitten lips and the tight clench of the jaw. As she took in the pair of them with their hangdog faces, her puffy eyes widened. One hand went to her mouth, the other to her breast. 'Oh God,' she said, her voice tremulous with the tears that were about to come again.

'Mrs Maidment? I'm Detective Chief Inspector—'

The rank told Tania Maidment what she didn't want to know. Her wail cut Patterson off in mid-introduction. She staggered and would have fallen had he not moved rapidly towards her, an arm round her slumped shoulders, letting her collapse into him. He half-carried her into the house, DC Patel at their heels.

By the time he lowered her into the plump living-room sofa, Tania Maidment was shaking like a woman on the edge of hypothermia. 'No, no, no,' she kept saying through chattering teeth.

'I'm so sorry. We've found a body we believe to be your daughter, Jennifer,' Patterson said, casting a desperate glance at Patel.

She picked up his cue and sat down by the distraught woman, taking her freezing hands in her own warm ones. 'Is there someone we can call?' she said. 'Someone who can be with you?'

Mrs Maidment shook her head, jerky but clear. 'No, no, no.' Then she gulped air as if she was drowning. 'Her dad . . . He's due back tomorrow. From India. He's already flying. He doesn't even know she's missing.' Then the tears came with a terrible storm of guttural sobs. Patterson had never felt more pointless.

He waited for the first barrage of grief to lessen. It seemed to last a hellish length of time. Eventually, Jennifer's mother ran out of energy. Patel, keeping her arm round the woman's shoulders, nodded almost imperceptibly at him. 'Mrs Maidment, we're going to need to take a look at Jennifer's room,' Patterson said. Heartless, he knew. There would be a forensic team there soon to strip the place properly, but he wanted first dibs on the dead girl's private space. Besides, the mother might be in bits now, but it wasn't unusual for parents to leap to the realisation that there might be elements of their children's lives they didn't want the world to know about. It wasn't that they wanted to impede the investigation, more that they didn't always understand the importance of things they considered irrelevant. Patterson didn't want that to happen here.

Without waiting for a response, he slipped out of the room and headed upstairs. Patterson thought you could gauge a lot about the condition of family life from its environment. As he climbed, he made his own judgements about Jennifer Maidment's home. There was a gloss to the place that spoke of money, but it lacked the sterility of obsession. A splay of opened mail was scattered on the hall table, a pair of discarded gloves lay on the shelf above the radiator, the vase of flowers on the windowsill of the half-landing needed winnowing.

Five closed doors faced him as he reached the first floor. A home where privacy was respected, then. First came the master suite, then a family bathroom, then a study. All

19

in darkness, not giving many of their secrets away. The fourth door revealed what he was looking for. He breathed in the scent of Jennifer Maidment's life for a moment before turning on the light – peach sweetness with a note of citrus scored through it.

It felt disarmingly similar to his daughter's room. If he'd had the money to let Lily have her head, he suspected she'd have ended up choosing the same sort of pink and white and pastel décor and furniture. Posters of boy bands and girl bands, dressing table a jumble of attempts at getting the make-up right, a small bookcase with novels he'd seen lying around his own living room. He assumed the pair of doors in the far wall led to a walk-in wardrobe which would be crammed with a mix of practical and fashionable items. Time enough for the SOCOs to go through all that. What he was interested in was the dressing table and the small desk tucked into one corner.

Patterson snapped a pair of latex gloves over his hands and started to work his way through the drawers. Bras and pants, fussy and frilly but pitiful in their essential innocence. Tights, a few pairs of socks rolled into tight balls, concealing nothing. Camisoles and spaghetti-strapped tops, T-shirts rendered improbably skinny by lycra. Cheap earrings, bracelets, pendants and necklaces arranged neatly in a tray. A bundle of old Christmas and birthday cards that Patterson scooped up and put to one side. Someone would need to go through those with Mrs Maidment when she was able to focus on something beyond her grief.

Nothing else caught his interest so he moved to the desk. The must-have Apple laptop was closed, but

Patterson could see from the indicator light that it was hibernating rather than turned off. The latest iPod was connected to the computer, its headphones in a tangled bundle next to it. Patterson unplugged the computer from the mains, wrote an evidence receipt for it and tucked it under his arm. A quick glance round the room to confirm that he hadn't missed anything obvious, then he went back downstairs.

Mrs Maidment had stopped crying. She sat upright, eyes on the floor, hands clenched in her lap, tears still glistening on her cheeks. Without lifting her eyes, she said, 'I don't understand how this could happen.'

'None of us does,' Patterson said.

'Jennifer doesn't lie about where she's going,' she said, her voice dulled and thickened by pain. 'I know everybody thinks their kids don't lie, but Jennifer really doesn't. Her and Claire, they do everything together. They're always here or at Claire's house or out together. I don't understand.'

Patel patted Mrs Maidment's shoulder. 'We'll find out, Tania. We'll find out what happened to Jennifer.'

Patterson wished he had her confidence. Heartsick and weary, he sat down and prepared to ask questions he suspected would mostly be in vain. Still, they had to be asked. And the answers weighed for truth and lies. Because there would be both. There always was.

CHAPTER 3

Carol hadn't lied. The Sancerre was delicious, tangy with the taste of gooseberries, cool and crisp. Even so, Tony wasn't in the mood for more than gentle sipping. If Carol was going to offer up information about his father in the spirit of a dog dropping a soggy newspaper at the feet of its human, he wanted to keep his wits about him.

Carol settled herself on the sofa opposite the armchair Tony had chosen. 'So, don't you want to know what I've found out about your father?'

Tony avoided her eyes. 'He wasn't my father, Carol. Not in any meaningful sense.'

'Half of your genetic inheritance comes from him. Even the most behavioural of psychologists has to admit that counts for something. I thought you'd want to find out all you could about him.' She swallowed a mouthful of wine and smiled encouragingly at him.

Tony sighed. 'I've managed to live all my life without knowing anything about my father except that he chose not to be in my life. If you hadn't had your wits about you and stepped in when my mother was trying to cheat me out of what he left me in his will, I'd still be none the wiser.'

Carol gave a snort of laughter. 'You make it sound like you wish I hadn't stopped Vanessa ripping you off.'

He thought she'd seldom come up with a more inspired guess. But that day in the hospital when she'd stopped Vanessa in her twisted tracks, Carol had been looking out for what she thought were his best interests. To suggest that she'd inadvertently created more problems than she'd solved would only hurt her. And he didn't want to do that. Not now. Not ever. 'I'm not being ungrateful for what you did. I'm just not sure I want to know anything about him.'

Carol shook her head. 'You just don't want to dismantle all the defences you've built up over the years. But it's OK, Tony. Vanessa might be a monster, but from what I've been able to find out, your father was the opposite. I don't think there's anything to be afraid of.'

Tony swirled the wine round his glass, his shoulders hunched defensively. One corner of his mouth twitched upwards in a bitter smile. 'There's got to be something, Carol. He walked away from me. And her, incidentally.'

'Maybe he didn't know about you.'

'He knew enough about me to leave me a house and a boat and a wedge of cash.'

Carol considered. 'If you're going to take his money, I think you owe him something.'

She had a point, he thought. But if the price of maintaining his ignorance was giving his inheritance to charity, it might be worth paying. 'I think he took a long time to make any contribution to what he owed me. I don't think the money even begins to touch it. He left me with Vanessa.' Tony put down his glass and clasped his hands tight. He spent much of his working life helping patients negotiate the treacherous shoals of their emotions. But all his listening had done nothing to ease the process for himself. Though he'd learned to construct the appropriate reactions for most social situations, he still didn't trust himself to come up with the correct emotional responses in the highly charged context of personal relationships. If he was ever going to fail at what he called passing for human, this was where it would happen. And yet, Carol deserved more from him than silence or flippancy. He drew himself together, shoulders rigid. 'You and me, we both know how fucked up I am. I don't blame Vanessa for what she did to me. She's as much a product of her environment and her genes as I am. But there's no doubt in my mind that she's a big part of the reason why I fit so badly in the world.'

'I don't think you're such a bad fit,' Carol said.

Kindness, he thought, trumping candour. 'Maybe so, but you've had at least a bottle of wine tonight,' he said, the attempt at humour too heavy-handed to survive the distance between them. She glared and he shrugged an apology. 'He could have mitigated my mother's impact and he didn't. Money all these years later doesn't begin to pay the debt.'

'He must have had his reasons. Tony, he really does sound like a decent man.'

He got to his feet. 'Not tonight. I'm not ready for this. Let me think about it, Carol.'

Her smile was forced. He knew her expressions in all their variety and he read the disappointment in this one. No matter that he'd helped her score success after success in her professional life; when it came to their personal relationship, he sometimes thought disappointment was all he'd ever left her with.

Carol emptied her glass. 'Till the next time,' she said. 'It'll keep.'

He sketched a little wave and made for the stairs that separated her basement flat from his house above. As he turned to say goodnight, he saw her smile soften. 'I know you,' she said. 'Sooner or later, you'll have to know.'

Alvin Ambrose wrestled his warrant card from the inside pocket of his jacket as he approached the house. He knew that his size, his colour and the fact that it was after ten o'clock would all conspire against him in the eyes of the people who lived in this 1970s 'executive detached'. Better to have the ID front and centre when the door opened.

The man who answered the doorbell was frowning at his watch. Then he made great play of peering at Ambrose's warrant card. 'What time of night do you call this?'

Ambrose bit back the smart-arsed retort and said, 'Mr David Darsie? Detective Sergeant Ambrose from West Mercia. I'm sorry to trouble you, but we need to speak to your daughter Claire.'

The man shook his head, sighing in an extravagant pantomime of incredulity. 'I don't believe this. Are you bothering us at this hour because Jennifer Maidment's out late? It's barely half past ten.'

Time to put the jerk in his place. 'No, sir,' Ambrose said. 'I'm bothering you at this hour because Jennifer Maidment's been murdered.'

David Darsie's expression shifted from irritation to horror as swiftly as if he'd been slapped. 'What? How can that be?' He looked over his shoulder as if expecting some fresh nightmare to appear there. 'Her mother only rang a while ago.' He ran his hand over his thinning dark hair. 'Jesus. I mean . . .' He swallowed hard.

'I need to talk to your daughter,' Ambrose said, moving closer to the open door.

'I don't know . . . This is incredible. How can . . . My God, Claire's going to be devastated. Can't this wait till morning? Can't you let us break it to her gently?'

'There is no gentle way. Sir, I need to talk to Claire tonight. This is a murder inquiry. We can't afford to waste time. The sooner I can talk to Claire, the better for our investigation. I'm very happy for both you and your wife to sit in on our conversation, but it needs to be tonight.' Ambrose knew he appeared obdurate to people who didn't know his weaknesses. When it came to moving an investigation forward, he was happy to use whatever means he had available. He lowered his voice, turning it into the dark rumble of tanks rolling down a street. 'Now. If you don't mind.' His foot was across the threshold and Darsie had no option but to back up.

'Come in,' he said, waving towards the first door on the right.

Ambrose led the way into a cosy living room. The furniture looked worn but comfortable. A shelf unit was stacked with DVDs and board games, an apparently random pile of kids' toys occupied the corner between one sofa and the widescreen TV. A coffee table was strewn with Meccano and a stack of children's books leaned against the end of the other sofa. The room was empty and Ambrose looked expectantly at Darsie.

'Sorry about the mess,' he said. 'Four kids, and we're all congenitally untidy.' Ambrose tried not to judge the man too harshly for caring about the state of the room when he'd just heard his daughter's best friend had been killed. He knew shock provoked unpredictable and off-kilter reactions.

'Your daughter?'

Darsie nodded vigorously. 'Just a minute, I'll get Claire and her mum.'

It took so little time for Darsie to return with his wife and daughter that Ambrose knew the cowardly bastard hadn't broken the news himself. Claire, skinny and waif-like in a fluffy white towelling dressing gown over flannel PJs and shocking pink Crocs, was still aiming for the aloof teenager look, while her mother looked tired rather than appalled. All three hovered by the door, waiting for Ambrose to take charge.

'Please, sit down,' he said, giving them a few moments to arrange themselves on the sofa. 'I'm sorry to disturb you, but it's important.'

Claire shrugged. 'Whatever. It's no big. Just 'cos Jen's busted her halo and stayed out late.'

Ambrose shook his head. 'I'm sorry, Claire. It's a lot worse than that.'

The panicked look hit her fast. These days, given what they saw online and on TV, it didn't take long to make the leap. Any pretence at insouciance had vanished before Ambrose could say anything further. 'Oh my God,' Claire wailed. 'Something really bad's happened to her, hasn't it?' Her hands flew to her face, fingers digging into her cheeks. She threw herself at her mother, who instinctively put a protective arm round her.

'I'm afraid so,' Ambrose said. 'I'm sorry to have to tell you that Jennifer died earlier this evening.'

Claire shook her head. 'I don't believe you.'

'It's true. I'm really sorry, Claire.' He braced himself as the girl burst into tears.

'Give us a minute,' her mother said, shock flushing her pink and white. 'Please.'

Ambrose left them to it. He sat on the stairs, waiting. People thought being a copper was all action – car chases and slamming suspects up against walls. They didn't understand that patience was what it was all about. Patterson got it. That was one of the reasons Ambrose liked his boss. Patterson didn't transfer the pressure from above for results to his team. It wasn't that he lacked a sense of urgency, just that he believed some things took their own time.

Ten minutes passed before David Darsie slipped out of the living room. 'They need a bit longer. Can I get you a brew?'

'Coffee, please. Black, two sugars.'

He nursed the coffee for a further ten minutes before Mrs Darsie joined him. 'She's very upset,' she said. 'So am I, come to that. Jennifer's a lovely girl. They've been best friends since primary. The Maidments are like a second family to Claire. Same with Jennifer. They were always together, here or at Jennifer's, or off out at the shops or whatever.'

'That's why Claire's such an important witness for us,' Ambrose said. 'If anybody knows what Jennifer had planned for this evening, it's likely to be your daughter. Talking to me is the best thing she can do for her friend now.'

'She understands that. She's just pulling herself together now, then she'll talk to you.' Mrs Darsie put a hand to her face, cupping her chin and cheek. 'God, poor Tania. She was an only child, you know. Tania and Paul had been trying for ages before Jennifer came along and they doted on her. Not that they spoilt her or anything. They were quite strict. But you only had to watch them with her to see how invested they were in her.'

'We were wondering where Mr Maidment was tonight,' Ambrose said, making the most of her apparent willingness to discuss the Maidments.

'He's been in India. He owns a company that makes machine tools, he's been out there drumming up business, trying to keep going through the credit crunch.' Her eyes swam with tears. 'He won't even know about this, will he?'

'I really couldn't say,' Ambrose said gently. 'My colleagues are with Mrs Maidment now, helping her through. They'll figure out the best way to get in touch with Mr Maidment.' He put a warm hand on Mrs Darsie's elbow. 'Do you think Claire might be able to talk to me now?'

Claire was curled in a tight ball on the sofa, face flushed and eyes puffy with tears. Shrunk into herself, she looked a lot younger than fourteen. 'You said Jennifer died,' she said as soon as Ambrose walked in. 'You mean somebody killed her, don't you?'

'I'm afraid so,' Ambrose said, sitting opposite her as her mother adopted a protective pose again. 'I'm sorry.'

'Did they . . . Did she . . . Did they hurt her? I mean, obviously they hurt her, they killed her, right. But was it, like, torture?' Her need for reassurance was obvious. Ambrose didn't generally lie to witnesses, but sometimes it was the most humane course of action.

'It would have been over very quickly,' he said, the low rumble of his voice a comfort in itself.

'When did it happen?' Claire asked.

'We can't be sure yet. When did you see her last?'

Claire took a deep breath. 'We came out of school together. I thought she was coming round here because we had some biology course work to do and we usually do science stuff here because my dad's a chemistry lecturer and he can, like, help us when we get stuck with stuff. But she said no, she was going home on account of her dad is coming home tomorrow and she wanted to make a cake. Sort of, welcome home, kind of thing.'

'That's nice. Did she usually do something special like that when her dad had been away?'

Claire shrugged. 'I don't know, really. I don't remember

her doing anything like that before, but I never paid much attention. He's always going away, her dad. Sometimes just for a couple of nights, but lately he's been away for weeks at a time.'

'It's because of the economies in China and India,' her mother interrupted. 'He needs to exploit the new markets, that's why he's been away so much.'

Ambrose wished Claire's mother would keep out of it. He always tried to get interviews to flow like a conversation. That was the best way to get people to reveal more than they intended. He hated it when other people broke across that flow. 'And that's all Jennifer said about her plans? That she was going home to bake a cake?'

Claire frowned, reaching back into her memory. 'Yeah. I was a bit miffed that she didn't say anything before. Because we've got this thing about not letting each other down. "Friends don't let each other down," that's, like, our slogan. I mean, she didn't even ask me to come back with her and help.'

'So, at the time, you thought it was a bit strange? Jennifer just announcing this out of the blue?'

'Kind of.' Claire nodded. 'I mean, no big, right? Just kind of not like her. But I wasn't going to fall out with her about it, you know? She wanted to do something nice for her dad, that's her business.'

'Where did you actually say goodbye to her?'

'Well, we didn't say goodbye. Not as such. See, we're at the bus stop and the bus arrives and I get on first, then Jennifer goes, "I forgot, I need to get chocolate for the cake, I need to go to the Co-op." There's this little local Co-op five minutes' walk from school, see? So I'm on the

31

bus already and she's pushing past people to get off and the next thing I see is her walking past the bus, down towards the Co-op. And she waves to me, all smiley. And she goes, like, "See you tomorrow." Well, that's what it looked like she was saying.' Claire's face crumpled and tears spilled down her cheeks. 'That's the last I saw of her.'

Ambrose waited while her mother stroked Claire's hair and gentled her back to composure. 'Sounds like Jennifer wasn't herself tonight,' he said. 'Acting a bit out of character, was she?'

Claire shrugged one shoulder. 'I don't know. Maybe, yes.'

Ambrose, the father of a teenage son, recognised this as adolescent-speak for 'absolutely'. He gave her a small confiding smile. 'I know you don't want to say anything that feels like you're letting Jennifer down, but there's no room for secrets in a murder investigation. Do you think she could have been going to meet somebody? Somebody she was keeping secret?'

Claire sniffed and wiped her nose with the back of her hand. 'She'd never keep anything like that from me. No way. Somebody must have got her on her way to the Co-op. Or on her way home after.'

Ambrose let it go. There was nothing to be gained by making Claire hostile to the investigation. 'Did you guys hang out online together?'

Claire nodded. 'We mainly used to go online at her house. She's got a better computer than me. And we talk all the time, instant messaging and texting and stuff.'

'Do you use a social networking site?'

Claire gave him a 'well, duh' look and nodded. 'We're on Rig.'

Of course you are. A few years back, it had been MySpace. That had been overtaken by Facebook. Then RigMarole had come along with an even more user-friendly front end, with the added bonus of free downloadable voice recognition software. You didn't even have to be able to type now to access a global community of like-minded peers and well-camouflaged predators. Ambrose tried to keep tabs on his own kids and their online circles, but he knew he was fighting a losing battle. 'Do you happen to know Jennifer's password? It would really help us if we could access her profile and messages as quickly as possible.'

Claire gave a quick sideways look at her mother, as if she had secrets of her own she didn't want to reveal. 'We had this kind of code. So nobody could guess. Her password was my initials, plus the last six digits of my mobile. Like, CLD435767.'

Ambrose keyed the code into his mobile. 'That's amazingly helpful, Claire. I'm not going to bother you much longer, but I need to ask you: did Jennifer ever talk about anybody she was scared of? Anybody she felt threatened by? It could be an adult, it could be somebody at school, a neighbour. Anybody at all.'

Claire shook her head, her face crumpling in misery again. 'She never said anything like that.' Her voice was piteous, her expression desolate. 'Everybody liked Jennifer. Why would anybody want to kill her?'

CHAPTER 4

Carol couldn't believe how quickly John Brandon's presence had been erased from his former office. His décor had been muted and unobtrusive, a single family photograph and an elaborate coffee machine the only real clues to the man himself. James Blake was clearly cut from a different cloth. Leather armchairs, an antique desk and wooden filing cabinets provided a faux country house feel. The walls were hung with unmissable pointers to Blake's success – his framed degree certificate from Exeter, photographs of him with two prime ministers, the Prince of Wales, a scatter of home secretaries and minor celebrities. Carol wasn't sure whether this was vanity or a warning shot across the bows of Blake's visitors. She'd reserve judgement till she knew him better.

Blake, looking buffed and spruce in his dress uniform, waved Carol to one of the tub chairs in front of his desk.

Unlike Brandon, he didn't offer tea or coffee. Or pleas-antries, it turned out. 'I'll get straight to the point, Carol,' he said.

So that was how it was going to be. No fake building of bridges, no pretence at common ground between them. It was evident to Carol that the use of her name wasn't the first step on the road to camaraderie, just a firm attempt at diminishing her by refusing to acknowledge her rank. 'I'm glad to hear it, sir.' She resisted the impulse to cross her arms and legs, choosing instead to mirror the openness of his pose. Some things had rubbed off from all those years of hanging around with Tony.

'I've looked at your record. You're a brilliant police offi-cer, Carol. And you've built a first-class team around you.' He paused, expectant.

'Thank you, sir.'

'And therein lies the problem.' Blake's mouth turned up in a smile that indicated how pleased he was at his own cleverness.

'We've never viewed our success as a problem,' Carol said, knowing that wasn't quite the response he'd been looking for.

'I understand the terms of engagement for your team are that you investigate major crime on our patch that doesn't come under the remit of any of the national squads?'

Carol nodded. 'That's right.'

'But when you're between major crimes, you investi-gate cold cases?' He couldn't hide his disdain.

'We do. And we've had some notable successes there too.'

'I don't dispute that, Carol. What I dispute is whether your talents are best deployed on cold cases.'

'Cold cases are important. We speak for the dead. We bring closure to the families and we bring people to justice after they've stolen years from society.'

Blake's nostrils flared, as if some unpleasant odour had wafted his way. 'Is that what your friend Dr Hill says?'

'It's what we all think, sir. Cold cases matter. Their impact on the public isn't negligible either. They help people to realise how committed the police service is to solving major crime.'

Blake took out a small box of breath mints and popped one in his mouth. 'All of that's true, Carol. But frankly, cold cases are for plodders. Carthorses, Carol, not thoroughbred racehorses like you and your team. It's perseverance that solves them, not the kind of brilliance you and your team bring to bear.'

'I'm afraid I don't agree with your assessment, sir.' She couldn't quite grasp why she was growing so angry. Only that she was. 'If it was that simple, these cases would have been resolved a long time ago. It's not just about applying new forensic techniques to old cases. It's about coming at the cases from fresh angles, about thinking the unthink-able. My crew are good at that.'

'That may be. But it's not an effective use of my budget. Your team represents a stupendous level of investment. You have a range and level of skills and knowledge that should be devoted to solving current cases. Not just major crimes, but other serious matters that cross the desks of CID. The people we serve deserve the best possible policing. It's my job to provide that in the most cost-effective way possible. So I'm putting you on notice, Carol. I'm going to leave things as they are for the time being, but your team will be coming under close examination. You're on trial. In three months' time, I'm going to make a decision based on a rigorous scrutiny of your caseload and your results. But I'm warning you now: all my instincts are to reabsorb you into the mainstream of CID.'

'Sounds like you've already made your mind up, sir,' Carol said, forcing herself to sound pleasant.

'It's up to you, Carol.' This time, the smile was undeniably smug. 'And one other thing – while we're on the subject of budget? You seem to commit a lot of money to consulting Dr Hill.'

Now the stirring of anger was rising to a flare. 'Dr Hill has been a key component in how we achieve our success,' she said, unable to avoid sounding terse.

'He's a clinical psychologist, not a forensic scientist. His expertise is replicable.' Blake opened a drawer and took a folder from it. He glanced at Carol as if surprised that she was still there. 'The National Police Faculty has been training police officers in behavioural science and profiling. Using their resources is going to save us a fortune.'

'They don't have Dr Hill's expertise. Or his experience. Dr Hill is unique. Mr Brandon always thought so.'

There was a long silence. 'Mr Brandon isn't here to protect you any more, Carol. He may have thought it was appropriate to pay your . . .' he paused and when he spoke again, it was freighted with innuendo '. . . *landlord* such a large chunk of Bradfield Police's budget. I don't. So if you need a profiler, use one who doesn't make us look corrupt, would you?'

Patterson could feel the first throb of a headache deep in his skull. It was hardly surprising; he'd had a scant two hours' sleep. Viewers who saw him on TV could be forgiven for thinking their TVs had been swapped for black-and-white sets, what with his silver hair and grey skin. Only the red eyes would be the giveaway. He'd had enough coffee to kick-start a Harley Davidson but even that hadn't helped him look like a man you'd want running your murder inquiry. There was nothing more dispiriting than holding a press conference with nothing to give other than the bare facts of the crime itself.

Maybe they'd get lucky. Maybe the media coverage would shake loose a witness who had noticed Jennifer Maidment after she'd waved farewell to her best friend. That would surely be the triumph of hope over experience. What was more likely was a stream of fantasy sightings, most of them delivered in good faith but just as useless as the attention seekers and the unfathomable bastards who simply liked to waste police time.

As the reporters filed out, he went in search of Ambrose. He found him looming over their tame forensic computer analyst. Gary Harcup had been dragged out of his bed just after midnight and put to work on Jennifer's laptop. Ambrose barely glanced up at his boss then turned back to the screen, screwing up his tired brown eyes to help him focus. 'So what you're telling me is that all of these sessions originated on different machines? Even though it says it's the same person talking to Jennifer?'

'That's right.'

'Well, how can that be?' Ambrose sounded frustrated.

'I'm guessing whoever was talking to Jennifer was using internet cafés and libraries. Never the same place twice.' Gary Harcup shared bulk with Alvin Ambrose, but that was all. Where Ambrose was taut, polished and muscular, Gary was plump, rumpled and bespectacled with a mop of tousled brown hair and matching beard. He looked like a cartoon bear. He scratched his head. 'He's using a free email address, impossible to trace. None of the sessions lasts more than half an hour, nobody is going to pay any attention to him.'

Patterson pulled up a chair. 'What's going on, lads? Have you got something for us, Gary?'

But it was Ambrose who replied. 'According to Claire Darsie, her and Jennifer used RigMarole all the time. And Gary here's been able to pull up a whole stack of their chat room and IM sessions.'

'Anything useful?' Patterson leaned forward so he could see the screen more easily. A whiff of fresh soap came from Ambrose, making Patterson feel ashamed of his own unwashed state. He'd not stopped to shower, settling for a swift pass of the electric shaver over his face.

'There's a lot of rubbish,' Gary said. 'The usual teenage chatter about *X Factor* and *Big Brother*. Pop stars and soap actors. Gossip about their mates from school. Mostly they're talking to other kids from their class, but there are some outsiders from other areas of RigMarole. Generally other girls of their age into the same boy bands.'

'I hear a "but",' Patterson said.

'You hear right. There's one that's a bit different,' Ambrose said. 'Trying to fit the mould but hitting the occasional bum note. Cagey about revealing anything that might pin them down geographically. Can you show us, Gary?'

Gary's fingers fluttered over the keys and a string of message exchanges started to scroll down the screen. Patterson read attentively, not quite sure what he was looking for. 'You think it's paedophile grooming?'

Ambrose shook his head. 'It doesn't feel like that. Whoever it is, they're drawing Jennifer and her buddies out, making friends. Usually with paedos, they're trying to cut one out of the herd. They play on general insecurities about looks, weight, personality, just not being cool enough. That's not happening here. It's much more about showing solidarity. Being one of the group.' He tapped the screen with his finger. 'It's not exploitative in any way.'

'And then it gets really interesting,' Gary said, scrolling down so fast the messages turned into a blur of text and smileys. 'This was five days ago.'

Jeni: Wot do u mean, zz?
ZZ: Evry1 has secrets, things theyr ashamd of. Things u'd die if ur crew new about.
Jeni: I don't. My best friend nos everything about me.
ZZ: Thats wot we all say and we all lying.

'The others weigh in and it turns into a general conversation,' Gary said. 'But then ZZ pulls Jennifer into a private IM session. Here we go.'

ZZ: i wanted 2 talk 2 u in priv8.

Jeni: Y?

ZZ: cuz i no u hav a BIG secret.

Jeni: U no more than me then.

ZZ: sumtimes we dont no wot our own secrets r. Bt i no a secret tt u wd not want anybody else to no.

Jeni: I don't no wot u r on about.

ZZ: b online 2moro same time & we'll talk abt it sum more.

'And that's where that session ends,' Gary said.

'So what happened the next day?' Patterson said.

Gary leaned back in his chair and rumpled his hair. 'That's the problem. Whatever ZZ had to say to Jennifer was enough to make her wipe the conversation.'

'I thought there was no such thing as wiping a computer's memory, short of hitting the hard disk very hard with a hammer,' Patterson said. The headache was bedding in now, a deep dull throb beating between his ears. He squeezed the bridge of his nose tight, trying to shut down the pain.

'That's about the size of it,' Gary said. 'Doesn't mean it's accessible at the click of a mouse, though. I'm assuming this lass didn't have a clue how to scrub her machine clean. But even so, I'm going to have to push a shedload of software through this baby to try and retrieve what she's tried to erase.'

'For fuck's sake,' Ambrose groaned. 'How long's that going to take?'

Gary shrugged, his whole chair moving with him. 'Piece of string, innit? I might crack it in a few hours, but it could take days.' He spread his hands in a gesture of helplessness. 'What can I say? It's not like servicing a car. There's no way I can give you a meaningful estimate.'

'Fair enough,' Patterson said. 'Can we just go back to where I came in? You were telling Alvin these sessions all came from different computers? Is there any way to find out where those computers are?'

Gary shrugged, then laced his fingers together and cracked his knuckles. 'Theoretically, but there's no guarantee. There's websites that hold the details of individual computers' IDs. But machines change hands.' He pulled the corners of his mouth down like a sad clown. 'Still, there's a fair chance you can track down some of them.'

'At least that way we might get some idea of where this bastard's based,' Patterson said. 'That also needs to be a priority for us now. Can you deal with that as well as analysing the computer? Or do we need to bring in some support?'

If Gary had been a dog, the ruff of hair at the back of his neck would have been standing erect. 'I can manage,' he said. 'While the programs are running on Jennifer's machine, I can start looking up the computer IDs.'

Patterson stood up. 'Fine. But if it's taking too long, we'll get you some help on the donkey work.'

Gary glowered at him. 'None of this is donkey work.'

Patterson managed not to roll his eyes. 'No, of course not. Sorry, Gary. No offence.' He resisted the temptation to pat him on the shoulder as he would his family's pet mongrel. He stood up. 'Alvin, a word?'

Out in the corridor, Patterson leaned against the wall, the lack of progress feeling like a physical weight on his shoulders. 'This is going bloody nowhere,' he said. 'We've not got a single witness. She got off the bus but never made it as far as the Co-op. It's like Jennifer Maidment vanished into thin air somewhere between the bus stop and the shop.'

Alvin's mouth twisted up in one corner and dropped down again. 'That's if she was ever going to the Co-op.'

'What do you mean? According to you, Claire Darsie said Jennifer was going to the Co-op to buy chocolate for her dad's cake. She saw her walking in that direction. Jennifer waved to her.'

'Doesn't mean she was telling the truth,' Ambrose said, his face impassive. 'Just because she started off walking that way doesn't mean she kept on going. Claire said the whole thing was out of character. So maybe Jennifer had other plans. Plans that had bugger all to do with the Co-op. Or her dad's cake. Maybe there wasn't a cake at all.'

'You think she was meeting somebody?'

Ambrose shrugged. 'You've got to wonder what would be important enough to make a teenage girl lie to her best mate. Generally, that comes down to a lad.'

'You think she realised the gatecrasher on Rig was a bloke?'

'I don't know. I doubt she was that sophisticated. I think she went to learn more about this so-called "secret".'

Patterson sighed. 'And until Gary works his magic, we don't have a bloody clue what that might be.'

'True. But in the meantime, it wouldn't hurt to have a chat with Mum and Dad. Find out if there were ever any plans for a cake.'

CHAPTER 5

Daniel Morrison had been indulged from well before the moment he'd been born. It would have been hard to imagine a child more wanted and neither expense nor consideration had been spared in the effort to make his life the very best it could be. During her pregnancy, his mother Jessica had forsworn not only alcohol and saturated fat but also hairspray, dry cleaning, deodorant and insect repellent. Everything that had ever been accused of being potentially carcinogenic had been banned from Jessica's environment. If Mike came home from the pub smelling of cigarette smoke, he had to strip off in the utility room then shower before he could come near his pregnant wife.

When Daniel emerged from his elective caesarian section with a perfect Apgar score, Jessica felt justified in every preventative step she'd taken. She didn't hesitate to share that belief with anyone who would listen and quite a few who wouldn't.

The drive to perfection didn't end there. Daniel's every stage of development was accompanied by the age-appropriate educational toys and other forms of stimulus. By four, he was enrolled in the best private prep school in Bradfield, encased in grey flannel shorts, shirt and tie, maroon blazer and a cap that wouldn't have looked out of place in the 1950s.

And so it continued. Designer clothes and fashionable haircuts; Chamonix in the winter, Chiantishire in the summer; cricket whites and rugby jerseys; Cirque du Soleil, classical concerts and theatre. Whatever Jessica thought Daniel needed, Daniel had. Another man might have put the brakes on. But Mike loved his wife – his son too, obviously, but not the way he adored Jessica – and so he chose the route that made her happiest. As she indulged Daniel, so he indulged her. He'd been lucky enough to get in on the ground floor of the mobile phone business back in the early nineties. There had been times when it had felt like the legendary licence to print money. That Jessica knew how to spend it had therefore never been an issue.

What was slowly beginning to dawn on Mike Morrison was that his fourteen-year-old son was not a very nice person. In recent months, it had become clear that Daniel was no longer happy to accept whatever Jessica decided was best for him. He was developing his own ideas about what he wanted, and the sense of entitlement that Jessica had bred into him meant he wasn't happy to settle for anything less than the prompt and total fulfilment of his desires. There had been some spectacular arguments, most of which had ended with Jessica in tears and Daniel in voluntary exile in his suite of rooms, sometimes refusing to emerge for days at a time.

It wasn't the arguments that bothered Mike, in spite of Jessica's frustration and anger. He recalled similar rows in his own teens as he'd tried to assert himself in the teeth of parental opposition. What made him anxious was a suspicion that was hardening to a certainty that he didn't have a clue what was going on in his son's head.

He remembered being fourteen. His concerns had been pretty simple. Football, both watching and playing; girls, both real and imagined; the relative merits of Cream and Blind Faith; and how long it would be before he could wangle himself into a party where there was alcohol and dope. He hadn't been a goody two-shoes and he'd been convinced that his own drift away from his parents' expectations would help forge a connection when Daniel hit adolescence.

He couldn't have been more wrong. Daniel's response to Mike's attempts at bonding by sharing had been a shrug, a sneer and a complete refusal to engage. After one too many rebuffs, Mike had reluctantly accepted that he had no idea what was going on inside his son's head or his life. Daniel's dreams and desires, his fears and his fantasies, his passions and his proclivities were unfathomable to his father.

Mike could only guess at what occupied his son during the long hours they were out of each other's presence. And because he didn't like what his imagination conjured for him, he'd chosen to try not to think about it at all. He guessed that was entirely fine by Daniel.

He couldn't have guessed that it was also just fine by his killer.

Some meetings were better held outside the workplace. Carol had always known it by instinct; Tony had provided her with a rational explanation. 'Take people off their territory and it blurs hierarchies. They're slightly off-balance but they're also trying to show off, to make their mark. It makes them more creative, more innovative. And that's essential in any unit where you want to keep ahead of the game. Keeping things fresh and inventive is one of the hardest things to achieve, especially in hierarchical organisations like the police.'

In a team like theirs, staying ahead of the curve was even more crucial. As James Blake had so pointedly reminded her, elite units were invariably under closer scrutiny than routine departments. Developing new initiatives that proved effective was one straightforward way to disarm their critics. Now the pressure was heavier than ever, but Carol trusted her crew to fight for their roles as hard as she would herself. Which was why she was taking orders for drinks in the private karaoke room of her favourite Thai restaurant.

More than that, she was practising something else she'd learned from Tony: choices and the way they're made have the potential for revelation, even in the smallest degree. So this was a chance for her to check perceptions against knowledge, to see whether the things she thought she knew about her team were corroborated by what they chose and how they chose it.

Stacey Chen had been a no-brainer. In the three years they'd been working together, Carol had never known their ICT wizard to drink anything other than Earl Grey tea. She carried individual sealed sachets in her stylish leather backpack. In bars and clubs whose drinks menu didn't stretch to tea, she demanded boiling water and added her own bag. She was a woman who knew exactly what she wanted and, once she'd figured out what that was, she was utterly uncompromising about getting it. Her consistency also made it difficult to gauge her state of mind. When someone never wavered in their preferences, it was impossible to figure out whether they were stressed or elated, especially when they were as good at keeping things hidden as Stacey. It felt uncomfortably like racial stereotyping, but there was no denying that Stacey managed inscrutable better than anyone Carol had ever known.

After all this time she still had almost nothing to add to the bare facts of Stacey's CV. Her parents were Hong Kong Chinese, successful entrepreneurs in the wholesale and retail food business. Rumour was that Stacey herself had made millions from selling off software she'd developed in her own time. She certainly dressed like a millionaire, with tailoring that looked made to measure, and there was an occasional flash of arrogance in her demeanour that showed another facet to her quiet diligence. If it hadn't been for her brilliance with technology, Carol had to acknowledge she would not have chosen to work at close quarters with someone like Stacey. But somehow mutual respect had developed and turned their connection fruitful. Carol couldn't imagine her team now without Stacey's flair.

DC Paula McIntyre was clearly weighing up her options, probably wondering if she had the chutzpah to order a proper drink. Carol reckoned Paula would reject the thought, needing her boss's good opinion more than she craved alcohol. *Right again.* Paula opted for a Coke. There was an unspoken bond between Paula and her boss; the job had inflicted damage on them both that went far beyond the normal experience of front-line police officers. In Carol's case, the injury had been compounded by the treachery of the very people she should have been able to count on. It had left her bitter and angry, close to quitting. Paula too had considered leaving the job, but in her case the issue had not been betrayal but unreasonable guilt. What they had in common was that their route back to comfort in their chosen profession had been mapped out with Tony Hill's help. In Carol's case, as a friend; in Paula's, as an unofficial therapist. Carol was grateful on both counts, not least because nobody was better at extracting information from an interview than Paula. But if she was honest, there had been a niggle of jealousy in there too. *Pathetic,* she chided herself.

And then there was Kevin. It occurred to Carol that, now John Brandon had retired, DS Kevin Matthews represented her longest professional relationship. They'd both worked the first serial killer investigation Bradfield Police had run. Carol's career had skyrocketed as a result; Kevin's had imploded. When she'd returned to Bradfield to set up the MIT, she'd been the one to give him a second chance. *He's never entirely forgiven me for that.*

All those years and still she couldn't buy him a drink without checking what his fancy was. One month it would be Diet Coke, the next black coffee, then hot chocolate. Or, in the pub, it would be cask-brewed real ale, or ice-cold German lager or a white-wine spritzer. She still wasn't sure if he was easily bored or easily swayed.

Two members of the team were absent. Sergeant Chris Devine was lying on some Caribbean beach with her partner. Carol hoped her thoughts were a million miles from murder, but knew that if Chris had an inkling of what was going on here she'd jump on the first flight home. Like all of them, Chris loved what she did.

The final member of the team, DC Sam Evans, was unaccountably missing. Carol had either told or texted them all about the meeting, but none of the others seemed to know where Sam was. Or what he was pursuing. 'He took a call first thing then he grabbed his coat and left,' Stacey had said. Carol was surprised she'd even noticed.

Kevin grinned. 'He can't help himself, can he? The boy could take Olympic gold in paddling your own canoe.'

And this isn't the time for demonstrating that the MIT isn't so much a team as a collection of bloody-minded individuals who sometimes end up looking like a line-dancing set by accident. Carol sighed. 'I'll go and order the drinks. Hopefully he'll be here soon.'

'Get him a mineral water,' Kevin said. 'Punishment.'

As he spoke, the door opened and Sam hurried in, a computer CPU under one arm and a self-satisfied look on his face. 'Sorry I'm late, guv.' He swung the bulky grey box out and brandished it in front of his chest like the Wimbledon Men's Singles plate. 'Ta-da!'

Carol rolled her eyes. 'What is it, Sam?'

'Looks like a generic PC box, probably early to mid-nineties, given it's got a slot for a five-inch floppy as well as a three-and-a-half-inch one,' Stacey said. 'Tiny memory by today's standards, but enough for basic functions.'

Paula groaned. 'That's not what the chief means, Stacey. What's it all about, that's what she's on about.'

'Thank you, Paula, but I've not quite been rendered speechless by Sam's arrival.' Carol touched Paula's shoulder and smiled, taking the sting out of her words. 'As Paula says, Sam, what's it all about?'

Sam plonked the CPU down on a table and patted it. 'This little baby is the machine that Nigel Barnes swore didn't exist.' He pointed a finger at Stacey. 'And this is your chance to put him away for his wife's murder.' He folded his arms across his broad chest and grinned.

'I still have no idea what this is about,' Carol said, knowing this was what she was meant to say and already halfway to forgiving Sam for his late arrival. She knew Sam's tendency to go out on a limb was dangerous and bad for solidarity, but she found uncomplicated anger hard to sustain. Too many of his divisive characteristics were precisely the ones that had driven Carol so hard at the start of her own career. She just wished he'd get past the naked ambition stage and realise you didn't always travel fastest when you were alone.

Sam tossed his jacket over a chair and perched on the table beside the computer. 'Cold case, guv. Danuta Barnes and her five-month-old daughter went missing in 1995. Disappeared without a single validated sighting. The feeling at the time was that her husband Nigel had done away with them.'

'I remember it first time around,' Kevin said. 'Her family were adamant that he'd killed her and the baby.'

'Spot on, Kevin. He didn't want the kid, they'd been fighting constantly about money. CID searched the house top to bottom, but they didn't turn up a single bloodstain. No bodies. And enough gaps in the wardrobe to back up his story that she'd just done a runner with the baby.' Sam shrugged. 'Can't blame them, they covered all the bases.'

'Not quite all of them, by the looks of it,' Carol said, a wry twist to her lips. 'Come on, Sam, you know you're dying to tell us.'

'It came across my desk six months ago, just a routine review. I went round to see Nigel Barnes, but it turned out the file wasn't up to date. He sold the house just over a year ago. So I asked the new owners if they'd come across anything unusual when they'd been doing the place up.'

'Did you know what you were looking for?' Kevin asked.

Sam tipped his head to him. 'I did, as it happens. Back in '97, some eagle-eyed SOCO noticed that the computer monitor and keyboard didn't match the CPU. Different make, different colour. Nigel Barnes swore blind that's how he'd bought it, but the Stacey wannabe knew he was lying because the monitor and keyboard came from a mail-order brand that only sold complete packages. So at some point, there had to have been another CPU. I wondered whether the hard drive was still knocking around somewhere. But the new owners said no, the house had been stripped bare. Tight bastard even took the lightbulbs and the batteries out of the smoke alarms.'

He pulled a clown's face of sadness. 'So I thought that was that.'

'Until your phone rang this morning,' Paula chipped in. By now, they all knew how and when to prompt each other through their war stories.

'Correct. Turns out the new owners decided to tank the cellar, which meant ripping off all the old plasterwork. And guess what was hiding behind the plasterboard?'

'Not the old computer!' Paula threw up her hands in mock amazement.

'The old computer.' Sam caught Stacey's eye and winked. 'And if it's got any secrets to reveal, we all know who's the woman to find them.'

'I can't believe he didn't destroy it,' Kevin said, his carrot-red curls catching the light as he shook his head.

'He probably thought he'd wiped the hard disk clean,' Stacey said. 'Back then, people didn't understand how much data gets left behind when you reformat the drive.'

'Even so, you'd think he would take it with him. Or dump it in a skip. Or give it to one of those charities that recycles old computers to Africa.'

'Laziness or arrogance. Take your pick. Thank God for them both, they're our best friends.' Carol stood up. 'Nice job, Sam. And we're going to need as many of those as we can muster over the next three months.' Their expressions ranged from bewilderment to resignation. 'Our new Chief Constable thinks MIT is too much of a luxury. That we don't earn our keep because anybody can deliver results in the cold cases we work on when we're not totally occupied with live jobs. That our talents should be at the service of the whole CID across the piece.'

The immediate response was a tangle of exclamations, none of them offering Blake's position a shred of support. Their voices died away, leaving Sam's, 'Twat,' to bring up the tail.

Carol shook her head. 'Not helpful, Sam. I don't want to go back to being part of a routine CID squad any more than any of you do. I like working with you all, and I like the way we structure our investigations. I like that we can be creative and innovative. But not everybody appreciates that.'

'That's the trouble with working for an organisation that rewards respect for the pecking order. They don't like legitimised individualism,' Paula said. 'Misfit outfits like us, we're always going to be in the firing line.'

'You'd think they'd appreciate our clear-up rate,' Kevin complained.

'Not when it makes them look less efficient,' Carol said. 'OK. We have three months to demonstrate that MIT is the most effective vehicle to achieve the things we do best. I know you all give a hundred per cent on every inquiry we take on, but I need you to find something extra to help me justify our existence.'

They exchanged looks. Kevin stood up, pushing his chair back. 'Never mind the drinks, guv. Better get cracking, hadn't we?'

CHAPTER 6

The rain was still teeming when Alvin Ambrose arrived to pick up his boss from the postmortem on Jennifer Maidment. Any chance of garnering trace evidence from the crime scene was long gone. The only source of physical information about Jennifer's fate was the girl's body itself. DI Patterson trotted to the car, head down and shoulders hunched against the sharp sting of the rain, and threw himself into the passenger seat. His face was scrunched up in disgust, blue eyes almost invisible between lids swollen from lack of sleep. Ambrose wasn't sure if the disgust was because of the weather or the autopsy. He nodded to the coffee carton in the cup holder. 'Skinny latte,' he said. Not that Patterson needed anything to make him skinnier.

Patterson shuddered. 'Thanks, Alvin, but I've not got the stomach for it. You have it.'

'How did it go?' Ambrose asked, easing the car towards the car park exit.

Patterson yanked on his seat belt and stabbed it into its slot. 'It's never good, is it? Especially when it's a kid.'

Ambrose knew better than to press for more. Patterson would take a few moments to compose himself, assemble his thoughts, then he'd share what he thought his bagman ought to know. They reached the main road and Ambrose paused. 'Where to?'

Patterson considered, never one to leap to judgement. 'Anything new come in while I've been in there?'

There had been plenty, a ragbag of bits and pieces signifying not a lot. Stuff that was going nowhere, bits and pieces that officers way down the totem pole would have eliminated by teatime. One of Ambrose's roles in their partnership was to sift through what came in and decide what was worth Patterson's attention. It was a responsibility he'd been apprehensive about when Patterson had first picked him out for his bagman, but he'd soon learned he had judgement worth trusting. That Patterson had known this ahead of him only cemented Ambrose's respect for his boss. 'Nothing that needs your attention,' Ambrose said.

Patterson sighed, his hollow cheeks puffing in and out. 'Let's go and see the parents, then.'

Ambrose turned into the traffic and summoned up a mental map of the best route. Before he'd made the first turning, Patterson began talking. It was, Ambrose thought, quick off the mark for his boss. A measure of how heavy Jennifer Maidment was weighing on his spirit.

'Cause of death was asphyxiation. The polythene bag over her head, it was taped tight to her neck. No sign of a struggle at all. No blow to the head. No scratches or bruises, no blood or skin under her fingernails.' His voice was leaden, the words slow and deliberate.

'Sounds like she was drugged.'

'Looks that way.' Patterson's face altered as anger replaced depression. Two dark flushes of colour tinted his cheeks and his lips were tight against his teeth. 'Of course, it'll be fucking weeks before we get the toxicology results. I tell you, Alvin, the way we do forensic science in this country, it's a joke. Even the crappy old NHS is faster. You go to the GP for a full set of blood tests and you get the results, what, forty-eight hours later? But it takes anything up to six weeks to deliver a toxicology result. If the bloody politicians really want to deter criminals and up the detection rate, they should throw money at the forensic services. It's insane that we can only afford the technology in a tiny percentage of cases. And even when the accountants let us have some access, it takes fucking for ever. By the time we get the results, nine times out of ten all it does is back up what we've already pulled off with old-fashioned coppering. The forensics should be there to help the investigation, not just to confirm we've arrested the right villain. That *Waking the Dead*? And *CSI*? I sit there in front of the telly and it's like some horrible black comedy. One episode and I'd have used up my entire budget for a year.'

It was a familiar rant, one of several that Patterson trotted out whenever he felt frustrated with a case. Ambrose understood that it wasn't really about whatever his boss was criticising. It was about what Patterson saw as his failure to deliver the sort of progress that might help the grieving families with their pain. It was about being fallible. And there was nothing Ambrose could say that would make either of them feel better about that. 'Tell me about it,' was all he said. There was a long pause while he gave Patterson time to compose himself. 'So what else did the doc have to say?'

'The genital mutilation was apparently the work of an amateur. A long-bladed knife, very sharp. Probably not anything exotic – could have been a carving knife.' Patterson made no attempt to disguise his revulsion. 'He inserted the blade into the vagina and twisted it round. The doc reckons he might have been trying to cut out the whole lot – vagina, cervix, uterus. But he didn't have the skill for it.'

'So we're probably not looking for someone with medical knowledge,' Ambrose said, calm and apparently imperturbable as ever. But under the surface, he felt the slow build of a familiar dull anger, a rage he'd learned to contain as a teenager when everyone assumed that a big black lad was always going to be up for a fight. Because when he gave in to it, the fact that he was a big black lad meant he was always going to be in the wrong, one way or another. Better to burn inside than end up taking the weight of everybody else's need to prove themselves. And that included teachers and parents. So he'd learned to box, learned to put the power of his fury under the discipline of the ring. He could have gone all the way, everyone said so. But he'd never enjoyed the demolition of his opponents enough to want to make a living out of it.

'The doc said he wouldn't even ask this one to carve a bloody turkey.' Patterson sighed.

'Any signs of sexual assault?' Ambrose signalled to turn into the Maidments' street. He knew how Patterson adored his Lily. There would be no mercy, no pity in this hunt if the killer had raped his victim too.

'Impossible to tell. No anal trauma, no sperm in her mouth or throat. If we get really lucky, there might be something in the samples that have gone to the lab. But don't hold your breath.' The car drew to a halt. When they caught sight of him, the lounging pack of journalists came to life and surrounded the door. 'Here we bloody go,' he muttered. 'Neither use nor ornament, most of them.' Patterson shouldered his way through the throng, followed by Ambrose. 'I've got no further comment,' he muttered.

'Give the family a break,' Ambrose said, spreading his arms to keep them at bay as his boss approached the house. 'Don't make me waste our time getting the uniformed guys down here to move you away. You back off now, we'll see what we can do about sorting out a press call with them, OK?' He knew it was a pointless request, but at least they might try and make themselves a little less conspicuous for a while. And his bulk did sometimes carry its weight in these situations.

By the time he got to the door, Patterson was already halfway inside. The man holding the door would probably pass for handsome in other circumstances. His hair was thick and dark, shot through with silver. His features were regular, his blue eyes had that slight downward angle that seemed to appeal to women. But today, Paul Maidment had the gaunt and haunted look of a man one step away from life on the streets. Unshaven, hair awry and clothes crumpled, he looked blankly at them through red-rimmed eyes as though he'd lost his grip on all the conventions of behaviour. Ambrose couldn't begin to imagine what it must be like to step off a plane thinking you're about to be reunited with your family only to discover that your life has been shattered beyond repair.

Shami Patel hovered behind Maidment. She made the introductions. 'I'm sorry I didn't get the door, I was in the kitchen making tea,' she added. Ambrose could have told her Patterson didn't care for excuses, but this wasn't the time.

They filed into the living room and sat down. 'We could all use some tea, Shami,' Ambrose said. She nodded and left them.

'I'm sorry I wasn't at the airport to meet you myself,' Patterson said. 'I had matters to attend to. Concerning Jennifer's death, you understand.'

Maidment shook his head. 'I've no idea what you people do, I just want you to get on with it. Find the person who did this. Stop them wrecking another family.' His voice caught and he had to clear his throat noisily.

'How's your wife?' Patterson said.

He coughed. 'She's . . . The doctor's been. He's given her something to knock her out. She managed to hold it together till I got home, but then . . . well, it's better that she's out of it.' He spread his hand over his face and gripped tight, as if he wanted to rip his face off. His voice came at them slightly muffled. 'I wish she could stay out of it for ever. But she'll have to come back. And when she does, this'll still be here.'

'I can't tell you how sorry I am,' Patterson said. 'I've a

daughter about the same age. I know what she means to me and my wife.'

Maidment dragged his fingers down his face and stared at them, tears spilling from his eyes. 'She's our only child. There won't be any more, not at Tania's age. That's it for us, this is where it ends. We used to be a family, now we're just a couple.' His voice cracked and shivered. 'I don't know how we get past this. I don't understand this. How could this happen? How could somebody do this to my girl?'

Carrying a tray loaded with steaming mugs, milk and sugar, Shami returned. 'Tea,' she said, handing round the drinks. It was a mundane moment that broke the mood and made it possible for Patterson to move the interview forward.

'According to Claire, Jennifer said she was planning to bake you a cake to welcome you home. That she had to go to the Co-op to get some chocolate for it. Was that something she usually did? Made a cake for you coming home?' Patterson said gently.

Maidment looked baffled. 'She'd never done it before. I didn't even realise she knew how to bake a cake.' He bit his lip. 'If she hadn't done that, if she'd just gone to Claire's like she was supposed to . . .'

'We're not convinced she was telling Claire the truth,' Patterson said, his voice gentle. Ambrose had always been impressed with Patterson's care for those left in the shadows of violent death. The only word he could think to apply to it was 'tender'. Like he was conscious of how much damage they'd already taken and didn't want to add to it. He could be tough, asking questions Ambrose would have struggled with. But underneath it, there was always a consideration of other people's pain. Patterson let his words sink in, then continued. 'We wondered if she was using that as an excuse so Claire wouldn't ask too many questions about where Jennifer was really going. But we had to check with you. To see if it was the kind of thing she did when you'd been away.'

Maidment shook his head. 'She'd never done anything like that. We usually went out for a celebration dinner if I'd been away for more than a couple of nights. All three of us. We'd go for a Chinese. It was always Jennifer's favourite. She never baked me a cake.' He shivered. 'Never will now.'

Patterson waited for a few moments, then said, 'We've been looking at Jennifer's computer. It seems she and Claire spent a lot of time online, both together and separately. Did you know about that?'

Maidment clutched his drink like a man possessed by cold. He nodded. 'They all do it. Even if you wanted to stop them, they'd still find a way. So we got together with the Darsies and insisted on the girls' computers having all the parental controls on. It restricts where they can go and who can get to them.'

Up to a point, thought Ambrose. 'She used RigMarole a lot,' he said, picking up the baton of the questioning. He and Patterson had been working together so long they didn't even have to discuss their tactics in advance. They knew instinctively how to let things flow between them. 'The social networking site. Did she ever talk to you about it?'

Maidment nodded. 'We're very open as a family. We try not to be heavy-handed with Jennifer. We've always made a point of talking things through, explaining the reasons why we don't let her do something or why we don't approve of some behaviour or other. It kept the lines of communication open. I think she talked to us more than most teenagers. At least, judging by what our friends and my colleagues say about their kids.' As often happened with the abruptly bereaved, talking about his dead daughter seemed to shift Maidment to a place where he could briefly disconnect from his grief.

'So what did she have to say about RigMarole?' Patterson said.

'They liked it, her and Claire. She said they'd made a lot of online buddies who're into the same TV programmes and music. I've got a page on RigMarole myself, I know how it works. It's a very straightforward way of making connections with people who share your interests. And their filters are very good. It's easy to shut somebody out of your community if they don't fit or they're breaking the boundaries you're comfortable with.'

'Did she ever mention someone with the initials Zed Zed? Or maybe Zee Zee?' Ambrose asked.

Maidment ran a finger and thumb across his eyelids then rubbed the bridge of his nose. He took a deep breath and exhaled. 'No. I'm pretty sure she didn't. You'd be better off asking Claire about that level of detail. Why are you asking? Has this person been stalking her?'

'Nothing like that, as far as we can see,' Ambrose said. 'But we recovered some message sessions between them. It looks as if ZZ was suggesting he or she knew some secret Jennifer had. Did she say anything like that to you or your wife?'

Maidment looked bewildered. 'I've no idea what you're talking about. Look, Jennifer isn't some wild child. She leads a pretty sheltered life, to tell you the truth. She's hardly ever given us a minute's worry. I know you've heard all that before, parents trying to make out their kid was a little angel. I'm not saying that. I'm saying she's stable. Young for her years, if anything. If she had a secret, it wouldn't be the sort of thing you're thinking about. Drugs, or sex, or whatever. It would have been a crush on some lad, or something silly like that. Not the sort of thing that gets you murdered.' The word brought reality crashing back down on Maidment, crushing him all over again. The tears began to creep down his cheeks. Without a word, Shami reached for a box of tissues and pressed a couple into his hand.

There was nothing else useful to be learned here, Ambrose thought. Not today. Maybe never. He glanced across at Patterson, who nodded almost imperceptibly.

'I'm sorry,' Patterson said. 'We'll be on our way now. I want you to know that we're throwing everything we've got at this. But we still need your help. Maybe you could ask your wife if Jennifer said anything about this ZZ. Or about secrets.' He stood up. 'If there's anything you need, DC Patel here will sort you out. We'll be in touch.'

Ambrose followed him from the house, wondering how long it would be before Paul Maidment could get through five minutes without thinking of his murdered daughter.

CHAPTER 7

Tony surveyed his living room, reflecting that it was a convenient proof of the second law of thermodynamics: entropy increases. He wasn't quite sure how it happened, but piles seemed to accumulate whenever his back was turned. Books, papers, DVDs and CDs, console games and controllers and magazines. All of these were more or less comprehensible. But the other stuff – he had no idea how that had gravitated there. A cereal box. A Rubik's cube. A small pile of red rubber bands. Six mugs. A T-shirt. A tote bag from a bookshop he was sure he'd never visited. A box of matches and two empty beer bottles he couldn't remember buying.

For a brief moment, he thought about tidying up. But what would be the point of that? Most of the chaos didn't belong anywhere specific in the house, so he would just be shifting the mess to another room. And all of them already had their own particular brand of disarray. His study, his bedroom, the spare room, the kitchen and the dining room were each the repository of a particular aspect of his turmoil. The bathroom wasn't bad. But then, he never spent time there that wasn't strictly functional. He'd never been one for reading on the toilet or working in the bath.

When he'd bought this house, he'd thought there was enough room to absorb his stuff without it spilling over into these uncontrollable little nests of miscellany. He'd had the whole house painted a sort of off-white bone colour and he'd even gone out and bought a job lot of framed black-and-white photographs of Bradfield's cityscape that he found both soothing and interesting. For about two days the house had looked quite stylish. Now he wondered if there might perhaps be scope for a Parkinson's Law of Thermodynamics: entropy expands to fill the space available.

He'd been so convinced that he had more than enough space that his first decision on moving in had been to convert the surprisingly light and spacious basement into a self-contained flat. He'd imagined letting it out to academics spending a sabbatical at Bradfield University, or junior doctors doing a six-month stint at Bradfield Cross Hospital. Nobody long-term, nobody who would impinge on his life.

Instead, he'd ended up with Carol Jordan as his tenant. It hadn't been planned. She'd been living in London at the time, holed up in a cool and elegant flat in the Barbican, holding the world at bay. A couple of years before, when John Brandon had persuaded her to return to front-line police work, she'd been reluctant to sell her London flat and commit to buying a place in Bradfield. Perching in Tony's basement was supposed to be temporary. But it had turned out to be an arrangement that suited them strangely well. They were careful enough of each other not to impose. But knowing the other was at hand was comforting. At least, he thought it was.

He decided against clearing up. It would only revert to type within days anyway. And he had better things to do. Theoretically, working only part-time at Bradfield Moor Secure Hospital was supposed to provide Tony with enough free time to work with the police and to read and write the articles and books that helped him stay connected with the community of his colleagues. In practice, there were never enough hours in the day, especially when he factored in the time he spent playing computer games, an indulgence he genuinely believed freed up his subconscious creativity. It was amazing how many apparently intractable problems could be solved after an hour adventuring with Lara Croft or building a medieval Chinese kingdom.

Things had grown worse lately, thanks to Carol. She'd had the brilliant idea that a Wii would help him eliminate the limp he still carried after an attack from a patient had left him with a shattered knee. 'You spend too long hunched over a computer,' she'd said. 'You need to get fit. And I know there's no point in trying to persuade you to go to the gym. At least a Wii will get you off your backside.'

She'd been right. Too right, unfortunately. His surgeon might have given the thumbs-up to the amount of time Tony now spent lumbering round his living room playing tennis, bowling and golf or indulging in surreal games against weirdly dressed rabbits. But Tony had a feeling her approval wouldn't be matched by the editors whose deadlines he was in serious danger of missing.

He was about to destroy the chief rabbit in a shoot-out on the streets of Paris when he was interrupted by the intercom that Carol had installed between her basement flat and his house above.

'I know you're there, I can hear you jumping,' her voice crackled. 'Can I come up or are you too busy pretending to be Bradfield's answer to Rafa Nadal?'

Tony stepped away from the screen with barely a pang of regret and pressed the door-release button. By the time Carol joined him, he'd replaced the game controllers on their charger and poured a couple of glasses of sparkling water. Carol took hers, looking sceptical. 'Is this the best you can do?'

'Yes,' he said. 'I need to maintain my fluid balance.' He walked past her, back towards the living room, his move calculated to make resistance easier.

'I don't. And I've had the kind of day that deserves a treat.' Carol stood her ground.

Tony kept on walking. 'And yet you came here, knowing I'm trying to help you move away from drinking so much. Your actions are saying the opposite of your words.' He looked over his shoulder and grinned at her, trying to take the sting out of thwarting her. 'Come on, sit down and talk to me.'

'You're wrong.' Clearly grumpy now, Carol followed him and plonked herself down on the sofa opposite his chair. 'I'm here because I have something important to talk to you about. Not because deep down I want to not have a drink.'

'You could have asked me to come down to your flat. Or to meet you somewhere that serves alcohol,' Tony pointed out. Finding the arguments was tedious, but helping her back to a point where she genuinely didn't need a drink was the best way he knew of demonstrating how much he cared for her.

Carol threw her hands in the air. 'Give me a break, Tony. I really do have something important to discuss.' It sounded like she meant it.

Another good reason why he wanted her to stop leaning on alcohol. Her need for a drink masked so many other things – something genuinely important to share with him, a truly difficult day – and that made it hard to read her. And not being able to read her was something he found very hard to bear. Tony leaned back in his chair and smiled, his blue eyes twinkling in the pool of light cast by a nearby reading lamp. 'Go on then. I'll stop being your nagging friend and revert to interested colleague. Has this got anything to do with your meeting with your new boss, by any chance?'

Carol's answering smile was sardonic. 'Got it in one.' She swiftly laid out the ultimatum James Blake had given her team. 'It's so unrealistic,' she said, frustration obviously gnawing at her composure. 'We're entirely at the mercy of what comes up over the next three months. Am I supposed to be wishing for some tasty murders, just so that I can show off how good my team is? Or fake evidence to clear up a few high-profile cold cases? You can't apply some time-and-motion study to a specialist investigative unit.'

'No, you can't. But that's not what's going on here. He's already made his mind up. This trial period's bogus, for precisely the reasons you've laid out.' Tony scratched his head. 'I think you're screwed. So you might as well just do things exactly as you would anyway.'

He saw her shoulders slump. But she knew better than to come to him for anything less than honesty. If they started down that road, the trust they'd spent years building would crumble faster than overcooked meringue. And since neither of them had anyone else in their life as close as the other, they couldn't afford that. 'That's what I'm afraid of,' she sighed. She took a long drink from her water glass. 'But that's not all.' She stared down into her glass, the thick tumble of her hair hiding her face.

Tony closed his eyes momentarily, rubbing the bridge of his nose. 'He's told you to stop using me.'

Galvanised by his acuity, Carol's neck straightened and her startled eyes met his. 'How did you know that? Has Blake spoken to you?'

Tony shook his head. 'It's the dog that didn't bark in the night.'

Carol nodded, getting it. 'He didn't speak to you. I introduced you, he didn't engage.'

'Which I took to mean that I'm not part of his budget or his plans.' He smiled. 'Don't worry about me, there's plenty of other chief constables who still think I'm money well spent.'

'I'm not worried about you, I'm worried about me. And my team.'

He spread his hands in the equivalent of a shrug. 'It's

hard to fight a man who reduces everything to the maximum bangs for his buck. The truth is, I'm not the cheapest option, Carol. You're turning out your own profilers these days. Your bosses think it's better to go down the American route – train cops in psychology – rather than rely on specialists like me who know nothing about the realities of policing the streets.' Only someone who knew him as well as Carol could have detected the subtle edge of irony in his tone.

'Yeah, well, you get what you pay for.'

'Some of them are pretty good, you know.'

'How do you know?'

He chuckled. 'I'm one of the people who's been training them.'

Carol looked shocked. 'You never said.'

'It was supposed to be confidential.'

'So why are you telling me now?'

'Because if you have to work with them, you should know they've had the benefit of input from some of the most experienced profilers around. Not just me, other people in the same field who I've got a lot of time for. And these bright young officers have not had their knowledge cluttered up by having to decide on treatment regimes. They're very focused on one aspect of psychology, and they're not stupid. Give them a chance. Don't dismiss them because they're not me.' There was another layer of meaning to his words which they both understood. Unfortunately for Tony, it wasn't a good time to remind Carol of the bond between them that underpinned all their professional ventures.

She covered her eyes with her hand, like a woman

shielding herself from the sun. 'Blake was really snide, Tony. He implied that my reasons for choosing to consult you are grubby and corrupt. He knows that I'm your tenant, and he made it sound like there was more to it than that, that we had something sordid to hide.' She turned her head away and drank more water.

It was hard to understand why a man in Blake's position would choose to undermine one of his most effective officers before he'd even seen for himself what she was capable of. But undermine her he had, and he couldn't have chosen a more effective pressure point if he'd consulted Tony himself. With any other pair of people who shared their history, the assumption that they were lovers would probably have been right on the money. But the emotional bond they'd shared from the earliest days of their professional connection had never spilled over into the physical. Right from the start, he'd levelled with her about the impotence that had consistently blighted his relationships with women. She'd had the good sense not to decide she was the woman who could redeem him. But in spite of their unspoken agreement to keep their feelings on a limited leash, there had been times when the forces pulling them together had seemed strong enough to overcome his fear of humiliation and her anxiety that she wouldn't be able to hide her disappointment. But each time, the world had thrown obstacles in their path. And given the atrocities that were commonplace in their world, those were not obstacles that could be overcome lightly. He'd never forget the one time she'd let her guard slip because of him, and the darkness it had unleashed. For a while, it had looked as if she could never make her way back from that particular abyss. That she had was, he believed, no thanks to him and everything to do with the power the job had over her. Tony doubted whether Blake knew anything real about their history, but the gossip factory had provided him with enough information to use him against her. He hated that that was possible. 'Stupid bastard,' Tony said. 'He should be making alliances, not alienating the likes of you.' He gave a thin smile. 'Not that there are many like you.'

She shifted in her seat. He thought she probably wished she smoked so she would have something to occupy herself with. 'Maybe it's time I thought about moving out. I mean, we both only ever meant it to be temporary. While I decided if I wanted to be back in Bradfield.' She raised one shoulder in a half-shrug. 'While I decided if I still wanted to be a cop.'

'You seem to have settled both those questions,' he said, trying to hide the sadness her suggestion had provoked. 'I can see why you might want somewhere that feels more like your own place. A bit more room. But don't feel you have to go on my account.' A lop-sided smile. 'I've almost got used to having someone around I can borrow milk from.'

Carol's smile was pained. 'That's all I am to you, is it? A source of midnight milk?'

A long pause. Then Tony said. 'Sometimes I wish it was that simple. For your sake as much as mine.' He sighed. 'I really don't want you to move, Carol. Especially if we're not working together. Living in different places, we'd hardly see each other. I'm not good at holding on to people and you work insane hours.' He stood up. 'So, do you fancy a glass of wine?'

Gary Harcup licked the grease from his fingers then wiped them on his jeans. The pizza had been cold for at least three hours, but he hadn't noticed. He ate from habit, he ate as a pause for thought, he ate because the food was there. Savour had nothing to do with it. He loved that he lived in a world where you could have food delivered to your door 24/7 without even having to pick up a phone. A click of the mouse would see him supplied with Chinese, Indian, Thai or pizza. Some days, he only left his computer to take in deliveries and to go to the bathroom.

In the community he inhabited, Gary's life was far from unique. Most of the people he knew lived a variation of his daily existence. Every now and then they had to emerge blinking into the daylight to interface with clients of one sort or another, but if they could avoid it, they did. If they'd been a separate species, they'd have died out in a couple of generations.

Gary loved his machines. He loved moving around in virtuality, travelling through time and space without ever having to leave the womb of his small, smelly flat. He found immense satisfaction in solving the problems his clients offered up, but he also knew the deep frustration of occasional failure.

Take this job for West Mercia. A lot of what they wanted from him was the product of simple number-crunching. Tracking down the whereabouts of particular machines, for example. It was the sort of thing where you keyed in information and set the software off and running. A child of five could do it.

But trawling through the scattered detritus of deleted files, that was a different matter. Pulling out fragments, identifying which belonged where, fitting them together like a vandalised jigsaw – that was man's work. After a cursory exploration, he'd reluctantly had to admit that his software wasn't up to it. He needed something better – and he knew just where to go. Over years of working in this twilight zone, Gary had built a network of allies and contacts. Most of them he wouldn't have recognised if they'd been sitting next to him on a train, but he knew their screen names and cyber-IDs. For what he needed today, Warren Davy was his man. Warren, the man who could almost always come up with the goods. When it came to masters of the virtual universe, Warren was one of the best. They'd known each other since the earliest days, back before there had even been an internet, when the only way for teenagers like them to communicate in the ether had been bulletin boards populated by hackers, phreaks and geeks. Warren, in Gary's view, was the man.

A quick email, then he'd have a shower. It had been a day or two, and he'd noticed he was itching in the places where a man welded to a computer chair inevitably overheated.

When he returned to his desk, dressed in clean boxers and T-shirt, the reply was already there. You could always rely on Warren, he thought. Not just one of the smartest tools in the box, but one of the most open-handed too. It was thanks to Warren that Gary had a lot of the software that allowed him such free access to other people's information.

> Good to hear from you, Gary. I'm stuck in Malta on a security set-up job, but I think we've got something that might do the trick for you. I can let you have it at cost. It's called Ravel and you can download it from the DPS site. Use code TR61UPK to login, we'll bill you at the end of the month as usual.

> You're right, there is something newer and shinier coming down the pike from SCHEN, but it's going to cost you about three times what Ravel does. I know Bradfield Police are beta-testing it, so maybe West Mercia could get you a deal when it's up and running.

> Good luck with the trawl.

Gary gave the screen the thumbs-up, relieved that he was going to be able to put on some kind of a show for Patterson. Warren had come through. But even though Warren was so on top of things, he had a pretty rose-tinted view of how closely cops co-operated. Whatever the deal was with SCHEN and Bradfield Police, Gary knew there was no way West Mercia would be getting in on the ground floor with it. SCHEN were totally notorious for playing their expensive cards close to their chest. Gary had been aware of them for years. He even knew the guy behind them used the screen name Hexadex. But he'd never been able to get alongside him. All he knew was that the guy had developed some shit-hot analytical software over the years and that he had some kind of deal with Bradfield cops, who always seemed to be the ones beta-testing any crime-fighting apps of SCHEN's new kit.

Gary sighed. He'd never had the kind of creativity that had propelled SCHEN to gigabucks and Warren to megabucks. But at least he had his clutch of steady clients who didn't know that he wasn't one of the big dogs. And thanks to mates like Warren, hopefully they'd never have to find out.

Daniel Morrison slumped in front of his computer, his blue eyes sulky and his wide, full mouth turned down in a scowl. His life was so fucking boring. His parents were, like, dinosaurs. His dad acted like they were living in the Stone Age, when there was nothing to do except go to football matches and listen to records. Records, for fuck's sake! OK, so some vinyl was retro and cool, but not the stuff his dad liked to spin on his turntable. And the way he talked about girls . . . Daniel rolled his eyes back in his head and let his head loll. Like they were innocent little dolls or something. He wondered if his dad had the faintest idea what went on with girls in the twenty-first century. It would blow his stupid little mind if he knew.

Daniel would've bet that every single one of the girls he hung out with had forgotten more about sex than his dumbfuck father had ever known. He could never decide whether to laugh or groan when his father tried to talk to him about 'respect' and 'responsibility' when it came to girls. Maybe he hadn't actually done it yet, but he'd come close, and he had a full range of coloured and flavoured condoms ready and waiting. He wasn't going to be lumbered with some screaming kid, no thank you. God. He'd tried telling his father that he knew what he was doing, but the old man wasn't hearing what he had to say. He still wouldn't let him go out clubbing or to gigs with his mates. Said he could only go if they went together. Like he was going to show up at some event with his sad dad in tow. Yeah, right. That would happen.

Usually, his mother let him do pretty much what he wanted. But lately she'd been sounding more and more like a clone of his dad. Talking about homework and focus and shit like that. Daniel had never given a toss about homework. He'd always been smart enough to get by without trying. Even if it wasn't as easy to bullshit his way through some subjects now he was heading towards GCSEs, he could still get by better than pretty much anybody else without doing all the grunt work they had to put in.

It wasn't like you needed exams for what he wanted to do. Daniel knew his destiny already. He was going to be the stellar comedian of his generation. He'd be sharper, darker and funnier than *Little Britain*, *Gavin and Stacey* and *Peep Show* put together. He'd take comedy where it had never gone before. All his mates said he was already the funniest guy they'd ever heard. When he'd tried to tell his parents about his ambition, they'd laughed too. But not in a good way. So much for, 'We'll always be there for you.' Yeah, right.

With a world-weary sigh, he pushed his heavy fringe out of his eyes and logged on to RigMarole. This was usually the best time of day to connect with KK. They'd been online buddies for a couple of months now. KK was cool. He thought Daniel was awesomely funny. And even though he was just a kid like the rest of them, he knew a couple of dudes on the comedy circuit. He'd told Daniel that he could help him meet up with people who could set him on the road to celebrity comedy. Daniel had been smart enough not to push him, and sure enough, KK had come through. They were going to meet up soon, and then Daniel's life would start to change, big time. He'd been hibernating in the darkness but soon he was going to burst into the spotlight.

It would be worth putting up with KK's occasional creepiness. Like lately, he'd been talking about secrets. When they'd been in a private chat space, he'd been going on about knowing Daniel's secrets. Knowing who he really was. im t only 1 who nos who u realy r, he'd said. More than once. Like Daniel didn't even know himself. Like KK had access all areas inside Daniel's life. It kind of weirded Daniel out. So what if he'd told KK a lot about himself, about his dreams, about his fantasies of making it mega? That didn't mean the guy knew all his secrets.

Still, if KK was going to be his route to the big time, Daniel reckoned the guy could say pretty much what he wanted. Like it would matter when Daniel was all over the TV and the internet.

It never crossed his mind that he might end up famous for a very different reason.

CHAPTER 8

One week later

Even though he was going through them for the third time, Alvin Ambrose was still totally absorbed by the witness interviews in the Jennifer Maidment case. School friends, teachers, other kids she'd communicated with via RigMarole. Officers from as far afield as Dorset, Skye, Galway and a small town in Massachusetts had talked to teenagers whose reactions ranged from freaked out to completely freaked out by what had happened to their correspondent. Ambrose had already sifted the information twice, his instincts on full alert for something that struck a bum note, oblivious to the buzz and hum of the squad room. So far, nothing had given him a moment's pause.

The interviewing officers had been briefed to ask about the elusive ZZ, but nothing had come of that either. ZZ only showed up on Rig; there was no reaction of familiarity from teachers or family or friends who didn't use the social networking site. Those who had encountered ZZ online knew nothing more than the police had already established from Jennifer's conversations. ZZ had managed to worm his way into her network but in the process had given away nothing that would help identify him. It was frustrating beyond words.

A shadow fell across his desk and he looked up to see Shami Patel pretending to rap her knuckles on a non-existent door. 'Knock, knock,' she said, her smile awkward.

If she'd made the effort to seek him out, the chances were she had something to say worth listening to. Besides, with her generous curves and hair waved in a long bob, she was easy on the eye. That wasn't something you could say about most of the human scenery in the CID office. Ambrose responded with an expansive gesture towards the flimsy folding chair that sat at the end of his desk. 'Have a seat,' he said. 'How's it going with the Maidments?' When it had become clear that the Maidments might be one of the few sources of leads in their daughter's murder, he'd checked her out with mates in the West Midlands, where she'd come from. He needed to be sure she wasn't going to miss anything crucial. But his sources soon set him straight on that score. They said Patel was probably the best family liaison officer they had. 'Too fucking sharp for holding hands, if you ask me,' one of them had said. 'Don't know what she's doing, leaving us for you turnips.'

Patel sat down and crossed one well-shaped leg over the other. There was nothing coquettish in the gesture, Ambrose noted, almost with regret. He was generally content in his marriage, but still, a man liked to know he was worth flirting with. 'They're exhausted,' she said. 'It's like they've gone into hibernate mode to conserve what they've got left.' She stared at her hands. 'I've seen it before. When they come out of it, chances are it'll be with all guns blazing at us. They've got nobody else to blame, so we'll be the ones who take the flak unless we find the person who killed Jennifer.'

'And that's not happening,' Ambrose said.

'So I gathered. What about forensics? Nothing there?'

Ambrose shrugged his massive shoulders, the seams of his shirt straining at the movement. 'We've got some evidential stuff. Not the sort that produces leads, the sort that you can build a case with once you've got a suspect. We're still waiting for the forensic computer specialist, but he's less and less hopeful with every day that goes by.'

'That's what I thought.' Patel bit her lip, frowning a little.

'Have you picked something up from the family? Is that why you're here?'

She shook her head hastily. 'No. I wish . . . It's just . . .' She wriggled in her chair. 'My bloke, he's a DC with West Midlands. Jonty Singh.'

It was a short sentence but Ambrose immediately constructed the story behind Shami Patel's apparently perplexing move to Worcester. A nice Hindu girl with traditional, devout parents who had her lined up for some nice Hindu boy. And she goes and falls for a Sikh. Either they'd found out and there had been a family bust-up or else she'd moved down here before the wrong person spotted her and Jonty in the back row of the pictures. By moving to Worcester, she could have a life where she wasn't constantly looking over her shoulder. 'OK,' Ambrose said cautiously, wondering where this was going.

'You remember that business in Bradfield last year? The footballer that got murdered, and the bomb at the match?'

Like anybody was going to forget that in a hurry. Thirty-seven dead, hundreds injured when a bomb ripped through the corporate hospitality booths during a Premier League match at Bradfield Victoria. 'I remember.'

'Jonty was involved on the periphery. Before the bombing. One of the initial suspects in the murder was an old collar of his. He stayed in touch with his contact on the investigation, a guy called Sam Evans. He's on Bradfield's MIT. Anyway, I was telling Jonty how frustrated we all were at the lack of progress with Jennifer. I know I shouldn't have, but he's in the job, he knows not to talk—'

'Never mind that,' Ambrose said. He trusted this woman's judgement. 'What did he have to say, your DC Singh?'

'He told me the Bradfield MIT work with a profiler who's been a key factor in their success rate.'

Ambrose tried to keep his scepticism from his face, but Patel picked it up anyway. Her words accelerated, bumping into each other. 'This guy, he sounds exceptional. Sam Evans told Jonty he's saved lives, solved cases that nobody else could get a handle on. He's the business, Sarge.'

'The boss thinks it's mumbo jumbo, profiling.' Ambrose's voice was a deep rumble.

'And you? What do you think?'

Ambrose smiled. 'When I'm running the shop, I'll have an opinion. Right now, there's no point.'

Patel looked disappointed. 'You could at least talk to Sam Evans at Bradfield. See what he has to say?'

Ambrose stared at the cluttered surface of the desk, his big hands curled like empty shells on the stacks of paper. He didn't like creeping around behind Patterson. But sometimes you had to take the back alley. He sighed and reached for a pen. 'What's this profiler's name, then?'

Carol walked into her squad room, feelings mixed when she saw her team already settled round the conference table, ready for the morning meeting. She was proud that they were pulling out all the stops in their bid to assure their future, but bitter because she felt it was futile. 'What's going on here?' she said, detouring to the coffee machine. 'Did the clocks go forward without me noticing?'

'You know we like to keep you on your toes, chief,' Paula said, passing a box of pastries round the table.

Carol sat down, blowing gently on the steaming coffee. 'Just what I need.' It wasn't clear whether she was referring to the drink or to being kept on her toes. 'So, anything in the overnights?'

'Yes,' and 'No,' said Kevin and Sam simultaneously.

'Well, which is it?'

Sam snorted. 'You know that if this kid was black and from a council estate with a single mum, this wouldn't even have made the overnights.'

'But he's not and it did,' Kevin said.

'We're just capitulating to white middle-class anxieties,' Sam said scornfully. 'The kid's with some girl or else he's had it up to here with Mummy and Daddy and taken off for the bright lights.'

Carol looked at Sam with surprise. The most nakedly ambitious of her team, he was generally first out of the starting blocks on anything that had the potential to raise his profile and improve his standing. To hear him spout a position that appeared to have its roots in class politics was akin to tuning in to the Big Brother house to hear them discussing Einstein's theory of special relativity. 'Any chance of anyone explaining what you guys are talking about?' she said mildly.

Kevin consulted a couple of sheets of paper in front of her. 'This came in from Northern Division. Daniel Morrison. Fourteen years old. Reported missing by his parents yesterday morning. He'd been out all night, they were worried stiff but assumed he was making some point about being a big boy now. They rang round his friends and drew a blank, but they reckoned he must be with somebody they didn't know about. Maybe a girlfriend he'd kept quiet about.'

'It's a reasonable assumption,' Carol said. 'From what we know of teenage boys.'

'Right. They thought they'd re-establish contact with him when he turned up at school yesterday. But he didn't show. That's when his parents decided they should talk to us.'

'I take it there's been nothing since? And that's why Northern are punting it our way?' Carol held her hand out and Kevin handed over the print-out.

'Nothing. He's not answering his mobile, not responding to emails, not activated his RigMarole account. According to his mother, the only way he'd let himself be that cut off is if he's dead or kidnapped.'

'Or else he doesn't want Mummy and Daddy to find him shacked up with some cutie,' Sam said, clamping his mouth shut in a mutinous scowl.

'I don't know,' Kevin said slowly. 'Teenage boys want to boast about their conquests. It's hard to believe he'd resist letting his mates know what he was up to. And these days, that means RigMarole.'

'My thoughts precisely,' Carol said. 'I think Stacey should check out whether his phone's switched on and, if it is, whether we can triangulate his position.'

Sam half turned away from the table and crossed his legs. 'Unbelievable. Some overprivileged white boy goes out on the razz and we're falling over ourselves to track him down. Are we that desperate to make ourselves look indispensable?'

'Clearly,' Carol said, her voice sharp. 'Stacey, run the checks. Paula, talk to Northern Division, see where they're up to, if they want any help from us. See if you can get them to send us any interview product. And by the way, Sam, I think you're wrong. If this was a black kid from an estate with a single parent who took his disappearance seriously, so would we. I don't know why you've got a bee in your bonnet about this, but lose it, would you?'

Sam blew out his cheeks in a sigh, but he nodded. 'Whatever you say, guv.'

Carol put the pages to one side for later and looked round the table. 'Anything else new?'

Stacey cleared her throat. There was a faint lift at the corners of her mouth. Carol thought it translated as the equivalent on anyone else of a shit-eating grin. 'I've got something,' she said.

'Let's hear it.'

'The computer Sam brought in from the old Barnes house,' Stacey said, pushing a stray strand of hair behind her ear. 'I've been working it pretty hard for the past week. It's been very instructive.' She tapped a couple of keys on the laptop in front of her. 'People are amazingly stupid.'

Sam leaned forward, accentuating the planes and angles of his smooth-skinned face. 'What did you find? Come on, Stacey, show us.'

She clicked a remote pointer and the whiteboard on the wall behind her sprang into life. It showed a fragmentary list, with missing letters and words. Another click and the gaps filled with highlighted text. 'This program predicts what's not there,' she said. 'As you can see, it's a list of steps for murdering Danuta Barnes. From smothering her to wrapping her in clingfilm to weighting her down to dumping her body in deep water.'

Paula whistled. 'Oh my God,' she said. 'You're right. Amazingly stupid.'

'That's very lovely,' Carol said. 'But any decent lawyer's going to point out that it's circumstantial at best. That it could be a fantasy. Or the outline of a short story.'

'It's only circumstantial till we find Danuta Barnes's body and compare the cause of death with what we've got here,' Sam said, reluctant to let go of the possibilities of his discovery.

'Sam's right,' Stacey said over the chatter that his words provoked. 'That's why this other file is so interesting.' She clicked the remote again and a map of the Lake District appeared. The next click revealed a chart of Wastwater that clearly showed the relative depths of the lake.

'You think she's in Wastwater.' Carol stood up and walked over to the screen.

'I think it's worth taking a look,' Stacey said. 'According to his list, he was planning on somewhere he could drive to but somewhere that was also quite remote. Wastwater fits the bill. At least, looking at the map, it looks like there's not many houses round there.'

'No kidding. I've been there,' Paula said. 'A bunch of us went up for a weekend break a few years ago. I don't think we saw another living soul apart from the woman who ran the B&B. I'm all for a bit of peace and quiet, but that was bloody ridiculous.'

'He had a kayak,' Sam said. 'I remember that from the original file. He could have draped her across the kayak and paddled out.'

'Good work, Stacey,' Carol said. 'Sam, get on to the underwater unit up in Cumbria. Ask them to set up a search.'

Stacey raised a hand. 'It might be worth asking the geography department at the university if they've got any access to ETM+.'

'What's that?' Carol asked.

'Landsat Enhanced Thematic Mapper Plus. It's a global archive of satellite photos managed by NASA and the US Geological Survey,' Stacey said. 'It might be helpful.'

'They can spot a body from space?' Paula said. 'I thought being able to watch my home TV in another country was about as far out as it gets. But you're telling me the geography department at Bradfield Uni can see underwater from a satellite? That's too much, Stace. Just too much.'

Stacey rolled her eyes. 'No, Paula. They can't necessarily see a body. But they can zoom in so far these days you can get a lot of detail. They might be able to narrow down where we should be looking by eliminating where there definitely isn't anything.'

'That's wild,' Paula said.

'That's technology. There's a geography faculty in the USA that reckons they've pinpointed where Osama Bin Laden's hiding by narrowing down possibilities from satellite photography,' Stacey said.

'You're kidding,' Paula said.

'No, I'm not. It was a team at UCLA. First they applied geographic principles developed to predict the distribution of wildlife – distance-decay theory and island biogeographic theory—'

'What?' Kevin chipped in.

'Distance-decay theory . . . OK, you start with a known place that fulfils the criteria this organism needs for survival. Like the Tora Bora caves. You draw a series of concentric circles out from there, and the further you get from the centre, the less likely you are to find those identical conditions. In other words, the further he goes from his heartlands, the more likely he is to be among people who are not sympathetic to his goals and the harder it is to hide. Island biogeographic theory is about choosing somewhere that has resources. So, if you were going to be stuck on an island, you'd rather it was the Isle of Wight than Rockall.'

'I don't understand where the satellites come in,' Paula said, frowning.

'They figured out the likely zone where Bin Laden might be, then they factored in what they know about him. His height, the fact that he needs regular dialysis so he has to be somewhere with electricity, his need for protection. And then they looked at the most detailed satellite imagery they could find and narrowed it down to three buildings in a particular town,' Stacey said patiently.

'So how come they've not found him yet?' Kevin pointed out, not unreasonably.

Stacey shrugged. 'I only said they reckoned. Not that they'd actually succeeded. Yet. But the satellite imaging is getting more detailed all the time. Each image used to cover thirty metres by thirty metres. Now it's more like half a metre. You wouldn't believe the detail the experts analysts can pick up. It's like having an overhead Google Street View of the whole world.'

'Stop, Stacey. You're making my head hurt. But if we can harness that, I will be eternally grateful. Have a word with the satellite bods,' Carol said. 'But let's concentrate on getting the Cumbria team on side. Anything else?' Glum looks round the table told her all she needed to know. She hated being in this position. What they needed was something big, something headline-grabbing, something spectacular. Only trouble was that what would be meat and drink to Carol and her team would be the worst kind of bad news for somebody else. She'd experienced too much of that sort of tribulation to want to visit it on anyone else.

They were just going to have to grin and bear it.

CHAPTER 9

Even the advent of his teens hadn't broken Seth Viner's habit of candour where his parents were concerned. He couldn't remember a time when he'd felt he needed to keep secrets from either of his two mothers. OK, sometimes it was easier to talk to one rather than the other. Julia was more practical, more down to earth. Calmer in a crisis, more likely to listen all the way through to the end. But she'd weigh things up and she wouldn't always come down on his side of the issue. Kathy was the emotional one, the one who rushed to judgement. Nevertheless, she'd always be in his corner – my kid, right or wrong. Still, she was the one who made him stick to things, the one who wouldn't let him take the easy way out when things were difficult. But he'd never regretted telling either of them something, even things he was embarrassed about. They'd taught him that there was no place for secrecy with the people you love most in the world.

The other side of the equation was that they'd always listened to his questions and done their best to answer them. Everything from 'Why's the sky blue?' to 'What are they fighting about in Gaza?' They never fobbed him off. It sometimes weirded out his teachers and made his friends give him the fish-eyed stare, but he knew all sorts of stuff just because it had occurred to him to ask and it had never occurred to Julia and Kathy not to answer. He reckoned it was something to do with their determination to be honest with him about how he'd ended up with two mothers.

He couldn't remember when it had dawned on him that it was pretty far out there to have two mothers instead of one of the more conventional arrangements like a mum and a dad or a stepdad, or a single mum and a bunch of grandparents, uncles and babysitters. Everybody starts out thinking their family is normal because they've no other experience to measure it against. But by the time he started school, he knew the family that embraced him was different. And not just because of the colour of Kathy's skin. Oddly enough, the other kids seemed almost oblivious to his difference. He remembered one time when Julia had picked him up from school during his first term. Kathy usually did the school run because she ran her website design service from home, but she'd had to go out of town for some meeting, so Julia had left work early to collect him. She'd been helping him on with his wellies when Ben Rogers had said, 'Who are you?'

Emma White, who lived on their street, had said, 'That's Seth's mum.'

Ben had frowned. 'No, it's not. I've met Seth's mum and this isn't her,' he'd said.

'This is Seth's other mum,' Emma had insisted.

Ben had totally taken it in his stride, moving straight on to the next topic of conversation. It had stayed like that – part of the landscape, how the world was, unremarkable – until Seth had been nine or ten, when his passion for football had brought him into direct contact with kids who hadn't grown up with the notion that having two mums was just part of the spectrum of family life.

One or two of the bigger lads had tried to use Seth's unusual domestic set-up to get some leverage against him. They soon found out they'd picked the wrong target. Seth seemed to move inside a bubble of invulnerability. He deflected insults with bemused good nature. And he was too well liked among the other boys to make a physical campaign possible. Confounded by his self-confidence, the bullies backed off and chose someone easier to victimise. Even then, Seth thwarted them. He had a way of letting those in authority know when bad things were going on without ever being seen as a grass. He was, it seemed, a good friend and a pointless enemy.

So he'd moved seamlessly into adolescence – kind, pop-ular and direct, his only apparent problem his anxiety not to fail. Julia and Kathy held their breath, waiting for the other shoe to drop. It seemed like they'd been doing that since the day Julia had been inseminated. There had been plenty of Jonahs ready with dire warnings. But Seth had been a happy, easy baby. He'd had colic once. Just once. He'd started sleeping through the night at an incredible seven weeks. He'd avoided childhood ailments apart from the occasional cold. He hadn't been the toddler from hell, partly because the first time he'd tried it in public, Kathy had walked away and left him standing red-faced and howling in the middle of a supermarket aisle. She'd been watching from round the end of the breakfast cereals, but he hadn't realised that at the time. The horror of abandonment had been enough to cure him of temper tantrums. He whinged sometimes, as they all did, but neither Kathy nor Julia responded in the desired way, so he'd mostly given that up too.

The personality trait that saved him from being too good to be true was the constant stream of chatter that often seemed to start when his eyes opened in the morning and only ended when they closed again at bedtime. Seth was so entirely fascinated by the world and his place in it that he saw no reason why anyone would not want a blow-by-blow account of his every action and thought, or a remarkably detailed recitation of the plot of whatever DVD he'd last seen, the more trivial the better. Occasionally, belatedly, he would register his audience's eyes rolling back in their sockets, or their whole faces glazing over as they waited for him to get to the point. It didn't give him even a flicker of hesitation. He carried on to the bitter end, even when Kathy would lay her head on the kitchen table and moan softly.

In the great scheme of things, it wasn't the worst character flaw. His mothers had both noticed it seemed not to have the same effect on his friends as it had on them. And they were grateful that the onset of adolescence hadn't turned their beautiful boy into a surly, monosyllabic hulk. Most of his friends made them shudder these days. Cute, loving boys who had scampered round their house engaged in all sorts of fantasy games had morphed into grunting, smelly creatures who regarded communication with adults as somehow letting the side down. It was, Kathy said, some kind of miracle that Seth had escaped this particular aspect of the rites of passage into manhood.

'He does have terrible taste in music,' Julia had pointed out more than once, as if that counterbalanced his better qualities. She had no idea where he'd acquired his taste for early grunge; she was just grateful that so far it hadn't infected his wardrobe too much.

'It could be worse,' Kathy always said. 'He could be into musicals.'

Seth's inability to keep anything to himself meant Julia and Kathy were relaxed about his computer use. Not so relaxed that they didn't have the appropriate parental controls bolted on, with all the extra security that Kathy used to protect the websites she designed. But they didn't physically look over his shoulder, though Kathy routinely checked his RigMarole page for weirdos and undesirables.

Not that there was much need for that. A lot of Seth's table talk revolved around Rig – who he was talking to, what they had to say about whatever people were twittering over that week, what fascinating new app he'd heard about.

The trouble with living life in a play-by-play mode is that other people eventually tune out in a kind of self-defence. These days, Julia and Kathy only half listened to Seth's news of the world. Much of what he had to say got lost in the slipstream of words that spilled round the kitchen table. The first time he mentioned a new Rig friend called JJ, Kathy registered the name and checked him out on Seth's pages. He seemed a regular geeky teenager analysing the lyrics of Pearl Jam and Mudhoney, full of a mixture of pomp and angst. Nothing to worry about there.

And so JJ became part of the background noise, just another set of references they could let wash over them. Naturally, then, when Seth casually mentioned that he was meeting up with JJ so they could go on a rare sounds quest in Bradfield's second-hand CD stores, no alarm bells rang.

When you're used to candour, it never occurs to you that what you're hearing is something less than the truth.

Tony googled the Worcester estate agent's website then clicked on the 'New Properties' button. The woman he'd dealt with at the agency had sounded like one of his bipolar patients in an unmedicated manic phase. She'd assured him two days ago that the photographs would be taken that very afternoon and the details placed on the website 'within hours'. It had taken him till now to work up the nerve to look at the information about the house he was selling without ever having seen.

Given the price the agent had suggested, he knew it must be a substantial property, but he wasn't prepared for the ample Edwardian villa that confronted him. It was a double-fronted house in mellow red brick with the deep bay windows and imposing doorway picked out in contrasting pale yellow. Heavy swags of curtains were visible at the margins of the windows, and the garden looked opulently landscaped. 'Unique opportunity to purchase fine family home overlooking Gheluvelt Park,' the strapline across the top shouted. 'Four beds, three recep, three bath. Fully fitted workshop with power.' Tony's eyebrows rose and his mouth puckered. It was a hell of a lot of house for a man living alone. Perhaps he'd liked to entertain. Or maybe he'd just liked to demonstrate to the world how well he'd done. Edmund Arthur Blythe obviously hadn't been short of a bob or two.

It occurred to Tony that this sale would mean the same for him. He already had £50,000 from the legacy sitting in his bank account, but that was a fraction of what the house would bring. He'd never imagined having this sort of cash at his disposal, so he'd never speculated about what he would do with it. He had no expensive tastes. He didn't collect art, drive fast cars or wear expensive suits. He wasn't good at taking holidays at the best of times, and he had no inclination towards exotic destinations where the weather was too hot, the drains were suspect and you had to have needles stuck into your arms and buttocks before you could board the plane. The things he enjoyed most happened to be what he was paid for – treating patients and profiling off-kilter minds. But soon he was going to be a rich man, whether he liked it or not.

'I can always give it away,' he said aloud. There were plenty of charities who would make something worthwhile out of a windfall like that. And yet, it didn't appeal to him quite as much as he would have expected it to. Apparently Cyndi Lauper was right when she sang that money changes everything. Impatiently, he turned his attention back to the screen.

There were more pictures available at the click of a mouse. Tony's finger hovered. He wasn't sure he was ready for this. He'd deliberately chosen not to explore the domain of the man who had contributed half of his genetic material. He didn't want to discover a happy and fulfilled life, to unearth a popular and well-balanced man, to find out that he'd been ignored by someone who could have transformed his childhood from a wilderness of misery to something approaching normality. Disinterring that truth could lead to nothing but bitter resentment. Being Vanessa's son had been a direct route to wretchedness. Both his mother and the grandmother who had carried most of the routine burden of raising him had left him in no doubt that he was beyond worthless, that he contained the seeds of iniquity, that he could hope to be nothing more than a pathetic apology for a man. What he had learned as a psychologist was that his childhood experiences were a blueprint for the sort of creature he spent his profiling life tracking. He was more like them than anyone else, even Carol, could have guessed. They hunted victims; he hunted them. They profiled victims; he profiled them. The need was the same, he suspected.

His needs would have been very different if Blythe had been part of his life. And he didn't want to think about what that would have meant. So he'd made all the arrangements by phone and email, having Blythe's solicitor send the keys directly to the estate agent. The solicitor had acted as if this had been perfectly normal behaviour, but Tony knew it wasn't. He understood only too well that he was building walls between himself and the man who hadn't been willing to be his father. There was no reason why he should put his own fragility at risk for the sake of someone who had only had the courage to acknowledge his son after death.

But still there was a nagging voice at the back of his head, telling him there would come a time when he would regret maintaining this distance. 'Maybe so,' he said aloud. 'But I can't do this now.' For a moment, he wondered if he should put the house sale on hold, so Blythe's home would remain intact, available for his scrutiny when he was ready for it. He dismissed the idea almost before it was fully formed. He might never be ready, and there was something morally wrong about leaving houses empty when people needed homes.

Impatient with his own lack of clarity, he shut down the house details and pulled a patient file towards him. Here was where he could make a difference, intervening in the lives of people whose behaviour had diverged disastrously from what the majority regarded as normal. His own history with his mother had given him an insider's knowledge of how different the world could look when the view had been dramatically distorted. He knew only too well what not belonging felt like, how terrifying it could be to negotiate a world whose rules and conventions were so at odds with the ones that had made survival possible. Since Tony had taught himself how to pass for human, he reckoned he could help others to overcome their damage. Too many of his patients were beyond repair, but some could be redeemed, rehabilitated and restored to something approaching normal life.

His reading was interrupted by the phone. Half distracted, he picked it up. 'Hello?' Carol had told him more than once that his phone greeting sounded astonished and wary, as if he was taken aback by a ringing piece of plastic that spoke when you lifted it. 'You remind me of a poem I read when I was at school,' she'd said. '"A Martian Sends a Postcard Home", it was called.'

The person on the other end of the phone was hesitant. It sounded like he'd have agreed with Carol, given half a chance. 'Is that Dr Hill? Dr Tony Hill?'

'Yes? Who is this?'

'I'm Detective Inspector Stuart Patterson. West Mercia CID.'

'We've not met, have we?' Tony always liked to get that out of the way. He was good with faces but names often escaped him. This wouldn't be the first time he'd thought he was talking to a complete stranger only to discover they'd sat together at some dinner a month before.

'No. I was told you were the person to talk to about profiling.'

'Well, I'm certainly one of them,' Tony said. He grimaced at the phone. 'I have some experience in the field.'

'We've got a case down here. I think we could use your help.'

'West Mercia? That's Worcester, right?' Now he sounded wary even to himself.

'And the surrounding area, yes. But the murder was on the outskirts of the city. Have you read about it? Is that why you're asking?' Patterson's words ran into each other in his haste, but Tony could distinguish an accent that had the faint burr he associated with the Borsetshire accents in *The Archers*.

'No, I just wasn't exactly sure . . . Geography isn't my

strong suit. So, what is it about this case that makes you think you need someone like me?'

Patterson took a deep breath. 'We've got a fourteen-year-old girl who's been murdered and sexually mutilated. We've been working the case for over a week and we've got nothing you could call a lead. We've covered all the obvious bases but there's nothing to go at. We're desperate, Dr Hill. I want to close this case, but we're not getting there by the numbers. I need a fresh approach.' There was a pause. Tony stayed silent, sensing there was more to come. 'I've been told you might be able to provide us with that.'

That was the second time Patterson had spoken of being told. So he was coming to Tony not from conviction but because he was under pressure. Faced with a crime like the one Patterson had described, Carol Jordan and a clutch of other homicide detectives Tony had worked with would have been on the phone to him within hours. That was because they were believers. Working with sceptics always doubled the amount of work on a profiler's plate. But on the other hand, it meant you couldn't get away with anything other than solid, evidence-based conclusions. It was always good to be dragged back to basics.

Then he thought, *Worcester*, and detected the hand of Carol Jordan. *She thinks she can't get me to take an interest in Blythe, so she's setting me up with a murder in Worcester so I have to go there. She thinks once I'm there, I won't be able to resist poking my nose in.* 'Do you mind me asking who suggested I might be able to help?' he asked, sure of the answer.

Patterson cleared his throat. 'It's a bit complicated.'

'I'm in no hurry.'

'Our FLO – Family Liaison Officer, that is . . . Her bloke's with West Midlands. One of the lads from Bradfield MIT, a DC called Sam Evans, he liaised with her bloke on the Bradfield bombings case last year. Anyway, the two of them stayed in touch, meeting up for the odd curry now and again. And this DC Evans, he's been singing your praises. My DS, he put a call in to DC Evans and got your number.' Patterson gave a small cough, clearing his throat. 'And my DS persuaded me it was time to think outside the box.'

'You didn't speak to DCI Jordan?' Tony couldn't believe it.

'I don't know a DCI Jordan. Is he DC Evan's boss?'

An assumption that might have annoyed Tony in other circumstances convinced him Patterson was telling the truth. This wasn't a Carol Jordan set-up. 'What was the cause of death?' Tony asked.

'Asphyxiated. She had a plastic bag over her head. She didn't fight, she was off her face on GHB.'

'GHB? How do you know? I thought you couldn't detect that because we've got it in our blood already?'

'Not at these levels. She hadn't been dead long when we found her, so it was more obvious,' Patterson said heavily. 'We're still waiting for a full tox screen, but at this point, it looks like she was given enough GHB to make the killer's job very easy.'

Tony was automatically scribbling notes as he listened. 'You said "sexually mutilated".'

'He took a knife to her. A long-bladed knife, I'm told. Made a right mess inside her. What do you think, Doc? Are you going to be able to help us?'

Tony dropped the pen and pushed his reading glasses up to rub the bridge of his nose. 'I don't know. Can you email me the crime-scene pictures and the summary reports? I'll take a look at them and get back to you first thing tomorrow. I'll know then if I can be of any use.'

'Thanks. If it's a yes, will you need to come down here?'

A man already worried about his budget. 'I need to see the crime scene for myself,' he said. 'And I'll probably want to talk to the parents. A couple of days at the most. Maybe one overnight. Two at the most,' he said, showing he understood. He gave Patterson his email address, took his phone number and arranged to talk to him in the morning.

Tony replaced the phone and leaned back in his chair, closing his eyes. West Mercia Police wanted him to go to Worcester on the very day when he'd set in train the sale of Edmund Arthur Blythe's house in Worcester. Some people he knew would build a whole edifice of predestination out of that. But he set no store by coincidence. He had patients who read all sorts of fateful meanings into coincidence; during his brief tenure as a university lecturer, he'd warned his students not to be sucked into those fantasies. How did it go again?

'We've all been there. On holiday, in some out of the way village or on a beach that isn't in the Lonely Planet guide or in some fabulous little seafood restaurant recommended by the locals. And we come face to face with somebody who plays football with our brother or catches our bus every morning or walks their dog in the same park as we do. And we're amazed. It's the thing we tell everybody when we get home – "you'll never believe who I ran into . . ." But stop and think about it. Think of the myriad moments of each day on your holiday when you *didn't* run into anyone you recognised. Come to that, think of the myriad moments of every single day at home when you don't run into anyone you recognise. Mathematically, the chances are that you are going to run into someone you recognise eventually pretty much wherever you go. The world is a shrinking contact zone. Every year that passes, our chances of these apparently meaningful encounters grows. But they are not meaning-ful. Unless of course you do have a stalker, in which case you need to disregard everything I am saying and call the police.

'So when your patients put forward some version of their mission that relies on assigning meaning to random events, remember that there is no meaning in coinci-dence. It happens. Accept it and ignore it.'

His computer beeped, announcing the arrival of a new email. DI Patterson being quick off the mark, he sus-pected. Tony let himself fall forward in his chair, opening his eyes and groaning. 'Accept it and ignore it,' he said out loud.

CHAPTER 10

It took Paula less than thirty seconds to appreciate that the only person in the Northern Division's CID room who thought it was a good idea to bring MIT into their missing person inquiry was the boss. She'd been told to report to DS Franny Riley in their central squad room for a briefing. When she turned up, the first person she spoke to shrugged and gestured over his shoulder with his thumb. 'Big bugger over there with the fag.'

Smoking had of course been outlawed in Bradfield Police offices for years. But the beefy detective pointed out to Paula had a cigarette dangling from one corner of his mouth. It was unlit, but the malevolent dark eyes that glanced up at her held the defiant threat of a man who would spark up his lighter at the slightest provocation. He looked like a refugee from the worst days of rugby league, Paula thought as she crossed the room. Busted nose badly repaired, unmatching ears and no neck visible. 'I'm DC

McIntyre,' she said. 'Paula McIntyre.' She held out a hand. Franny Riley hesitated for a moment, then engulfed her hand in his. His grip was strong but his skin surprisingly soft.

'Franny Riley. I thought you lot were supposed to be the crack squad. Don't know what the fuck the boss is thinking. Wastes your time, makes us look like fucking imbeciles.' His scowl deepened. Between the jut of his eyebrows and the flabby pouches under his eyes, Paula wondered how he could see.

'Let's hope so.'

He cocked his head, puzzled. 'You what?'

'I'd be very happy if this turns out to be a waste of time for both of us when Daniel Morrison turns up safe and sound with a just-fucked look on his face. Wouldn't you?' Paula gave him the full-on charm and pulled her cigarette pack from her jacket. 'So where do we have to go to smoke around here?'

The roof of Bradfield Police's Northern Division HQ had one of the best views in the city. Built at the top of Colliery Hill, it commanded the surrounding neighbourhoods. On a clear day, you could make out landmark buildings in the city centre, as well as Bradfield Victoria's distant stadium and the parks that had acted as green lungs since the Industrial Revolution. To the north, the moors spread-eagled across the horizon, ribbon roads weaving through the gaps between their rounded summits. Somehow, a Perspex bus shelter had found its way on to the roof, protecting smokers from wind and rain and providing them with what was probably the most scenic smoking area in Bradfield.

'Nice one,' Paula said, perching on the narrow plastic bench that ran the length of the shelter. 'Has anyone reported their bus shelter missing yet?'

Riley snorted with laughter. It was a peculiar sound, like a clogged drain when it's rodded. 'As if.' He inhaled deeply, his cigarette an apparent life-support system. 'The chief super's terrified of heights, so chances are we're safe up here. So, what are you after from me, DC McIntyre?'

'I hoped you could brief me on where you're up to with Daniel Morrison. That way I can avoid covering the same ground twice.'

He grunted. 'I thought that was how you elite buggers did it? Start right from the beginning, go over everything that's already been covered, then claim the credit?'

'You must be thinking of some other bunch of wankers, Sarge.' Paula turned to shelter the flame as she lit up her own cigarette. She felt herself relax as the nicotine did its dizzy dance in her brain. She had a knack for getting under the guard of people she was interviewing. She knew it was at the heart of why Carol Jordan valued her so highly, but she tried not to analyse the process too much in case the wheels came off. So now, without thinking too hard about it, she flashed Franny Riley a complicit smile. 'I reckon you're on top of this.'

She could see Riley visibly loosen up. 'Smart lass.'

'You don't seem very anxious about Daniel. Does that mean you think he's a runaway?'

Riley shrugged his meaty shoulders. 'Not exactly a runaway. More a lad on a bit of an adventure. Like you said, he'll likely turn up with a well-shagged look on his face.'

'What makes you say that?'

Riley took an aggressive drag on his cigarette and spoke through the exhale. 'Spoilt little shit. Mummy and Daddy's little darling. No reason for him to do a runner when he gets everything his own way at home.'

Paula let that lie for now. In her experience, you didn't generally get anything like the whole picture from the family in the first couple of days of a disappearance. It might seem on the surface as if Daniel wanted for nothing, but sometimes that also meant a kid had more to deal with than he'd bargained for. 'You've ruled out abduction?'

'If it was a kidnap, either the parents wouldn't be talking to us or we'd be seeing a ransom demand by now. Besides, the dad's not ransom material. He's got plenty, but not the kind of plenty that makes kidnap worth the candle.' Riley sucked the last of the cigarette down to the filter and crushed the butt underfoot with an air of finality.

'What's the last sighting?'

Riley yawned and stretched then reached for another cigarette. 'He's a pupil at William Makepeace. He rode into town on the bus after school on Monday. He was by himself, but a couple of other lads from his year were sitting near him. They all got off the bus at Bellwether Square. The other lads went to the computer game shop. They say Daniel walked off across the square in the opposite direction.'

'Towards Temple Fields?' In spite of herself, Paula felt the hair on her arms prickle. It was nothing to do with the chill wind slanting down from the moors.

'That's right.'

'And after that?'

Riley shrugged. 'Well, we've not put out an appeal, so we've not got five hundred time-wasters giving out from Land's End to John O'Groats about how they've seen him.' He walked to the mouth of the shelter and looked out across the city, apparently through with his report. Just when Paula was about to write him off as a lazy bastard, Riley surprised her. 'I took a look at the city-centre CCTV,' he said. 'The lads were telling the truth. Daniel crossed the square and cut down a side alley that takes you into Temple Fields.' He turned his head and gave her an appraising look. 'You know what that's like better than most. Am I right?'

For a moment, Paula wasn't sure whether he was referring to her sexuality. 'Sorry?' she said, her tone sharp enough to indicate she wasn't going to let homophobia go past without a fight.

'You are the one, aren't you? The one who got caught in the crossfire when that undercover in Temple Fields went tits-up?'

Paula would almost have preferred the sexism she'd mistakenly ascribed to him. She'd nearly died in a scummy room in that maze of streets and alleys because of a killer who had been smarter than even Tony Hill had realised. Dragging herself back from the brink had been a harsh and hazardous journey, one she knew she couldn't have managed without Tony's support. Even now, more or less recovered as she was, she still hated that it was part of her history. 'I'm the one,' she said. 'And I'm aware that the CCTV coverage in Temple Fields is still shit.'

Riley gave a one-finger salute with a dip of the head, acknowledging her admission. 'Bad for business. We call it the gay village and pretend it's gone respectable with its trendy bars and its poncey restaurants, but you and me, we know the truth. The sex shops and the hookers and the pimps and the dealers don't want their customers on camera. So as soon as Daniel disappears into Temple Fields, we're fucked.'

'No chance of catching him leaving?'

Riley scratched his belly. 'Too many options. Too much manpower to throw at a missing teenager. You know how it is. And still no guarantees. He could be in there right now, sacked out in somebody's bloody warehouse flat. Or he could have left in the back of somebody's car and we'd be none the wiser.'

'Not good.' Paula got to her feet and joined Riley in his scrutiny of the city below. Somewhere out there was the key to Daniel Morrison's disappearance. It might as well have been in Iceland for all the use it was to them right now. 'Not good at all.'

'What are you going to do about it? Talk to the family?'

She shook her head. 'It's not up to me. But I'll be advising my chief to let it lie till something changes. It sounds like you've covered the bases already.'

Riley seemed taken aback. 'Right you are,' he said, failing to hide a note of surprise. 'If we're no further forward by tomorrow morning, we'll likely wheel the parents out at a press conference. I'll give you fair warning.'

Paula stubbed out her cigarette. 'Thanks, Sarge.' She felt his eyes on her back as she crossed the roof to the fire stairs. She reckoned she'd made a new friend. The day had not been wasted.

*

Tony looked around the crowded curry house. He and Carol had been coming to the same Indian restaurant on the fringes of Temple Fields since the first case they'd worked together, and in spite of changes of décor and chef, it was still one of the busiest and the best. He'd once been concerned that the tables were so close that people would be put off their food by the conversations he and Carol shared, until he'd realised there was so much background noise that eavesdropping was impossible. And so it had become a regular rendezvous. Tony suspected they both appreciated its neutrality, a no man's land where neither had territorial advantage in the complicated skirmishes of their relationship.

He glanced at his watch again and this time when he looked up he spotted Carol threading her way through the packed tables towards him. Her cheeks were pink from the chill of the evening, making her eyes seem bluer. Her thick blonde hair was ready for a cut, the layers growing shaggy and disordered. If pressed, Tony would have admitted he preferred the current look to the groomed perfection of a fresh cut. But then, nobody was likely to press him, least of all Carol.

She dropped into her chair with a whoosh of a sigh, shrugging off her coat and reaching for the sweating bottle of Cobra sitting in front of her. She clinked it against Tony's and took a long swallow. 'That's better,' she said. 'Thirsty work, getting here on time.'

'Good day?' Tony knew the answer; they were here because the text she'd sent had invited him here to celebrate.

'I think so,' Carol said. Their waiter glided to a halt by

the table and they both rattled off their orders without having to consult the menu. 'We may just have the key to a fourteen-year-old cold case.' She outlined the fresh evidence against Nigel Barnes. 'The good news is that Stacey's managed to narrow down the possible zones for the body dump, so Cumbria's underwater search team are willing to take a crack at it. I've sent Sam up there to liaise with them.'

'Well done. That should get you the kind of headlines to keep Blake off your back.'

The corners of her mouth turned down. 'I don't know. I suspect he'll just write it off as something that would have happened whoever was doing cold cases, but he'd be wrong. See, most detectives, when they heard Nigel Barnes had moved house, they wouldn't bother following up the way Sam did. They'd regard it as an excuse to let the whole thing drop. But my team are special. They think in tangents, not straight lines. It's hard to explain to a man like Blake what that means on the ground.'

'Especially if he doesn't want to understand,' Tony said.

Carol gave a wry smile. 'Quite. But let's not think about that tonight, let's just enjoy the fact that my team are on the verge of another success.'

'You do a good job. It's hard, having to tell families their worst nightmares have come true, but at least you end the uncertainty. And bringing killers to justice, that's always worth something. It's the old cliché, but it's true. You're there to speak for the dead, to act on their behalf.' He smiled at her, his eyes crinkling up at the corners. He was glad the evening had got off to a good start. He had a feeling it might not continue so smoothly.

A plate piled with vegetable and fish pakoras arrived and they both helped themselves. There was a respectful silence as they worked their way through. At last, Tony sighed in satisfaction. 'I didn't realise how hungry I was.'

'You always say that,' Carol mumbled through her last mouthful of crisp batter and soft cauliflower.

'It's always true.'

'So, how's your day been?'

Wary now, Tony said, 'Well, I'm pleased to say that even if James Blake doesn't want me, there are others who do. I had a call today asking me to consult on a murder, so it looks like I'm still in demand.'

'That's great. Anyone I know?' Carol looked genuinely pleased. He imagined that might not last.

'A DI called Stuart Patterson.'

Carol frowned and shook her head. 'Name doesn't ring a bell.'

'From West Mercia.'

Surprise flashed across her face, freezing her expression. 'West Mercia? You're going to Worcester?' The accusation he'd expected was there in her voice.

'That's where I'm needed, Carol. I didn't chase this. It chased me.' He didn't want to sound defensive but he knew he did.

'You didn't have to say yes.'

Tony threw his hands in the air. 'I never have to say yes. And I always have to say yes. You know that. Like I just said, we're the only ones left to speak for the dead.'

Carol hung her head. 'I'm sorry. You're right. It just seems . . . I don't know. When I tried to talk to you about your father, you cut me off at the knees. You didn't want

113

to deal with it. And yet here you are, first chance you get, off to the city where he lived most of his adult life. You'll be walking the streets he walked, seeing the buildings he saw, maybe even drinking in the same pubs as people who knew him.'

'I can't help that, Carol. It's not like I drove down to Worcester to murder and mutilate a teenage girl on the off-chance West Mercia would call me in to do them a profile. This is what I do best, this is what makes me come alive. I'm good at it and I can help.' He stopped speaking as the waiter arrived with their main courses.

Once they were alone again, she said, 'So are you going to pretend you've got no connection with the place once you're there?'

'That wouldn't be a pretence. I don't have any connection.'

Carol gave a dry laugh as she loaded a piece of naan with karahi chicken. 'Apart from owning a house and a boat there.'

'That's an accident, not a connection.'

She gave him a long look, compassionate and tender. 'You won't be able to resist, Tony. If you try to, it'll eat a hole in your heart.'

'That's a bit melodramatic for you,' he said, trying to deflect her concern. 'Where's my pragmatic detective chief inspector?'

'Trying to get you to accept your own needs for once. You spend your life trying to fix what's broken. You do it for your patients. You do it when you profile for us. You do it for the people you care about, people like Paula. And me. All I want is for you to be selfish this time and do it for yourself.' She reached out and put a hand over his. 'We've known each other a long, long time, Tony. We know a lot of the ways we're both fucked up. When you've spotted opportunities to help me, you've taken them. Why won't you let me do the same for you?'

He felt his throat swell, as if he'd swallowed a naga chilli whole. He shook his head, pushing his plate away. 'I just want to do my job.' Getting the words out was a strain.

'I know that.' Carol spoke gently, almost inaudible against the background noise. 'But I think you'd do it better if you acknowledged your need to come to terms with your history.'

'Maybe.' He drank some beer and cleared his throat. 'Maybe you're right.' He managed a weak smile. 'You're not going to let this go, are you?'

She shook her head. 'How can I? I don't like to see you hurting because you're in denial.'

Tony laughed. 'Excuse me, but I'm supposed to be the psychologist here.'

Carol pushed his plate back towards him. 'And I'm a good learner. Now eat your dinner and let me tell you what I've managed to find out.'

'You win,' he said meekly, reaching for his fork.

'It's not like it's anything approaching the whole picture,' Carol said. 'But it's somewhere to start. The first good thing is that he didn't have a criminal record. He even had a clean driving licence, though he did have a couple of speeding convictions in 2002. Probably down to the installation of speed cameras on the nearest main road.'

'And then he learned to be careful.' Tony slowly began to eat, one tiny morsel at a time.

'The second good thing – at least, I think it was probably good for him, if not for the people who were close to him – is that his death was very quick. No lingering illness, no long period of debilitation. The cause of death was a massive heart attack. He'd been at some sort of canal boat rally and he was walking back to his boat when he collapsed on the quayside. By the time the ambulance arrived, he was beyond help.'

Tony imagined what that must have been like. The paralysing grip of sudden pain. The loss of control. The agonising understanding that this was it. The darkness descending. The terrible loneliness, the absence of anyone he cared about. No chance to say goodbye. No chance to make amends. 'Did he know he was likely to have a heart attack?'

'Not really. He'd been diagnosed with ischaemic heart disease, but it didn't seem to have had any impact on the way he lived. He played golf, he spent a lot of time pottering about on the canals in his narrowboat, and he went to work. He smoked a cigar most evenings, he drank the best part of a bottle of red wine every day and he enjoyed eating out in expensive restaurants several times a week. Not the way you behave if you've got an eye on a long and healthy life.'

Tony shook his head. 'How did you find this stuff out?'

'I'm a DCI. I called the coroner's officer.'

'And they just told you all this? Didn't they wonder why you wanted to know?' Tony knew he shouldn't be surprised by the lack of privacy the state offered its citizens, but there were still times when it amazed him how easy it was to garner information that was supposed to be confidential. 'You could have been anybody,' he added.

'He did wonder, yes. I reassured him that we didn't think there was anything untoward about Edmund Blythe's death, just that we were looking into the possibility that someone on our patch had stolen his identity. So naturally I needed some details.' She grinned and helped herself to a spoonful of tarka daal.

'You're very devious. I'd never have thought of that.'

Carol raised her eyebrows. 'You're one to talk. I've seen you be more twisted than a corkscrew in the interview room. I'd never come up with some of the stuff that comes second nature to you when you're trying to get inside someone else's skin.'

He tipped his head in acknowledgement of her accuracy. 'True. Well, thanks for that. You're right, it's not the end of the world to know this.'

'There is more. You up for it?'

Again he felt wariness rising, a constriction in his gut. 'I'm not sure.'

'I don't think there's anything in what I've found out that could cause you a problem,' Carol said carefully. 'I wouldn't be pushing you so hard if I thought it was going to fuck you up.'

He looked across the restaurant at the crammed tables. Judging by the faces of the diners, all human life was here. Romance, business, disagreement, friendship, joy, sadness, family ties, first dates. Everyone in the room had the potential for all of these aspects of relationships. What was he so afraid of? What could hurt him about a dead man who'd known nothing about him when he'd been alive? He turned back to Carol. Her eyes seemed not to have left his face. He was, he thought, lucky to have her in his life, even if her persistence sometimes drove him crazy. 'OK,' he said.

'He was a smart bloke, your father—'

'Not my father,' Tony interrupted, instantly angered. 'Please, Carol. No amount of pushing's going to make that acceptable.'

'I'm sorry, I'm sorry. It wasn't meant to be a push. I just wasn't thinking, that's all. What do you want me to call him?'

Tony shrugged. 'Edmund? Blythe?'

'His friends called him Arthur.'

'Then Arthur will do.' He glared at his food. 'I'm sorry I snapped at you. But I can't think of him that way. I really can't. I've said it before: "father" implies a relationship. Good or bad, honest or dishonest, loving or hating. But we didn't have any kind of relationship.'

Carol's expression was apology enough. 'Arthur was a smart bloke. He set up his company, Surginc, a couple of years after you were born. I'm not sure what he was doing before that. The woman I spoke to at Surginc has worked there for thirty-odd years, but she didn't know anything about Arthur's life before he came to Worcester except that he came from up north somewhere.'

A twist of a smile. 'That would be Halifax, we assume, since that's where my mother was living at the time. So what does this Surginc do?'

'It's all a bit technical, but the gist of it is that they make disposable surgical instruments. Where Arthur was ahead of the game was that he developed a series of recyclable disposable instruments made from a combination of plastics and metal. So instead of them being single use, the materials could be reclaimed and reused. Don't ask me what's so special about the process they use, but it's apparently unique. He had a patent on it. One of several he held, apparently.' Her smile softened the lines of her face, reminding him of why people often underestimated her toughness. 'Turns out you're not the first innovative thinker in your bloodline.'

Against all his determination, Tony couldn't help feeling pleased at Carol's news. 'For all her faults, so's my mother. It's good to know I don't get all my creativity from her.'

Carol's expression tightened at the mention of his mother. Tony wasn't surprised. The antagonism between the two women had sparked on first meeting. Tony had been in hospital, recovering from a brutal attack at the hands of a Bradfield Moor patient. He'd been in no fit state to act as a buffer between the two women, and the fact that Carol had intervened to stop Vanessa ripping him off over Arthur Blythe's estate had cemented their mutual loathing. 'Well, there's one big difference between Arthur and Vanessa,' she said. 'From all accounts, Arthur was one of the good guys. As well as being smart, he was apparently a good employer – his firm even had a profit-sharing system with the workers. He was very sociable, good company, generous. He employed about twenty-five people, but he knew all about their families. Always remembered their kids' names, that sort of thing. When he sold the company two years ago, he took the entire staff and their partners off to a country-house hotel for a weekend break. No expense spared.' Carol paused, expectant.

Tony summoned up an anodyne response. 'No wonder they liked him.'

'The one thing none of them could work out was why he stayed single. In all the years this woman worked for him, he never turned up at an office event with a woman on his arm. One or two of them thought he was gay, but she didn't think so. He appreciated women too much, she thought. She wondered if maybe he'd been widowed or divorced when he was really young. So I checked out the records at the Family Records Centre. He never married.'

Tony gave a laugh. 'Sounds like he was as good at relationships with women as me.' *And probably for the same reason. We were both fucked up by Vanessa.*

As if reading his thoughts, Carol said, 'Well, there is a common factor there.'

Tony reached for his beer. 'Vanessa's toxic. But I can't blame her for everything.'

Carol looked as if she didn't agree. 'Well, one thing we can say is that, once Arthur moved out of her orbit, he really made something of his life. I know you can't set aside the fact that he ignored your existence while he was alive, but from what I've learned about him . . . I don't know, it feels like there must have been a good reason for his absence. And if anyone knows what that is, it must be Vanessa.'

'In that case, it can stay a mystery. I've no plans to talk to her in the foreseeable future.' Tony pushed his plate to one side and signalled to the waiter. He hoped Carol would read his desire to change the subject. 'You want another beer?'

'Why not? When are you going down to Worcester?'

'Probably tomorrow or the day after. I need to talk to DI Patterson again in the morning, once I've taken another pass through the stuff he sent me. I don't imagine I'll be gone for more than a couple of days. Nobody's got any budget for luxuries like me any more,' he added drily.

'It's that teenage girl, right? I've seen the news coverage. How are they doing?'

He ordered the beers and gave her a crooked smile. 'How do you think? They're calling me in. That should tell you all you need to know.'

'So, bugger all to go on, then?'

'Pretty much.'

'I don't envy you.'

'I don't envy myself. One body, it's always hard to draw strong conclusions. You know how it goes. The more deaths, the better I get.' It was, he thought, the worst thing about profiling. It gave a whole new meaning to profiting from someone else's misery. One of the hardest things he had ever had to come to terms with was that he was in the only job where he relied on serial offenders to make him look good.

It didn't help him sleep at night.

CHAPTER 11

Paula picked her way across the oblong plastic stepping stones that provided an authorised route from the periphery of the crime scene to its heart. It was bloody bleak up here. She wondered what it had been about this barren hillside that had convinced some speculative builder to develop the site. Even a nature lover would struggle to find much appeal up here. There was a distant cluster of trees, through which she could make out what looked like a low stone house. A hill farm, probably, given the sheep grazing the slopes above and beyond the building site that had become the focus of such intense activity.

'At least it's not raining,' Franny Riley greeted her as she reached the knot of people at the end of the pathway. The unlit cigarette in his mouth bobbed up and down as he spoke.

'Good morning to you too, Sarge,' Paula said. A couple

of the other detectives at the scene gave her a curious glance, but the white-suited forensic team didn't even raise their eyes. They were more concerned with the dead than the living. 'Thanks for the heads-up.' She'd been less than thrilled when her day-off, lie-in sleep had been broken by the insistent bleat of her mobile, but Franny Riley's news had certainly been worth a wake-up call.

'I think we've found him,' he'd said, his voice sombre so she knew it wasn't the good kind of finding. 'I'll text you directions.'

She'd called Carol, showered in four minutes and a further twenty minutes later she'd given her name to the officer running the access to the crime scene. He'd clearly been expecting her, reinforcing her sense of Franny Riley as an effective copper. And now here they were, standing a few feet away from a concrete-lined trench where the presumed body of Daniel Morrison lay.

'Who found the body?' she asked.

'Anonymous phone tip. He sounded very fucking frightened.' Franny gestured with his thumb towards the tarmac drive. 'There's some fresh tyre tracks where somebody's pulled off. Fresher than the body, apparently. And a mess of bootprints. All since yesterday afternoon when it rained, the lads who know about these things are saying. It's looking like some gobshite drove up here on the off-chance of finding something worth robbing and got more than he bargained for.'

'Do we know for sure if it's Daniel Morrison?'

'Chances are.' Franny rolled his beefy shoulders inside his anorak. 'Come on, let's get outside the cordon so we can have a fag and I can bring you up to speed.' Without waiting for a response, he was off across the plastic plates like a man on a mission. As soon as they were clear of the police tapes, his cigarette was lit. Joining him, Paula caught a couple of disapproving glances from uniformed officers. These days, it felt like smoking was up there alongside child abuse on the list of social crimes. She kept meaning to give up, but somehow it always slipped off the agenda. She'd stopped before, but after she lost a friend and colleague to the dangers of the job and came close to death herself, she'd embraced nicotine like a lover returned from peril. It was a better drug in times of crisis than others she'd seen claim friends and colleagues. At least it didn't impair your judgement or lead you into compromising positions with scumbag dealers.

'So, what's down there in the trench?' Paula said.

'A young lad. Answering Daniel's description. Wearing the right school sweatshirt.'

'Don't you have photographs?'

Riley sighed a stream of attenuated smoke. 'We've got pics. But until we get the body on the slab, that's not a huge help. He's got a plastic bag over his head. Taped tight round his neck. Looks like that's how he died, judging by the state of him.' He shook his head. 'That's not the worst of it, though.'

Paula's stomach contracted. She'd seen enough to understand what that short sentence might comprehend. 'Mutilated?'

Riley looked over her shoulder towards the distant trees, his battered face a forbidding mask. 'Just a bloody hole where his cock and balls should be. No sign of them in there with him, but we won't know for sure till we lift him.'

She was glad she hadn't had to look at the body. She knew only too well the pity and horror that always walked hand in hand with the bodies of the violently dead, particularly young victims. They always looked so short-changed, their vulnerability an accusation. 'What's your boss saying?' she asked. 'I mean, this is about as major as it gets.'

Riley snorted. 'He's crapping himself. I think we can safely say it's pass-the-parcel time. We'll carry on processing the scene, but you need to tell your guv'nor it's all yours now. I'll make sure all the paperwork's in order and over to your office soon as.'

'Thanks,' Paula said, reaching for her phone. A chance to prove themselves to Blake, she thought. But Daniel Morrison had paid a hell of a price for that chance. And his family hadn't even made the down-payment yet.

What had always driven Carol Jordan was her desire for justice. It infused her personal life as much as her professional one. When it came to the people she loved, she felt deeply the responsibility to put right whatever wrongs afflicted them. In Tony's case, she'd mostly been frustrated because the roots of his damage lay too deep for her to grasp, far less put right. But meeting Vanessa Hill had opened up possibilities. Never mind that the woman was a shallow, selfish bitch who should never have been allowed to raise a child. Carol would have swallowed the woman's insults and insinuations if she'd thought it would help her to help Tony. But when she had uncovered

Vanessa's devious scheme to deprive her son of his inheritance from the father he'd never known, she knew Vanessa had burned any bridges that might possibly lead to co-operation.

And yet, Carol couldn't resist the idea that she had to try. Even though Tony thought it wasn't what he wanted, she needed to do her best for him. It wasn't easy to go against his wishes, but his reaction the night before had persuaded her she was right to swallow her doubts. She was convinced that the information she'd been able to garner about Arthur Blythe had meant something positive to Tony. But there was still so much to discover. She wanted to know where Blythe had been before he popped up in Worcester and what he had been doing. She assumed he'd been in Halifax, where Tony had grown up in his grandmother's house. It was where Vanessa's recruitment and training consultancy was still based. Carol wondered how she was doing in a job market that seemed to be contracting daily as the global recession bit deeper into every area of employment. If anybody was likely not merely to survive but to come out ahead of the game, it was Vanessa Hill.

Going head to head with Vanessa was not something Carol relished. But there was no escaping the fact that Tony's mother was the primary source for information on Arthur Blythe. No detective worth their salt would put her anywhere but number one on the list of people to talk to about Arthur's history. Sure, you'd take everything with a pinch of salt, but you couldn't ignore her potential.

So first thing, she'd told Kevin Matthews to cover her back if Blake came looking and set off to drive over the

Pennines to Halifax. The motorway route might have been quicker, but it was almost twice the length of the cross-country drive. Carol hesitated to call it the pretty way; there were too many remnants of the area's polluted industrial past scattered across the dramatic landscape to qualify it for that description. But there was no denying the dramatic approach into Halifax, a long spiral down from the high ridge of the moors to the dark sprawl held in the bowl of the valley.

Vanessa Hill's company HQ was a squat brick building on the outskirts of the town. Carol parked in a visitor's slot and had barely turned off the engine when her phone rang. The display told her it was DS Matthews. 'Bugger,' she said, opening the line. 'Kevin, what's happening?'

'Paula's just been on. She's at a Northern Division crime scene. Anonymous tip, looks like Daniel Morrison. They want to punt it over to us.'

Duty dictated that Carol should turn round and drive straight back to Bradfield. But she'd come this far and she suspected her interview with Vanessa Hill wasn't going to take long. And Northern Division's patch was at least on the right side of Bradfield. 'OK, Kevin. Text me directions. I'll be there soon as I can. Tell Paula to hold the fort. You get over there now, make sure we're in the loop. And when they get a positive ID, I want you to go with the FLO to tell the parents.'

'Got it. Do you want me to alert Tony?'

A routine inquiry, because her team knew that Tony preferred to see the body where it lay if there was any possibility of it being a case where they could use his expertise. But Tony was off limits now. And probably on his way to West Mercia to work for someone who was allowed to appreciate his skills. 'No, that's fine. I'll see you shortly.'

With a fresh sense of urgency, Carol walked up to the steel and glass doors, where she was brought up short by the need to announce herself via the intercom. She hadn't expected that. Nothing for it but to go for the full pomp of rank. 'Detective Chief Inspector Carol Jordan to see Ms Hill,' she said.

There was a long silence. Carol imagined consternation followed by consultation. 'Do you have an appointment?' a female voice crackled at her.

'We don't normally consider an appointment necessary,' Carol said as frostily as she could manage. Another silence, then the door buzzed. She found herself in a vestibule that led to a small reception area furnished with discreet comfort. The woman behind the desk looked startled. Carol read her name badge and smiled as she said, 'Good morning, Bethany. I'm here to see Ms Hill.'

Bethany cast a swift look over her shoulder towards the door that led into the main part of the building. 'Can I see your ID?' she said, a spasm of a smile flashing across the lower part of her face.

Carol fished it out of her bag and held it up for Bethany to see. Before she could react, the door swung open and Vanessa Hill swept in. At first glance, she hadn't changed much since Carol had last seen her. She was still keeping the years at arm's length, thanks to a hairdresser with a discreet hand on the golden brown dye and her own good eye for the judicious amount of make-up. She remained slender, her figure flattered by a beautifully cut suit whose narrow skirt revealed legs still shapely. However, the lines on her face that had revealed her less than generous nature seemed to have been smoothed out. Botox, thought Carol, marvelling again at the vanity that would persuade a woman that injecting poison into her face was a good move.

'It's the police to see you,' Bethany said, apprehensive as a menopausal shoplifter confronted by a store detective.

Vanessa's mouth curled in a contemptuous smile. 'This isn't the police, Bethany. This is my son's girlfriend. Nothing to be worried about here.' Wrong-footed, Carol struggled in vain to find a response. Seeing her discomfort, Vanessa carried on. 'Come through, Carol. Let's not discuss family business in front of the staff.'

Bethany looked relieved. Grateful not to have committed some unwitting gaffe, Carol thought, following Vanessa through the door into an open-plan office bustling with focused activity. She couldn't see a man in the place, and none of the women even glanced up from their computers or their phones as they passed.

Vanessa's office was at the far end of the room. It was smaller than Carol expected, and more functional. The only trace of luxury was an electric massage pad attached to the chair behind the desk.

'I'm not Tony's girlfriend,' Carol said as Vanessa closed the door behind her.

Vanessa sighed. 'Of course you're not. More's the pity.' She passed Carol and settled into her chair, waving at a comfortless visitor's chair opposite. 'Let's not pretend we like each other, Carol. What are you doing here?'

'Edmund Arthur Blythe.' At the sound of his name,

Vanessa compressed her lips and narrowed her eyes. Undaunted, Carol continued. 'Tony wants to know more about him. How the two of you met, what he was doing in Halifax, that sort of thing.'

'No, he doesn't. You might want to, but Tony's got no interest. He'd have been happier if you hadn't interfered in the first place. Letting him sign Eddie's estate over to me would have been the best thing for him.' Vanessa squared her shoulders and folded her hands on the desk.

'Apart from the small matter of, what – half a million or so?'

Vanessa made a noise that might have been a laugh. 'If you think my son gives a toss about money, you know a lot less about him than I gave you credit for. Trust me, you sticking your nose in our business has led to nothing but grief for Tony. You don't understand the first thing about him. Whatever he might have told you, I'm the one who knows what's best for him because I'm the one who knows what makes him tick. I shaped him, not you.' She stood up. 'Now, if that's all that's on your mind, I think it's time for you to sling your hook.'

'Why won't you tell me? It's ancient history. It's no skin off your nose now. It's not like you can sink any lower in my estimation. What's the big secret? Tony deserves to know why his father didn't want to stick around.'

'And I deserve my privacy. This conversation is over, Carol.' Vanessa walked past her and threw open the door. 'Next time you come here, you better have a warrant.'

Furious and frustrated, Carol walked past Vanessa, head held high. A humiliating waste of time, that's what this had been. But as she slammed her car door, Carol vowed that Vanessa Hill would not defeat her. Now she had an added spur in her search for Edmund Arthur Blythe's story. Not just to help Tony but to spite his mother. Right now, it was hard to say which gave the stronger impetus.

CHAPTER 12

It made sense to take the train to Worcester. More time to reread the case information. The possibility of arriving fresh rather than frazzled from negotiating the maze of motorways round Birmingham. A no-brainer. Normally, Tony wouldn't have thought twice about it. But without a car, he'd be at the mercy of West Mercia Police. If he wanted to drive past Arthur Blythe's house or take a look at his factory, he'd have to embark on an awkward explanation to some police driver. And if he felt the need to visit the crime scene in the middle of the night when he couldn't sleep, he'd earn himself a reputation for being even more weird than they were expecting. He decided freedom was worth the trade-off.

By the time he pulled into his hotel in Worcester, he'd lost count of the number of times he'd cursed his own stupidity. Why hadn't he thought of hiring a car once he'd arrived? He'd estimated two hours' driving; it had taken three and a half and left him feeling like he'd had the worst kind of workout. Tony laid his head on the steering wheel and tried in vain to loosen the muscles of his neck and shoulders. He dragged himself out of the car and checked in.

He'd barely closed the door behind him when he felt the heavy hand of depression settle on him. He knew there were hotels whose rooms gladdened the heart. He'd even stayed in a couple over the years, mostly when deluded companies had hired him under the misapprehension that he could help motivate their management teams. This was not one of those rooms. The décor – no, you couldn't call it décor, not in any meaningful sense of the word; there were various dead shades of brown in the room, ranging from cheap-and-nasty milk chocolate to tobacco. The window was too small and looked out on the car park. The TV had only seven channels and the bed had all the give of a wooden pallet. He understood the exigencies of police budgets, but surely there must have been a better option than this?

Sighing, Tony dumped his bag and sat on the bed facing a print of the African veldt. The connection between Worcester and wildebeest was lost on him. He took out his phone and called DI Stuart Patterson. 'I'm at the hotel,' he said without preamble.

'I don't know how you go about this,' Patterson said. 'I think you said you wanted to see the crime scene?'

'That's right. It's a good first stop for me. I'd like to talk to the parents too, if that's possible.'

Patterson offered to send DS Ambrose over to pick him

up. Tony would have preferred a face-to-face with Patterson himself, but working with new teams always meant adjusting to the way they ran the game. So he'd settle for the bagman for now and build a bridgehead from there.

With half an hour to kill, Tony decided to take a walk. The hotel was on the fringe of the city centre and five minutes' walk brought him to a street of banks, estate agents and the sort of chain stores that had replaced traditional small shopkeepers, selling the same chocolates, shoes, greetings cards, alcohol and dry-cleaning services as every other high street in the country. He ambled along, vaguely looking in the windows until he was brought up short by the familiar name of the estate agency he'd been dealing with.

Front and centre in the window were the details of the very house he was trying to sell. 'For a man who doesn't believe in coincidence, I seem to be confronting a few. Might as well roll with it, eh?' The sound of his voice broke the moment and before he could stop and think, he walked into the agency. 'Good morning,' he said cheerily. 'Can I talk to someone about that house in the window?'

Paula had never been more relieved to see her boss. The police surgeon and the forensics team were eager to remove Daniel Morrison's body, but she'd enlisted Franny Riley's support to insist that it stayed where it was till the DCI had seen it. 'You can't shift the cadaver till the SIO has signed off on it,' she'd protested. 'I don't care if your guv wants rid. It stays till DCI Jordan gets here.'

Kevin Matthews had turned up in time to back her up.

But the atmosphere was growing increasingly hostile as time drifted past and Carol failed to appear. Finally Paula saw her striding up the drive towards them, looking decidedly more chic than usual. Wherever she'd been, she'd made a definite effort to impress. 'Sorry to keep you all waiting,' Carol said, charm on full beam. 'I got stuck behind an accident on the Barrowden road, right down in the valley where there's no mobile signal. Thank you all for being so patient.'

When she was on form like this, there was nobody like Carol Jordan. She had everybody scrambling to please her, to earn that look of approval. It didn't hurt that she was easy on the eye, but the set of her mouth and the directness of her gaze meant nobody was ever going to take her for a bimbo. Paula knew she was a little bit in love with her boss, but she'd learned to live with that as an exercise in futility. 'It's this way, chief,' she said, leading the way over to the trench, introducing Riley on the way. 'DS Riley's been my liaison, it would be helpful if we could keep him on board,' she said. Code for 'he's one of us, in spite of appearances.'

She stood at Carol's shoulder, looking down at the grievous distortion of humanity lying at the bottom of the ditch. Dirt and blood smeared the boy's clothes, and his head inside the transparent plastic looked unreal, like some hideous prop from a straight-to-DVD horror flick. 'Christ,' Carol said. She turned her face away. Paula could see a faint tremble shiver through her boss's lips. 'OK, let's have him out of here,' she said, stepping aside and beckoning the others over to join them.

'We're going to assume that we're looking at Daniel

Morrison here,' Carol said. 'The body answers the description of the missing boy and he's wearing the William Makepeace sweatshirt under his jacket. That means we're sixty hours out from the last time Daniel was seen by someone who knew him. So we've got a lot of catching up to do. Once we get an approximate time of death, we'll know how many hours we need to fill in. But I want those hours accounted for. Paula, you liaise with DS Riley, make sure we have all their product. Kevin's going to go with the FLO to break the news to the parents, but I also want you to do the follow-up, Paula.' Carol started to walk back to the perimeter of the scene, her team at her heels.

'For now, Paula, you take the school. Teachers and friends. It's a private school, you're going to come up against more than your fair share of wankers, but they're not going to wind you up and you are going to find out exactly what kind of lad Daniel Morrison was. We'll get Stacey on to his computer. Oh, and Paula? I want a fingertip search of the roadside from the end of the drive to the main drag. Tell DS Riley I said so.' At the end of the plastic panels, she turned back to face them, her smile weary. 'We owe Daniel a result. Let's do it.'

'Do I need to pick up Tony at Bradfield Moor?' Paula asked. Over Carol's shoulder, she saw Kevin make the throat-cutting gesture with one finger.

The muscles of Carol's face tensed. 'We're going to have to manage without Tony this time. If we think we need a profiler, we'll have to rely on someone from the National Police Faculty.'

She hid her disdain well, Paula thought. You'd have to

really know the chief to realise how little store she set by the Home Office's blue-eyed boys and girls.

'One more thing,' Carol said. 'We need to check out who knew about this place. Kevin, as soon as you're clear, get on to the builder, get a list of his crew, also architects, surveyors, the whole kit and caboodle. I'll arrange some bodies from Northern to cover the initial background checks and interviews, then we can review what comes up.' She ran a hand through her hair in a gesture Paula recognised. It was her boss's way of buying herself some time. 'Anything I've missed?' she asked. Nobody spoke. One day, Paula dreamed she'd come up with something remarkable, something that hadn't occurred to Carol or anyone else. She turned away and reached for a cigarette. Unfortunately it wasn't going to be today.

The house looked more attractive in reality than it had in the photo. There was a better sense of its proportions, an awareness of its relationship to the garden, a context for its solid Edwardian lines. Tony opened the gate and walked up the drive, his feet crunching uneven on the gravel. It made him aware of the slight limp that still afflicted him after his encounter with an unmedicated patient and a fire axe. They'd offered him further surgery, but he'd said no. He'd hated being incapacitated, loathed the awareness of how little control he had over his life when his physical movement was compromised. For as long as he could manage without an operation, he would.

He was early for the viewing appointment with the agent so he walked round the side of the house and found himself in a formal rose garden. The bushes were little more than bare contorted twigs at this time of the year, but he could picture how they would look in summer. He knew nothing about gardening, but it didn't take much knowledge to see this was a well-tended arrangement, designed for pleasure. Tony sat down on a stone bench and gazed out across the roses. Arthur Blythe would have done the same thing, he imagined.

His thoughts would have been very different, however. He wouldn't have spent the middle of his day pacing a muddy lay-by, trying to climb inside the mind of a killer who had chosen this particular spot to dump his teenage victim. Alvin Ambrose, Patterson's bagman, had been helpful, giving Tony useful background about the area and the condition of the victim. The mutilation had occurred postmortem. 'But not here,' Tony had said. 'He'd need privacy.'

'Plus the weather,' Ambrose added. 'It was lashing with rain and blowing a gale. The weather set in late afternoon, round about the time Jennifer left her pal Claire. Frankly, you wouldn't want to be walking the dog in it, never mind . . . you know. What he was doing.'

Tony looked up and down the lay-by. 'He'd need somewhere sheltered from the weather and from prying eyes. But she was already dead, so he didn't have to worry about being overheard. I suppose he could have worked on her here, in the back of a van or a truck.' He closed his eyes for a moment, summoning up what the lay-by would be like under cover of darkness. 'That would let him pick the perfect moment to dump her. Better than just driving in on the off-chance . . .' His voice tailed off and he clambered through the undergrowth towards the sheltering trees. It smelled of loam and pine resin and stale urine. It suggested nothing to him, so he made his way back to Ambrose, patient by his car. 'Either he's used it before, or he's deliberately scouted it out. Not that there's any way of telling which it is. And if he has used it before, there's no reason to believe it was for criminal purposes. He could just have stopped to take a leak or have a catnap.'

'We're coming by every night, talking to whoever's parked up here, asking if they've noticed anything unusual,' Ambrose said, clearly knowing it wasn't enough. Tony liked that the sergeant showed none of the contempt or arrogance that often met his profiling sorties. Ambrose seemed stolid and unemotional, but his silence wasn't the silence of the dull. He spoke when he had something to say, and so far what he'd had to say had been worth listening to.

'Hard to think what would qualify as unusual to a bunch of truckers,' Tony muttered. 'The dump site is a problem, though. The weight of probability is on it not being a local. So hauling in the usual suspects isn't going to get you anywhere.'

'Why do you think it's not a local?' Ambrose sounded genuinely interested in the answer.

'I imagine there's a lot of better places to dump a body round here that a local would know about – more out of the way, less busy. Just safer all round for the killer. This is a relatively high-risk dump site. I think that, even if he did scout it out before, this was essentially a site of opportunity for someone who didn't know anywhere better and didn't want to risk driving any distance with a dead body on board.'

'Makes sense.'

'I try to,' Tony said wryly.

Ambrose grinned, his impassivity disappearing in an instant. 'That's why we brought you in.'

'Your first mistake.' Tony turned back and prowled along the fringe of the lay-by again. On the one hand, this killer planned carefully. He'd spent weeks grooming Jennifer, setting her up to take his bait. He'd captured her, apparently avoiding witnesses and suspicion. And according to Ambrose, he'd left no forensic traces that had any investigative value. And then he'd dumped her by the side of the road, apparently not caring when she would be found. 'Maybe he's just not very strong,' he called to Ambrose. 'Maybe he couldn't carry her very far.' As he drew closer, he continued. 'We tend to ascribe super-human qualities to this kind of offender. Because deep down we think they're monsters. But they're mostly pretty average in terms of physique. Now you, you'd have no trouble carrying a fourteen-year-old girl all the way into those woods, back where she might not be found for weeks or months. But me? I'd struggle to get her out of the car and off the roadway. So maybe that's the reason for the apparent contradiction.'

That had been his most profound conclusion from his crime-scene visit. He hoped for more from the Maidments, but they couldn't see him till later that afternoon. Her father had apparently decided he needed to spend some time back at work, so he wouldn't be available till four. If Tony had been given to believing in signs and portents, he would have had to chalk that up as another one. He'd been fully prepared to cancel his arrangement with the agent if it had clashed with meeting Jennifer's parents. Instead, their availability had dovetailed perfectly with his plans.

Ambrose had dropped him at the hotel. He probably thought Tony was poring over witness statements, not sitting in a rose garden waiting for an estate agent to show him round a house he already owned. That wasn't normal, by any standards of behaviour. Not as crazed as murdering teenage girls, but still a long way from normal.

It was, Tony thought, as well that Ambrose didn't know the truth.

CHAPTER 13

In her lowest moments, Carol imagined the worst fate James Blake could have in mind for her. Promotion. But not the sort of promotion that would let her lead her troops into battle. The sort that would have her sitting behind a desk, fretting about policy, while all the important work was being done elsewhere.

Like those times, thankfully rare, when her team were occupied on the front line, doing what needed to be done to find Daniel Morrison's killer and she was sitting in her office trying to fill the time before she was due at the boy's postmortem. Usually she tried to occupy her mind with administration and paperwork. But today, she had something more pressing on her mind.

Leading her team in their cold-case work had added new weapons to Carol Jordan's detective arsenal. She'd always been good at digging into the backgrounds of victims and suspects, but now she'd learned how to direct her archaeological skills backwards to a time when there were no computerised records or mobile phone bills to speed the plough. Like the years when Edmund Arthur Blythe had been living and presumably working in Halifax. Libraries were the most fruitful source, often leading to living experts who could fill in remarkable details. But there were also obscure electronic gateways to information. And Carol had access to the best of those.

Stacey was surrounded by a battery of screens. She'd now built a barricade of information between herself and the rest of the team. She'd started with two, expanded to three, and now there were six monitors arrayed in front of her, each of them showing different processes in action. Even though she was currently concentrating on filtering the city-centre CCTV footage through the face-recognition software, other applications were running, whose function was a mystery to Carol. Stacey glanced up as her boss approached. 'No luck yet,' she said. 'The trouble with these CCTV cameras is that they're still not very high res.'

'We'll just have to keep plugging away,' Carol said. 'Stacey, is there somewhere online where I can access old telephone directories?' She made a mental bet with herself that Stacey would show no signs of surprise at the request.

'Yes,' she said, her eyes returning to the screens. Her fingers flew over the keyboard and one of the screens changed to display a map with a flashing cursor.

'And that would be?'

'Depends how far back you want to go.'

'The early 1960s.'

Stacey's hands paused above the keys for a moment. Then they started typing again. 'Your best bet is one of the genealogy sites. They've digitised a lot of public domain social information: phone books, street directories, electoral rolls. They're also really user-friendly because they're aimed at—'

'Idiots like me?' Carol said sweetly.

Stacey allowed herself half a smile. 'Non-ICT professionals, I was going to say. Just google "old phone books" and "ancestors" and you might find something. Don't forget, back in the early 1960s, most people didn't have phones, so you might not get lucky.'

'I can only hope,' Carol said. She was pinning her hopes to the fact that Blythe had re-emerged in Worcester as an entrepreneur. Perhaps he'd started in business back when he'd been courting Vanessa.

Half an hour later, she was thrilled to be proved right. It was there, on the screen, in black and white in the 1964 directory. *Blythe & Co., Specialist Metal Finishers.* Carol checked the years either side and discovered the company was listed for only three years. So when Blythe left, the company ended. It looked like a dead end. What were the chances of tracking down anyone who had worked there forty-five years before, never mind someone who had known him well enough to remember anything useful?

Still, she'd faced more hopeless pursuits. Now it really was time for the library. A quick online search and she had the number of the local reference library. When she got through, she explained that she was looking for a local history expert who might know about small businesses in the 1960s. The librarian um-ed and ah-ed for a moment, had a muffled conversation with someone else and finally said, 'We think you need to talk to a man called Alan Miles. He's a retired woodwork teacher, but he's always been very keen on the industrial history of the area. Hang on a mo, I'll get you his number.'

It took Alan Miles almost a dozen rings to answer his phone. Carol was about to give up when a suspicious voice said, 'Hello?'

'Mr Miles? Alan Miles?'

'Who wants to know?' He sounded old and cross. *Great, just what I need.*

'My name is Carol Jordan. I'm a detective chief inspector with Bradfield Police.'

'Police?' Now she could hear anxiety in his voice. Like most people, talking to the police provoked worry, even for those who had nothing to worry about.

'I was given your number by one of the staff at the central library. She thought you might be able to help me with some background research.'

'What sort of background research? I know nowt about crime.' He sounded eager to be gone.

'I'm trying to find out anything I can about a man called Edmund Arthur Blythe who ran a company of specialist metal finishers in Halifax in the early 1960s. The librarian thought you were the best person to talk to.' Carol tried to sound as flattering as she could.

'Why? I mean, why do you want to know about that?'

God preserve me from suspicious old men. 'I'm not at liberty to say. But my team specialises in cold cases.' Which was nothing less than the truth, if not the whole truth.

'I don't like the phone,' Miles said. 'You can't get the measure of a person over the phone. If you want to come over to Halifax, I'll talk to you face to face.'

Carol rolled her eyes and suppressed a sigh. 'Does that mean you can help me with information about Blythe and Co?'

'Happen I can. There'll be stuff I can show an' all.'

Carol considered. Everything here was under control. They were nowhere near arrest or interview on anything. Unless something very unusual happened at the post-mortem, she could easily disappear for a couple of hours in the evening. 'How are you fixed this evening?' she asked.

'This evening? Seven o'clock. Meet me outside Halifax station. I'll be wearing a fawn anorak and a tweed cap.'

The line went dead. Carol glared at the phone, then saw the funny side and smiled to herself. If it took her further forward on her quest for Tony's not-father, dealing with grumpy Alan Miles would be more than worth it.

When Ambrose arrived to take him to meet Jennifer Maidment's parents, Tony could barely hide his relief. After the estate agent's tour, he'd struggled to focus his thoughts on the crime scene he'd visited earlier. He knew something was nagging at him about this killer, but he wasn't sure what it was, and the more he tried to think about it, the more his mind's eye was invaded by images of Arthur Blythe's home. Tony was seldom influenced by his immediate surroundings. The notion of interior design had never planted itself in his consciousness. So he was all the more bemused by the inescapable fact that he envied Arthur Blythe this house. It went beyond mere comfort. It felt like a home, a place that had grown organically round one man's idea of what mattered to him. And although he hated to admit it, it pierced Tony that Arthur Blythe had cast him off and gone on to make a home that felt so complete in itself. Nobody would ever feel like that about his house. He certainly didn't. He didn't have that absolute sense of himself that had clearly invested the man he never got to call his father.

So Ambrose's arrival felt like a liberation from his troublesome thoughts. It wasn't a relief that lasted for long. 'Did you bring the RigMarole print-outs?' Tony asked as soon as he'd settled into the car. When he'd heard about ZZ, he'd asked Ambrose to bring copies of whatever they'd salvaged from the sessions so he could study them.

Ambrose stared straight ahead. 'The boss doesn't want them to leave the office. He's happy for you to read them, but he wants you to do it in-house.'

'What? He doesn't trust me? What does he think I'm going to do with them?'

'I don't know. I'm just telling you what he said.' Ambrose's hands were tight on the steering wheel. His discomfort was like a vibration in the air.

'It's not because he's worried I'm going to sell them to the *Daily Mail*,' Tony said, irritated out of proportion to the offence. 'It's about control. He's afraid of losing control of his investigation.' He threw his hands in the air. 'I can't work like this. It's a waste of my energy to get caught up in this sort of pettiness. Look, Alvin, I work the way I work. I can't concentrate the way I need to if I've got somebody looking over my shoulder. I need to be away from the bustle, the running around. I need to study this stuff and I need to do it on my terms.'

'I get that,' Ambrose said. 'The DI isn't used to working with somebody like you.'

'Then he needs to get on the learning curve,' Tony said. 'It might help if he was keener to meet me face to face. Can you sort this out, or do I need to talk to him?'

'Leave it with me,' Ambrose muttered. 'I'll see what I can do.' They travelled the rest of the way in silence, Tony trying to bury everything that was standing between him and the next step of this process of discovery. Right now, all that mattered was drawing the Maidments out of their pain so they could tell him what he needed to know.

The man who opened the door held himself stiff and brittle as a dried reed. Ambrose introduced them and they followed Paul Maidment into the living room. Tony had often heard it said that people took grief differently. He wasn't sure he agreed. They might outwardly react in different ways, but when you got right down to it, what grief did was tear your life in half. Life before your loss and life after your loss. There was always a disconnect. Some people let it all hang out, some people rammed it into a hole deep inside and rolled a heavy stone over it, some people pretended it wasn't happening. But speak to them years later and they were always able to date memories in terms of their loss. 'Your dad was still alive then,' or 'That was after our Margaret died.' It was as precise as BC and AD. Come to think of it, that had been about grief and loss too, whatever your views on the authenticity of Jesus as the son of God.

In his role as a profiler, he mostly got to meet people when they were on the wrong side of the chasm of grief. He seldom knew what they'd been like before their lives had been torn in half. But he could often make an educated guess at what had existed on the other side of the gap. His consciousness of what had been lost formed a crucial part of his ability to empathise with where they were now, stranded in unfamiliar territory, trying to make sense of the map with part of the compass missing.

His first impression of Paul Maidment was of a man who had decided to draw a line under his daughter's death and move on. It was a decision he was clearly struggling to stick to. At this point, Tony thought, he was close to going under for the third time.

'My wife . . . she'll be down in a minute,' he said, looking around him with the air of someone who is seeing his environment for the first time and isn't quite sure how he got there.

'You went back to work today,' Tony said.

Maidment looked startled. 'Yes. I thought . . . There's too much to be done, I can't leave it to anyone else. Business . . . it's really not good just now. And we don't need to lose the business on top of . . .' He tailed off, distracted and distressed.

'It's not your fault. This would have happened whether you'd been home or not,' Tony said. 'You and Tania, you're not to blame for this.'

Maidment glared at Tony. 'How can you say that? Everybody says the internet's dangerous for teenagers. We should have taken better care of her.'

'It wouldn't have made any difference. Predators like

this, they're determined. Short of locking Jennifer up and never letting her communicate with anyone else, there was nothing you could have done to stop this.' Tony leaned forward, drawing Paul Maidment into his space. 'You need to forgive yourselves.'

'Forgive ourselves?' The woman's voice came from behind him, slightly slurred from drink or drugs. 'What the hell do you know about it? You've lost a child, have you?'

Maidment buried his head in his hands. His wife moved to the centre of the room with the exaggerated care of someone who is sufficiently in control to know they are slightly out of it. She looked at Tony. 'You'll be the shrink, then. I thought it was your job to analyse the bastard who killed my daughter, not us.'

'I'm Tony Hill, Mrs Maidment. I'm here so I can learn a bit more about Jennifer.'

'You're a bit late for that.' She subsided into the nearest chair. Her face was a mask of perfectly applied make-up but her hair was tangled and unkempt. 'A bit late to get to know my lovely girl.' Her voice trembled a little under the careful articulation.

'And I'm very sorry about that,' Tony said. 'Maybe you can help me. How would you describe her?'

Tania Maidment's eyes grew moist. 'Beautiful. Clever. Kind. That's what everyone says about their dead child, isn't it? But it was true about Jennifer. She was no trouble. I'm not stupid enough to say things like "We were each other's best friend" or "We were like sisters", because we weren't. I was her parent, her mother. Mostly, we got on. Mostly she told me what she was doing and who she was doing it with. Nine days ago I'd have said she always told me. But obviously I was wrong. So I might have been wrong about all the other stuff too. Who knows any more?'

Maidment raised his head, tears sparkling on his cheeks. 'She was all of those things. And more too. We dreamed of a child like Jennifer. Bright, talented, good fun. And that's what we got. A dream daughter. And now the dream's gone, and it's worse than if it had never come true.'

There was a long silence. Tony could find nothing to say that didn't seem banal. It was Ambrose who broke the moment. 'There's nothing we can do to bring Jennifer back, but we are determined to find the person who killed her. That's why Dr Hill's here.'

Grateful for the way in, Tony said, 'I know you've already spoken to the police, but I wanted to ask you what Jennifer said about RigMarole. How she talked about it, what she said she used it for.'

'She went on about it for ages,' her mother said. 'You know that thing they do, teenagers? "Mum, everybody's got—" whatever it is. And you ask around and actually, nobody has whatever it is, they're all just desperate to get it. She was like that with RigMarole, dying to have her own account. Claire was the same. I spoke to her mum and we talked it over with the girls. We said they could both have an account, provided that they installed all the privacy controls.'

'Which they did,' Maidment said bitterly. 'And that lasted for a matter of days. Just long enough for us all to be convinced they were being responsible about it.'

'They were being responsible as they saw it, Paul,' Tania said. 'They just didn't understand the risks. You don't at that age. You think you're invulnerable.' Her voice crashed and broke, catching in her throat like a crumb going down the wrong way.

'Did she ever say anything that suggested there might be something going on that made her uncomfortable with Rig?'

The both shook their heads. 'She loved it,' Maidment said. 'She said it was like it opened the world up for her and Claire. And of course, we all assumed that was in a good way.'

'Had she ever met anyone previously that she'd got to know online?'

Maidment shook his head and Tania nodded. 'You never said anything about that,' he said, the accusation inescapable.

'That's because it was completely innocuous,' Tania said. 'Her and Claire met up with a couple of girls from Solihull. They went for an afternoon out at Selfridges in Birmingham. I spoke to the mother of one of the girls beforehand. They had a good laugh and said they'd do it again.'

'When was this?' Tony asked.

'About three months ago.'

'And it was just the four of them? You're sure of that?'

'Of course I am. I even asked Claire again. After you lot started going on about RigMarole. She swore there had been nobody else involved.'

But someone else could have electronically eavesdropped the arrangements. There could have been a fifth pair of eyes taking in everything they did. It would have taken a crueller man than Tony to voice those thoughts. 'Jennifer sounds like a very sensible girl.'

'She was,' Tania said softly, her fingers stroking the arm of her chair as if it were her daughter's hair. 'Not in a boring, goody-two-shoes way. She had too much spirit for that. But she knew the world could be a dangerous place.' Her face crumpled. 'She was so precious to us. Our only child. I made sure she understood that there were times when it made sense to be cautious.'

'I understand that,' Tony said. 'So what would entice her to meet someone in secret? What would make her ignore her good sense and meet a stranger? What would tempt her so much she had to lie to her best friend? I mean, we all lie to our parents from time to time, that's the way the world works. But teenage girls don't lie to their best mates without a very pressing reason. And I'm struggling to think what that might be. Was there any-thing – anything at all – that Jennifer wanted so badly she'd throw caution and good sense out of the window?'

The Maidments looked at each other, nonplussed. 'I can't think of anything,' Tania said.

'What about boys? Could there have been somebody she was infatuated with? Somebody who could have per-suaded her to keep him secret?'

'She'd have told Claire,' Tania said. 'I know they talked about the boys they fancied. Telling Claire wouldn't have counted as breaking a promise.'

She was probably right, he thought. What she was describing was standard operating procedure for females, particularly teenagers. Tony got to his feet. There was nothing more for him here. The police had already searched Jennifer's room. It would be too disturbed now to tell him anything useful. 'If you think of anything, call me,' he said, handing Paul Maidment a card with his mobile number. 'Or if you just want to talk about Jennifer. I'm happy to listen.' The Maidments both looked non-plussed at the abrupt ending to the conversation. Tony thought they probably expected an extended outpouring of compassion. But what would be the point of that? He couldn't make them feel better, even if they wanted to. Still, Tania Maidment wasn't taking anything lying down right now.

'That's it?' she said. 'Five minutes of your precious time and you're out of here? How the hell can you have learned anything about my daughter in five minutes?'

Tony was startled. The recently bereaved who wanted to lash out generally picked on the police, not him. He was accustomed to sympathising with Carol, not taking it on the chin himself. 'I've been doing this a long time,' he said, trying not to sound defensive. 'I'll be talking to her friend Claire, I'll be reading her emails. You're just one of the sources for my picture of Jennifer.'

Tania looked as if he'd knocked the wind out of her. She made a noise that on another day might have been a contemptuous snort. 'That's what it's come to, is it? I'm just one of the sources for my daughter's life.'

'I'm sorry,' Tony said abruptly. Staying would merely prolong the immediate pain for the Maidments. His only value to them lay elsewhere. So he simply nodded to them both and walked from the room leaving Ambrose to scramble after him.

The detective caught him up halfway to the car. 'That

was a bit hairy,' he said. 'I think they thought you were a bit curt.'

'I'm not good at small talk. I said what I needed to. They've got something to think about now. That might shake something loose in their memories. Sometimes what I do, it looks brutal. But it works. Tomorrow, I want to talk to Claire. Jennifer might have spoken to her.' He gave a wry smile. 'I promise to play nice.'

'What do you want to do now?' Ambrose asked.

'I want to read the messages you got from her computer. Why don't you drop me at my hotel and bring me the paperwork as soon as you can persuade your boss that if he wants to get what his budget is paying for he should let me do things the way that works for me.' He put a hand on Ambrose's arm, realising how brusque he had sounded. He still got it wrong more often than he liked when it came to responding like normal people. 'I really appreciate your help with this. It's not easy to explain how the profiling works. But it does involve thinking myself inside someone else's skin. I don't like being around other people when I'm going there.'

Ambrose ran a hand over his smooth skull, his eyes troubled. 'I don't imagine you do. Tell you the truth, it's all a bit spooky to me. But you're the expert.'

He spoke as if that were something to be pleased about. Tony stared up at the Maidments' house, wondering what sort of messy head had wrecked their lives. Soon he'd have to pry his way in there and find out. It wasn't an enticing prospect. For a brief moment, he missed Carol Jordan so much it made him feel nauseous. He turned back to Ambrose. 'Somebody has to be.'

CHAPTER 14

Paula watched another adolescent boy slouch out of the small room they'd been allocated to conduct interviews in. 'Were you like that when you were fourteen?' she asked Kevin.

'Are you kidding? My mother would have slapped me if I'd spoken to an adult like that. What I can't decide is whether it's a generation thing or a class thing. Seems to me that working-class lads have got an attitude too, but there's something different about these pillocks. I don't know if it's a sense of entitlement or what, but they're really pissing me off.'

Paula knew exactly what he meant. She'd been in schools after kids had died in knife attacks, the sudden nightmare that seemed to happen out of nowhere, almost at random. She'd felt that sense of shock that permeated the corridors, seen the anxiety on teenage faces as they wondered whether death was going to touch them next, heard the fear under the defiance in pupils' voices. There was none of that here. It was as if Daniel's death was something that had happened far from them – an item on the news, something parents talked about as a remote threat. The only person who'd seemed at all upset was Daniel's form teacher. Even the headmaster of William Makepeace had behaved as if this were a minor inconvenience rather than a tragedy. 'If I had kids, this is the last place I'd be sending them,' Paula said.

'You ever think about it? Having children, I mean.' Kevin cocked his head to one side, considering her.

Paula puffed her cheeks and blew her breath out. 'Nothing like the big questions, eh, Sarge? To be honest, I've never felt the ticking of the biological clock. What about you? You like being a dad?'

He looked surprised at having his question turned back on him. 'It's the best thing and it's the worst thing,' he said slowly. 'The way I love my kids, Ruby especially – it's total, unconditional, forever. But the downside is the fear of loss. Cases like this, where parents end up burying their kids? It's like a nail in your heart.'

A knock at the door interrupted their exchange and another teenage boy walked in without waiting to be invited. Slim and dark, he was the shortest lad they'd seen all morning by several inches. Perfect skin the colour of roasted almonds, a thick mop of glossy dark hair, a Viking longship prow of a nose and a rosebud mouth – an off-kilter arrangement of features that demanded a second look. 'I'm Asif Khan,' he said, dropping into a chair. Hands in pockets, legs thrust straight out and crossed at the ankles. 'And you're the cops.'

Here we go again. Kevin introduced them both and got straight down to business. 'You know why we're here. Was Daniel a friend of yours?' He wasn't expecting much; the boys identified as having been close to Daniel had been the first half-dozen sent in to talk to them. There had been another eight or nine since, none admitting to more than acquaintance.

'We was bruvvahs, innit?' Asif said.

Paula leaned right forward in her chair, her face close to the boy. 'Do me a favour, Asif. Cut it out. You're a pupil at William Makepeace, not Kenton Vale. Your daddy's a doctor, not a market trader. Don't give me the fake street shit. Talk to us properly, with respect, or we'll be doing this at the police station, on our turf, on our terms.'

Asif's eyes widened in shock. 'You can't talk to me like that – I'm a minor. I should have an adult present. We're only talking to you because the school said it would be best.'

Paula shrugged. 'Fine by me. Let's get your dad down to the station too, see how impressed he is with his boy's big talk.'

Asif held Paula's stare for another few seconds, then dropped one shoulder and half turned away from her. 'OK, OK,' he muttered. 'Daniel and I were mates.'

'Nobody else seems to think so,' Kevin said as Paula retreated back into her chair.

'I didn't mix with that bunch of wankers Daniel hung around with, if that's what you mean. Me and Daniel, we did other stuff together.'

'What kind of stuff?' Kevin said, his imagination stumbling over the possibilities.

Asif uncrossed his feet and tucked them under his chair. 'Comedy,' he said, apparently embarrassed.

'Comedy?'

He fidgeted in his seat. 'We both wanted to be stand-ups, OK?'

One of the other lads had mentioned Daniel's interest in comedy, but hadn't mentioned this ambition. 'That's pretty wild,' Paula said. 'Not on the curriculum here, I bet.'

A ghost of a smile lit Asif's eyes. 'Not until we get our BBC3 series and make it respectable,' he said. 'Then it'll be right up there in drama class.'

'So you and Daniel shared this ambition. How did you find out you both wanted to do that?' Kevin asked.

'My cousin, he manages a club in town. They have a comedy night once a month. My cousin, he lets me in, even though he shouldn't. So I was going in one night, and there's Daniel arguing with the guy on the door, making out he's eighteen. Which he wasn't going to get away with, not even with the fake ID. So I ask him what's going on and he says there's one of the acts he really wants to see, he heard him on the radio and he wants to see his routine. So I talk my cousin into letting him in, and we get talking and that's when I find out he totally wants to get into the comedy game. So we start meeting up every couple of weeks round my house, trying out our material on each other.' He rubbed a hand over his face. 'He was pretty funny, Daniel. He had this great routine about adults who try to be, like, down with da kids. And he had this, like, presence.' He shook his head. 'This is so bad.'

'We think Daniel went to Temple Fields after school on Tuesday,' Kevin said. 'Did he say anything to you about meeting anybody there?'

Asif frowned. 'No.'

'You don't sound very sure.'

'Well, he didn't say anything about any specific meeting,' Asif said. 'But the last time we got together, last week, he said he'd met somebody online who was setting up some radio show to showcase young comedy talent. Like, kids who were too young to get on stage on the club circuit.' He shrugged. 'Kids like us. I asked if he could get me in on it and he said, sure, but he wanted to meet the guy first, get his feet under the table.' He looked suddenly miserable. 'I got a bit pissed off with him, I thought maybe he was trying to cut me out, keep it for himself, like. But he said, no, it wasn't like that, we were mates and he still owed me for getting him into the club in the first place. He just wanted to make the first contact, sort it all out, then bring me in afterwards.' Sudden light dawned and his eyes widened. 'Shit. You think that's what got him killed?'

'It's too early in the investigation to say,' Kevin said hastily. 'At this stage, we don't know what might be relevant. So it would be helpful if you could tell us anything about this contact of Daniel's. How did they meet, do you know?'

Asif nodded. 'It was on RigMarole. You know, the networking site? They were both in a *Gavin and Stacey* mosh pit – that's what we call a sort of fan group. They liked a lot of the same stuff so they got talking in a private sidebar and that's when it came out about him being a comedy producer.'

'Did Daniel mention his name?'

'No. That was one of the things I got pissed off about. He wouldn't even tell me the guy's name. He was, like, the guy didn't want it spread around in case somebody jumped the gun on him. So I never knew his name. Only that he made programmes at the BBC in Manchester. Supposedly,' he added.

'You weren't convinced?' Kevin asked.

'It just seemed like a funny way to go about things,' he said. 'I mean, he'd never heard Daniel do his schtick. How could he know he was good on his feet? But you couldn't tell Daniel anything. He was, like, his own law.'

'Did Daniel say where they were meeting? Or when?' Kevin tried.

'I told you. He was acting like it was a state secret. No way he was going to let the details slip. What I told you, that's all I know.'

It was, Paula thought, a start. Not much of one, but a start at least.

Ambrose felt his spirits give a little lift when he walked into Patterson's office to find his boss closeted with Gary Harcup. He hadn't been looking forward to attempting to put an upbeat gloss on the odd little profiler from Bradfield. But with Gary here, there would be something to divert Patterson's attention. There might even be a bit of something to get their teeth into.

Looking at Patterson, Ambrose saw a man who desperately needed some good news. He was pale and wan, his eyes heavy-lidded and baggy, his hair lifeless and stiff. It was always the same when they weren't moving forward fast enough on a case. Patterson absorbed all the pressure and all the pain till you thought he was going to crack up. Then something inside him would shift, he would see possibilities begin to open up and suddenly he'd be upbeat and full of confidence again. It was just a matter of waiting it out. 'Come on in,' Patterson said, waving Ambrose forward and gesturing to a chair. 'Gary's just this minute got here.'

Ambrose nodded to the chubby computer expert, who looked as dishevelled as ever. Hair awry, T-shirt crumpled, something adhering to his beard that Ambrose didn't want to examine too closely; he didn't exactly inspire confidence. But he'd come through for them often enough in the past for Ambrose not to care how he looked. Maybe he should suspend his judgement on Tony Hill. Not leap to conclusions just because the guy seemed kind of unorthodox in the way he approached things. He should wait and see if he too came up with the goods the way Gary did. 'All right, Gary?' he said.

Gary nodded so vigorously his belly shook. 'Doing good, Alvin. Doing good.'

'So, what have you got for us?' Patterson asked. He sat back in his chair, gently tapping the desk with a pencil.

Gary produced a couple of transparent plastic envelopes from his backpack. Each contained a few sheets of paper. 'It's a bit of a mixed bag. This—' he slapped the first '—this is a list of the machines I was able to identify. I only got about half of them. The others are out there in no man's land, passed on second- or third-hand.'

Patterson took the papers from the folder and scanned the top sheet. When he'd done, he passed it to Ambrose. It didn't take them long to look through the list of seventeen machines Gary had identified. Internet cafés, public libraries and one airport. 'It's all over the place,' Patterson said. 'Worcester, Solihull, Birmingham, Dudley, Wolver-hampton, Telford, Stafford, Cannock, Stoke, Stone, Holmes Chapel, Knutsford, Stockport, Manchester Airport, Old-ham, Bradfield, Leeds . . .'

'I wasn't completely accurate when I said he used a different machine every time,' Gary said. 'When I went back and analysed all the messages we've still got, I found some of them were double or triple use. The ones he went back to twice are Worcester, Bradfield and Stoke. He used Manchester Airport three times. But they're all public-access machines.'

'It's the motorway network,' Ambrose said, seeing the roads unfurl in his mind's eye like veins on a forearm. 'M5, M42, M6, M60, M62. These are all easy access off the motorway. If he was stalking Jennifer, Worcester was one end of his journey.' He looked up, eyes bright with a fresh idea. 'And Leeds was the other end. Maybe that's where he lives.'

'Or maybe that's where his next target lives,' Patterson said. 'He used Manchester Airport three times. Maybe that's the one that's nearest to where he actually lives. You need to run this past our profiler, see what he thinks. Don't they have some kind of computer program for figuring out where the killer lives? I'm sure I heard about that when they had that pair of random snipers in America.'

Gary looked dubious. 'I don't know if geographic pro-filing would work on something like this. Plus, it's a pretty specialist field.'

Suddenly animated, Patterson sat up straight and waved a hand at the papers. 'Get him in, let him have a look. That's what we're paying him for.'

Ambrose almost said something, then realised it wasn't the moment to raise Hill's demands to see the material on his ground. He'd have to wait till Gary had left. 'What's the other stuff, Gary?' he asked.

'Not quite so good,' Gary said, placing the other file on the desk. It looked pretty thin. 'But before I get to that, I wanted to tell you one other thing I did try. I thought that since ZZ was using Rig to contact Jennifer, he must have a page of his own. It turns out that he did, but the page was deactivated around four o'clock on the afternoon Jennifer disappeared. He was burning his bridges behind him.'

'Is there any way of getting at what was on the page?'

Gary shrugged. 'You'd need to get Rig on board. I don't think they'd give you anything without a warrant. And you've got a whole issue around data protection. They don't actually own the personal data people put up there. After the trouble Facebook got into over ownership of what's on the member pages, all the networking sites have been very careful to put up Chinese walls between their customers and themselves. So if there is some residual information on Rig's servers, you might not be able to get at it even with a warrant. Not without fighting their lawyers.'

'That's insane,' Patterson protested.

'That's the way it goes. These companies, they don't want to be seen as a pushover when the cops come calling. There's all sorts of stuff going on in their private sidebars. If you guys can just walk in and take what you want, they're going to have no clients in about five minutes flat.'

'God help us,' Patterson muttered. 'You'd think they wanted to encourage murderers and paedophiles to use their sites.'

'Only if they're got valid credit cards and like to shop online,' Ambrose said. 'Thanks anyway, Gary. I'll talk to the people at Rig and see what they have to say. So, how did you get on with the fragments you found on the hard disk?'

'I've managed to pull out some of the last conversation between Jennifer and ZZ. The one she erased. It's only partial, but it's something. There's two copies in there,' he added.

Thin divided by two, then. Ambrose took the two sheets of paper Patterson offered him.

ZZ: . . . 4 . . . king 2 me . . . priv8 here &no . . .

Jeni: Y u want 2 be . . .

ZZ: . . . ke I sd . . . BIG secr . . .

Jeni: no i don't

ZZ: u don't no wo . . .

Jeni: . . . noth . . .

ZZ: . . . i no truth . . .

Jeni: . . . ow . . . my biz

ZZ: cuz i no wh . . . 2 find stuf . . . idd . . . aces t look 4 inf . . . u don . . .

Jeni: . . . makin it up?

ZZ: cuz when i . . . no its tr . . . ul c . . .

Jeni: . . . so spill

ZZ: take a deep breth

Jeni: u mak . . . nd big deal

ZZ: ur . . . ur real . . .

Jeni: . . . fkd in t hed

ZZ: i can prove . . .

Jeni: LIAR

ZZ: . . . et me 2moro . . . @ ca . . . el u, show . . .

Jeni: . . . lieve u?

ZZ: cuz we need 2 . . . 30 @ c . . . nt tel . . .

Jeni: . . . b ther. U btr not b ly . . .

Patterson frowned. 'It's not exactly easy to read,' he said. 'It's hardly bloody English. It's like a different language.'

'It is. It's called textspeak. Your Lily would be able to read that like it was a newspaper,' Ambrose said. 'Basically, ZZ is saying he knows Jeni's big secret. He says something that Jennifer is totally pissed off about. She says he's fucked in the head and then she shouts that he's a liar. That's what the capital letters mean, she's shouting.'

'Mental,' Patterson muttered.

'Then I think he's saying they should meet tomorrow. He gives her a time and place and tells her not to tell. And she says she will be there and he better not be lying,' Gary said.

'So where's he telling her to meet?' Patterson said, pink with frustration.

Gary shrugged. 'Who knows? Somewhere beginning with "ca". Café? Car park? Castle Street? The cathedral?'

'You can't narrow it down any more than that?'

Gary looked hurt. 'You've got no idea, have you? It's taken me more than a week to get this much. I had to beg a mate for some software that's still in development to get this far. Given what there was on that computer, it's a miracle we've got this much. At least now you can rule out a lot of places where she didn't go.'

Patterson chewed the skin by his thumbnail in an act of suppressed rage. 'I'm sorry, Gary,' he grunted. 'I know you've done your best. Thank you. Send us your bill.'

Gary extracted himself from the chair with an attempt at dignity, grabbed his backpack and marched to the door. 'Good luck,' was his parting shot.

'He's an annoying little twat, isn't he?' Patterson said when the door closed.

'But he does deliver.'

'Why else do you think I give him houseroom? So, we need to narrow down everywhere in the city that begins with "ca" and check what CCTV cover there is from nine days ago. Plenty there for the team to get stuck into.' Patterson was vibrant with energy now. He'd turned the corner from despair to optimism. It was, Ambrose thought, the perfect moment to pitch him on Tony Hill's behalf.

'Since we're going to be flat out on this,' he began, 'we're not going to want any extra bodies cluttering the place up. Are we?'

CHAPTER 15

Carol had lost count of the number of times she'd stood in a pathology suite watching a pathologist performing their precise and grisly duty. But she'd never grown inured to the pitiful nature of the procedure. Seeing a human being reduced to their component parts still filled her with sadness, but it was always tempered with the desire to deliver justice to whoever was responsible for bringing the cadaver to this place. If anything reinforced Carol's need for justice, it was the morgue rather than the crime scene.

The pathologist today was a man who had become her friend. In a reflection of his mixed heritage, Dr Grisha Shatalov ran his department at Bradfield Cross Hospital with a paradoxical blend of White Russian authoritarianism and Canadian moderation. He believed the dead merited the same respect as the living patients whose histology slides he studied under the microscope, but that didn't mean things had to be run with chilly formality. Right from the start, he'd welcomed Carol into his world and made her feel part of a team whose goal was to bring secrets from obscurity into the light.

Lately, Grisha had begun to share the pallor of his subjects. Long hours coupled with a young baby had left his skin grey, his long triangular eyes surrounded by dark patches like the bandit mask of a racoon. But today, he'd recovered his colour, almost seeming healthy and fit. 'You look good,' Carol said as she settled herself against the wall to the side of the dissecting table. 'Have you been on holiday?'

'I feel like I've had a vacation. Finally my daughter has learned how to sleep for more than three hours at a time.' He grinned at her. 'I'd forgotten how wonderful it feels to wake up naturally.' As he spoke, his hand moved automatically to the tray beside him, instinctively selecting the first of a chain of instruments that would expose what was left of Daniel Morrison to their prying eyes.

Carol let her thoughts run down their own roads as Grisha worked. She didn't need to pay close attention; he would make sure he alerted her to anything she needed to know. Her team were liaising with Northern Division to make sure all the routine elements of the investigation were in place. Something might leap out from those initial interviews and inquiries. Stacey's brilliant computer skills might produce a loose thread for them to pick at. But that would only be if they got lucky. There was little else that could be done now until the information started flowing back to their squad room so they could pore over it, trying to identify something that didn't fit. You could never explain in advance what that bad fit might turn out to be. There were no guidelines, no training, no checklist. It was a mixture of experience and instinct. It was an indefinable quality that each of her officers possessed, and one of the main reasons they were on her squad. Each of them had different areas where their antennae were most finely tuned, and together they were more than the sum of their parts. What a bloody waste it would be if Blake had his way and they were scattered to the four winds.

She was so absorbed in her own thoughts that the post-mortem flashed past. She could hardly believe it when she heard Grisha invite her through to his office to go over the key points again. 'Again?' she said as she followed him, sparing a glance for the body on the table. An assistant was closing the long incisions that Grisha had made on Daniel's torso. When it was possible these days, he used a keyhole approach to the task, avoiding the traditional Y-incision that left everyone looking like a victim of Baron von Frankenstein. That wasn't possible when he was dealing with a murder victim. Shuddering in spite of herself, Carol wished it was.

'It makes it easier on the families,' he'd explained to her. 'They've got this horrible image in their head of what a cadaver looks like after a postmortem, so if we can explain that it won't be like that, they're more inclined to agree to postmortems when it's a medical rather than a forensic exercise.' Looking at Daniel now, she could see the force of his argument.

Carol followed him into his office. It was hard to believe, but there seemed to be even less room for Grisha and his visitors than the last time she'd been there. There was paper everywhere. Charts, folders, periodicals and stacks of books filled shelves, stood in piles on the floor and leaned precariously against the computer monitor. When Carol shifted a mound of computer print-outs to sit on the visitor's chair, she could barely see Grisha behind the desk. 'You're going to have to do something about this,' she said. 'Don't you have a PhD student with nothing better to do?'

'I swear to God, I think other people have started dumping their shit in here. Either that or the peer-reviewed stuff is breeding.' He shifted a heap of folders so he could see her better. 'So, your boy Daniel . . .' He shook his head. 'It always feels wrong, looking at a bunch of organs that have seen so little use. It's hard not to think of all the good things he's missed out on. The things we enjoy doing that leave their nasty repercussions waiting to ambush us.'

Carol had no response that didn't feel sentimental or trite. 'What's the verdict, then? Cause of death?'

'Asphyxiation. Heavy-duty polythene bag taped over his head effectively cut off his oxygen supply. No signs of a struggle, though. No blood or skin under his nails, no bruising anywhere apart from a mark on his thigh which looks about three or four days old and is, in my opinion, completely not sinister.'

'Do you think he was drugged?'

Grisha frowned at her over his glasses. 'You know I don't know the answer to that. We won't have any kind of answer till we get the tox screens back, and even then we'll be none the wiser if it was GHB because the levels we already have in our blood rise after death. If I was dumb enough to make guesses about this kind of thing, I would guess he was incapacitated by drugs. Not drink, because there was no smell of alcohol in the stomach. His last meal, incidentally, consisted of bread, fish, salad and what looks like jelly babies. Probably a tuna salad sandwich, and probably eaten no more than an hour before he died.'

'And the castration?'

'Judging by the blood loss, I'd say postmortem, but not by long. He'd have bled out if he'd still been alive.'

'Amateur or professional?'

'This is not the work of a surgeon. Nor of a butcher, I'd say. Your killer used a very sharp blade, a scalpel or something similar with a small cutting edge. But in spite of that he still didn't get it off in one clean slice. He didn't hack at it, but it took him three or four separate movements of the blade. So I'd say this is not something he's had a lot of practice at.'

'First timer?'

Grisha shrugged. 'I couldn't say. But he was thorough, he didn't just slash at it. Have the penis and testes turned up? Were they at the scene?'

Carol shook her head. 'No.'

'Trophies. Isn't that what your Dr Tony would say?'

Carol gave a tired smile. 'He's not my Dr Tony, and I would never be crazy enough to second guess him. I wish he was here to weigh in with his tuppence worth, but that's not going to happen this time out.' Her voice was edgy.

Grisha stretched his neck so his head moved backwards, like a man avoiding a blow. 'Whoa, Carol. What's he done to upset you?'

'Not him. Our new Chief Constable, who thinks if I want profiling expertise I should stay in-house.'

Grisha's mouth made an O shape. 'And we don't like that idea?'

Whatever Carol was planning to say was overtaken by a knock at the door. The familiar ginger curls of DS Kevin Matthews appeared round the edge of the door. 'Sorry to interrupt,' he said, wincing a smile at Grisha.

'You looking for me?' Carol said, getting to her feet.

'Yeah. There's another teenage lad on the missing list. Central patched it straight through to us.'

Carol felt a heaviness in her stomach. There were times when this job felt too much to bear. 'How long?'

'His parents thought he was having a sleepover. Only, he wasn't.'

Long enough, thought Carol. More than long enough.

CHAPTER 16

Julia Viner sat on the edge of a generous armchair, poised for movement, her fingers constantly working in her lap. Wiry dark hair threaded with grey was pulled back from her face to reveal fine-boned features and olive skin lightly scored with fine wrinkles. Her eyes were sharp and dark, like those of a small bird accustomed to the gloom of hedgerows and suspicious of the light. She wore a full skirt and a fine woollen jumper in dark burgundy. Kathy Antwon sat on the arm of the chair, one hand on Julia's shoulder, the other thrust into the pocket of her jeans. Carol could see the bunch of her fist through the material. She had the angry scowl of someone who is afraid but daren't let herself acknowledge the fear. Her light brown skin was flushed darker along the high cheekbones, her lips pressed tight together.

'What do you need to know? How can we help you find Seth?' Julia asked, her voice tense.

'We need you to be absolutely honest with us,' Carol said. 'Sometimes parents don't want to tell us the whole story when children go missing. They don't want to get their child into trouble, or they don't want to admit that they have rows, like every other family in the world does. But honestly, the best thing you can do for Seth is not to hold anything back.'

'We've got nothing to hide,' Kathy said, her voice rough and heavy with pent-up emotion. 'We'll tell you anything you want to know.'

Carol glanced at Kevin, who had readied his notebook and pen. 'Thank you. The first thing we need is a recent photo of Seth.'

Kathy jumped to her feet. 'I've got some I took at the weekend. They're on my laptop, hang on, I'll get it.' She hurried from the room. Julia looked after her, her expression slipping momentarily into bereavement. She'd pulled herself together by the time she turned back to face Carol. 'What do you need to know?' she repeated.

'When was the last time you saw Seth?'

'When I left for work yesterday morning. It was the same as any other morning. We had breakfast together. Seth was talking about some history homework project he wanted me to help him with. My degree is in history, you see. He thinks I know everything about anything that happened before the middle of last week.' She spoke on a faint, breathy attempt at a laugh. 'Then I left for work.'

'Where is it you work?' Carol said.

'I run the education department at the city council,' she said.

That went some way to explaining how they afforded

the sprawling ranch-style bungalow on its corner plot in the section of Harriestown known as the Ville. Back in the 1930s, it had been the home of De Ville Engineering Works, a vast sprawl that had built engines for planes, commercial vehicles and racing cars. In the 1980s, the last of the de Villes had seen where the future lay and exported the whole business to South Korea, selling the site to a local builder whose daughter had just married an architect whose heart belonged to Frank Lloyd Wright and the American Southwest. The result had been a land-scaped development of forty houses that became an instant hit with style magazines round the world. Nobody could quite believe it, but those who had bought their houses off-plan soon found they had acquired some of the most sought-after real estate in the north of England.

'And I'm a graphic designer,' Kathy said as she returned carrying an open laptop. 'That's how we ended up here. I designed all the original brochures for the Ville, so I knew to buy in ahead of the crowd.' She turned the screen to face Carol, revealing a full-screen head-and-shoulders shot of a smiling dark-haired boy with his mother's olive skin and dark eyes. His hair was long, roughly parted on one side and falling halfway across one eye. A scatter of spots across his chin, a chipped front tooth and a slightly crooked nose finished the thumbnail sketch Carol was already drawing in her mind. 'That was taken on Sunday.'

'Is it possible for you to email it to my team? That's probably the quickest way to get it out there.' Carol was already fishing in her pocket for a business card.

'No problem,' Kathy said, putting the laptop on a side table and running her finger across the mousepad. Carol handed over her card, which included the generic email for MIT. They all waited while Kathy set the upload in motion. 'Done and dusted,' she said, returning to her partner in the armchair. Carol, acutely aware of Seth's eyes on her, hoped the screen-saver would cut in sooner rather than later.

'DCI Jordan was asking when we last saw Seth,' Julia said, reaching up to clasp Kathy's hand.

'After Julia left for work, I walked down to the bus stop with Seth. Usually he goes off to school on his own. It's only a three-minute walk to the bus stop. But we were low on bread and I decided to walk across to the supermarket. So we set off together. The bus arrived almost as soon as we got to the stop, and I waved him off. That must have been about twenty to nine. He'd already arranged to have a sleepover with his pal Will, so he had clean pants and socks and shirt with him.'

'And as far as you know, he was at school all day?'

'When he didn't come home today as usual, I called the school,' Kathy said. 'They told me he hadn't been in at all today. So I asked about yesterday. And he was in all his classes. I admit, I wondered if he'd sneaked off somewhere with his girlfriend and Will was covering his back. It wouldn't have been like either of them, you understand? They're not wild lads. But you wonder, don't you?'

'It's only natural. We've all been teenagers,' Carol said. 'I certainly didn't tell my parents all I got up to.'

'So I checked with Will and with Lucie, his girlfriend. That's when I found out he wasn't at Will's and never had been. Will said Seth had told him yesterday morning that he wanted to take a rain check, he had other plans.'

'And Will didn't ask what those other plans might be?'

Kathy's brows furrowed. 'Not that he's telling me. He might be a bit more forthcoming to someone with an official reason for asking, though.'

'That's not fair, Kathy,' Julia protested. 'You've no reason to believe Will hasn't told you all he knows.'

Kathy rolled her eyes skywards. 'You're so trusting. If Seth told him not to say anything, he's not going to tell me, is he?'

Carol let the moment settle, then said, 'Have you heard anything from Seth at all since he left yesterday morning? A text? An email? A phone call?'

The two women checked with each other, then both shook their heads. 'Nothing,' Kathy said. 'Not that that's unusual. He doesn't usually make contact unless there's a reason. Like a change in arrangements. Which he didn't communicate to us this time.'

Kevin cleared his throat. 'Is his girlfriend at home?'

'Yes. I spoke to her on the landline at her house,' Kathy said. 'The last she saw of him was at lunchtime yesterday. They ate together in the school canteen – they're in different streams so they didn't see each other in class. But he didn't say anything to Lucie about not going to Will's. She still thought the sleepover was on.'

'Did he often have a sleepover on a school night?' Kevin asked.

Kathy looked as if she wanted to slap him. 'Of course not. We're not the kind of wishy-washy liberals who let their kids run the game. Last night was out of the usual run of things. Will and Seth are big grunge fans, and one of their favourite bands was doing a live webcast. We said they could hang out together to watch it for a special treat.' Her breath seemed to stick in her throat and she coughed helplessly. When she recovered, eyes streaming and face suffused with blood, she gasped, 'Some fucking treat.'

Julia put her arm round her and leaned her head against her arm. 'It's OK, Kathy. It's going to be OK.'

'Is there anybody else you can think of that he might have gone to visit or gone to meet?' Carol said.

'No,' Kathy said wearily. 'We've already tried his other school friends, but nobody's seen him since yesterday.'

Carol wondered if there was a tactful way to broach the subject of Seth's biological parentage and realised there wasn't. Still, it had to be dealt with. 'What about his father?' she asked.

'He hasn't got a father,' Kathy said, weariness tempering what was obviously a source of irritation to her. 'He's got two mothers. End of story.'

'Seth was conceived via AID,' Julia said, her arm tightening round her partner. 'Back in the days of anonymous donors. All we know about the donor is that he was five foot eleven inches tall, slim build, with dark hair and blue eyes.'

'Thanks for clearing that up,' Carol said with a smile.

'Is that all they tell you?' Kevin said. 'I thought you got a sort of pen portrait. What they did, what their hobbies were, that sort of thing?'

'It varies from clinic to clinic,' Julia said. 'The one we used only gives you the bare minimum.'

'So there's no way the father could track down his kid and make contact? Or Seth could track down his father?' Kevin asked.

'It's donor, not father. No, it's completely anonymised. Not even the clinic knows the name of the donor. Just their code number,' Julia said. Her patience was clearly thinning.

'And why would Seth do that? He's never shown any curiosity about his donor. He's got two parents he loves and who love him. Which is more than a hell of a lot of kids can say,' Kathy said, openly belligerent now.

'We appreciate that. But we do have to explore every possibility.'

'Including homophobia,' Kathy muttered. To Julia: 'I told you what it would be like.' Before Carol could respond, the doorbell pealed out. 'I'll get it,' Kathy said, bounding out of the room. They heard the murmur of voices, then Kathy returned with Stacey Chen in tow. 'It's another one of your lot.'

'DC Chen is our ICT expert. We'd like your permission to examine Seth's computer,' Carol said.

'It's in his room. I'll show you,' Kathy said.

'I need a word with DCI Jordan first, if you'll excuse us?' Stacey said.

As Carol left the room, she heard Kevin's loyalty kick in. 'She's not got a homophobic bone in her body,' he said. 'Two of her team, two of her closest colleagues are both lesbians. She chose them, and she trusts them.'

Nice one, Kevin. I bet that cuts absolutely no ice with Kathy. She'll have Paula and Chris pegged as a right pair of Uncle Toms. Carol closed the door behind her and raised her eyebrows at Stacey. 'News?'

'The wrong sort. Daniel Morrison's home computer isn't web-configured. He only uses it for gaming and schoolwork. He's got a webbook for all his online stuff. And he keeps that in his backpack when he's out of the house. So we've got no electronic starting point.'

'What about his email address? RigMarole account? Facebook?'

Stacey shrugged. 'We might be able to backtrack some stuff. But he could have a dozen or more email addresses and web presences we know nothing about. It's a big blow. There's only so much I can do with so little.'

'Any joy with the CCTV?'

She shook her head. 'Nothing after he leaves Bellwether Square. I think he must have left in a vehicle.'

'OK. Concentrate on Seth for now. Better we try to take care of the living.' *If he is still living, which in the light of Daniel's death, I seriously doubt.* 'His mother's just emailed a recent photo to our address, can you get that out force-wide asap?'

'I'll do it right now.'

'Thanks. Keep me posted,' Carol said, turning back to the living room, where the atmosphere was no easier than when she'd left. 'I'm sorry about that,' she said. 'Perhaps you could show DC Chen where to find Seth's computer? And we'll need your formal permission to search it, since he's a minor.'

'Do whatever you need to do,' Julia said as Kathy made for the door. 'She didn't mean to insult you, Chief Inspector. She's just upset, and when she gets upset it comes out as anger.'

Carol smiled. 'I'm not easily insulted, Ms Viner. All I'm concerned about here is that we do everything we can to bring Seth home.'

Julia visibly drew herself together. 'When I was driving home. After Kathy called. On the radio. There was something about a murdered teenage boy.' Her hand flew to her mouth and she bit down on her knuckles.

'That wasn't Seth, Ms Viner. We've positively identified that boy, and it is definitely not Seth.'

Kathy walked back into the room in time to hear Carol's words. 'See, I told you, it couldn't be Seth.'

'Always the optimist.' Julia clung to her arm.

'We'll be talking to Will and Lucie, and to Seth's other friends. And we'll be putting his photo out on our website and releasing it to the media. This is our number one priority right now,' Carol said, getting to her feet. 'Kevin will stay with you. If there's anything else you can think of that will help us find Seth, tell him. I'll be on the end of a phone if you need to talk to me.'

Julia Viner looked up at her, eyes pleading. 'Just bring him home. I don't care why he's disappeared or what he's done. Just bring him home.'

Her words echoed in Carol's head all the way to the car. There was only so much she could do, but that was all at Julia and Kathy's disposal. The thing was, thanks to her Bluetooth phone, she could make her phone calls as easily from her car as from her office. And there was another lost boy she owed some answers to. Carol started the engine and headed out of town on the Halifax road.

CHAPTER 17

Sam was not impressed with the moody grandeur of Wastwater. He found the mountains oppressive and the dark waters of the lake depressing. Why anyone would choose to come here for a holiday was beyond him. Walking was all well and good if you were on a Caribbean beach like his sergeant was right now. But the amount of freezing rain they got here must make it more of a misery than a pleasure. And what was there to do in the evenings? Sam loved to dance. He wasn't picky; it didn't have to be one particular club or one specific DJ or a distinct style of music. He just loved to feel the rhythm course through him, to lose himself in the beat and to move with an abandon he revealed nowhere else in his life. He wouldn't mind betting there wasn't a dance venue within twenty miles of here. Unless it was Morris dancing, which was to dancing what the ploughman's lunch was to food.

He'd spent most of the day huddled in his car or in the underwater search team's support vehicle. They weren't a talkative lot. They'd taken Stacey's list of co-ordinates and gone into a huddle over a chart, marking sections that he assumed corresponded to the search areas she'd suggested following her consultation with the satellite-imaging experts at Bradfield University. Some had donned wet-suits and strapped tanks of air to their backs then headed for the boat with its fat black inflatable rim. Sam hadn't the faintest idea how they would go about the search. He'd never had any interest in diving. He couldn't see the point. If you wanted to watch tropical fish, you could check out a David Attenborough DVD and never have to leave the comfort of your own living room.

The day had dragged wearily on. Divers disappeared under water, spoke incomprehensibly via their radio link to the control team in the support vehicle, surfaced and disappeared again somewhere else. Occasionally, the boat would return to shore and the divers would swap with another team. Sam was almost beginning to regret being so diligent with the Danuta Barnes case.

But then towards the end of the afternoon, everything changed. It was, he thought, the fifth dive. One of the resting divers walked briskly across to his car and made a circle with his thumb and first finger. Sam wound down his window. 'Looks like we've found something, mate,' the diver said cheerily.

'What sort of something?'

'A big bundle, wrapped in plastic. According to our boys, it's tied to a bag made of what looks like fishing net, filled with rocks.'

Sam grinned. 'So what happens now?'

'We'll rope it, get airbags underneath then winch the lot up. Then we'll take a look inside.'

The recovery process seemed to take forever. Sam tried to suppress his impatience, but he couldn't keep still. He walked the shoreline, climbing up a low bluff from where he could get a better view of the boat a few hundred yards away. But he was too far away to see much of what was going on. At last, a black-wrapped lump the size of a Portaloo began to emerge, sluicing water in its wake. 'Christ, that's big,' Sam said aloud, transfixed by the struggles of the dive team to get it on board without capsizing their boat.

The sound of their engine split the hush of the late afternoon and Sam hustled back down to the rough scree of the little beach they'd launched from. The boat nosed right on to the shore but Sam hung back, not wanting to ruin his shoes unnecessarily. It took five of them to manhandle the constantly shrinking bundle from the boat on to dry land, staggering up the beach to lay it down on the grass by the support vehicle. Water still leaked generously from all sides.

'What now?' Sam asked.

The dive team leader pointed to one of his men emerging from the support vehicle with a camera. 'We take photos. Then we cut it open.'

'You don't take it to a secure area first?'

'We don't take it anywhere until we know what the appropriate destination might be,' he said patiently. 'It might be rolls of carpet. Or dead sheep. No point in hauling them off to the mortuary, is there?'

Feeling stupid, Sam just nodded and waited while the officer with the camera took a couple of dozen shots of the oozing package. At last he stepped back and one of the divers took a long knife from a sheath at his waist and slit the package open. As he peeled the plastic back, Sam held his breath.

The remaining water flowed away. Inside the black plastic, three packages were sheathed in polythene turned opaque by time and water, bound with duct tape.

Sam had been expecting Danuta Barnes and five-month-old Lynette. This was clearly more than he'd bargained for.

While Tony might not have appreciated Carol's characterisation of him as a lost boy, it wasn't so far off the mark. In the hour since Alvin Ambrose had delivered his hard-won bundle of papers, Tony had barely been able to string two thoughts together. The couple in the next room had concluded their blazing row with equally blazing sex. Through the other wall someone was listening to some sort of motorsport that involved throaty engines and squealing tyres. It was intolerable.

It almost made him believe in fate.

Except that he knew deep down that if it hadn't been the noise, it would have been something else. After all, there was plenty to choose from. The poor lighting. The hardness of the bed. The chair that was the wrong height for the desktop. Any one of them would have justified the decision he was about to make. The decision he had, if he was honest with himself, made that afternoon when, as soon as he'd freed himself from the estate agent, he'd paid a visit to a firm of solicitors whose office was also within easy walking distance of the hotel.

Tony picked up the papers and slipped them into his still-packed bag. He didn't actually check out. That could wait till morning. He got into his car and retraced the route he'd driven earlier, only making a couple of mistaken turns along the way. Hell, there were days when he made more errors than that between Bradfield Moor Secure Hospital and his own front door.

He parked on the street outside the house he supposed he could call his. Although that seemed too presumptuous. This was unquestionably Edmund Arthur Blythe's house still. And yet, Tony imagined that if his benefactor had a ghost it wouldn't mind his presence.

The keys the solicitor had handed over turned smoothly in the twin mortise locks and the door swung open without the faintest creak. Inside, it was blissfully quiet. Discreet double glazing smothered the traffic noise and not even the ticking of a clock disturbed the silence. Tony gave a contented sigh and made his way through to the drawing room he'd admired earlier that afternoon. Its deep bay window gave on to the garden, though at this time of day there wasn't much to be seen through the growing dark. From upstairs, there was a view of the park, but at this level, the garden felt secluded and isolate, a private space for the house and its owner to enjoy.

He turned away and his eye caught a tall cabinet filled with CDs. As he approached, light flooded the shelves, startling him. He looked up and caught sight of a motion sensor on the front of the cabinet. 'Clever,' he murmured, casting an eye over a collection that encompassed nine-teenth-century classical music and the more melodic twentieth-century jazz. He'd clearly enjoyed something with a tune, Tony thought. Out of curiosity, he turned on the CD player. Rich, smooth saxophone with a swing to its rhythm, the last music Edmund Arthur Blythe had chosen to listen to. A ticker display across the front of the CD player's illuminated panel said, 'Stanley Turrentine: "Deep Purple"'. Tony had never heard of the man but he recognised the tune and liked the way the sound made him feel.

He walked away and switched on a standard lamp, perfectly placed to cast its light over a high-backed armchair with a convenient side table next to it. The ideal arrangement for a man who wanted to read and perhaps to make the occasional note. Tony took the papers out of his bag and settled into the chair. For the next hour, he sat with the transcripts and unobtrusive saxophones, trying to get a feel for ZZ and to make sense of the fragmentary final session. 'ur . . . ur real . . .' he read over and over. 'Your what? You are what? You are who? You're really, what? Your real what?' He puzzled over '. . . el u, show u.' 'Tell, that's it. I'll do more than tell you, I'll show you. Of course, that's it. You want to show her, don't you? But what? What do you want to show her?'

He got to his feet and paced, trying to find some hypothesis that would cover those imponderable gaps in the conundrum. The more he could read into this exchange, the closer it might bring him to both victim and killer. 'Tell you you're really what? Show you you're something . . . But what? What's the secret? The secret she doesn't even know she's got? What kind of secret can we have that we don't even know about?'

His prowling brought him face to face with a drinks table. Not the predictable heavy crystal tumblers that would have been of a piece with the slightly old-fashioned, comfortable furniture, but modern, stylish glasses that fit the hand in the most unassertive of ways. He picked one up and enjoyed the heft of it. On the spur of the moment, he poured himself a small Armagnac. It wasn't a drink he'd normally have chosen, but the presence of three different varieties on the table convinced him that this had been the preferred tipple of Edmund Arthur Blythe. It felt appropriate to raise a glass of the old man's favourite drink to his memory. Well, not to his memory as such, since Tony had no memory of him at all. Maybe to his attempt to make amends from beyond the grave. Even if it was a doomed attempt.

He sipped as he paced, mulling over everything he'd learned about Jennifer Maidment and her killer. Something stirred at the back of his mind. Something that had nibbled at the edge of his thoughts earlier. What had it been? He returned to his bag and took out the material Patterson had initially emailed to him. Crime-scene photos and the postmortem report, that's what he was interested in.

He studied each photograph carefully, paying particular attention to the shots of Jennifer's mutilated body on the autopsy table. Then he read the original crime report again, taking particular note of the times. 'The last confirmed sighting is quarter past four. The missing report comes in just after nine. And unless all the truckers are lying, you couldn't have dumped her after half past seven, when the first two HGV drivers pulled in together. Really, you only had her for a couple of hours.' He put down the report and paced again, coming to rest by the ornate wooden fire surround. He leaned on the mantel and stared down into the empty grate, trying to ease his way into the mind of Jennifer's killer, trying to feel what he'd felt, know what he'd known.

'You had to get her away from people, drug her, suffocate her with the plastic, mutilate her and get her to the dump site,' he said slowly. 'Where's the pleasure for you? Where's the why? What are you getting off on? Possessing her? Controlling her?'

He turned away and walked back to the window, frowning into the gloom. 'It's just not long enough. You spent weeks grooming her. For what? A couple of hours? I don't think so. You commit that much planning, that much time, that much energy, you want more than a snatched couple of hours. You've lusted after her. You need to slake that thirst. But not you, apparently. You just killed her, cut her and dumped her. That doesn't make any sense . . .' Everything he knew told him killers like this relished the time they spent with their victims. They set up their hiding places away from prying eyes so they could satisfy themselves again and again and again. They didn't take all the risks involved in capturing a victim only to turn their backs on the possibility of stretching the pleasure to the max. The ones who liked live prey held them captive, violating them again and again, torturing them and savouring the chance to make their fantasies flesh and blood. Often with the emphasis on the blood.

The ones who preferred the passivity of a corpse often went to great lengths to keep the body as fresh as possible for as long as possible. The early stages of decomposition were seldom a deterrent to the seriously screwed up.

But that's not what happened with Jennifer. 'Killed her, cut her and dumped her,' he repeated. 'No time to play. Something happened to stop you. But what?' It had to be something unforeseen. Perhaps he'd lost access to the place where he'd planned to take her. Or else something had erupted in his other life that made it impossible to carry out his plans. Whatever it was, it must have been compelling. Nothing less than that would keep a killer from his satisfaction, not once he had his victim in his power.

It made sense, Tony thought. But not the sort of sense that satisfied. 'Killed her, cut her and dumped her,' he muttered under his breath as he walked back to the drinks table and poured himself a taster of the second Armagnac bottle. He took a tiny sip and returned to his pacing.

Suddenly he stopped short. 'Cut her. Cut her.' Tony slapped his forehead. He hurried back to the photographs, confirming what he thought he remembered. 'You cut out her vagina, ripped up her cervix, slashed her uterus. You went to town on her. But you didn't bother with her clitoris.'

Tony drained his glass and returned for a refill. The conclusion that was rattling round his head seemed inescapable. Any investigator of this kind of crime would think it absurd in its counter-intuitiveness. But he'd never been afraid to accept possibilities that others shied away from. It was one of the reasons Carol Jordan had always prized his mind. Somehow, he didn't think DI Stuart Patterson would be so generous. But there was no getting away from it. It was the only thing that made sense of the two incongruities he'd recognised.

'This isn't a sexual homicide,' he declared to the empty room. 'There's nothing sexual about it. Whatever's going on here, it's not about someone getting their rocks off.'

Which begged a question that was, to Tony, even more disturbing. If it wasn't about sex, what was it about?

CHAPTER 18

Alan Miles wasn't hard to spot. He was the only person standing outside Halifax station in a gentle mist of rain wafting down from the Pennines that defied the canopy. Carol parked where she shouldn't and walked briskly over to the slightly stooped figure peering out at the world through the kind of glasses she hadn't seen anyone wear since the NHS stopped doing free prescription pairs. Heavy black plastic across the top, steel wire round the rest of the lenses, and thick as milk-bottle bottoms. Face like an Easter Island slab. She could imagine him giving the bottom-stream fourth-year boys hell. 'Mr Miles?' she said.

He turned his head with the articulation of an elderly tortoise and appraised her. Evidently he liked what he saw for a smile of extraordinary sweetness transformed him utterly. His hand went to the brim of his cap and he raised it fractionally. 'Miss Jordan,' he said. 'Very prompt.

I like that in a woman.' In the flesh, he sounded like a basso profondo version of Thora Hird.

'Thank you.'

'I hope I wasn't rude to you on the telephone. I have no telephone manner. It's a device that completely flum-moxes me. I know I sound most off-putting. My wife tells me I should leave it alone and let her deal with it.'

'If I had the choice, I would leave it to somebody else to deal with,' Carol said. She meant it; she'd spent the last twenty minutes talking to division commanders, press officers and her own team, making sure everything that could be done to find Seth Viner was being done. And that nobody was forgetting about Daniel Morrison either. The guilt at jumping ship was tremendous. But not enough to divert her from her other mission.

'Now, I see you've arrived by car, which is perfect, really,' Miles said. 'If you don't mind driving, we can make our way to the very premises where Blythe and Co held sway. That'll give you a sense of the place. There's a very pleasant public house a few streets away where we can have a small libation while I outline what I've got for you. If that's acceptable to your good self?'

Carol struggled to keep a straight face. She felt as if she'd stumbled into a BBC TV series by one of the other Alans – Bennett or Plater – who specialised in Yorkshire eccentrics. 'That would suit me fine, Mr Miles.'

'Call me Alan,' he said with a roguish look. If he'd had mustachios, he would have twirled them, Carol thought as she led the way back to her car.

He sat stiffly in the passenger seat, a whiplash of a man leaning towards the windscreen, the better to see where they were going. He directed her through a convoluted one-way system, leaving the town centre behind and climbing a steep road flanked by small stone-faced terraced houses. They turned off about halfway up the hill into a warren of narrow streets. The final turn brought them into a dead end. On one side Carol could see a line of brick houses whose front doors opened directly on to the street. Opposite was the side wall of what looked like a warehouse or a small factory. It was obviously not a recent construction, being made of stone with a slate roof. Beyond the building was a small yard for vehicles, cut off behind a high chain-link fence. A metal sign said, *Performance Autos – Yorkshire*. 'There you go,' Miles said. 'That used to be the premises of Blythe and Co, Specialist Metal Finishers.'

It was hard to feel excited about so prosaic a building, but it did mark a real step forward in her journey. 'That's quite something, Alan. Seeing it still standing.' If he wanted to, Tony could make this journey and send his imagination travelling through time. Somehow, she thought he might give it a miss. 'So what have you got to tell me about Blythe's and its owner?'

'Shall we repair to the public house?'

'With great pleasure,' Carol said, wondering why she was starting to sound as if she too inhabited TV Yorkshire. *I'll be ordering a port and lemon next.*

The Weaver's Shuttle huddled down a lane near an old Victorian mill that had been converted into apartments. The pub had avoided a makeover, its exposed stone walls and low beams stubbornly enclosing an old-fashioned bar where couples sat and talked quietly, old men played dominoes and a group of middle-aged women were having a very decorous darts match. The barman nodded to Miles as they walked in. 'Evening, Alan. The usual, is it?' Reaching for a half-pint glass and a wooden pump handle.

'Indeed, landlord. What can I get you, young lady?' Miles removed his cap, revealing a gleaming bald dome fringed with steel-grey curls.

'Let me, Alan.' Carol smiled. 'I'm thinking of a dry white wine,' she said, doubting whether the wine would come up to the class of the real ales whose badges were lined up on hand pumps along the bar.

'I've got a South African Sauvignon Blanc or a Pinot Grigio open tonight,' the barman said. 'Or I've a Chilean Chardonnay cold.'

'I'll try a glass of the sauvignon,' she said, realising how ready she was for a drink. It had been a while since she'd gone this late in the day before having her first glass. Maybe she really was getting past the point where alcohol had been the one reliably bright element in her days. Something else that might please Tony.

When it came, the wine was cold and vivid with the smell of grass and the taste of gooseberry. Alan Miles was watching her attentively as she took her first mouthful. He chuckled. There was no other word for it, Carol thought. 'Not what you expected,' he said.

'So little in life is,' she said, surprised at her candour.

'When you say it like that . . . well, that's a pity, Miss Jordan,' he said. 'But enough of us. You want to know about Blythe's. Eddie Blythe was nearly a local lad, grew up down the road in Sowerby Bridge. A bright lad, by all accounts. He went to the technical college in Huddersfield and showed a lot of aptitude in the field of metallurgy. Whether it was by chance or design, he happened on a new process for coating metals that was very useful in the field of medical instruments. Scalpels and forceps and the like, as I understand it. He patented his bright idea and set up the factory to manufacture his products. He was doing very well, apparently. And then suddenly, in the spring of 1964, he sold up, lock, stock and barrel, to some steel firm in Sheffield. Within weeks, they'd moved production to Sheffield. They took the key workers with them. Paid their removal costs and everything.' He paused and supped some of his glass of mild.

'That seems very generous,' Carol said.

'Supposedly it was part of the deal Eddie Blythe made.' He took a slim envelope out of his inside pocket. 'Here's a photocopy of a newspaper article.' He passed it to her.

'Local firm sold,' the headline read. The few paragraphs said little more than Miles had already related. But there was a photograph across two columns. The caption read, 'Mr E.A. Blythe (L) shakes hands on the deal with Mr J. Kessock (R) of Rivelin Fabrications.' She squinted at the photograph, strangely moved. There was, she thought, a look of Tony in the set of his shoulders, the angle of his head, the shape of his face. She took out a pen and scribbled down the date of the article.

'He left town after he sold up,' Miles said. 'I couldn't find anybody that knew him personally, so I don't know what lay behind him getting rid of the business and leaving town. You might want to check out the archives of the Triple H.'

'The Triple H?'

'Sorry. I'm forgetting you're not from round here. The *Halifax and Huddersfield Herald*. They've been digitising their back numbers.' Miles spoke the unfamiliar word as if it were in a foreign language. 'My special interest is the wool industry and I've found quite a few gems with their "search engine". They let you use "text strings" and the like. Regrettably I couldn't get on the library computer to check this afternoon. We've not got the internet at home,' he said. Carol sensed a wistfulness he was reluctant to admit to.

'Thanks for the suggestion. I'll take a look when I get back.' If nothing else, she might find a better version of the photocopy Miles was folding up and replacing in its envelope. 'You've been very helpful,' she said.

He made a self-deprecating face. 'Nowt you couldn't have found out for yourself.'

'Maybe. But it would have taken me a lot longer. Believe me, I'm always grateful to people who save me time.'

'It'll be a hard job, yours,' he said. 'Hard enough for a man, but you women are always having to prove your-selves, eh, lass?'

Her smile was wintry. 'No kidding.'

'So, has this helped you with your cold case?' he asked, his glance shrewd.

'It's been very instructive.' Carol finished her drink. 'Can I give you a lift anywhere?'

Miles shook his head. 'I'm only five minutes down the road. Good luck with your investigation. I hope, like the Mounties, you get your man.'

She shook her head, wondering where Tony was and

what he was doing. 'I'm afraid it might be too late for that. That's the trouble with cold cases. Sometimes the people involved are beyond our reach.'

Nobody ever volunteered for the last ID. No matter how many times you asked people to put a name to their dead, it still felt like shit. Every CID team had its own rules of engagement. Some left it to the Family Liaison Officer; some SIOs always insisted on doing it themselves. In Carol Jordan's MIT, the same rule applied to this as to everything else – the person best equipped for the task was the designated officer. And so it was that Paula dealt with more than her fair share.

Given that she was stuck with it, she always preferred to carry out the job alone. That way she didn't have to concern herself with anyone but the grieving person who was going to have to confront a lifeless body and decide whether or not it was the remains they feared most.

The FLO had been with the Morrisons since that morning. They'd been told the chances were that the body found earlier had been their son. But Paula knew that they'd still be in denial, still convinced there had been some grotesque muddle at the crime scene, that some total stranger had been misidentified as their beloved boy. Until they saw Daniel's body for themselves, they'd be clinging to those shreds of hope. Paula was the one who would have to rip that prospect from them.

The FLO showed her into the kitchen, where the air was thick with cigarette smoke. Jessica Morrison sat at a marble-topped table, staring out through the conservatory at the darkness beyond. An untouched cup of tea sat by her folded hands. Her make-up sat on her skin like the icing on a cake. Her eyes were bloodshot and wild, the only clue to the pain saturating her.

Her husband perched on a high stool at the breakfast bar, a full ashtray next to his mobile and the landline handset. When Paula walked in, he couldn't keep the look of bruised hope from his face. She shook her head slightly. He opened his mouth, but no words came out. He took a pack of cigarettes from the pocket of his crumpled shirt and lit up. 'I haven't smoked for the best part of twenty years,' he said. 'Amazing how it comes back to you as if you'd never stopped.'

If there was an easy way to do this, Paula still hadn't found it. 'I'm afraid I need one of you to come with me. We need to be certain that it's Daniel we found earlier today,' she said. 'I'm sorry, but it has to be done.'

Jessica got to her feet, stiff as an arthritic old lady. 'I'll come.'

'No.' Mike jumped off the stool and held up his hand. 'No, Jess. You're not up to this. I'll do it. I'll go with her. You stay here. You don't need to see him like this.'

Jessica looked at him as if he were mad. 'It's not Daniel. So it makes no odds. I'll go.'

He looked stricken. More in touch with reality, Paula thought. 'What if it is him? I can do this, Jess. This is not a job for you.' He put his hand on her arm.

She shrugged him off. 'If it is Daniel, which I don't believe for a minute, then I need to see him. I'm his mother. Nobody else has the right to say goodbye.' She walked straight past him, down the hall towards the door.

Mike Morrison looked at Paula beseechingly. 'She's

not strong enough to handle this,' he said. 'It should be me.'

'I think you should come too,' she said. 'She's going to need you. But I think she's right. She needs to see him for herself.' She gave him a fleeting pat on the arm and followed Jessica out to the car.

Paula was thankful it was a short drive to Bradfield Cross Hospital, which housed Dr Grisha Shatalov's pathology suite. The atmosphere in the car was grim, the silence swelling to fill all the space available. Paula parked by the bay reserved for the mortuary van and led the way into the building by the discreet rear entrance. The Morrisons followed her like beasts to the slaughter. She led them into a small room decorated in muted colours with a long couch facing a wall-mounted monitor. 'If you'd like to take a seat,' she said. 'Once you're settled, the screen will show you the image we need you to identify.'

'I thought we would see . . .' Mike's voice tailed off. He didn't know what to call the body Paula presumed was his son.

'We find it's less traumatic this way,' Paula said, as if she believed it. What could possibly make this less traumatic was beyond her powers of imagination. She waited till they sat down. 'I'll be back in a minute.'

She left the Morrisons and went down the hallway to the technicians' room. 'We're ready for Daniel Morrison. The body that came in this morning?'

'We're all set up,' one of the mortuary techs confirmed. 'You just need to switch on the monitor.'

Back in the viewing room, Paula checked the Morrisons were composed and ready. Then she switched on the

201

screen. It turned silvery grey then Daniel's face appeared. They'd done a good job, she thought. Asphyxiation didn't leave pretty victims, but they'd managed to make him look less swollen and engorged than he'd appeared earlier. His eyes were closed, his hair combed. By no stretch of the imagination did he look peaceful, but at least he didn't look nearly as fucked up as he had done when they'd found him.

'That's not Daniel,' Jessica said loudly. 'That's not my son.'

Mike put his arm round her shoulder and gripped her tight. 'It's Daniel,' he said, his voice bleak. 'It's Daniel, Jess.'

She pulled away and staggered to her feet, approaching the monitor. 'It's not Daniel,' she screamed, clutching her chest. Suddenly her face contorted in terrible pain. Her body twisted and bent and her mouth opened in a silent cry of agony. She fell to the ground, her body in spasm.

'Jess,' Mike yelled, falling to his knees beside her. 'Get help,' he shouted at Paula. 'I think she's having a heart attack.'

Paula sprinted from the room and threw open the technicians' office door. 'She's having a heart attack, call a code.'

They looked blankly at her. 'We're not on the system,' one said.

'Well, get her on a fucking gurney and into the main hospital,' Paula shouted. 'Now. Do it!'

Afterwards, she'd have been hard pressed to catalogue the events of the next few minutes. The technicians were galvanised into action, loading Jessica on to a trolley and racing through the corridors to A&E, Mike and Paula at their heels. Then the Casualty staff sprang into action with unflustered aplomb and Paula was banished to the family waiting area with Mike.

Paula made sure he was settled and the receptionist knew where he was and where she would be, then headed for the ambulance bay and a nicotine hit. She had one hand on the door and the other on her cigarettes when a faintly familiar voice said, 'Detective McIntyre?' She swung round and found herself staring at warm grey eyes and a tentative smile.

'Dr Blessing,' she said, unable to resist the grin spreading across her face. 'Elinor, I mean,' she added, remembering that the last time they'd met she'd been granted that privilege.

'It's good to see you,' Elinor said, wrapping her white coat more tightly around her as they stepped out into the chill air.

'You too.' Meaning it more than she'd meant anything in a while. When the two women had met on a previous case, Paula had felt a frisson between them. She'd even thought Elinor might have been flirting with her, but it had been so long since she'd had to decode those messages and she'd been so tired; it had all been too hard. She'd planned to follow up later, but life had, as usual, got in the way.

'You still working with DCI Jordan on the Major Incident Team?' Elinor asked.

'That's right. Attached by an umbilical cord to the worst that human beings can do to each other. And you? Still on Mr Denby's team?'

'For now. Though I'm due a move soon. But right now I'm on my way to Starbucks,' Elinor said. 'If I drink another cup of junior doctor coffee I'll need to have my stomach pumped. Can you join me?' She caught sight of the cigarette pack in Paula's hand. 'They have tables outside.'

Paula felt a flash of irritation. 'I'd love to. But I can't.' She gestured back towards A&E. 'Work. I need to stay close at hand.' She spread her hands in defeat.

'No problem. It's only two minutes' walk. How would it be if I brought you something back?'

Paula felt a warm glow in her stomach. She'd been right, this was a woman after her own heart. 'A grande skinny latte would be a beautiful thing.'

'Coming up.' Elinor hustled off down the driveway, a white blur in the streetlights.

Paula lit her cigarette and took out her phone. Positive ID on Daniel Morrison. Mum had heart attack. Am @ A&E with Dad, she keyed in and sent the message to Carol. That should cover her back for long enough to have an exploratory coffee with the lovely Dr Blessing. Work might be shit, but it looked as if her personal life might just be taking a turn for the better.

CHAPTER 19

It wasn't that she missed him when he was away. It wasn't like they lived in each other's pockets. When they were both busy, they could easily go for a week without spending an evening together. But Carol was always conscious of the emptiness of the house above her basement flat when Tony was away. Their lives were separate, their space private, the doors at the head and foot of the internal staircase creating a sort of airlock between them.

And yet . . . She knew when he was not there. Maybe there was a genuine reason; perhaps his movements created a vibration at some subliminal level in the house's fabric and whose absence unsettled her reptile brain. Or maybe they were, as Blake had implied, a little too closely in tune. Carol shivered at the thought. Her feelings for Tony were a complicated web whose strength and fragility she preferred not to test.

So she told herself it was just as well that he wasn't

here, as if his presence would somehow hamper her exploration of his history. Certainly it would be more than likely to sharpen the nag of guilt she felt at continuing to go behind his back and against his expressed wishes. Nevertheless she logged on to Google and soon found herself on the home page of the *Halifax and Huddersfield Herald*. First she tried 'Eddie Blythe' but got no result. But when she replaced the first name with Edmund, a string of results unrolled on the screen.

The first on the list, the most recent in terms of date, was the story Alan Miles had shown her in the pub. Frustratingly, the photograph hadn't been scanned in. The next result was a story about the proposed sale of Blythe's company to the Sheffield firm. Halfway through the story was a paragraph that stopped her in her tracks. 'The factory's owner, Mr Edmund Blythe, was unavailable for comment. Mr Blythe is recovering from a recent violent assault, as reported in this newspaper.'

A violent assault? Alan Miles hadn't mentioned anything about that. Carol hastily scrolled down the rest of the results, looking for something that wasn't about the factory. A few stories down, she hit pay dirt.

VIOLENT ATTACK IN SAVILE PARK

A Halifax businessman was recovering in hospital last night after a brutal attack as he walked home through Savile Park with his fiancée.

Edmund Blythe, 27, the managing director of Blythe & Co, Specialist Metal Finishers, was stabbed by a thug who attempted to rob him at knife-point.

When he refused to hand over his wallet, the man struck out with his weapon and hit Mr Blythe in the chest. According to hospital staff, the blow came close to his heart and it was a matter of pure luck that the consequences were not fatal.

Mr Blythe, of Tanner Street, and his fiancée were returning to her parents' home after spending the evening with friends who live on the far side of the park.

His distraught fiancée, who has asked not to be named, said, 'It was a terrible shock. One minute we were walking along arm in arm, minding our own business. Then a man stepped out from the shadow of some bushes and brandished a knife. I could see the blade gleaming in the moonlight.

'I was terrified. He told Edmund to hand over his wallet, but he refused. Then the man rushed at him and there was a struggle. I started screaming and the man ran off.

'It was too dark for me to see him clearly. He was about six feet in height and wore a flat cap pulled down over his hair. He sounded local, but I doubt I should be able to recognise his voice again. It was all so frightening.'

Detective Inspector Terrence Arnold said, 'This man is clearly very dangerous. We advise members of the public to be on their guard when walking in secluded areas after dark.'

'Bloody hell,' Carol said aloud as she reread the article. Why on earth had Vanessa failed to mention this dramatic incident? It wasn't like her to miss the chance for a touch of the limelight. Not to mention the sympathy she'd elicit for being involved in such a terrifying attack.

It did go some way to explain why Blythe had decided to abandon Halifax for Worcester. An unprovoked assault like that would make anyone anxious about the place they were living. But she'd have expected him to want to take his fiancée with him. Of course, if Vanessa hadn't wanted to leave Halifax, no amount of persuasion would have shifted her.

Carol poured herself a fresh glass of wine. She checked the other articles, but there was no more about the attack. Clearly no arrest had been made. Not entirely surprising, with no description of any value. Doubtless the usual suspects had been dragged in and slapped around a bit, but nothing had come of it. And Blythe himself had clearly been unwilling to discuss it. It seemed he'd sold up and left town almost immediately. It was all very sudden.

It was beginning to look as if Carol might have to pay another visit to Tony's mother. Only this time, she wouldn't be taking no for an answer. The only thing that stopped her heading straight back to Halifax and Vanessa's lair was a text from Paula.

'Oh shit,' Carol said. Strictly speaking, she didn't need to turn out on this one. But her sense of obligation was heightened by her earlier dereliction. I'll be there within the half hour, she texted back to Paula. Hold the fort till then.

Niall Quantick hated his life. He hated his useless mother. He hated the scuzzy streets round their spazoid flat. He hated never having any money. He hated school, hated that he had to show up every day, thanks to his arsehole mother's deal with the head teacher that, if he didn't show, he wouldn't get even his pitiful allowance from her. OK, so he planned to play the system to get away from her and her fucking hateful little life, but he didn't want her to know that. He would have gone to school anyway, but his small rebellion against the machine last term had totally paid off. Pretty much the one thing he didn't hate about his life was that he was clever enough to outsmart everybody who tried to get one over on him.

He took a toke off the joint he indulged in every day after school when he walked the stupid dog to get out of the flat so he could chill out in the crappy park with its used needles and scumbags and glue bags and dogshit. What a fucking life.

Most of all, he hated his fuckwit arsehole father for turning his life into this drudged-out hell. His life might not feel so shit if he couldn't remember a time when it had been different. The other kids he hung out with didn't seem as pissed off with their lives as he was and he thought that might be because they didn't have anything better to contrast it with. Oh sure, they thought they knew what it would be like to have a flash car and a big gaff and holidays where the sun shone every day. But that was just fantasy footballer world to them. Not to Niall. Niall remembered what it was like to have all of those things.

Before this scummy flat in a part of Manchester so bad that jobseekers had to lie about their postcode, they'd lived in a detached house on the outskirts of Bradfield. Niall had had his own bedroom plus a playroom. He'd had a PS3 and an Xbox. There had been a room full of gym equipment with a plasma-screen TV at the end of the treadmill. His dad's Mercedes had sat in the double garage next to his mum's Audi. They'd had season tickets for Manchester United, they'd gone abroad on holiday three times a year and Niall couldn't keep track of his Christmas and birthday presents.

Then three years ago, it had all come crashing down. His mum and dad had been fighting like *EastEnders* for months. He couldn't figure out what the trouble was, just that they couldn't seem to get through a day without being at each other's throat. Finally, his dad had taken them on holiday to Florida, supposedly to patch things up. But he'd walked out of the rented villa on the third night after yet another row. His mum had said to hell with him, they were going to enjoy the rest of the holiday. They came home ten days later to find the house sold, the rooms stripped bare, the cars gone and the locks changed. He'd sold the house out from under them and taken their clothes in bin bags round to Niall's mum's parents' house in Manchester.

It was breathtakingly evil. Niall had thought so at the time and he thought so still.

His mum got lawyered up, but it didn't do her any good. It turned out that his dad's company owned the house and everything else. On paper, his dad didn't have a pot to piss in. And so now, neither did Niall or his useless mother.

He was amazed at his dad's capacity for pure evil. His mother had dragged them both round to his car dealership one afternoon, trying to shame him into giving them more than the fifty quid a week he was shelling out for

Niall. They'd shut Niall out of the room, leaving him with the clueless receptionist while they screamed at each other. But he could still hear every word. 'He's not even my kid,' his dad had yelled at the height of the row.

His mum hadn't said anything, but Niall heard a loud crack, like something glass being thrown at a wall. Then the door had opened and he'd seen a spider web of cracks where the big plate-glass window on to the showroom should have revealed gleaming rows of cars. 'Come on,' she'd said, grabbing his arm and making for the door. 'We don't want money off that despicable lying bastard anyway.'

Speak for yourself, Niall had thought. All the more reason for taking his money, him being a despicable lying bastard. Who the fuck did he think he was, making out that Niall's mum was some sort of slut who'd have another man's kid and pass it off as his? She might be a useless cow, but he knew she wasn't a slag. Unlike his dad, who would do anything rather than put his hand in his pocket to support his wife and kid.

So thanks to him they were stuck in the shit, no way out till Niall could carve out his own possibilities. He'd keep his nose clean and turn his life around, then show his dad what a man was.

But meanwhile, he was stuck in this shitty life that he hated. There was only one little flicker of light at the bottom of the mineshaft. He wanted to learn Russian because he wanted to work for some oligarch and learn how to get rich himself. Those guys didn't give a shit whose toes they stood on. Hell, they'd break them just to pass the time. But none of the teachers at his poxy school could teach Russian. So he'd gone looking for some free Russian tuition locally. And then DD had turned up on his RigMarole page, offering to help out.

Niall didn't know what DD stood for. Probably some Russian first name and patronymic. But DD was the real thing. He'd given Niall some basic lessons online to make sure he was serious. And this week they were going to meet up for the first time. They'd have their first lesson face to face, and Niall would be on the road to riches. And maybe even his own football team.

That'd show the despicable lying bastard a thing or two.

Posing the question was one thing. Finding the answer was another entirely. His difficulty was not that he was in a strange place; Tony felt paradoxically relaxed in Blythe's home. It had the sort of tranquil, organic feel he'd have chosen himself, if he ever could have roused himself to take enough interest in his surroundings.

What bothered him was his inability to find a plausible reason for the attack on Jennifer Maidment. It was hard to imagine a personal motive against a fourteen-year-old girl that would lead to murder. If it had been a peer-group killing, it would have been a knife attack on the street or some back alley. There would almost certainly have been witnesses or, at the very least, other teenagers or family members who knew about it after the fact. But this was far too organised. Far too mature a killing method. And besides, the killer had to have had access to a vehicle. And there would have been no genital mutilation in a peer-group murder.

It was possible that Jennifer's death was the most brutal

of messages to either parent. Or both, perhaps. But on the surface, it was hard to see how the Maidments could intersect with the sort of person who would regard murdering and mutilating a teenager as a proportionate response to anything. He ran an engineering company, she was a part-time teacher of children with special needs. And again, if it was a message killing, it was a bloody strange way to go about it. The relatively peaceful death followed by the brutal mutilation. No, whatever this was about, it wasn't about coercion or revenge or any other obvious message to the parents.

As his thoughts picked over possibilities and rejected them almost as soon as he'd developed them, he ranged through the house, moving from room to room without thinking about it, not even conscious of how at ease he was with his surroundings. When his mind finally stopped churning over, he found himself in the kitchen and realised he was hungry. He opened a couple of cupboards, looking for something to eat. There wasn't much choice, but Tony had never considered himself a gourmet. He chose a packet of oatcakes and a tin of baked beans and sat down at the breakfast bar with a spoon and plate. Absently, he loaded the oatcakes with cold beans and ate the result with more relish than it warranted. There was something satisfying about this – he felt like Hansel and Gretel secretly exploring the witch's cottage. Only for him there would be no witch.

Once he'd satisfied his appetite, he went back to the armchair where he'd left the paperwork and crawled through it again. He looked at the locations of the various computers used to send messages to Jennifer Maidment and vaguely recalled Ambrose saying something about hoping they could use them to narrow down a location for the killer. Tony hadn't paid a great deal of attention because that sort of analysis wasn't something he used himself. He trusted his own observations and his own capacity for empathy, his own experience and his own instincts. He was uncomfortable with the idea of reducing human behaviour to a set of algorithms, even though he knew it had produced startling results on occasion. He just didn't feel comfortable with it.

But he knew a woman who did.

Fiona Cameron's number was stored in his phone. They'd met at various conferences over the years, and she'd called him in for a second opinion on a case she'd been working in Ireland. There had been nothing he could fault her on, but he had been able to offer a couple of helpful suggestions. They'd worked well together. Like Carol, she was intelligent and diligent. Unlike Carol, she'd managed to marry a demanding professional life with a long-term relationship. Tony glanced at his watch. Just after nine. She'd probably be doing whatever it was normal people did at this time of the evening. He wondered what that might be, exactly. Finishing off dinner? Watching TV? Sorting the laundry or just sitting talking over a glass of wine? Whatever it was, she probably wouldn't appreciate a call from him.

Knowing that had never stopped him before, and it wasn't going to stop him now. The phone rang out. Just when he was about to give up she answered, sounding a little flustered. 'Tony? Is that really you?'

'Hi, Fiona. Is this a bad moment?'

'No, not at all. I'm stuck in a hotel room in Aberdeen.' So, not like normal people, then. Just like him. All alone and a long way from home. 'I was just putting my room-service tray out in the hall, I nearly locked myself out. So, how are you?'

'I'm in Worcester,' he said, as if that was an answer. 'Something's come up on a case I'm working on and I wanted to ask you if you thought it was something that was susceptible to that geographic profiling program you use.'

She chuckled, the distance doing nothing to diminish the warmth in her voice. 'Same old Tony. Absolutely no small talk.'

She had a point, he thought. But he'd never bothered trying to pretend otherwise with a woman as acute as Fiona. 'Yeah, well, leopards and spots, what can I say?'

'It's OK, I don't mind. Anything to take my mind off the yawning tedium of the evening ahead. I daren't leave my room. I'm doing a seminar tomorrow and there are a couple of colleagues down in the bar I would slit my wrists to avoid. So I'm very happy to have something to pass the time with. What is it?'

'It's the murder and mutilation of a fourteen-year-old girl. And it's a killer who's going to do it again if we can't stop him. We've got an unidentified suspect who's been spending time online with our victim. He uses public-access computers spread across a hundred miles or so. Mostly single use but some of them more than once. So it's not offences, as such. Just locations that we know he's used. Is that something you can do anything with?'

'I'm not sure till I see it. Can you fire it over to me?'

'I'll have to type it in. I've only got a hard copy.' *And Patterson will have a nervous breakdown if I ask for an electronic copy so I can send it to someone right outside the loop.*

'Poor you. I hope it's not too long a list.'

'I'll get it to you in the next hour or so.'

'I'll look out for it. Take care. Good to talk to you.'

He pulled out his laptop and booted up, pleased to see that Blythe's wireless broadband appeared still to be functional. It didn't really matter whether Fiona Cameron could help. He was doing something positive, and experience had taught him that starting down that road always freed up the part of his brain that came up with the inspired connections that made him so effective a profiler.

There was a reason why Jennifer Maidment had died the way she had. And Tony sensed he was edging closer to it.

CHAPTER 20

Paula knew she was the best interviewer on the team. But still she felt ill at ease when she was confronted with teenage girls. Her own adolescence had been so atypical, she always felt she had no common ground to build on. It was ironic, she thought. She could find a starting point to reach out to violent sex offenders, to paedophiles, to stone-hearted people traffickers. But when it came to teenage lasses, she always found herself at a loss.

Unfortunately, she didn't have a choice. Carol Jordan had turned up at Bradfield Cross just in time to catch a harassed Casualty officer breaking the news to Mike Morrison that his wife hadn't made it. Not surprisingly, the poor bastard looked like a lost soul. Wife and son ripped out of his life without warning, everything solid turned to mist. Thank God the chief had stepped up to the plate and taken over, sending Paula off on the thankless task of trying to elicit information from Seth Viner's girl-friend.

Still, she couldn't be too glum. She'd had a cup of coffee with Elinor Blessing and a promise that they'd get together soon for a bite to eat. It seemed Paula's interest wasn't all one way. It was such a cliché, though. Cops and doctors or nurses. They were always hooking up. It was partly because the only person who could understand the madness of your work demands was someone who had the same insanity in their own professional life. And it was partly because they were the only people you ever met who weren't villains, victims or patients. And maybe it was also partly to do with the fact that a lot of people became cops or health professionals because they gen-uinely wanted to help people, so there was some semblance of common ground.

Whatever the reason, Paula hoped the affinity would work for her and Elinor. It had been a long time since she'd been in a relationship, but it had only been relatively recently that she'd even considered she'd moved far enough past her own issues for it to be a possibility.

'Cart before the horse,' she muttered to herself as she walked up the short path from the pavement to Lucie Jacobson's house. A brick terrace, one grade up from the basic no-garden variety. These had a single-storey arched ginnel that ran between every other house from front garden to back yard, making them look almost like semis. The Jacobson's house had a little porch tacked on to the front, not much bigger than a cupboard. One side of it was jammed tight with what looked in the gloom like a press of bodies. When Paula rang the bell, the light snapped on and they were revealed as nothing more sinister than coats and waterproofs, baseball caps and bike helmets. Paula held up her ID and the woman who'd appeared in the doorway nodded and opened up.

'I've been expecting one of your lot,' she said with a resigned cheerfulness Paula didn't encounter that often. 'You'll have come about Seth. Come in.' She ushered Paula into a cramped living room where everything of necessity had its place. It was as organised as the cabin of a ship, with shelves and cabinets crammed with books, videos, CDs, vinyl and box files, neatly labelled with titles like, 'Utilities', 'Bank', and 'VATman'. An unmatched pair of sofas and a couple of chairs occupied the remaining space, facing a bulky TV attached by umbilical cables to the usual assortment of peripherals. 'Have a seat,' she said. 'I'll just get Lucie. Her brothers are out with their dad, playing basketball, so we'll have a bit of peace and quiet. They're twins. Sixteen. They take up a disproportionate amount of room.' She shook her head and made for the door. 'Lucie,' she called. 'There's someone here to talk to you about Seth.'

She turned back into the room, leaning on the doorpost. 'I'm Sarah Jacobson, by the way. I've already spoken to Kathy and Julia. They're in a right state.' She sighed and ran a hand through her short dark curls. 'Who wouldn't be? God, it's hard enough getting through their teens anyway, without a nightmare like this.' Feet thundered on stairs behind her and she stood back to let her daughter through. Lucie Jacobson had the same mop of curls, though in her case they formed a mass around her head, corkscrewing over her shoulders in an amazing cascade. Her face peeped out from her hair, narrow and sharp-featured, deep blue eyes given extra definition by wide lines of kohl along the lids. She was striking, not pretty, but Paula suspected she might grow into a beauty. Black jeans and black T-shirt completed the nice middle-class version of the junior Goth look.

'Is there any news?' she demanded, glaring at Paula as if she were personally responsible for Seth's disappearance.

'I'm sorry. There's been no sign of Seth.' Paula stood up. 'I'm Paula McIntyre, Detective Constable. I'm one of the team assigned to find him.'

'Just a constable? Are you important enough to be doing this? Because it's really important that somebody finds Seth,' Lucie said, coming in and throwing herself into a sofa opposite Paula.

'Lucie, for God's sake,' her mother said. 'Nobody's impressed.' She glanced at Paula. 'Tea? Coffee?'

'Not for me, thanks.'

Sarah Jacobson nodded. 'I'll be in the kitchen if you need me.' She gave her daughter a hard stare. 'I'm leaving you alone with Ms McIntyre so you can say what you need to say without being worried about what I think. OK?' And she left them to it.

'Like I'm worried about what she thinks about anything.'

'Course you're not. You're a teenager,' Paula said drily. She made an instant decision not to treat this one with kid gloves. 'And here's the thing. I really couldn't give a shit about anything right now except finding Seth. So whatever little secrets you've got up your sleeve that you think might get either of you into trouble? It's time to tell. If you help us find Seth, your grubby sins and transgressions are going to be forgotten. I don't care about drugs, or drinking or shagging, OK? I just want to know what you know that might help us find Seth.' She met Lucie's defiant gaze and stared her down. 'Whatever the two of you have got up to, you can bet I have heard it, seen it or done it before.'

Lucie sighed and rolled her eyes. 'Like that's got anything to do with anything. There's nothing we do that's remotely got to do with Seth not being here, OK? Me and him, we're cool. What you need to know is that yes, Seth does have a secret.'

Paula tried not to show how much of her attention Lucie had grabbed. 'And you know what it is?'

'Course I do. He's mine and I'm his.'

'So, what is this secret?'

Lucie looked her up and down, as if making a decision. 'You a lesbian, then? Like Seth's mums?'

'To quote you, "Like that's got anything to do with anything,"' Paula parried.

'So you are, then.' Lucie smiled as if she'd scored a point. 'That's cool. We don't trust people that totally buy into the system,' she said. 'I wouldn't trust you if you weren't a lesbian. You need something to offset the whole cop thing.'

Paula so wanted to say, 'Whatever,' in that totally teenage way but she restrained herself. 'You need to be telling me Seth's secret.'

Lucie squirmed into the soft cushions. 'It's no big. Really.'

'So tell me.'

'He's been writing songs. Mostly lyrics, but some of them, the whole thing. Music and everything.'

It seemed a strange thing to be ashamed of. 'And that was a secret?'

'Well, yeah. I mean, it's just one step away from writing poetry, for God's sake. And how lame would that be?'

'OK. So, had he played his songs to anybody? Or shown them the lyrics?'

'Well, duh. Obviously, he showed me. But see, that's what all this might be about. Because, like on Rig— You know about Rig, right?'

'RigMarole? I know about Rig, yeah.'

'Well, on Rig, there was this dude and he was like, with Seth, "I know your dirty little secret," and Seth was really freaked. So they got into a sidebar and Seth is like, "How did you know about my songs?" and the dude goes, "You need to be more careful what you leave lying around." So obviously Seth had dropped one or something and this dude had picked it up and he only works in the music business.'

Paula's spirits were sinking by the minute. She could see how it had played out. Seth had been lured into giving away his own secret and the killer had turned that back on the boy to create a dream Seth would buy into. 'And he said he could get Seth a deal?'

Lucie tutted. 'Nobody would be that thick, to believe a scam like that,' she said. 'He said he could introduce Seth to a couple of bands that are on the way up, bands who've got stuff online but don't have a record deal yet. Bands that might like to work with him on their way to making it big. He said he was going to fix something up for Seth.'

'And that's who Seth was meeting last night?'

She looked away. 'Maybe. He was supposed to tell me, but he didn't. He just said he was going to Will's but not to call me because they might have stuff going down.'

Paula let that settle for a minute, then said, 'What can you tell me about this guy?'

'He uses JJ as his Rig username. He totally knows his stuff. He's a real expert on the whole grunge scene, which is Seth's big thing too. He said JJ knew stuff only a real insider would know.'

Except, how would you know what that is? He could have made it all up and you sweet babes would have fallen for it. 'Is there anything else you know about him? Where he lives? Where he works?'

For the first time, Lucie looked distressed. 'No, all I know is his screen name. He never talked about himself. He came on to talk about music, not to do the personal stuff.'

'Did you ever check out his page on Rig?'

Lucie frowned. 'I never did, no, but Seth checked it out. He said it was full of great music stuff.' Her face cleared. 'Of course. That's the way to find him. JJ, like letters, not spelled out.'

'Bear with me a second,' Paula said, holding up one finger. She took out her phone and called Stacey. 'Paula here,' she said.

'I know,' Stacey said. 'It's what caller ID is for.'

God save me from geek humour. 'Seth Viner was in communication with somebody on RigMarole about music. The guy used the name JJ, letters only. It's possible JJ lured him into a meeting. Can you take a look?'

'I'm looking right now . . .' A pause. 'Nothing here. Leave it with me. I'm going to have to back-door it.'

'Do I want to know what that means?' Paula asked.

'No.'

The line went dead. 'Thanks, Lucie,' Paula said. 'I think this might be a big help to us.' *And I wish you'd told someone as soon as you knew he was missing.* 'Is there anything else you think I should know about?'

Lucie shook her head. 'He's one of the good guys, Seth. You need to find him and bring him home. This is not a good place to be right now. I'm scared something bad is happening to him.'

'I understand that. And it's OK to show you're scared. Your mum, she seems like she'd be there for you, you know?'

Lucie snorted. 'She works for the BBC. For radio. I mean, stuff like *You and Yours*. How embarrassing is that? It's like, the definition of straight.'

'Give her a chance,' Paula said, getting to her feet. 'I know you won't believe me, but she was once like you are now.'

Lucie nodded. Her eyes were wet. She had the look of someone who would wail if she tried speaking. Paula knew exactly how that felt. It wasn't so long ago that she'd had to deal with losing one of her closest friends. There had been plenty of times when grief and fear had threatened to overwhelm her too. She fished out a card.

'Call me if you think of anything. Or if you just want to talk about Seth. OK?'

Minutes later, she was in her car, heading back to the office to pass the watches of the night with Stacey. She had a horrible feeling that whatever lay ahead of Lucie Jacobson, a joyful reunion with her boyfriend wasn't going to be on the agenda.

CHAPTER 21

Birds were singing. Singing their heads off. One sounded like a squeaky wheel, another like it had something grievous stuck in its throat. Tony slowly surfaced from a thick blanket of sleep. He couldn't remember the last time he'd slept straight through the night, undisturbed by dreams, unaffected by anxieties. He'd struggled with sleep for years. Since he started investigating the contents of truly messy heads, if he was honest.

At first, he luxuriated in the unfamiliar feeling of being rested. Then he had a moment of bewilderment as he opened his eyes and couldn't think where he was. Not home, not a hotel, not the on-call room at Bradfield Moor . . . Then memory kicked in. He was lying in the bed of Edmund Arthur Blythe, the man who had contributed half of his DNA, in the master suite of a substantial Edwardian villa by a park in Worcester. A bit like Goldilocks, he thought.

Tony glanced at his watch, then shook his wrist in disbelief. Almost nine o'clock? He couldn't believe it. He'd been asleep for ten hours. He hadn't slept that long since he'd been an undergraduate and stayed up all night to finish an essay. Other people partied, Tony studied. He propped himself up on one elbow and shook his head. This was insane. Alvin Armstrong was due to pick him up at his hotel in just over half an hour. He'd never make it. He'd better call him and rearrange the pick-up. Thirty-three minutes to come up with the sort of story that wouldn't make him sound like one of the lunatics who've taken over the asylum.

He was about to reach for his phone when it startled him by springing into life. Tony juggled it off the bedside table and to his ear. 'Yes? Hello? Hello?' he gabbled.

'Did I wake you?'

It took him a moment, then he was orientated. 'Fiona,' he said. 'No, I'm wide awake. I was just picking my phone up to call someone else. You startled me, that's all.'

'Sorry. I just thought I'd let you know, I ran those locations you gave me through my programs.'

'Fantastic. That's really quick work.'

Fiona chuckled. 'We have moved on since the age of the abacus, Tony. They make the calculations pretty quickly these days. Even on a laptop in a hotel room.'

'I know, I know. But humour me. It still feels like magic to me.'

'Well, I don't feel entirely magical about this. I don't think these results are definitive, because we're looking at a different choice mechanism from the criminal committing

227

an offence. The locations of actual crimes are conditioned by the availability of victims. As we both know, some criminals have very restricted criteria for their crimes. A rapist likes a certain type of woman. A burglar only does first-floor entries . . .'

'I'm with you, yes,' Tony said. He knew she didn't mean to teach him to suck eggs but he wished she'd get to the point. He didn't need a seminar, only a result.

'So his choice of locations is limited much more than someone who's just looking for a public-access computer. Because they're everywhere. I expect even you've noticed that.'

'I've even used them, Fiona.'

'My, we'll get you into the twentieth century yet, Tony. So, with the proviso that these results are not backed up with the kind of solid research that underpins the criminal geographic profiling, I'm prepared to say that I think the person using these internet nodes lives in South Manchester, near to the M60. I've got a map with a red zone that I'm about to email over to you. It's apparently where Didsbury, Withington and Chorlton come together. Whatever that means demographically.'

'They read the *Guardian* and listen to Radio 4. Shop locally and feel wistful about John Lewis.'

Fiona laughed delightedly. 'Not your usual sexual homicide territory, then?'

'No. But I don't think this is sexual. I think it's going to go serial, but there's something else going on here that I can't get at. You know that feeling?'

'Oh yes. Not a good one. Anyway, if there's anything else I can help you with, give me a ring.'

'Thanks, Fiona. I owe you a big drink next time I see you. Are you going to the Europol thing next month?'

He never found out what Fiona was going to say. With no warning, the door opposite the bed swung open and the estate agent who had shown him round the day before walked in, talking over her shoulder to someone behind her. 'And I think you'll agree the master suite here is stunning.' Then she turned into the room and gawped at Tony, clutching the duvet to his chest.

'I've got to go, Fiona,' he said to the phone. Then he tried on a smile and said, 'I know this looks weird, but I can explain.'

That was when the estate agent started to scream.

Bethany didn't quite have the nerve to refuse Carol entry, but she clearly didn't want to reveal her arrival to Vanessa. 'She's very busy,' the receptionist said. 'I doubt she'll be able to fit you in at short notice today. You were very lucky that she was able to make time for you when you were here before,' she gabbled.

Carol didn't bother turning on the charm. If this woman had worked for Vanessa for any length of time, fear would be a better spur than the desire to please. 'This is a police matter,' she said. 'Tell Ms Hill that I am here in my capacity as commander of the cold case review team.' She turned away, giving Bethany no option but to pick up the phone.

'I'm sorry, Vanessa,' Carol heard her say plaintively. 'That policewoman is here again. She says she needs to talk to you on a police matter. Something about a cold case review?' A long pause. Then the sound of the phone

229

being replaced. 'She'll be with you as soon as possible,' Bethany said in the gloomy voice of a woman who knows she's caught between a rock and a hard place.

Time slipped by. Carol checked her watch, her phone and her email. She'd stopped by the Northern Division incident room on the way here to issue instructions for the day's operations and she'd left messages for all her team that the morning conference would be at ten instead of nine. But still she couldn't quite believe she was pursuing this while she was in the middle of two major cases, not to mention the Wastwater search.

If Blake found out how she was spending her time when she should have her hand on every aspect of ongoing investigations, he'd have all the ammunition he needed to close down her operation. But even that knowledge couldn't budge her from this path. It was as if she lacked the strength to continue playing the role of the cop who put the job ahead of everything else. For years, she'd done what was asked of her, and more. She'd put her life on the line, she'd faced degradation and damage and dragged herself back into the front line. It had been a struggle to return to the job but, having made her comeback, she hadn't hesitated to confront whatever had been thrown at her.

But now she'd been utterly blown off course by the demands of her feelings for Tony. Because she cared more about him than the job that had provided her with so much meaning? Or because she wanted to be defiant, to assert her right to do her job the way she wanted in the teeth of a boss who wanted to run her like a clockwork mouse?

Whatever the answer, she'd have to find it another day. For finally, Vanessa Hill was standing before her, clearly in imperfect control of her anger. The toe of her high-heeled shoe tapped a tattoo on the carpet. 'I thought we'd concluded our business,' she said, her voice low but sharp.

Carol shook her head. 'My business is never concluded till I get to the truth,' she said. 'And so far, that's been a commodity in scarce supply where you're concerned.' She glanced at Bethany. 'I don't think you want to have this conversation in a place where it's likely to end up as cloakroom gossip.'

This time, instead of taking Carol back to her office, Vanessa led her to a small room off the reception area. Two generously upholstered leather sofas faced each other across a granite coffee table. The walls were decorated with prints of Gustav Klimt's opulent paintings. A room dressed to impress, Carol thought. She wasn't.

Vanessa threw herself down on one of the sofas. 'I thought I made it clear to you that I was done with this bizarre quest of yours,' she said in a bored voice.

Carol refused to be derailed. 'Part of my job as commander of the Major Incident Team is to investigate cold cases. I've been looking at an old case involving an assault in Savile Park. Ring any bells?'

Vanessa's composure barely flickered. 'Get to the point,' she said.

'You were with your fiancé, Edmund Arthur Blythe. You told the police you were accosted by a man who wanted Eddie's money. Things got out of hand and Eddie was stabbed. Almost fatally. And the next thing that happened was that Eddie left town.'

'Why are you bringing this up?' There was a dangerous edge to Vanessa's voice. Carol remembered the Bob Dylan line about the woman who never stumbles because she's got no place to fall. Except that with Vanessa it was more like never stumbling because she refused to admit falling was a possibility.

'Because you never have. Tony deserves to know why his father walked out on you both. If you won't tell me the truth about what happened, then I will reinvestigate this case with full vigour. Your statement seems to me to be very thin. I promise you I will turn your life upside down and I will give a statement to the effect that all these years later you tried to swindle your son out of his inheritance. It's enough to open an investigation. Believe me, Vanessa, I am every bit as tough as you, and I will cheerfully be a thorn in your side till you give me some answers.'

'This is harassment. I'll have your badge if you try it.' Vanessa couldn't keep the fury from her face. Carol knew she'd won.

Carol shrugged casually. 'And how long will that accusation stand up? I can make your life uncomfortable for a very long time. I don't think you want that. I don't think you want your name dragged through the mud. Or your company's name. Not at a time when the economy's on the floor and people are counting every penny they spend on recruitment and training.'

'He should have grabbed you with both hands,' Vanessa said. 'Pitiful excuse for a man. Just like his father before him.' She crossed her legs, folded her arms and glared at Carol. 'So what do you want to know?'

'I want to know what happened that night to make Eddie run away. And I want to know why you've never told Tony.'

Vanessa gave Carol a hard, calculating stare. 'How would you feel if the man you'd agreed to marry revealed himself to be a spineless coward? The minute that lad produced his knife, Eddie turned to jelly. He was offering his wallet, begging him to leave us alone. He was crying. Can you believe that? Tears running down his cheeks, snot running down his face like a little boy. He was pathetic. And that bastard lapped it up. He was laughing at Eddie.' She paused. Her left foot moved up and down to a private internal beat, the gleaming leather catching the light. 'He demanded my jewellery. My engagement ring, a gold bracelet Eddie had given me. So I kicked him in the shins. That's when he turned on Eddie. He stabbed him, then he ran for it.'

'Did you blame yourself for what happened?' Carol asked, knowing what the answer would be.

'Blame myself? It wasn't me that grovelled to that bastard. I was the one who stood up for us, the way Eddie should have. He was a coward, and that mugger knew it. It wasn't me he went for, because he knew I wouldn't stand for it. All I blame myself for is not realising what a bloody wimp Eddie truly was.' Contempt dripped from her words like blood from a slaughterman's knife.

'Why did Eddie sell up and leave town?'

'He was mortified. Thanks to the paper, everybody knew he'd let himself down. And me. He was a laughing stock. The big-shot businessman who couldn't stand up to a late-night mugger. He couldn't take the shame. And I'd dumped him by then, so there was nothing to keep him here.'

'You dumped him? While he was in hospital?'

Vanessa looked unconcerned. 'Why bother waiting? He wasn't the man I thought he was. Simple as that.'

Her ruthless egotism was breathtaking, Carol thought. She couldn't imagine anything denting Vanessa's self-belief. It was a miracle Tony had survived as well as he had. 'Nobody was ever arrested,' Carol said.

'No, you lot were as useless then as you are now. To be honest, I didn't think they were that bothered. If he'd tried to rape me, they might have summoned up some interest. But to them, Eddie was just a pathetic rich bugger who didn't know how to take care of himself and deserved what he got.'

Carol struggled to believe that. Back in the less violent 1960s, the police would have taken such an attack seriously, even given an alleged class divide that didn't square with Alan Miles's account of Eddie as a local lad made good. But Vanessa's version gave Carol a stick to beat her with, which made it irresistible. 'You didn't give them much of a description to go on.'

Vanessa raised her eyebrows. 'It was dark. And he didn't hang around. He sounded local. You of all people must know how little witnesses actually see when they're being attacked.'

She had a point. But then smart operators like Vanessa usually did. 'So why did you never tell Tony the truth? Why let him believe that Eddie leaving was something to do with him?'

'I've no control over what my son chooses to believe,' Vanessa said dismissively.

'You could have told him the whole story.'

A cold, malicious smile lifted the corners of her mouth. 'I was protecting him from the truth. I didn't want him to know how pathetic his father was. First, because he couldn't stand up to a lad who was probably as scared as he was. And second, because he cared so much about what people thought of him that he ran away rather than face the music. Do you think it would have helped Tony to know that his father had a yellow streak a mile wide? That he'd been abandoned by a man who made the lion in *The Wizard of Oz* look like a hero?'

'I think it would have been more helpful than growing up thinking his father left because he didn't want anything to do with his child. Did Eddie never show any interest in the fact that he had a son?'

Vanessa breathed heavily through her nose. 'I didn't know he knew. I certainly never told him. How he found out, I don't know.'

Carol couldn't keep the astonishment from her face. 'You never told him? He didn't know you were pregnant?'

'I was only three months gone when the attack happened. I wasn't showing. Back then, you didn't advertise that you were expecting. And as it turned out, it's just as well. He'd have rushed me to the altar and I'd have been stuck with the pathetic little coward. I'd never have had all this,' she added with absolute conviction, waving her arm proudly to encompass her offices. 'Eddie did us a favour when he cleared off.'

This, thought Carol, was where self-belief teetered over

into self-delusion. 'You don't think he was entitled to know his son?'

'You get what you take in this world. Entitled's got bugger all to do with it.' With that brutal line, Vanessa got to her feet. 'This time, we're really done. I've nothing more to say to you. You can tell Tony or not. I couldn't care less.' She opened the door with a flourish. 'You really could do better for yourself, you know.'

Carol smiled in her face as she walked out. 'I almost feel sorry for you. You have no idea what you're missing.'

CHAPTER 22

Friday was the best day of Pippa Thomas's week. Since she'd cut her working week at the surgery to four days, she'd found a space in her life for her. One whole day when she didn't have to poke and prod, drill and fill to improve other people's smiles. One whole day when Huw was at work and the kids were at school and she was free. And she loved it.

But most of all, she loved the Friday Morning Club. There were five of them. Monica, who worked afternoons and evenings at the Citizens Advice Bureau; Pam, who looked after her demented mother and chose to spend her limited respite budget to liberate her for Friday mornings; Denise, who was a Lady Who Lunched except on Fridays; and Aoife, who ran the front of house at the Bradfield Royal Theatre. Rain or shine, they met in the car park of the Shining Hour inn, high up on the moors between Bradfield and Rochdale. And rain or shine, they would run a dozen miles over some of the roughest terrain in the north of England. They'd first met on a Breast Cancer Fun Run one Sunday in Grattan Park. 'Talk about oxymoron,' Denise had muttered as the five of them searched in vain for a toilet that was unlocked. 'Fun and breast cancer. Yeah, right.' They'd ended up acting as lookouts for each other as they squatted in the rhododendrons to empty their middle-aged bladders before they could run. By the end of the afternoon, the Friday Morning Club had been born.

That Friday it was a bright blue day with an exfoliating edge to the north-east wind that knifed its way across the Pennine moors. Pippa hugged herself inside her lightweight top. Soon she'd feel that delirious sense of her body moving freely through this amazing landscape. As soon as they set off Pippa assumed the lead. Denise took up position on her shoulder and they exchanged a few catch-up sentences. But soon they needed all their breath to feed oxygen to their muscles for the long, slow climb up to the summit of Bickerslow.

Head down, Pippa felt her quads stretch and swell as they carried her onwards. No time for the view now. All her focus was on reaching the marker cairn, where they would wheel west and find the shelter of the hill's shoulder and metalled surface, a brief respite from rough going. They'd barely started up the single-track road that dribbled across the moor top when Pippa stopped in her tracks. Denise cannoned into her, almost sending them both flying. 'What the hell is it?' Denise demanded.

Pippa said nothing. She just pointed at the soaking

bundle lying in a gully by the road. In spite of the bag that covered one end of the filthy cloth, there was no doubting that it was the remains of a human being.

Fridays would never be the same again.

Paula helped herself to a mug of the coffee someone had already brewed and parked herself behind her desk. Although it was only half past nine and the chief had rearranged the morning briefing for ten, the team were already here. At least, she thought Stacey was here. The battery of screens was so effective that she was almost invisible. But the faint tap and click of mouse and keys indicated her presence. As usual. Paula sometimes wondered if Stacey ever went home. Or even if she had a home to go to. Paula had never worked with anyone more secretive than Stacey. One way or another, she'd been in the home of everyone on the squad except for her. It wasn't that she was unfriendly. Just from another planet. Though lately, Paula thought she'd seen signs of Stacey thawing a little where Sam was concerned. Nothing major. Just making him the occasional brew and actually volunteering information about where he was and what he might be doing. Which she never did about anyone else.

Paula reminded herself there were more important things to think about this morning than her colleagues' personal lives. Every police station she had ever worked in had been a gossip factory. It was as if they had to make up for the unpleasantness of most of their work with an obsessive curiosity about the possible secrets of everyone else in the place. Overheated imaginations ran riot, perhaps because they were supposed to be bound so tight by fact in their professional lives.

She switched on her computer, but before she could check the overnights for any further progress, Sam Evans, freshly returned from the Lake District, perched on the corner of her desk. He was fractionally too close, just marginally in her personal space. It was a thing that men did unconsciously to diminish women, she thought. To put us on the back foot.

But with Sam, it never bothered her. He was one of those few men who were entirely relaxed around lesbians. There was nothing threatening in his closeness. If Paula was honest, she liked Sam. She knew he was nakedly ambitious, always out for number one. What amused her was that he thought nobody apart from the chief had sussed him. And if you knew what somebody's weakness was, it was easy to circumvent it. She liked Sam's quick mind. And, curiously, she liked his smell. His cologne was spicy, with a hint of lime, but it didn't completely erase the maleness of his natural odour. Mostly it was the smell of individual women that pleased Paula, but Sam was a rare exception and she knew it made her more susceptible to his charm.

'So,' he said. 'Ten o'clock briefing in the middle of a high-profile murder. What's going on with the guv'nor?'

Paula pulled a face. 'No idea. I assumed she was briefing the incident room at Northern about Daniel Morrison and talking to Central about the search for Seth Viner.'

Sam shook his head. 'She was at Northern at half past eight. Sorted out the actions for the day and she was out the door by ten to nine. My spies tell me she's not been at Central yet.'

Kevin was openly eavesdropping on their conversation. 'And she was on the missing list yesterday morning. When you called in from the crime scene, she wasn't here.' He went to refill his coffee, then joined Paula and Sam.

'Where was she?' Paula asked.

'Don't know. It took her a while to get there, though. So not anywhere in the immediate vicinity.'

'And she wasn't around yesterday evening,' Sam said.

'She was,' Paula said. 'When I texted her about Jessica Morrison's heart attack, she was there soon as.'

'Earlier, I mean. I came back here, thinking she'd be around. I've got news and I wanted to talk to her, but she wasn't here. Stacey said she'd been and gone. Not a word about where.' Sam folded his arms confidentially and said, 'You think its lurve? You think her and Tony have finally noticed what everybody else has known for years?'

Paula snorted. 'Give me a break. Those two are never going to be an item. He'd analyse it to death. He'd have diagrams all over his whiteboard.'

'I don't know,' Kevin said. 'She can be very imposing. Very commanding. If anybody can get Tony to shut up shop and pay attention to her, it's the guv'nor.'

'Maybe that's the real reason he's not working this case,' Sam said. 'Maybe it's got nothing to do with budget. You know what she's like. She wouldn't have him working with us if they were getting it on in their spare time. She'd see it as a conflict. And she'd knock it into touch.

She's a law unto herself when it comes to running a case, but as far as internal discipline is concerned, she doesn't like it when we step out of line.'

'Don't I know it,' Kevin muttered. Years ago, Carol had been instrumental in his disgrace and demotion. That she had also been the agent of his rehabilitation made him feel he would never escape being in her debt. He'd tried hard to like her, but he'd never quite succeeded. 'If that's what's going on, she's chosen the worst possible time for it. With Blake on our backs, we need all the help we can get. I know I used to think Tony was a weird fuck, that he didn't have any place on our team. But I've learned different. And I think we need him now.'

As he spoke, Sam straightened up, cleared his throat and said loudly, 'Morning, ma'am.'

Carol swept in, coat spreading around her as she strode to the conference table. How much had she heard? Paula wondered. 'I couldn't agree more, Kevin,' Carol said, dumping bags and coat on the floor by her chair. 'But Mr Blake says we need to cut our budget. So if we need expertise, we have to find it on the cheap. Apparently the National Crime Faculty has some baby profilers they'd like to try out in the field. Halle-fucking-lujah.' She looked at them all in turn and grinned complicity. 'Is there any coffee in this godforsaken hole?'

Five minutes later, they were all settled in their usual positions. Paula couldn't help wondering whether Sam was right. Or half right, maybe. Perhaps there was a man in Carol's life. Just not Tony. One who brought out her appetite for battle, apparently, if her energy this morning was anything to go by. She took their reports one by one, filleting the key elements and suggesting new avenues of approach. But it was clear by the end of their accounts that there was almost nothing to take them any further forward in the case of Daniel's murder and not much more as far as Seth's disappearance was concerned.

Kevin had followed up on Asif Khan's tale of the comedy producer who was looking for young talent. He'd spoken to commissioning editors at the BBC in Manchester, Glasgow, London and Cardiff, but nobody had ever had a pitch remotely like this. And there was certainly nothing in the pipeline that might fit even loosely the version Daniel had given his friend. 'So it's a dead end.' He pushed his notebook from him. 'To be honest, I thought it'd go nowhere, but you gotta cover the bases.'

'You do,' Carol agreed. 'And we do it better than most.'

Paula lifted her hand a few inches. 'Can I just check, chief? Are we working on the basis that these two cases are linked? Daniel and Seth?'

Carol nodded. 'Good question, Paula. I think we have to acknowledge that there's a strong probability we're looking at one perp. We need to be cautious at this stage. Because coincidences do happen. And so do copycats.'

'But from what Seth's girlfriend said to me, this JJ's been stalking Seth online for ages. Surely that precludes a copycat?' Paula said.

'That's making a lot of assumptions,' Sam said, amazingly up to speed for a man who'd been a hundred miles away for days. He was such a hot dog, Paula thought with a trace of resentment. 'It's assuming Seth's been abducted, not just gone underground for some reason nobody knows about or nobody's letting on about. It's also assuming that, if he has been abducted, it's the person he's been talking to online, this JJ. Who might just be straight up.' He held up a hand to still their noisy protests. 'He might be. It's possible. I'm just agreeing with the guv'nor. We need to keep an open mind. And it could be an opportunist copycat.'

'No, it couldn't,' Kevin said. 'Seth was already missing before we found Daniel's body.'

'We'd released Daniel to the media as a missing person,' Stacey pointed out. 'It's possible.'

Paula watched Carol cover her eyes with her hand and wished she'd kept her mouth shut. 'Point taken,' she said hastily.

Carol looked up and gave her a faint smile. 'You lot are very feisty this morning,' she said.

'Picking it up from you, boss,' Kevin said. 'So where do we go from here?'

'Let's hear what Stacey has to say first,' Carol said.

Stacey treated them all to a neat little smile. 'I've not had much luck with facial-recognition software and the city-centre CCTVs. They're too low-res, and the angles are pretty crap, frankly.'

'I sometimes wonder why we bother with all this surveillance,' Carol said. 'Whenever we need it, nine times out of ten it's as much use as a chocolate teapot.'

'If Stacey was running the game, none of us would have a single secret left,' Sam said.

Stacey looked surprised and pleased at what she took as a compliment. 'The cameras would work a lot better, that's for sure,' she said. 'As far as the other stuff goes, RigMarole seemed to be the place to start. I've had access to Seth's computer and there's a lot of chat with this JJ character. On the surface, it's all pretty innocuous, and very similar to shedloads of other online chatter. But he is definitely holding out a hand to Seth. And the interesting thing is that his personal pages on Rig have disappeared. They were closed down the afternoon Seth went missing. Which gives more weight to Paula's assumption, I'm afraid.'

'Have you been able to find out any more about this JJ?' Carol asked.

'I spoke to RigMarole yesterday. They say they don't own the data posted by individuals on their personal pages. They say they don't have access to it either. They say we need a warrant and that's no guarantee that we can access anything on their server.'

'Bastards,' Kevin said.

'So I went in anyway.'

Carol rolled her eyes. 'I wish you wouldn't tell me this stuff, Stacey.'

'I have to tell you, otherwise you can't distinguish between what's evidential and what's stuff we're not supposed to know.' There was a certain sense to Stacey's logic, Paula thought. Shame it made Carol green around the gills.

'What did you find that I'm not supposed to know?' Carol said, her earlier bounce starting to fade.

'All the personal data JJ used to set up the account is bullshit. None of it checks out. And he used a popmail account that doesn't need any ID to set up. So, in essence, he's a straw man.'

'Another dead end,' Paula said. 'He's a clever bastard, this one.'

'Possibly too clever by half,' Stacey said. 'There is one

strange thing, though. You all know who Alan Turing is, right? The guy who cracked the Enigma code and basically invented modern computers?'

'Who killed himself because of the shame of being prosecuted for being homosexual,' Paula said. 'In case you'd forgotten that bit.'

Kevin groaned. 'Not even the boss was in the job back then, Paula. What about Alan Turing, Stacey?'

'There's a famous photograph of him as a young man, still a student, I think, running at an athletics meeting. Anyway, JJ has cropped the head shot out of this picture, cleaned it up a bit and used it as his photo on his personal page. I'm not sure what that tells us, but it's not random, is it?'

This is when we need Tony, Paula thought. They were capable of making guesses and advancing hypotheses, but they had no way of weighing them against each other. 'So, do we think JJ's gay, then?' she asked.

'Or a geek,' Sam said. 'Would you say, Stacey?'

'Well, Turing's a bit of a geek hero,' she said. 'But it might just be a red herring. If he's that clever.'

'Did we get anywhere with Daniel?' Carol asked. 'I know we don't have his webbook, but I wondered if you'd been able to access his email account at all?'

Stacey looked slightly shamefaced. 'Well, while I was poking around behind the scenes at Rig, I thought I'd check out Daniel's account.'

Carol closed her eyes momentarily. 'Of course you did. And what did you find?'

'The person who's been talking to him in a sidebar about the comedy circuit calls himself KK.'

'Oh fuck,' someone breathed.

'And KK's pages were cancelled the afternoon Daniel went missing. He used a different Turing photo, with a Photoshopped haircut so he doesn't look so 1940s. Sorry to burst your balloon, Sam, but I think there's not much room for doubt. We're looking for the same person in both cases.'

They all wore the same look of desperation. 'It's not very likely that Seth's still alive, is it?' It was Paula who said what they were all thinking.

'We still have to operate as if he might be,' Carol said firmly. 'But the one thing we all know from past experience is that a killer like this isn't going to stop at two. Sam, do I take it the fact that you're back means nothing much is happening up in Wastwater?'

Sam looked pleased at having the attention turned back on him. 'Um, no. The opposite, in fact. But I thought you'd like to hear what's happened face to face. Plus what I need to do, I can do better from here.'

Carol gave him a hard stare. *He's on the verge of undermining her authority and I'm not sure he even knows it.* Paula sat back and waited to see whether Sam would save himself or not. 'What has happened?' Carol said, all the warmth gone from her voice.

'The kind of result you can't argue with,' he said. 'Late yesterday afternoon the divers pulled a plastic-wrapped bundle out of Wastwater, in one of the exact places Stacey had identified.' He paused to beam at them all.

'Do I take it we have a victim?' Carol said repressively, reminding them all that finding a body could never be cause for celebration.

The realisation that he'd struck entirely the wrong note dawned visibly on Sam. He rearranged his face and cleared his throat. 'More than one victim, I'm afraid.'

'Mother and daughter, wasn't it?' Carol said.

'Yes. And they did find the remains of a very young child. But—' He couldn't help himself. He just had to pause for dramatic effect.

'But?' Carol was definitely on the wrong side of cross now.

'But that's not all. There was a third set of remains. If that's Danuta Barnes and her daughter, there's another person down there with them. And it's probably a bloke.'

CHAPTER 23

Tony stared down at his shoes, shoulders in a defensive hunch. 'Thanks, Alvin,' he mumbled, feeling like a barely tolerated idiot. 'I appreciate you coming down to vouch for me.'

Ambrose had a look of angry disgust on his face. 'I stuck my neck out to get the DI to bring you on board. And now this? This is the stuff of legend. And not in a good way. Now I look like a complete twat for even suggesting you. That'll be my rep all over this force now: "Alvin Ambrose, the twat who hired the profiler that got arrested for being an intruder in his own house." Thanks, Doc.'

'I mean it, I'm really sorry.'

'Why didn't you just tell me about your dad?'

Tony sighed. 'He wasn't my dad. That's the problem, really.' Explaining himself to Ambrose, that was the worst of it. He'd spent his life building walls against the world, keeping to himself the things he wanted no one else to know. And all it took to bring the walls crashing down was one act of madness. This must be how his patients felt.

It had been the stuff of comedy, though there had actually been nothing funny about it. The screams of the estate agent had galvanised Tony, sending him diving out of bed in his boxers to grab his clothes. Unfortunately, it had also galvanised the house viewers, who had had the presence of mind to call the police and report an intruder.

The police had arrived in an amazingly short time. Tony was barely dressed, the estate agent still freaked out, the viewers with her on the other side of the door, refusing to let him out. In vain he had tried to explain that he had every right to be in the house. The fact that he had keys cut no ice with the cops. What made sense to them was the estate agent's story that he'd viewed the house as a prospective buyer the previous day and now he was claiming he lived there. He had to admit, he'd have believed her. He'd have thought the madman in the bedroom definitely needed to be taken down to the police station till either he could be sectioned or his story could be verified. Or not, as they were pretty sure would be the case.

Once they were at the nick, it had all been sorted out very quickly. A call to his solicitor and another to DS Ambrose had straightened things out. He'd been released, with a none too gentle warning that next time he wanted to sleep in a house for sale, he should tell the estate agent beforehand. When he'd emerged, chastened and embarrassed, Ambrose had been waiting for him, his expression a lot less friendly than it had been to date.

'What do you mean, he wasn't your dad?' Ambrose demanded as they drove off.

'I never knew him. I didn't even know his name till he died and left me the house.'

Ambrose gave a long whistle. 'That'd fuck with your head.'

Especially if your head was already fucked up to start with. 'You could say that.'

'So this job must have felt like you were getting a message from beyond the grave to come and check out his ground, right?'

'I wouldn't put it quite like that. More that it was a chance I couldn't ignore. I'm sorry. I should have told you. I just didn't expect the house to have such an effect on me.' *I thought it would be alien, distant, untouchable.* Instead, it had felt like a homecoming, which was a reaction too uncomfortable for Tony to want to revisit right now.

'All the same, the DI's not going to be thrilled when he hears about this. He already thinks you're on the wrong side of normal.'

'A perceptive man, your DI Patterson. However, he might be a bit happier when you tell him that I do have some suggestions about your killer.'

Ambrose took his eyes off the road and gave him a quick appraising glance. 'Terrific. How do you normally go about this?'

Tony smiled with relief. The fact that Ambrose was interested in the process of profiling suggested that he'd decided to forgive him. And given that there was nothing more fascinating to Tony than what he did professionally and how he did it, there was plenty of scope for satisfying Ambrose's curiosity. He was off and running. 'There's two parts to it, I suppose. The first part is a sort of reverse logic – instead of reasoning from cause to effect, I go the other way. I start with the victim. Getting a picture of who they are and what it is in their life that might make them attractive to a predator. Then I look at what's been taken from them. Their lives, obviously. But also the other aspects. Their individuality. Their gender. Their power. That sort of thing. And finally, I look at what's been done to them. The actuality of what the killer has done and the order he's done it in. And when I've absorbed all that, I start going backwards. I ask myself questions. If I'm the killer, what's in it for me? What do these actions mean to me? What am I getting from this? Why does it matter to me that I do these things in this particular order? Then I go further back. What is it that happened to me in the past that makes this meaningful? And by that stage, I'm hopefully well on the way to figuring out what's going on in the killer's head.' His hands were making patterns in the air, a physical representation of the twists and turns going on inside his head.

'And then I look at the probabilities. What sort of life is possible for a person with this sort of history? What impact has their damage had on their life? What kind of relationships are possible for them?' He spread his hands and shrugged. 'It's not an exact science, obviously. And every case throws up different questions.'

Ambrose sighed. 'Fascinating. But that wasn't actually what I meant. What I was asking was how you present your profile. On paper or in person?'

'Oh.' Tony knew Ambrose's response should have knocked the wind from his sails but he was unabashed. One thing he didn't envy the normal world was what he saw as a depressing lack of curiosity. As far as he was concerned, Ambrose should have been pleased to be on the receiving end of his explanation. But if all he wanted was the prosaic, Tony could provide that too. 'Usually I write it up on the laptop, then fire it over to the SIO. If they want clarification, I'll go through any points they're not clear on. But I'm not quite ready to profile. I've not got enough of a sense of Jennifer yet. I really want to talk to the best friend, Claire thingie.'

'Darsie. Claire Darsie.'

'Yes, of course, sorry.'

'That's where we're headed now,' Ambrose said. 'I cleared it with the school for her to get out of class to talk to you. You can take a walk through the school grounds, or find a quiet corner to sit down in.'

'Perfect. Thanks.'

'So, what can you tell me now? About what you think?'

'Not much. Because at this point, I'm not thinking very much that's concrete.' There was one thing that he had to drive home, though, and it was so counter-intuitive, Tony knew he'd have to lay the ground for it. 'I mean, I'm thinking this is not as straightforward as we first thought, and I'm wondering if that's deliberate or incidental.'

'What do you mean?'

Tony pulled a face. 'I'm not convinced this is a sexual homicide.'

'Not sexual?' Ambrose was incredulous. 'He virtually raped her with that knife. How can that not be sexual?'

'See, this is what I mean. I'm not ready to do a full pro-file yet so I've not got all my ducks in a row. But humour me for a moment. For the sake of argument, let's say this isn't about sexual gratification.' He looked expectantly at Ambrose, who sighed again.

'OK. It's not about sexual gratification. For the sake of argument.'

'But he cut her vagina, really drove that knife deep into her. Like you said, he made it look like she'd been raped with the knife. What I need to work out is whether he did that deliberately to make us think it was sexual. Or whether he did it for another reason and the fact that it looks sexual is just by the by.'

'That's crazy,' Ambrose said.

He wasn't the first cop who'd had that response to some of Tony's wilder ideas. Not all of them had been wrong, but they were in the overwhelming majority. 'Possibly,' Tony said. 'But like I said, I don't know enough yet for a full profile, and theories based on half the information are more likely to be half baked. However, when you get away from the unscientific stuff that I specialise in and turn to the hard science options, you can get a lot further with not much to go on.'

'What do you mean?'

'Algorithms. I spoke to a colleague who's more familiar with the geographic profiling process than I am. It's her view that your killer probably lives in South Manchester.'

'Manchester? You serious?'

'My colleague is. And she knows this stuff better than anyone. If you remember, when we were at the dump scene I said I thought the location made most sense if the killer wasn't from round here? Well, it looks like I was right on that at least. Well, if we believe Fiona, I was.'

'Manchester, though? She can be that accurate?'

'She's cautiously confident. She's sending me a map with the red zone marked on it. It's the part of town that thinks it's hip. Students, green politics, vegan grocery store, artisan bakery, media types and lawyers. Very cool. Not the natural stomping ground for a stalker killer, I'd have said. But the algorithms don't lie. Although because a trail of computer use has different criteria from a series of crimes, they maybe don't tell quite as accurate a story as usual.'

'I didn't know serial killers had a particular habitat,' Ambrose said.

Tony pondered for a moment. 'They tend towards rented accommodation. Mostly because they're not very good at holding down jobs long-term. So their employment history isn't helpful when it comes to getting a mortgage. So yes, the balance of probabilities is that he lived in rented accommodation.'

'That makes sense.'

Time to turn back to the one thing he knew was important. 'And so does what I said before, Alvin. I know you said it was crazy, but the more I think about it, the more I believe that really, truly, you need to listen to me on this one. And not just for the sake of argument. This is not a sexual homicide.'

Again, Ambrose took his eyes off the road to look at Tony. This time the car jittered in a slight swerve before he righted it. 'It still sounds crazy to me.' He sounded completely incredulous. 'How could it not be a sexual homicide? Did you not look at the crime-scene photos? Did you not see what he did to her?'

'Of course I did. But he didn't spend any time with her, Alvin. He spent weeks getting alongside her, lulling her into a false sense of security. If this was about sex, he'd have kept her for days. Alive or dead, depending on his tastes. He wouldn't have got rid of her in the time scale we're talking about here.'

Ambrose gave Tony the look reserved for madmen and weirdos. 'Maybe he panicked. Maybe the reality was way more extreme than he'd fantasised about. Maybe he just wanted rid.'

It was a possibility Tony had considered as he'd been dropping off to sleep. And he'd dismissed it almost immediately. 'If that had been the case, he wouldn't have taken the time and trouble to perform the mutilation. He'd just have killed her and dumped her. Believe me, Alvin, this crime is not about sex.'

'So what is it about, then?' Ambrose's jaw set in a stubborn line, muscles tight, lower lip jutting.

Tony sighed. 'Like I said. That's what I don't know yet. I can't read it at this point.'

'So you know what it's not, but you can't tell us what it is? Help me out here, Doc. How is this supposed to help us?' Ambrose sounded angry again. Tony understood why. They'd hoped he'd wave a magic wand and make things better but, so far, all he'd done was create more problems.

'At least it stops you wasting time in the wrong places. Like your local sex offenders. That's not who you're looking for here.'

'So when will you have a profile that might help us find out who we are looking for?'

'Soon. Later today, hopefully. I'm hoping Claire will help me understand Jennifer better. Maybe then I can get a sense of what might have motivated someone to kill her. The victim's always the key, Alvin. One way or another.'

DC Sam Evans was glad to be back in what he regarded as fully fledged civilisation. A place where coffee and bacon butties were possible, where it never got truly dark and where there was always somewhere to shelter from the rain. It didn't hurt that he'd had the rare pleasure of leaving everybody at the morning briefing gobsmacked.

The only problem now was following up on the small bombshell of the extra body in the lake. He had to walk a tightrope here. While he was waiting for the forensic team to come up with some leads, he had to make it look as if he was busy. If she thought he was twiddling his thumbs, Carol Jordan would reassign him to some donkey work on the live caseload. And if he was out of the office when the forensic evidence came in, someone else could pinch the case from under his nose and nick the glory. And that was something he wasn't prepared to put up with.

Sam took out his notebook and flicked back a couple of pages, looking for the number of the Cumbrian DI he was supposed to be liaising with. He was about to call him when his mobile rang. He didn't recognise the number. 'Hello?' he said, never willing to give anything away for free.

'Is that DC Evans?' It was a woman. She sounded brisk, youngish, confident.

'Speaking.'

'Are you the officer who emailed me a set of dental records?'

'That's right.' CID had obtained a set of records from Danuta Barnes's dentist back when she'd first gone missing and, at the suggestion of one of the Cumbrian cops, Sam had forwarded it to the University of Northern England at Carlisle.

'Good. I'm Dr Wilde, forensic anthropologist at UNEC. I've been taking a look at the remains from Wastwater. I'm not done yet, but I thought you'd appreciate an update.'

'Anything you can give me,' Sam said. *Thank you, God.*

'Well, the good news, depending on your perspective, I suppose, is that the dental records match the smaller adult skeleton, which I am pretty certain is that of a woman aged between twenty-five and forty.'

'She was thirty-one,' Sam said. 'Her name was Danuta Barnes.'

'Thank you. I've got my students working up DNA for all three sets of remains. We should be able to establish whether she's the mother of the child. Who is aged between four and six months, I'd estimate,' Dr Wilde continued.

'Lynette. Five months,' Sam said. He'd been struck by the pitifully small bundle sandwiched between the two larger ones. He wasn't given to sentiment, but even the hardest heart couldn't avoid being touched by so early and unnecessary a death.

Dr Wilde sighed. 'Hardly a life at all. Not much of an epitaph, is it? "Lived for five months: made a great teaching aid." Anyway, as soon as I can confirm that connection, I'll let you know.'

'Appreciate it. Anything you can tell me about the other body?' Not that he was expecting much from a bag of bones and some slurry whose components he didn't want to think too much about.

Dr Wilde chuckled. 'You'd be amazed. For example, I can tell you his name was Harry Sim, and he died some time after June 1993.'

Sam was thrown for a second. Then he laughed. 'What was it? Credit card or driving licence?'

She sounded disappointed. 'Smarter than the average DC,' she said in a cod American accent.

'I like to think so. Which was it, then?'

'Credit card. A Mastercard that ran from June 1993 to May 1997 in the name of Harry Sim. That should give you something to chase. I hope you're pleased.'

'You have no idea,' Sam said with heavy emphasis. 'Will you be checking his DNA against the kid as well?'

'Oh yes,' Dr Wilde said. 'It's a wise child who knows its father.'

'Anything on cause of death?'

'They make them greedy down Bradfield way,' she said, not so amused now. 'Impossible to say at this point. No obvious trauma to any bones, so probably not shot, strangled or battered with a blunt instrument. Could have been poisoned, asphyxiated. Could have been natural causes, but I doubt it. I suspect we'll never be able to establish a cause of death. If you're hoping for a murder charge, you might have to settle for circumstantial evidence.'

That was never good news. But he had no grounds for whining about it, given how much Dr Wilde had already given him. Who knew what he'd find when he started unpeeling the layers of Harry Sim's life and mysterious death? He thanked Dr Wilde and hung up, already knowing the next stop on his journey.

CHAPTER 24

The only time Carol ever minded being driven was when she was en route to crime scenes with bodies at their centre. Even with the most competent of chauffeurs, which Kevin undeniably was, the journey invariably seemed interminable. Her mind raced ahead, wanted to be there at the scene, calculating what would need to be done. It didn't matter that the victim was beyond the constraints of time. Carol was determined not to keep them waiting.

Kevin turned on to a narrow moorland road, the twisting turns forcing him to lower his speed. Carol looked around her. Her earlier visit to Vanessa had brought her near here earlier this morning. Although this landscape had been used as a burial site in the past, most notably by Brady and Hindley, the Moors murderers, it had never crossed her mind then that she might be passing the place where Seth Viner's killer had chosen to dump him.

'He likes isolation, this killer,' she said, hanging on to the grab handle as Kevin threw them round another bend.

'You think he's local?'

'Depends what you mean by local,' Carol said. 'A quarter of the population of the UK is within an hour's drive of the Peak District National Park. We're not that far north of there. This place looks empty, but it's a huge recreational area. Walkers, runners – like the ones who found the body – picnickers, orienteers, bikers with their stupid road races, people out for a drive on Sunday . . . There's a lot of legitimate reasons for knowing the moors quite well.'

'It should be over the next hill,' Kevin said, glancing at the satnav.

'Let's hope West Yorkshire aren't going to get all possessive on us,' Carol said. Although Seth had gone missing from Bradfield, his body had been found about four miles over the border in the neighbouring force's area. She'd never worked directly for West Yorkshire but she'd managed to piss off most of their senior CID officers a few years before when she'd been working off the books with Tony on a serial killer investigation nobody but them would take seriously. 'They're not very keen on me over there,' she added.

Kevin, who knew all about the history, grunted. 'You can't really blame them. You made them look a right bunch of wankers.'

'I'd hope they'd be over it by now. It was a long time ago.'

'This is Yorkshire. They're still feeling aggrieved about the Wars of the Roses,' Kevin pointed out as they breasted a rise. About a mile down the road they could see their destination, unmistakable in its array of vehicles, pale green tent, neon yellow tabards and white body suits. 'If you're lucky, all the ones you really pissed off will have retired.'

'I should be lucky – I'm certainly not rich.' They pulled up on the verge behind an ambulance whose doors were open to reveal a group of women huddled under thermal blankets, hands cupped round steaming drinks cartons. Carol gathered herself together, took a deep breath and headed for the uniformed constable manning the entrance to the crime scene. 'DCI Jordan, Bradfield MIT,' she said. 'And this is DS Matthews. I've got other officers on their way.'

He checked their ID. 'Sign in, ma'am.' He proffered his clipboard and pen, then waved them through. 'DCI Franklin's the SIO. He's in the tent.'

The tent erected by the forensics team to protect the scene sat right at the edge of the road. 'They never make you think of camping holidays, do they?' Carol muttered as they approached. She pulled the flap back to reveal the familiar scene. Forensic technicians in white, detectives in leather jackets of varying design but absolute predictability. Some things clearly never changed in West Yorkshire.

Heads turned as they entered and a tall cadaverous man peeled off from the group of detectives and came towards them. 'I'm DCI John Franklin. I don't know who you are, but this my crime scene.'

The usual friendly greeting, Carol thought. 'I'm DCI Carol Jordan,' she said again. 'It may be your crime scene, but I think he's my body.' She pulled a sheet of paper from her bag and unfolded it to reveal Kathy Antwon's photo of her son. 'Seth Viner. He was wearing black jeans, a white polo shirt, a Kenton Vale school sweatshirt and a dark navy Berghaus anorak when he went missing.'

Franklin nodded. 'Sounds about right. Come and have a look. The photo won't be much use to you, though. He doesn't look like that any more.'

Charm and diplomacy. The hallmarks of the Yorkshire male. Carol followed Franklin past the knot of detectives, Kevin at her shoulder. Close by the edge of the road, the earth fell away into a shallow gully a couple of feet wide. It wasn't really a ditch, more a depression in the ground that ran for about fifteen feet. It was just deep enough to conceal the body from anyone passing in a car. But the runners hadn't been so lucky.

It was a pitiful sight. Mud and blood caked his legs and lower torso. His head was encased in a plastic bag, taped tight round his neck. It was like a rerun of Daniel Morrison's body. Only the clothes were different. But even through the filth and corruption it was possible to recognise Seth's clothes. His jacket was missing, but the dark green sweatshirt and the black jeans were enough for Carol to feel certain she was looking at Julia and Kathy's son. 'Poor kid,' she said, her voice low and sad.

'You'll be wanting a joint operation, then,' Franklin said. There was no compassion about the man. That didn't mean he didn't feel it, just that he was determined not to show it in front of women and junior officers.

'Actually, I want to claim it,' Carol said. 'It's an identical MO to a murder on our patch earlier this week. You'll have heard about it – Daniel Morrison.'

264

Franklin's face contracted in a frown. 'This is our ground. So it's our case.'

'I'm not disputing the territory. But this is just a body dump. He was abducted from Bradfield, chances are he was killed in Bradfield. I've got an identical crime in Bradfield just days ago. It makes no sense to duplicate efforts.' Carol struggled to keep a grip on her temper. 'We've all got budgets. We all know what a murder inquiry costs. I'd have thought you'd have been gagging to get rid.'

'We're not like you. We don't try to offload our cases first chance we get. We've all heard about you and your MIT in Bradfield. Glory hunters, that's what we hear. Going head to head with the terrorist cops, grabbing the headlines over the Bradfield bombing. Well, if there's glory to be had for this one, it'll be shared. If you're lucky.' Franklin turned on his heel and returned to his own men. Heads came together and the low rumble of indeterminate conversation reached them.

'That went well,' Carol said grimly. 'Remind me I need to revisit my diplomatic skills.'

'How do you want to play it?'

'You stay here. The others will be along soon. Keep a watching brief, build some bridges. Make sure we're kept in the picture. I'm going back to talk to the Chief Constable, get him to iron this out so we don't spend the next week in mindless arguments about turf.' She turned back to look at Seth and felt despair. 'Those poor women,' she said. 'Make sure you or Paula goes with them to tell the parents. When this hits the news, they're going to be besieged. They need all the help we can give them.'

'I'll see to it.'

Carol gazed out across the moors. 'We need to stop this. We need to warn the kids and we need to catch this bastard before he does it again.' And thought the unspoken, the unsayable. *I wish Tony was here.*

The sky was clouded over, the promise of rain in the air. But still Claire Darsie wanted to be outside. Ambrose had introduced Tony, then left them to it. Tony was impressed by the policeman's gentleness. The more he saw of Ambrose, the more he liked him. He suspected the feeling wasn't mutual. Not after that morning's fiasco.

Claire led the way out of the school building. 'We can walk round the playing fields,' she said. 'There's a sort of gazebo thing we can sit inside if you want.' She was clearly aiming for unconcerned, but there was a brittleness about her that suggested her detachment wasn't even skin deep.

She set the pace, a brisk walk along a gravel path. In the summer, it would be heavily shaded by the mature trees that lined the boundary fence. But today there was plenty of light to reveal the strain in Claire's face. Tony made sure he kept a good distance between them. She needed to feel safe, and the first step towards that was staying out of her space.

'You and Jennifer, have you been friends a long time?' Stick to the present tense, avoid rubbing her nose in the permanence.

'Since primary school,' Claire said. 'I fell over in the playground on the first day and cut my knee. Jen had a hanky and she gave it to me.' She raised one shoulder in a half shrug. 'But even if that hadn't happened, she would have been the one I would have wanted to be friends with.'

'Why's that?'

'Because she was a nice person. I know people say you shouldn't speak ill of the dead, but that's not how it is with Jen. It was what people always said about her. She was kind, you know? She didn't have a mean bone in her body. Even when people pissed her off, she would end up seeing things from their point of view and let them off the hook.' Claire made a noise that might have been disgust. 'Not like me. When people piss me off, I make a point of getting my own back. I don't know why Jen puts up with me, you know?' Her voice wobbled and she tucked her chin into her neck. She upped the pace and pulled ahead of him. He let her go, catching up with her on the steps of the little wooden shelter at the end of the hockey pitch.

They walked inside and sat down facing each other. Claire curled in on herself, hugging her knees to her chest, but Tony stretched his legs out, crossing them at the ankles. He let his hands fall into his lap, an open position that made him unthreatening. Now he could see clearly the shadows under her eyes and the skin round her fingernails, bitten till it had bled. 'I know how much you love Jen,' he said. 'I realise you're missing her all the time. There's nothing we can do to bring her back, but we can maybe make things a bit better for her mum and dad if we can find the person who did this.'

Claire gulped. 'I know. I keep thinking about it. What she would have done if things had been the other way around. She'd have wanted to help my mum and dad.

But I can't think of anything. That's the problem.' She looked anguished. 'There's nothing to tell.'

'That's OK,' he said gently. 'None of this is your fault, Claire. And nobody's going to blame you if we don't find the man who took Jen away. I just want to have a chat. See if you can help me know Jen a bit better.'

'How will that help?' Natural curiosity overcame her anxiety.

'I'm a profiler. People don't really understand what I do, they think it's like something on the telly. But basically, it's my job to figure out how Jen came into contact with this person, and how she would have responded. Then I have to work out what that tells me about him.'

'And then you help the police to catch him?'

He nodded, a crooked smile crossing his face. 'That's the general idea. So, what was Jennifer interested in?'

He sat back and listened to a catalogue of teen music, fashions, TV shows and celebrity culture. He heard that Jennifer generally did what she was told – homework in by the due date, home on time when they went out in the evening. Mostly because it had never really occurred to Claire and Jennifer that they could do anything else. They lived a sheltered life in their selective girls' school, ferried around by parents, existing in an orbit that didn't intersect with the bad girls. Time passed and Tony's relaxed questioning finally helped Claire to relax. Now he could probe deeper.

'You make her sound a bit too perfect,' he said. 'Didn't she ever go just a bit mad? Get drunk? Try drugs? Want a tattoo? Have her navel pierced? Mess around with boys?'

Claire giggled, then put her hand to her mouth,

ashamed to be so light-hearted. 'You must think we're really boring,' she said. 'We did have our ears pierced the summer we were twelve. Our mothers went mad. But they let us keep them.'

'No sneaking out after hours to gigs? No smoking behind the bike sheds? Did Jen have a boyfriend at all?'

Claire gave him a quick sideways look but said nothing.

'I know everybody says she's not going out with anybody. But I find that hard to believe. A good person who was fun to hang out with. And pretty. And I'm supposed to believe she didn't have a boyfriend.' He spread his hands wide, palms upwards. 'I need you to help me here, Claire.'

'She made me promise,' Claire said.

'I know. But she's not going to hold you to that promise. You said yourself, if it was the other way round, you'd want her to help us.'

'It wasn't a proper boyfriend. Not like going on dates and stuff. But there was this guy on Rig. ZeeZee, he called himself. Just the letters, though. Like, two zeds.'

'We know she talked to ZZ on Rig, but they just seemed to be friends. Not boyfriend and girlfriend.'

'That was what they wanted everyone to think. Jen was paranoid about her parents finding out about him because he's four years older than us. So she used to go to the internet café near school to talk to him online. That way her mum couldn't check up on her. According to Jen, they were getting on really well. She said she wanted them to meet up face to face.'

'Did she tell you about any plans they might have had?'

Claire shook her head. 'She'd sort of gone quiet about

269

him. Whenever I tried to get her to talk about it, she'd change the subject. But I think maybe they'd made arrangements.'

'Why do you think that?' Tony kept his voice free of urgency, making it sound like the most casual of inquiries.

'Because ZZ was saying something on Rig about secrets and how we all have secrets that we don't want anyone to know. And then him and Jen went into a sidebar. And I thought she was telling him off for hinting at what was going on between them.'

But she hadn't been. She'd been pitched into that meeting they'd been skating round, according to Claire. It made sense of why a well-behaved girl like Jennifer would behave so recklessly. This was something that had even more of a build-up than they'd suspected. This was a killer who wasn't taking any chances. The last time he'd encountered a killer who planned so carefully or over so long a time had been the first case he'd worked with Carol and it had taken a terrible toll. He really didn't want to go into that dark place again. But if that was what it took to bring Jennifer Maidment's killer to justice before he could kill again, he would do it without hesitation.

CHAPTER 25

The caravan site wasn't going to win any beauty contests. Boxy vans in pastel shades squatted on concrete pads surrounded by weary grass and tarmac paths. Some residents had attempted window boxes and flowerbeds, but the prevailing winds off the bay had defeated them. But as Sam got out of his car, he had to admit the view made up for a lot. A watery sun added charm to the long expanse of sand that stretched almost to the horizon, where the sea twinkled at the fringes of Morecambe Bay. He knew this was a double-crossing beauty. Dozens had perished out there over the years, not understanding the speed and the treachery of the tides. From here, though, you'd never suspect a thing.

Sam made for the office, an incongruous log cabin that would have looked more at home in the American Midwest. According to Stacey, Harry Sim had last used his Mastercard ten days before Danuta Barnes had been

271

reported missing. He'd used to it buy ten pounds' worth of petrol at the garage two miles down the road from the Bayview Caravan Park. The bill had been settled by a cash payment at a Bradfield city-centre bank three weeks later. Also according to Stacey, this was an anomaly, since Harry Sim normally settled his account by posting a cheque to the credit-card company. How she managed to find out this sort of thing was little short of miraculous, he thought. And possibly not entirely legal.

The billing address for the card had been this caravan site. And that had been the last trace either Stacey or Sam had been able to find of Harry Sim. Computer searches, phone calls to Revenue and Customs, banks and credit-card providers had turned up a big fat zero. Which wasn't entirely surprising, since Harry Sim had apparently been lying on the bottom of Wastwater for the last fourteen years.

Sam knocked on the office door and walked in, his ID front and centre. The man behind the desk was playing some kind of word game on the computer. He glanced round at Sam, froze the screen and lumbered to his feet. He looked in his mid-fifties, a big man whose bulk had started to sag into fat. His hair was a mixture of sand and silver, too dry to readily submit to brush or comb. His skin had acquired a papery texture from years of salt air and stiff winds. He was neatly dressed in a flannel shirt, a scarlet fleece and dark grey corduroy trousers. 'Officer,' he said, nodding a greeting.

Sam introduced himself and the man looked surprised. 'Bradfield?' he said. 'You've come a few miles, then. I'm Brian Carson.' He waved a vague hand at the window. 'This is my site. I'm the owner.'

'Have you been here long?' Sam asked.

'Since 1987. I used to be a printer, down in Manchester. When we all got made redundant, I sunk my money into this place. I've never regretted it. It's a great life.' He sounded sincere, which left Sam feeling baffled. He couldn't imagine many more tedious occupations.

'I'm pleased to hear it,' he said. 'Because the person I need to ask you about lived here fourteen, fifteen years ago.'

Carson perked up. 'By heck, that's going back. I'll need to look in the records for that.' He turned and pointed to a door behind him. 'I keep all the files in the back. Not that I need the files. I pride myself on knowing my tenants. Not the holidaymakers so much, but the ones who keep their vans on, I know all of them. What's occurred that you're looking for someone from that far ago?'

Sam gave a lazy, rueful smile, the one that generally got people on his side. 'I'm sorry, I'm not allowed to discuss the details. You know how it is.'

'Oh.' Carson looked disappointed. 'Well, if you can't, you can't. Now, what's the name of this person you're interested in?'

'Harry Sim.'

Carson's face brightened. 'Oh, I remember Harry Sim. He stuck out like a sore thumb round here. Most of our long-term tenants, they're older. Retired. Or else they've got young families. But Harry was unusual. A single bloke, in his mid-thirties, I suppose he must have been. He kept himself to himself. He never came to barbecue nights or karaoke or anything like that. And his unit was right out at the very back. He didn't have much of a view, but he did get peace and quiet. The units down there are always the hardest to let, on account of they've not got the benefit of the bay view.' He flashed an awkward smile. 'With a name like ours, that's what people expect. A bay view.'

'I imagine,' Sam said. 'You said he lived alone. I don't suppose you remember if he had many visitors?'

Carson was suddenly crestfallen. 'It's not that I don't remember,' he said. 'It's just that I've no idea. Where he was, down at the end there – well, there's no way of seeing whether people were visiting or not. And in the summer, I know it's hard to believe, looking at it today, but it's mayhem out there. There's no way I could keep track of any individual's visitors unless they're right out there where I can see them through the window.'

'I appreciate that. Did you have much to do with him?'

Carson sank even further into gloom. 'No. Obviously, when he took up the tenancy, we spoke then, to make the arrangements. But that was pretty much it. He never stopped by for a chat, only came in if there was a problem, and since we pride ourselves here on there not being problems, we didn't see much of him at all.'

Sam almost felt sorry for the man, obviously so eager to help but with so little to offer. Except that he was the one losing out because of Carson's deficiency. 'How long did he live here?'

Carson brightened again. 'Now that I can tell you. But I'll have to look at my records to be precise.' He was already halfway through the door into the back office. Sam could see a row of filing cabinets, then he heard a drawer being opened and closed. Moments later, Carson re-emerged with a slim hanging file. 'Here we are,' he said, laying it on the counter. The label on the file read *127/Sim*.

'You've got quite a system here,' Sam said.

'I pride myself on keeping proper records. You never know when someone like yourself is going to be in need of some information.' Carson opened the folder. 'Here we are. Harry Sim took out a year's lease in April 1995.' He studied the sheet of paper. 'He didn't renew the lease, he only had the unit for the year.'

'Did he leave anything behind? Any papers, clothes?' *The remains of a life that had been snuffed out by someone else?*

'There's no note of anything. And there would be if he hadn't cleared it out, believe you me.'

Sam did. 'And you've no idea when specifically he left?'

Regret on his face, Carson shook his head. 'No. The keys were left on the table, it says here. But nothing to show how long they'd been there.'

This was looking like a very dead end. Harry Sim had gone, but nobody knew when or where or why. Sam knew where he'd ended up, but not where he'd begun. There was one last question left to try. 'When he took on the rental, did you ask for references?'

Carson nodded proudly. 'Of course.' He pulled out the bottom sheets from the file. 'Two references. One from the bank and one from his former boss, a Mrs Danuta Barnes.'

To Carol's relief, Blake was available almost immediately. She was surprised to find him behind his desk in full dress uniform. She'd grown accustomed to John Brandon only wearing the full rig when it was absolutely necessary, much preferring the comfort of a suit. Blake clearly liked to make sure nobody in the room forgot exactly how important he was.

He waved her into a chair, steepled his fingers and leaned his chin on them. 'What brings you here, Chief Inspector?'

Carol resisted the childish temptation to say, 'My own two feet.' Instead, she said, 'I need you to intervene on our behalf with West Yorkshire.' She outlined the situation clearly and succinctly. 'This is a murder inquiry, sir. I haven't got the time to play silly buggers with my oppo. We need not to waste any more time.'

'Quite. They should be happy to hand it off to us. It'll save them money and, if we're successful, I've no doubt they'll claim at least half the credit. Leave it with me, Chief Inspector. I'll get it sorted.'

Carol was pleasantly surprised at Blake's lack of fuss. And that he took her side so readily. But then, there might be serious credit further down the line, which would suit a man with his presumed ambitions. 'Thanks,' she said, starting to rise from her chair.

Blake waved her back down again. 'Not quite so fast,' he said. 'These two murders are definitely connected, in your professional opinion?'

She felt a sense of trepidation. Where was he going with this? 'I don't think there's any room for doubt. Identical MO, similar victims, same sort of body dump. It looks pretty clear that Seth Viner was stalked online and we've been told something similar went on with Daniel Morrison. We were careful not to release any details of what happened to Daniel, so we can rule out a copycat. I don't see how it can be anything but the same killer.'

He gave her a small tight smile that bunched his cheeks into a pair of crab apples. 'I trust your judgement,' he said. 'That being the case, what you need to do now is to bring in a profiler.'

Carol struggled with her composure. 'You told me my budget didn't run to that,' she said, her words clipped and tight.

'I told you your budget didn't run to Dr Hill,' Blake said, managing to invest Tony's name with disdain. 'What we have access to are the profilers from the National Faculty. Once I've dealt with West Yorkshire, I will arrange it.'

'I can do that, sir,' Carol said, hastily trying to wrest some control back. 'You shouldn't be wasting your time on admin like that.'

This time, Blake's smile had an air of cruelty. 'I'm happy to help,' he said. 'You have two murders on your plate. I know how easy it is for things to slip through the cracks when you're so occupied.'

The bastard was suggesting she'd deliberately ignore an order. Anger fizzed underneath her polite demeanour. 'Thank you, sir.' She couldn't manage a return smile.

'You'll be amazed how well you manage without Dr Hill.'

Carol stood up and nodded. 'After all, sir, we're none of us indispensable.'

Ambrose had dropped Tony back at the house so he could pick up his car. 'You're not planning on going back there tonight?' Ambrose asked as he unloaded Tony's overnight bag from the boot. 'Because if you are, you need to tell the estate agent to call you before she brings more people round.'

'I won't be there. I promise you won't have to bail me out again.'

'That's good news.' Ambrose popped a piece of chewing gum in his mouth and shook his head in a more genial way. 'Not the best way to start the day. So, what're your plans now?'

'I'm going to find a quiet pub where I can sit in a corner with my laptop and write up my profile. I should have it with you late this afternoon. Then I'll have something to eat, so hopefully I'll miss the rush hour in Birmingham when I drive back to Bradfield. If that's all right with you. Obviously, if there are issues with the profile that you need me to resolve, then I'll stick around. If there's one thing I'm pretty sure about with this killer, it's that he's going to do it again. I'll do whatever it takes to help you stop that happening.'

'You really think so?'

Tony sighed. 'Once they get the taste for it, guys like this need the buzz.'

'But when we were talking about him dumping the body so fast, didn't we talk about him maybe doing that because it freaked him out – doing it for real?' Ambrose leaned against the car, arms folded across his chest, a physical manifestation of his reluctance to accept that they were only at the beginning.

'That was your suggestion, Alvin. And it was a good thought because it makes sense of the evidence. But my experience says that's not how it goes. Even if it did freak him out, he's still going to want to try again. Only this time he'll want to make it better. So we need to operate like we're working against the clock.'

Ambrose looked disgusted. 'I tell you what. I'm glad I'm inside my head and not yours. I wouldn't want to have all that stuff swilling around all the time.'

Tony shrugged. 'You know what they say. Find what you're good at and stick to it.'

Ambrose shrugged himself upright and extended his hand. 'It's been an interesting experience, working with you. I can't say I've enjoyed it all, but I've been very interested in what you have to say about the killer. I'm intrigued at the prospect of working with my first profile.'

Tony smiled. 'I hope it doesn't disappoint. You've not seen me at my sparkling social best, it's true. But if I'm honest, I should tell you that life around me does tend towards the bizarre.' He pointed to his leg. 'You might have noticed the limp, for example. That was, literally, a mad axeman. One minute I was sitting in my office reading a Parole Board brief; next thing I know, I'm confronting a man with a fire axe who thinks he's harvesting souls for God.' His expression was pained. 'My colleagues seem to avoid these extreme situations. Somehow, I don't.'

Looking uneasy, Ambrose started to head for the driver's door. 'We'll be in touch,' he said.

Tony waved, then tossed his bag in the car. He hadn't been entirely truthful with Ambrose. There would be a pub where he was going, but that wasn't his primary destination. He'd collected more than one set of keys from

Blythe's solicitor. He knew absolutely nothing about boats, but apparently he was now the owner of a fifty-foot steel narrowboat called *Steeler*, which came with its own mooring at the Diglis Marina. 'Used to be the Diglis Canal Basin,' the solicitor had said with distaste. 'Complete with warehouses and Royal Worcester Porcelain. Now it's got waterside apartments and light industrial and commercial units. The march of time, and all that. All that's left of the way it used to be is the lock-keeper's cottage and the Anchor Inn. You'll like that. It's a proper, old-fashioned boozer. Arthur was a regular there. They've got a traditional wooden Worcestershire skittle alley. He was in one of their league teams. Pop in there and introduce yourself. They'll be pleased to see you.'

He'd save the pub for another day, he thought as he consulted the map and figured out how to get to the marina. Today he wanted to settle down in a corner of Blythe's boat and write his profile. Maybe mooch around the boat, see if Arthur had left any clues to himself tucked away there.

He parked as close as he could get to the moorings, then spent ten minutes wandering around looking for the boat. Eventually he found her, tucked away at the far end of a row of similar craft. *Steeler* was painted in traditional bright green and scarlet, her name picked out in flowing gold and black. Four solar panels were fixed to the roof, a tribute to Blythe's ingenuity. So power wouldn't be an issue, if he could figure out how to work the bloody thing.

Tony clambered aboard, his feet clattering on the metal deck. The hatch was secured with a couple of sturdy padlocks, whose keys the solicitor had cheerfully handed over. 'Be good to see the boat properly looked after,' he'd said. 'Lovely example of the type. Arthur was a stalwart of all the rallies round the Midlands. He loved messing about on the water.' That obviously wasn't something transmitted in the genes. Tony had no affinity whatsoever for water or boats. He didn't anticipate keeping *Steeler* for long, but now he'd come this far down the trail, he wanted to experience what Arthur had made of his other environment.

The hatch slid back smoothly, allowing him to open the double doors that led below. Tony climbed cautiously down the high steps and found himself in a compact galley, complete with microwave, kettle and stove. Moving forward, he emerged into the saloon. A buttoned leather banquette sat against one bulkhead, a table before it. A big leather swivel chair sat on the other side, arranged so it could face either the table or the TV and DVD player. In one corner stood a squat wood-burning stove. There were nifty little cupboards and shelving everywhere, making the maximum use of every inch of space. A door at the end led to a cabin containing a double bed and a wardrobe. The final door at the end took him into a compact bathroom, complete with toilet, washbasin and shower cubicle, all gleaming white tile and chrome. To his amazement, it smelled fresh and clean.

He wandered back to the saloon. He wasn't sure what he'd expected, but it wasn't this rigid functionality. There was no personality here. Everything was so regimented, so neat and tidy. The effect the house had had on him was completely absent. In a way, that was a relief. There would be nothing to distract him from the profile he had to write.

And there would be nothing to deter him from selling it in due course.

In spite of his general cack-handedness, Tony found it pretty straightforward to work out how to access the electricity. Soon, he had the lights on, and power to his laptop. No question, it made a great little office. All it lacked was wireless. For a wild moment, he considered driving the boat through the canal network to Bradfield and using it as an office. Then he considered the books and realised it was impossible. Not to mention the sort of thing that would send the likes of Alvin Ambrose running for the hills. The thought of how many things could go wrong between Worcester and Bradfield was truly terrifying. He'd settle for an afternoon's work and then send her off to the broker. Did narrowboats have brokers? Or was it an informal network where deals were done over a game of skittles?

'Get a grip,' Tony said aloud, booting up the laptop. He loaded his standard opening paragraphs:

The following offender profile is for guidance only and shouldn't be regarded as an identikit portrait. The offender is unlikely to match the profile in every detail, though I would expect there to be a high degree of congruence between the characteristics outlined below and the reality. All of the statements in the profile express probabilities and possibilities, not hard facts.

A serial killer produces signals and indicators in the commission of his crimes. Everything he does is intended, consciously or not, as part of a pattern. Discovering the underlying pattern reveals the killer's logic. It may not appear logical to us, but to him it is crucial. Because his logic is so idiosyncratic, straightforward traps will not capture him. As he is unique, so must be the means of catching him, interviewing him and reconstructing his acts.

He read it through, then deleted the second paragraph. As far as they knew, this killer wasn't serial yet. If Tony could help Ambrose and Patterson do their job, the killer might not get to the crucial 'three plus' that officially made him a serial. In Tony's world, that was what passed for a happy ending.

On the other hand, if they didn't succeed, there would be more. It was all a question of time. Time and skill. Just because they were in at the start didn't mean this wasn't a serial killer. With a sigh, he reinstated the paragraph then continued.

His fingers flew over the keys as he outlined in detail the conclusions he'd already run through with Ambrose at the body dump and earlier in the car. He paused for thought, then got up and explored the galley. He found instant coffee and creamer in jars and when he turned the tap on, water emerged. Cautiously he tasted it and decided it was fit to drink. While he waited for the kettle to boil, he searched for a mug and a spoon. The second drawer he opened contained cutlery. As he reached in to get a teaspoon, his thumb snagged on something. He looked more closely and found a thick white envelope the size of a postcard. When he turned it over, he was shocked to see his name on the front in neat block capitals. Arthur had written DR TONY HILL on an envelope and stuffed it in the cutlery drawer of his boat. It made no sense to him. Why would anyone do that? If he wanted Tony to have something, why leave it here, where it could so easily be missed, and not with the lawyer? And did Tony really want to know what the envelope contained?

He felt the envelope. There was something more than paper inside. Something light but solid, maybe ten centimetres by four, about the thickness of a CD box. He put it down while he made his coffee, constantly aware of its presence in his peripheral vision. He took the coffee and the envelope back to the table where he'd been working and set them down. He stared at the envelope, wondering. What had Arthur chosen to leave in so uncertain a way? And how would it help Tony to know what it was? He was sure there were things he didn't want to know about Arthur, but unsure what knowledge he did want to possess.

In the end, his curiosity won over his doubt. He ripped open the envelope and shook out its contents. There was a sheet of A4 made from the same heavy paper stock as the envelope. And a tiny digital voice recorder, the type Tony used himself these days when he was dictating patient notes for his secretary. He pushed at it with one finger, as if expecting it to burst into flames. Frowning, he unfolded the paper. Across the top, Arthur Blythe's name was engraved in copperplate script. He took a deep breath and started to read the neat handwriting that covered the page.

Dear Tony, it began.

The fact that you're reading this means that you've chosen not to ignore your inheritance. I'm glad about that. I failed you while I was alive. I can't make up for that, but I hope you can use what I've left you to give yourself some pleasure. I want to explain myself to you but I understand that you owe me nothing and you might not want to hear my self-justification. For a long time, I never knew you existed. Please believe that. I never intended to abandon you. But since I found out about you, I've watched your progress with a pride I know I have no right to. You're a clever man, I know that. So I leave it up to you whether you choose to hear what I have to say.

Whatever decision you make, please believe that I am sincerely sorry you grew up without a father in your life to help and support you. I wish you all kinds of happiness in the future.

Yours truly,

(Edmund) Arthur Blythe

In spite of his determination not to be moved, emotion closed his throat. Tony struggled to swallow, touched by the simple honesty of Arthur's letter. This was far more than he'd expected and he thought it might be more than he could bear. At least for now. He reread the letter, taking it line by line, feeling the weight of the words, imagining Arthur putting it together. How many drafts had he taken to get it right? His precise engineer's hand crossing out first and second and third attempts, trying to strike the right note, making sure he said what he meant, not leaving room for misunderstanding. He could picture him in the house, at the desk in his study, the lamp casting a pool of light over his writing hand. It suddenly occurred to him that he had no clear idea what Arthur had looked like. There had been no photographs on display in the house, nothing to indicate whether father and son shared any physical resemblance. There must be some; he made a mental note to look next time he was in the house.

Next time. As soon as he had the thought, Tony understood its significance. There would be a next time. Something had shifted inside him in the previous twenty-four hours. From wanting to maintain the distance between him and Arthur, he now wanted connection. He didn't know yet what form that would take. But he'd know when he got there.

What he did know was that he wasn't ready for Arthur's message yet. He might never be. But right now, he had work to do. Work that was more important than his own emotional state. He turned back to his laptop and started typing again.

'The killer is likely to be white,' he wrote. Almost invariably this kind of killer stayed within their own ethnic group. 'He is aged between twenty-five and forty.' Twenty-five, because it needed a level of maturity to engage in this degree of planning and to sustain the plan once the killing started. And forty, because the rule of probabilities stated that by then they'd either been caught, killed or calmed down.

He is not a lorry driver – several of the locations where he has used public-access computers are not convenient for lorry parking, e.g. Manchester Airport and the shopping centre in Telford. But he certainly owns his own vehicle – he would not risk leaving traces in a vehicle owned by a third party. It's likely to be a reasonably large car, probably a hatchback. I don't think he's a commercial vehicle driver, even though that is a hypothesis that has some attractions. It would certainly account for his movements up and down the motorway network. But given the tight schedules of commercial drivers, I doubt whether this would give him the degree of flexibility or free time to have set Jennifer up, then abduct her.

He is likely to be educated to university or college level. His awareness of computer technology and his level of familiarity with its possibilities indicates a high level of skill in this area. I believe he is an ICT professional, probably self-employed. The electronics industry is a loosely knit community of consultants who have a great deal of flexibility in their working hours and the locations of the companies they contract to.

In terms of personality, we're looking at a high-functioning psychopath. He can mimic human interaction but he has no genuine empathy. He's likely to live alone and to have no deep emotional ties. This will not mark him out as particularly unusual in his work community, since many ICT professionals appear similar although in fact many of them are perfectly capable of emotional interaction. They just prefer their machines because that takes less effort.

He may well be addicted to computer gaming, particularly to violent online multi-user games. These will present him with an outlet for the nihilistic feelings he has towards other people.

Tony read over what he'd written without any sense of satisfaction. Apart from his highlighting of the fact that this was not a sexual homicide, he felt he'd come up with nothing that wasn't either textbook or plain common sense. There was much more to be deduced about this killer, he was sure of that. But until someone came up with the connection between the killer and the choice of victim, they were all dancing in the dark.

CHAPTER 26

After the tragedy of Jessica Morrison's death, the last thing Paula wanted to do was sit down with another set of grieving parents. What was worse was having to do it on her own. Whatever had happened at top level, West Yorkshire had backed right off, to the point where they didn't want anything to do with the death knock. And Kevin was busy setting up protocols for collating all the West Yorkshire intel. So here she was, doing what she liked least. But if she'd learned one thing from her own encounters with grief, it was that avoidance never worked. What they said about having to get back on the horse was right. That still didn't make it feel any easier.

The woman who opened the door looked like she was at war with the world. Her dark eyes were angry, her skin tone faded to jaundiced yellow, her mouth set in a tight line. 'We've got nothing to say,' she snapped.

'I'm not a journalist,' Paula said, trying not to feel

insulted by the mistake. 'I'm Detective Constable Paula McIntyre from Bradfield Police.'

The woman's hands clawed at her cheeks. 'Oh fuck. No, tell me this is just routine.' She stumbled backwards, caught by a second woman who had appeared behind her. They fell into a tight hug, the second, slightly taller woman meeting Paula's eyes with a look of naked terror.

'If I could just come in?' Paula said, wondering where the hell the FLO was.

The women edged backwards and Paula slipped inside. 'Are you on your own?' she asked.

'We sent your liaison person away. We couldn't settle with her here. I'm Julia Viner,' the second woman said, postponing what she must know was inevitable with the gloss of social convention. 'And this is Kathy. Kathy Antwon.'

Kathy turned to look at Paula, tears streaming down her face. 'This is bad news, isn't it?'

'I'm sorry,' Paula said. 'A body was found earlier today. From the description of what he was wearing, we believe it's Seth.' Her mouth opened but she could find nothing else to say so she closed it again.

Julia's eyes closed. 'I've been waiting for this,' she sighed. 'Ever since we realised he was missing. I knew he was gone.'

They clung together wordlessly for what felt like hours. Paula stood there, dumb as a rock and feeling about as much use. When it was clear they weren't going to speak any time soon, she slipped past them and found the kitchen, where she put the kettle on. Sooner or later there would be a need for tea. There always was.

There was a teapot on the worktop nearby. All she needed now was to find the tea. She opened the cupboard above the kettle and saw a ceramic jar marked *tea*. She took it down and opened it. Instead of tea, she found it contained two five-pound notes, a few pound coins and a scrap of paper. Curious, she took it out. In a barely legible scrawl, it said, IOU £10. JJ taking me to meet band, need money for train. X Seth.

This was new, she was sure of it. She needed to run this past Julia and Kathy, but who knew when they were going to be up to that? Stepping to the far end of the kitchen, she pulled out her phone and called Stacey back at the office. 'I'm at Seth Viner's house,' she said. 'Something's come up. The person who was talking to Seth on Rig was called JJ, right?'

'Yes. The initials, not spelled out.'

'I think Seth arranged to meet him at the station.'

'Bradfield Central?'

'It doesn't say. But we should start there. Can you have another look at the CCTV?'

'Sure. If I've got a specific time and place to look at, I can try enhancing it with the predictive software and see what happens. Thanks, Paula, that's a real help.'

Paula closed her phone and squared her shoulders. Now all she had to do was find the real tea.

Sam was at the door of the Lexus before the woman had even turned off the engine. He'd been waiting for three hours for Angela Forsythe because he wanted to catch her on the back foot rather than pussyfoot his way past receptionists and PAs. He wasn't about to make a hash of his big chance because his witness was forewarned and forearmed.

One of the curiosities about the Barnes file was that the report of Danuta's disappearance had come not from Nigel, her husband, but from Angela Forsythe. She'd been the house lawyer at the private bank where Nigel Barnes, his wife Danuta and Harry Sim had all worked before Danuta had chosen motherhood over climbing the greasy pole. If anyone knew what the scoop was between Harry Sim and Danuta Barnes, chances were it was Angela. And the good thing about lawyers was that, even when they changed jobs, you could always track them down via the Law Society. As soon as Sam had discovered the connection between the two adult bodies in the lake, he'd been on to Stacey, asking her to find Angela for him. She'd got straight on it. For some reason, she never hung about when he asked her for stuff. He reckoned it was because she'd identified him as the one on the team with ambition, the one who was going places. And she wanted to make sure her career went meteoric alongside his.

And so, thanks to Stacey, he'd been staking out a personal parking space in the converted 1920s cigarette factory that had recently become one of the most desirable addresses in Bradfield. Only minutes' walk from the heart of the city's office district, it sat in its own park with a view across the canal to the restored Victorian merchant area where wool and cloth dealers had done business and taken their more public pleasures.

Angela Forsythe looked startled to see a well-built mixed-race man looming over her car. Her first reaction softened as she took in his suit, his smile, but mostly his warrant card. Still with the engine running, she lowered her window a few inches. A faint aura of something floral and spicy floated across to Sam. 'Is there a problem, officer?'

'I hope not, ma'am,' he said, opting for the excessive respect that he suspected might appeal to this expensively groomed woman with the tired lines round her eyes. He thought the dark green suit and cream shirt were well chosen, making her look sober but stylish. 'I wondered if I might talk to you about Danuta Barnes?'

A lesser woman would have gasped, he thought. But this one was trained not to give much away. 'Have you found her, then?'

It was a question he didn't really want to answer. He wanted the element of surprise intact when he confronted Nigel Barnes, and years of dealing with human duplicity had taught him not to trust witnesses, even if they seemed virulently hostile to the suspect. 'We're pursuing a new line of inquiry.' He smiled.

She wasn't taken in. 'It's all right. I'm not going to tell bloody Nigel,' she said, winding up the window and turning off the engine. She opened the door and slid out, her short but shapely legs almost knocking Sam out of the way. 'You'd better come up,' she said.

The flat was on the third floor, the original metal-framed Art Deco windows augmented by an additional plain glass panel to muffle any noise from outside. The living room was like Angela Forsythe herself – warm, colourful and sophisticated. He suspected she considered her effects carefully. She waved him to a comfortably overstuffed sofa and settled in a wing chair opposite.

Clearly there was to be no hospitality or small talk. 'Danuta was my best friend,' she said. 'I imagine your file tells you I was the one who reported her missing?'

'That's right.'

She nodded, crossing her legs with a whisper of friction. 'Nigel said he hadn't called the police because he thought she'd left him. Supposedly there had been a note but he'd been so upset that he'd burned it.'

All of which Sam knew already. 'That's not what I wanted to ask you about.'

Her eyebrows rose. She pushed her bobbed dark hair behind one ear, her head tilting to one side. 'No? That's interesting.'

'I wanted to ask if you knew Harry Sim.'

The name demolished her lawyer's guard. 'Harry Sim? What in God's name has Harry Sim to do with Danuta?'

Sam held his hands up, palms facing her. 'Ms Forsythe, I'm pursuing a new line of inquiry. I really don't want to disclose any details at this point. Not because I think you might be in cahoots with Nigel Barnes, but because I don't want to prejudice people's responses in any way. So I would really appreciate it if you could indulge me by answering my questions even if they seem strange or pointless to you.' He couldn't remember the last time he'd been this polite. Carol Jordan would have to give him credit for this.

Her smile was wry. 'You're rather good at this,' she said. 'With a bit of work, you could be a lawyer. Fine, Mr Evans. Fire away. I will do my best to answer you as objectively as possible.'

'How do you know Harry Sim?'

'He worked at Corton's. I was already there when he joined us, so it must have been around '91 or '92. Danuta and Nigel were account service managers and Harry was in investments. He worked for both of them, dealing with their client deposits.'

'What was he like?'

She chewed her lower lip for a moment, considering. 'He wasn't really a team player, Harry. Limited social skills. That didn't much matter, because he wasn't front of house and he was good at his job. Danuta really rated him.'

'Were they friends?'

Angela held her breath then let it out in a sigh. 'I wouldn't say friends, no. Not exactly. When he had his crack-up, Danuta was incredibly kind to him. But more the way you would be to a distant relative than a friend. Obligation rather than genuine affection, if you see what I mean.'

Sam's antenna stood to attention. 'His crack-up?'

'Let me see . . . It must have been late '94. He'd been under a lot of pressure to help us outperform our rivals and he'd made a few bad judgement calls. Harry always took things very personally, and he just went to pieces. One of the partners found him curled under his desk, sobbing. And that was the end of the line for poor Harry.'

'They just dumped him?'

Angela gave a little peal of laughter. 'Good God, no. Corton's was always tremendously paternalistic. They made sure he had the best of care in some discreet clinic. But of course, they couldn't take him back at the bank. You can't take chances with the customers' money.' This time, the laugh was bitter. 'That sounds pretty bloody hollow in today's financial world, doesn't it? But it was how they thought back then at Corton's.'

'So what happened to Harry?'

She shrugged. 'I don't really know. I drew up the severance papers, so I do know he went out the door with a year's money. And he would have had his own portfolio. So money wouldn't have been an issue. Not for a while, anyway. Danuta visited him in the clinic.' Angela frowned, rubbing the bridge of her nose. 'I vaguely remember her saying something about him selling his house and moving away,' she said slowly. 'But I wasn't really paying attention. I wasn't that bothered about Harry, to be honest.'

'It sounds like Danuta was.'

She shook her head. 'Not really. She felt sorry for him, that's all. She was always much kinder than me.' Matter of fact, not the overemphasis of someone protecting her friend.

'Is there any chance they could have been having an affair?'

There was nothing artificial about Angela's reaction. She threw her head back and roared with laughter. 'Christ,' she spluttered. 'Leaving aside the fact that Harry had all the emotional intelligence of a starfish, you obviously haven't seen a photo of him. Trust me, Danuta was several divisions out of his league. No, Mr Evans. Nobody who knew Danuta could believe that for a nanosecond.' She swallowed, recovering herself. 'I don't know who's set you off on this track, but you are so barking up the wrong tree.' Then suddenly she was sober and serious again. 'I so hoped you were bringing me news. Even bad news would have been better than the uncertainty, believe me. I still think of her.' She sighed. 'I so hoped someone was finally going to nail that bastard Nigel Barnes.' A sharp look at Sam. 'He killed her, you know. I've never doubted that for a minute.'

'What makes you so sure of that?'

'He's always been ruthless. As far as business is concerned, he'd cut your throat before he'd let you get one over on him. Danuta was his trophy wife. Smart, beautiful and not quite as successful as him. But after the baby was born, that all changed. She decided she didn't want to work any more. She wanted to be a full-time mother. Not wife and mother, just mother. She was entirely focused on her child.' She looked embarrassed. 'To tell you the truth, I found the whole thing pretty tedious. I hoped the novelty would wear off and the old Danuta would come out to play again. I've always thought Nigel couldn't stand the competition. So they had to go.'

'He could just have got divorced, surely?'

'Money and reputation,' Angela said. 'Nigel wouldn't want to part with either.'

'He'd have lost a lot more than that if he'd killed them and been caught.'

Angela Forsythe gave him a long, level stare. 'But he hasn't been, has he?'

CHAPTER 27

Tim Parker had never been to Bradfield before. All he knew about it was that they had a Premier League football team that usually bumped along somewhere in the middle of the table. Raking up history lessons from school, he vaguely remembered it had grown rich in the nineteenth century on textiles, though he couldn't recall whether it was cotton or wool. Or something else altogether. Had there been anything else in the nineteenth century? Linen, he supposed. Well, whatever.

Nominally a detective sergeant, Tim liked to think of himself as above and beyond the narrow confines of rank. He'd taken a first in PPE at Jesus College, Oxford, and had raced through the graduate fast-track process of the Metropolitan Police. He'd never had any intention of pounding the beat. He knew he was too smart for that. His goal had always been the cool end of the job, working in intelligence of one sort or another. He didn't much mind whether it was NCIS or SOCA or Europol. As long as it provided a challenge and made him feel like he was one of that handful who truly made a difference. He'd sort of slipped sideways into the profiling stream at the National Police Faculty and found he'd had a knack for it. He'd sailed through his courses and impressed most of his instructors. Well, the academic ones, anyway. The clinical psychologists who actually worked in secure mental hospitals hadn't been quite so glowing. Especially that weird little fuck from Planet Vague who talked about messy heads and passing for human. Like that had any scientific rigour.

Now he was more than ready for the real thing. It was just a pity it had to kick off on a Saturday. He and his girl-friend had tickets for Chelsea at home to Villa. A bunch of them were supposed to be meeting up for lunch before the game, then going on afterwards for a night out. But instead he was on his way to Bradfield. Susanne had been disappointed, but she'd got over it. By the time he'd left, she'd already fixed up for her pal Melissa to take his place.

The train was travelling through some pretty drab sub-urbs now. Grey council flats, red-brick terraces straggling up and down hills like you always saw on TV dramas set in the North. He'd once been to Leeds for somebody's stag night and vaguely remembered something similar. They crossed a canal basin, then suddenly the great cast-iron and glass arch of Bradfield Central came into sight round a curve in the line. It was, he had to admit, impressive. He hoped the team he'd be working with matched up to it.

Tim had heard of the DCI. Carol Jordan had a reputa-tion for cracking cases that, if she'd been a Met detective, would have given her legendary status. But Bradfield and gender combined to relegate her to the level of an operator who was owed respect. But the case notes that had been emailed to him overnight had not impressed him much. When you stripped out all the meaningless background noise from friends and family, there really wasn't much substance. No wonder they needed his help.

He descended from the first-class carriage he'd insisted on so he could have some privacy with the files and looked for his driver. A bored-looking uniform was deep in conversation with a railway staff member, paying no heed to Tim or the other passengers. Shouldering his rucksack, Tim marched down the platform and tapped the constable on his shoulder. 'I'm Tim Parker,' he said.

The officer's face was blank but his voice held a faint note of sarcasm. 'That's very nice, sir. I'm PC Mitchell. Is there something I can help you with?'

'Are you not my driver?'

The cop and the railway worker exchanged an amused smile. 'I'm a British Transport Police officer,' he said. Tim finally registered the man's insignia and felt deeply foolish. 'I don't drive anybody except my wife,' the officer continued. 'If you're expecting someone to meet you, I suggest you go over there.' He pointed to a large hanging sign that read *Meeting Point*. A uniformed constable was standing beneath it with a sign. Even from this distance, it was possible to make out Tim's name. Though not his rank.

Cross and embarrassed, he muttered something and walked away. At least he managed to make it to police HQ without making even more of an arse of himself. The driver knew nothing about the case or about the MIT. She didn't even know where their office was. Her job was done when he was delivered to reception. He had to sit and kick his heels for another ten minutes before anyone arrived to fetch him. He'd expected Jordan herself to come down and greet him, but she'd sent some DC with a sharp suit and a definite touch of attitude. He hoped DC Evans wasn't Jordan's idea of impressive.

The MIT squad room was a pleasant surprise. Cleaner, neater and better decorated than any CID office he'd ever been in. Probably something to do with having a woman boss. He knew that wasn't an appropriate thought, and he wouldn't have spoken it, but he reckoned it was likely to be the truth. One corner was inhabited by an ICT station. He could hear the sound of keys being rapidly struck but all he could see was the back of six monitors arranged like a barricade. He'd never seen anything so specialised in a mainstream operation. Another half-dozen desks dotted the room, apparently at random. None of them was occupied. Whiteboards covered with crime-scene photos and scrawled notes lined one wall. One for Daniel Morrison and one for Seth Viner.

'The guv'nor's in her office,' Sam said abruptly, leading him down to the far end of the room where a glass-walled room had its blinds drawn. 'Everybody else is out working.' He opened the door and followed Tim in.

His first impression of Carol Jordan was that she looked like most SIOs in the midst of a double murder – sleep-deprived, depressed and desperate. Her blonde hair had a dishevelled look, there were shadows visible under her eyes through the light cast of make-up, and there were two half-empty coffee cups on the desk. But when he looked closer, he realised that the hair was deliberately shaggy and her eyes had a sparkle of energy. Her tailored shirt was crisp and clean, and the make-up was free from smudges. Tim congratulated himself on seeing past the first impression to the woman beneath. He held out a hand. 'DS Tim Parker,' he said. 'Call me Tim.'

Carol looked faintly amused but shook his hand. 'DCI Jordan. Call me ma'am. Or chief. Or even guv.'

So that was how it was going to be. Put the new boy in his place, never mind that he's here to pull you out of the shit and make you look good. Without waiting for an invitation, he sat down. 'I've had a preliminary pass through the material you emailed me,' he said. 'The first thing I want is to see the crime scenes.'

'That's going to be a bit difficult,' Carol said. 'Because we don't know where the crimes took place. We can take you to the body dumps, if you like,' she added, apparently helpfully.

'That's what I meant,' Tim said, starting to feel seriously annoyed now. 'I'd also like to talk to the families.'

'That's not going to be quite as straightforward as we would like. Daniel Morrison's mother collapsed and died yesterday at the identification. His father's in meltdown and medicated from here to Christmas,' Carol said. 'But I expect we can arrange for you to talk to Seth's mums. I'll organise a uniform to drive you round.'

'It would be easier if I went with one of your team,' he said. 'Then I can ask questions as they come up.'

'I'm sure it would be easier for you, but we're at full stretch here. My team is very small and very specialised. I can't spare a detective to ferry you around. DC Evans

302

here will be your liaison, you can call him with any questions.'

'Do me a favour and save them up so you can ask them in a bunch,' Sam said. 'I'm already juggling two cases.'

By now, Tim was thoroughly pissed off with both of them. 'I understood I'd be working directly with you, ma'am.'

'I can't help that,' Carol said sweetly. 'You'll have access to me when it's necessary, but Sam knows what's going on. Except when he doesn't and then he knows who does.'

'We hope,' Sam added.

'I'm not used to—'

'As I understand it, you're not used to anything,' Carol said. 'I'm sure you checked us out before you came up here, Tim. Because I did the same thing. And I know this is your first time in the field.'

'That doesn't mean—'

'No, it doesn't mean you don't have valuable insights to offer us. But you're here on our terms, not yours. I run the game here, not you. Are we clear on that?'

He felt like an impotent ten-year-old being ticked off by his mother. Which was really unfair because this woman definitely wasn't old enough to be his mother. 'Yes, ma'am,' he said. Even to his own ears it sounded insincere.

'So when will you have something for me?'

'Since I've already had a chance to digest so much of the investigative material, I should have a prelim for you later today.' Now he was on familiar territory, he could feel his confidence overpowering his anger.

'Let's say five o'clock back here, unless you hear otherwise. Sam, fix Tim up with a driver. Where do you want to work? We've booked you a hotel room. You can work there, or we can find you a desk somewhere in the building. It's up to you.'

He hadn't even thought about it. He'd presumed he would be here, at the nerve centre of the operation. 'What about here?'

Carol looked surprised. 'Sure. I don't see why not. I just thought you'd prefer . . . There's a couple of spare desks. I'll see you later.'

She'd turned back to her computer monitor before he and Sam had left the room. 'She seemed surprised I want to work here,' Tim said, following Sam to a desk in the furthest corner of the room.

'The profiler we usually work with always writes his profiles in his own office,' Sam said, off hand. 'He can't think in here, he says. Too chaotic.'

'Who do you usually work with?' Tim asked.

'Dr Hill. Tony Hill.'

The freaky little fuck who thought Tim needed more empathy. Great. 'I know him,' he said.

'Great guy,' Sam said. 'He's been a real asset to the team.'

If he was that great, how come they'd chosen a newbie over him, then? Obviously Dr Hill had screwed up somehow and ended up being dumped. 'I'll do my best to fill his shoes,' he said.

Sam's face broke into a grin that carved deep lines round his mouth. 'Apart from anything else, you're about a foot taller than Tony. You'd look bloody silly in his shoes.

Just make yourself at home here, I'll sort out a minder for you.' He walked over to one of the other desks and picked up the phone.

Tim took out the pad where he'd started to make notes for his profile. So far, nothing had really turned out the way he'd expected. Now he needed to stamp his authority on the area of this investigation where he could make an impact. Carol Jordan had made it clear he wasn't high on her respect totem pole. If anyone could help them crack this case, it was Tim Parker. It was time to show DCI Ma'am he wasn't someone to be taken lightly.

Tony yawned his way downstairs and into the kitchen. The effect of the Worcester house clearly only worked when he was actually there. It had gone one o'clock when he'd reached Bradfield but not even the drive or the late hour had been enough to provoke the sort of deep and even sleep he'd experienced the night before. He put the coffee on and parked himself in a kitchen chair. Sitting on top of the usual clutter on the table was the slim chrome recorder he'd brought back from the narrowboat. He'd picked it up and put it down half a hundred times. He'd checked the contents – one audio file – but he hadn't attempted to listen to it.

The other new addition to the pile was a large manila envelope. Its contents were the result of a search of Arthur Blythe's desk. Tony rested his fingertips on the envelope and considered it. 'Coffee first,' he said aloud. As he fussed with the milk steamer, he wondered where Carol was. Not surprisingly, her flat had been dark when he'd come home. He'd hoped they could get together for coffee this morning, but then he'd heard her car engine in the drive about half an hour before. Either something had landed on her plate at work or she was heading up to the Yorkshire Dales to spend the day with her brother Michael and his partner. She'd mentioned the other day that she owed them a visit. It was a shame she wasn't around. She'd have been fascinated by the contents of the envelope, he was certain.

Coffee to hand he sat down again and emptied the envelope on the table. The urge to compare Arthur's features to his had sent him back to the house after he'd finished the profile and dealt with Patterson's questions. In spite of his own dissatisfaction with the work he'd done, the West Mercia detective seemed happy enough. Maybe he'd heard about the events of yesterday morning and he was just eager to get Tony off his patch.

A quick walk through the house had confirmed what Tony had thought. There were no photographs on display anywhere. Arthur wasn't a man who needed to show off his encounters with celebrity or prove he'd stood in front of the seven wonders of the world. But surely there must be something somewhere, even if it was only a passport or a driving licence?

The obvious place to begin the search was the study. And the starting point had to be the desk. Which of course was locked. Tony studied the bunch of keys he'd been given by the lawyer, but none of them looked as if they would fit the little brass locks in the drawers of the battered and scarred desk. He threw himself into the old wooden swivel chair, spinning himself round in irritation.

'Where would you keep the desk keys?' he shouted. 'Where would you put them, Arthur?'

On the third circuit, he saw them. On a shelf, sitting on top of the books. Obscured by the shelf above if you were standing up, but perfectly visible if you were sitting on the chair. Hidden in plain sight, as in all the best detective novels. Which, Tony noticed, were well represented on the study shelves. Reginald Hill, Ken Follett and Thomas Harris, predictably enough. But also, surprisingly, Charles Willeford, Ken Bruen and James Sallis. No women except for Patricia Highsmith, though. He reached for the keys and started with the top left-hand drawer.

The second drawer on the right was the first to yield anything that wasn't stationery or bank statements. An old chocolate box sat on top of a pile of paper wallets from photo-processing companies layered with the sort of formal folders you got at weddings and awards ceremonies. Tony opened the chocolate box and found a treasure trove of personal information. Here was Arthur's birth certificate; cancelled passports; graduation certificate from the college in Huddersfield; a certificate saying he had passed his silver medal in rescue and personal survival at Sowerby Bridge Public Baths; and other gems from which he could construct elements of a life. It was surprisingly moving.

Tony closed the box and placed it on top of the desk. Nobody but him would find meaning in this. He lifted out the bundle of photographs and turned them over, thinking that would bring the oldest to the surface. The first wallet contained twelve deckle-edged prints, a mere two and a half inches by four. Various adults held a baby in their arms, all looking immensely proud. Tony turned them over: *Mum with Edmund aged twelve weeks; Dad with Edmund; Gran with Edmund; Uncle Arthur with Edmund.* He replaced the photos and carried on. He wasn't that interested in the baby pictures. They didn't show what he wanted to see.

He sifted through school photos and the occasional family holiday roll of film, charting Arthur's progress through childhood. There weren't many photos of Tony as a child, but he thought he detected similarities. Something about the shape of the head, the cast of the eyes, the line of the jaw.

It seemed to him the resemblance grew through adolescence and hit its strongest point in Arthur's graduation photo. Sitting there holding his scroll, he looked like Tony's more relaxed brother. The likeness was striking. But after that, their faces diverged rather than coming closer with age. It was like watching a demonstration of quantum physics or the road less travelled by. The map of his father's face unfurled over sixty years and told a story of what Tony himself might have been had his experiences been different.

He'd spent a long time with the photographs, just letting them sink in. Thinking about nothing, not feeling much either. Simply accepting them into his consciousness. At last, he selected a dozen or so, from the formal presentation of some golf trophy to a casual shot of three men sitting round a pub table, glasses raised in a toast. Something concrete to have by him. And maybe to show Carol.

And now she wasn't here to share them with. Well,

there would be time for that later, if he was still in a sharing mood.

Tony got up to refill his coffee and turned on the radio as he passed it. The teeth-jarring ident of Bradfield Sound filled the room, the precursor to the news. The announcer's voice stepped on the tail of the jingle. 'And on the hour, all you need to know. News from Bradfield Sound, your local information station. Police have confirmed that the body found on Bickerslow Moor was that of missing teenager Seth Viner. Seth was last seen after school on Wednesday. He was supposed to be at a friend's house for a sleepover but he never made it. Seth is the second Bradfield teen to be found dead in a remote location in the past week. Detective Chief Inspector Carol Jordan, the commander of the city's Major Incident Team, spoke about these terrible murders to Bradfield Sound.'

And then that voice he knew as well as his own. 'We believe that both Seth Viner and Daniel Morrison were murdered by the same person,' she said, her voice carefully modulated to suggest respect for the dead as well as the urgency of her investigation. 'Our deepest sympathy goes out to their families and friends. We're asking everyone in Bradfield to think back very carefully over the last few days to see if you remember seeing Daniel or Seth on the days they disappeared. We need your help.'

Back to the announcer, who sounded far too chipper for his subject. 'DCI Jordan also issued a warning to young people and their parents.'

Carol again. 'We believe the killer may have made contact with both Seth and Daniel via a social-networking internet site. We urge young people and their parents to be

309

vigilant. Make sure the people you are interacting with are who they say they are. And if you've got any doubts at all, block their contact with you and get in touch with Bradfield Police.' She rattled off the number for the contact line.

That explained why she had taken off at the crack of dawn. A double murder inquiry didn't leave a lot of time for sleep. Or anything else. She had her ticking clock now, just like Patterson and Ambrose. But still, he was surprised she hadn't been in touch. OK, Blake wasn't prepared to pay for his help. But she was his friend. She should know by now she could count on him.

So why the silence?

He didn't have the chance to wonder for long. The doorbell rang, cutting across his brooding. To his surprise, he found Sam Evans on his doorstep, half-turned away from the door as if he wasn't that bothered about getting an answer. Tony couldn't help his spirits lifting. At last, a way in to whatever Carol was up to. 'Nice to see you, Sam,' he said, stepping back to let him walk inside.

As usual, Sam didn't beat around the bush. He'd barely made it as far as the living room before he spoke. 'I need your help,' he said.

Tony shrugged. 'I thought you lot couldn't afford me any more.'

Sam snorted. 'In my book, we can't not afford you. But they've sent us some pillock from the National Faculty instead. Tim Parker.' Tony couldn't keep the dismay from his face. Sam grunted. 'I see you know him. So you'll know he's a balloon. And I'm not dealing with the likes of him on this case. You know what we need most of all right now, don't you?'

Another man might have felt intimidated by Sam's vehemence. But Tony knew him well enough to read it as the bluster of a man who sees his dream under threat. 'You need results,' he said calmly, sitting down and adopting a relaxed pose. No need to let Sam see how mutual the need was. 'You need to show James Blake that your way of doing things is the best way.'

'Exactly. And that's why I'm here. I need your help. I need some ideas about a line of questioning.'

'I'm presuming Carol doesn't know you're here?'

Sam gave him a look. 'DCI Jordan doesn't have to know about it. Here's what I know, Doc. This team is DCI Jordan's life. Without it, she'd struggle.' His mouth twisted in a dark smile. 'And without DCI Jordan, you'd struggle.' He perched on the arm of a chair like a big bird ready for the off at the first threat.

Tony couldn't deny the discomfort Sam's truth provoked in him. 'So you're appealing to my self-interest?'

Sam shrugged. 'I've always found it a good place to start.'

'Carol won't like you sharing live case details with me.'

Sam frowned. 'Who said anything about a live case? What I want to ask you about is a cold case.'

Tony tried to hide his disappointment. 'You're not working on the murdered boys?'

'Well, yeah. Obviously. But I've got a cold case coming to the boil so I'm juggling, you know? And I'm struggling. Struggling and juggling. You know how it is.'

Tony couldn't remember Sam ever acknowledging that he needed help. Given his ambition and drive, Tony reckoned he was only here today because it was off the books and eminently deniable. Still, a favour to Sam might pay off down the line. 'Why don't you tell me about it?' he said.

It didn't take long. Sam had always had the knack of pulling out the key points in an investigation and ordering them logically. 'So you see my problem,' he said. 'I've no physical evidence of murder. And I've nothing apart from the computer to link Nigel Barnes to the death of his wife, his daughter and Harry Sim. Not to mention that I've no idea how Harry Sim fits into the picture.' He slapped his hands on his thighs in frustration.

'Harry Sim's the easy part,' Tony said, enjoying Sam's irritated frown. 'He's Nigel Barnes's get-out-of-jail-free card.'

'What are you talking about?'

Tony settled deeper into his chair, comfortable and confident as he only ever was when he was navigating other minds. 'If we know one thing about Nigel Barnes, it's that he's a planner. He figured it all out ahead of time. A meticulous man would make sure he already had his escape route in place before he started. And that's exactly what Harry Sim was.'

Sam made a sharp sound of frustration. 'I don't understand. How is Harry Sim a get-out-of-jail-free card?'

'Here's what will happen when you confront Nigel Barnes with the discovery of the bodies in the lake. There'll be some story about his wife leaving him and him going after her and finding the three of them dead in some sort of bizarre suicide pact. And he panicked because he thought he'd be blamed, so he got rid of the bodies. And by chance, it so happened that the disposal method he chose destroyed all forensic traces but left enough behind for us to identify the bodies. How very fortunate that Harry happened to have a credit card on him. I bet if you check back, it was Nigel Barnes who provided those dental records too.' As he spoke, Sam's aggravation grew more obvious.

'Fuck,' he exploded. 'So how the hell do I nail him?'

'He'll wriggle out of the computer. He'll talk about finding out she was having an affair and fantasising about what he was going to do about it,' Tony said with conviction. 'So all you're left with is his word against the circumstantial evidence.'

'I realise that. How do I break him down, Tony? You're the one who gets under their skin. What's going to blow Nigel Barnes apart?'

Tony leaned forward, the adrenalin fizz of the chase buzzing in his blood. 'You've got one chance, and one chance only . . .'

CHAPTER 28

DI Stuart Patterson read the profile one more time. He didn't much like what it had to say, but he had to admit it made sense of the information they'd gathered. It suggested new avenues of investigation. The only problem was that they weren't within his control. The world of ICT professionals, as far as he was aware, was populated by the likes of Gary Harcup, men who weren't renowned for their networking skills. As Dr Hill had himself pointed out, the characteristics exhibited by a psychopathic serial killer wouldn't exactly make him stand out among the geeks and anoraks.

And then there was the Manchester connection. Patterson couldn't argue against the reasoning that said his killer wasn't a local. There were plenty of places around Worcester where you could dump a body with much less risk than that lay-by. OK, its approach wasn't covered by cameras, but it was still a busy location.

However, while cameras might not have been much use when it came to catching the killer with his victim, Patterson was hopeful that they might give him something else to work with. On the main artery from the motorway to the city, the logical approach from the north, there were number-plate recognition cameras on either side of the road. In theory, there was a record of every vehicle that drove in and out of Worcester on that road. Given the hypothetical Manchester connection, he had told Ambrose to get hold of the list from the day of Jennifer Maidment's disappearance. Then he'd have to talk to DVLA in Swansea and ask them to go through the list and identify all the cars and vans registered to addresses in Manchester. It wasn't foolproof – this killer had demonstrated that he was clever enough to cover his tracks, and he might have had enough foresight to register his vehicle to another address. And sometimes people were simply slack. Vehicles changed hands and somehow the paperwork never made it to the DVLA. But at least it was a place to start. And since he was now going to have to ask Manchester for help, it wouldn't hurt to show willing on his part.

Patterson eyed the phone as if it were his enemy. He'd asked his boss to sort things out with Manchester. But his boss was an idle sod who passed every buck he could on the alleged principle of empowering his officers. All he'd done for Patterson was to authorise his approach to the other force. Now he'd have to play phone tag with Manchester's force control on a Saturday morning to find out who he should be talking to. The perfect use of his time.

It took the best part of an hour before Patterson was finally connected to someone who was prepared to accept any responsibility for liaising with him on Jennifer Maidment's murder. DCI Andy Millwood, the duty SIO in their Serious Crimes Unit, was a marked contrast to the other officers Patterson had spoken to. 'Happy to help,' he'd said. 'They're a bastard, these cases. Everybody wants results and they want them yesterday. It'd drive you up the wall.'

Tell me about it. Every time Patterson looked at his daughter, he felt a tidal wave of guilt and helplessness. Every time he saw one of the local rag's posters of Jennifer in a shop window, it seemed like an accusation. He knew that if he didn't resolve this case, it would turn into one of the ones that gnawed away at you, nibbling at your self-belief and pushing you ever closer to the brotherhood of ex-cops who preferred to deal with the world through the prism of a bottle. He also understood Dr Hill's conviction that, if they didn't stop this killer, he would do it again. And he didn't want more guilt on his back. 'I appreciate it,' he said.

'You say there's reason to believe your killer might be from our turf?'

'That's right. He'd been stalking Jennifer online and we traced nearly twenty public-access computers he used to do it. When the boffins ran the details through their geographic profiling software, it put South Manchester in the middle of the picture for his base. I can email you the map with the hotspot.'

'That'd be a start,' Millwood said. 'So, have you got anything else? Witness description? Anything like that?'

Patterson explained what he'd initiated with the number-plate recognition. 'Also, we've been working with a profiler. He thinks the killer works in ICT. Some sort of freelance consultant, he reckons. So maybe once we've got our vehicle check results, you could help us narrow it down? I'm happy to send up a couple of our lads to help out.'

'I won't deny that'd be useful,' Millwood said. 'It's a bit thin, mind. I'll talk to intel, see if they've got any nonces with ICT connections.'

'Erm . . .' Patterson interrupted. 'The profiler? He says it's not a nonce. He says it's not sexual. Even though he took a knife to her vagina.'

'Not sexual? How does he work that out?'

'Something to do with the killer not spending enough time with her. And not actually . . . Well, not actually cutting off her clitoris.' It was embarrassing having this conversation. Not because he felt uncomfortable talking about a victim's private parts, but because he knew how daft it sounded. He knew it sounded daft because that's what he'd thought when Tony Hill had first come out with his conclusion. But as he'd listened to the explanation, it had made a kind of sense.

Millwood made an explosive noise. 'Tchah,' or something like that, it sounded to Patterson. 'And you go along with that?' His scepticism was obvious.

'Well, the way he explained it, I could see what he was getting at. The trouble is, we don't have any other motive to go on. It's not like she ran with a wild crowd or anything.'

'So you don't want me chasing down the nonces?'

'Not unless they turn up on our licence-plate trawl.'

Millwood grunted. 'That's one less thing for us to worry about. OK, then. Once DVLA have given you the list, send your lads up with it. We'll give them a hand.'

It wasn't quite what Patterson had had in mind. He'd thought his detectives would be giving Millwood's officers a hand, not the other way around. But at least it felt like a small step in the right direction.

Tony was amazed that Carol had actually agreed to meet him for a late lunch. Normally in the heat of a murder inquiry, she barely made time to snatch a sandwich at her desk. But after Sam had left, having avoided telling him anything useful about the live case, he'd rung and suggested it. She'd sighed and said, 'Why not? The Thai on Fig Lane's usually quiet on a Saturday, it's all offices round there.'

She was, of course, late. He didn't mind. He understood the pressures and knew she would be there as soon as she could be. He sat by a window in the upper section of the restaurant and watched the quiet street below, sipping a Singha beer. There were worse ways to spend a Saturday afternoon. And the football didn't kick off till four, so he wasn't even going to miss that unless she was horrendously late. As that thought crossed his mind, he spotted Carol striding down the street, her coat flaring out like a superhero's cape with the speed of her movement. Something inside him quickened at the sight of her. A swift glance over her shoulder as she approached, and then she disappeared under the restaurant awning.

She emerged from the stairwell in a burst of cold air,

leaning across to brush her lips against his cheek. Her skin was cold, but flushed with the sudden heat of the restaurant. 'Good to see you,' she said, tossing her coat over the chair and sitting down. 'How was Worcester?'

'I nearly got arrested,' he said.

Carol laughed. 'Only you!' she said. 'How did you manage that?'

'Long story, later. The job was—' he held a hand out flat and waggled it. 'Sort of OK. Not straightforward in terms of profiling. They're going to struggle with this one. And he'll kill again if they don't close in.'

'That's disappointing. I know you like to feel you've made a difference.'

He shrugged. 'Sometimes it's not up to me. But what about you? I heard you on the radio this morning. Sounds like you've got plenty on your plate.'

'No kidding.' Carol picked up the menu. 'I don't know why I look. I know I'm going to have spring rolls and Pad Thai Gai.'

'Me too.' He waved a hand at the waitress and they both ordered, Carol adding a large glass of wine to her food. 'How's it looking?' he said.

'Like your guys in Worcester, we're going to struggle with this one. Damn all to go on. We're just praying forensics come up with something.'

'I know Blake says I'm off-limits. But we can talk unofficially, surely? I'll give you all the help I can,' Tony said.

She looked down at the table and fiddled with her chopsticks. 'I appreciate that.' A pause, then she met his eyes, her expression unreadable. 'But I can't accept.'

'Why not?'

'Because it's wrong. If we're not paying you, we've no right to your expertise. I'm not prepared to exploit our friendship.'

'That's precisely why it's not exploitation. Because we're friends. Friends help each other. Friends are there for each other.'

'I know that. And I hope you'll be there for me personally. I want your support, I want to be able to come and sit with you and have a glass of wine at the end of the day and say the things I would be able to say to someone who cares about me. But I can't tell you the stuff you want to know as a profiler.' Her wine arrived and she took a long drink.

He couldn't deny he liked that she thought of him as the shoulder to lean on. But he struggled with the logic of her professional position. 'That's daft. If I thought it would help me with my profile for West Mercia, I'd run it all past you. Because you're the best detective I've ever worked with. I don't care where I take help from. I've already picked Fiona Cameron's brains on this one, and she's not being paid,' he protested.

'That's up to you and Fiona. Tony, if Blake thinks that taking you off the payroll means he gets the product of your brilliance because of our relationship, then he's got to be shown he's wrong. Until he understands that, I'm not talking to you about the details of these cases. You'll have to be like everyone else and read about them in the papers.' She placed her hand over his and her voice softened. 'I'm sorry.'

'I don't understand,' he said. 'I mean, I get your point about not wanting to take advantage of our relationship.

Not wanting Blake to get something for nothing. But this is people's lives we're talking about, Carol. This is a killer who is going serial unless you can stop him. Surely we have to do what we can to stop that? Isn't that more important than making a point?'

For a moment, he thought his appeal to her finer instincts had won her over. She bit her lip and fiddled some more with her chopsticks. Then she shook her head. 'This isn't about cheap point-scoring. It's about a bigger picture. It's about making sure my team is properly resourced. It's not just a question of what happens in this case. If we don't settle this nonsense now, a lot more people are going to die and not have any kind of justice. I can't work with one hand tied behind my back for ever, and Blake has to be made to see that. You're right, there are lives at stake. And that's why I have to take a stand here.'

He remembered that he wasn't supposed to know about Tim Parker. He thought for a moment about how he'd have reacted if he'd genuinely been ignorant. 'So you're doing this without any outside help? A potential serial and you're going back to the old ways of thinking only coppers know how villains think?' He aimed for disbelief and annoyance, not sure how hammy he seemed.

Carol looked away. 'No, we've got someone from the faculty doing a profile.'

Tony groaned. 'I've done myself out of a job, haven't I? So who is it? Tell me it's one of the better ones.'

'Tim Parker.'

He put his head in his hands. His voice came out muffled. 'And what did you make of Tim?'

The waitress shimmered up in her tight satin kimono

with a platter of spring rolls and placed it between them. Carol picked one up and bit into it. 'Ah,' she gasped. 'Hot!' She chewed open-mouthed, swallowed and drank more wine. 'We used to have an expression when I was a teenager: NBB.'

'NBB?' Tony nibbled more gingerly.

'Nice Bloke, But . . .'

'And that meant what, exactly?'

'Pleasant enough. But something missing. Charisma, looks, smarts, personality, sense of humour. One or more of the above. Fatally flawed as a potential boyfriend, basically.' Seeing him about to respond with more mystification, she clarified her meaning. 'Not that I was thinking of Tim as potential boyfriend material. What I meant was that he's perfectly personable, clearly not stupid and knows how to take an order gracefully. But it's obvious he's not got what it takes.'

'And I have?'

Carol laughed. 'Apparently.'

Tony shook his head, laughing with her. 'That's more than a little worrying.'

'So do you know young Tim? Am I wrong? Does he have what it takes?'

Tony debated what to say. Should he tell her the truth, that Tim had about as much empathy as a tabloid journalist? He didn't care about Tim, but he did care about not undermining Carol and her team. So he settled for unfamiliar diplomacy. 'He's got some ability,' he said. That was stretching it as far as he was prepared to go.

They ate in silence. Then Carol said, 'If he's no good, I'll know,' she said.

'I know you'll know. The question is what you'll do about it.'

She gave a wry smile. 'I'll tell him. And then I'll raise merry hell with Blake. And hopefully he'll let me bring you in from the cold.'

He'd always loved her optimism. It had taken a battering over the years, but still she clung to the belief that things would work out for the best. He knew he should be grateful for that. Why else would she have clung on to him all this time? 'I'll make sure I've got my thermals on,' he said. 'It might take a while.'

'We'll see.' Carol finished the last of the spring rolls and sat back, wiping her lips with the napkin. 'So tell me about nearly getting arrested.'

Tony obliged, playing up the slapstick to lift her spirits. 'The amazing thing is that they still paid attention to my profile,' he finished.

'I wish I'd seen the look on the estate agent's face,' Carol said.

'She screamed like a train whistle,' he said. 'It was not a good experience.'

'What about visiting the house? Was that a good experience?'

Tony tilted his head back as if seeking inspiration on the ceiling. 'Yes,' he said, considering. 'Yes, it was.'

'What was it like?'

'A home,' he said. 'A place where someone lived comfortably. Nothing for show, everything because it was what he wanted, what he needed.' He sighed. 'I think I might have liked him.'

Carol's eyes were soft with sympathy. 'I'm sorry.'

'It can't be helped.' He loaded his fork with noodles and filled his mouth. It was as good a way of avoiding conversation as any.

Carol was looking troubled. She'd stopped eating and was signalling to the waitress for more wine. 'I found out some stuff when you were gone,' she said. He raised his eyebrows in a question. 'Stuff about Arthur. Why he left.'

Tony stopped chewing. His food seemed to have expanded into an impossibly large lump. He forced himself to swallow. 'How did you find that out?' *And why did you do it?* Because she couldn't help herself. Because she was the best detective he knew.

'I started with old phone books. I found his factory. He was brilliant, Tony. He developed a new method of electroplating surgical instruments. He patented it, then sold the business to some big outfit in Sheffield. He was pretty amazing.'

He studied his plate. 'He did well down in Worcester too. He had a factory there. He carried on inventing new stuff. And selling out.' He was well aware of the ambiguity of his final sentence. It matched his ambivalence towards Blythe.

'I also found out why he left,' she said, digging into her bag and coming out with a print-out of the story from the Triple H. She handed it over in silence and waited till he'd read it.

'I don't understand,' Tony said. 'Why did he leave town? He was the victim here. Are you saying there was something more to this? Was he being threatened or something?'

'No, nothing like that. According to Vanessa—'

'You talked to Vanessa about this? Carol, you know how I feel about involving Vanessa in my life.' His raised voice was drawing attention from the handful of other diners in the upper room.

'I know. But there's nobody else to ask, Tony.' She reached across the table and grabbed his hand. 'I think you need answers. Sleeping in Arthur's bed and working in his living room isn't going to tell you what you really need to know. There's no way you can make peace with yourself, with him, until you know why he ran away.'

Tony was so angry he didn't dare open his mouth. How could she understand so little about him? Had he been fooling himself all these years, investing her with qualities she didn't possess because he needed her to have them? He wanted to shout at her, to make her see how far she had trespassed. He knew he could devastate her and drive her from him with a handful of well-chosen sentences. And part of him wanted to do just that. Part of him wanted to banish her and her presumptions from his life. He'd travel further and faster and lighter without her. Then an appalling thought battled through his anger. *You sound just like Vanessa.*

'What's wrong?' Carol said urgently, her face mirroring what he realised she was seeing on his. Fear and horror in equal proportion, he suspected.

He breathed deeply. 'I'm not sure I can find the words for what I'm feeling,' he said. 'It scares me sometimes, how much of Vanessa there is in me.'

Carol looked as if she was going to burst into tears. 'Are you crazy? You couldn't be less like your mother. You're like polar opposites. She cares about nobody but herself. You care about everybody except yourself.'

He shook his head. 'I'm her son. Sometimes that terrifies me.'

'You're what you're made yourself,' Carol said. 'What I've learned about profiling from you is that people are shaped by what happens to them and how they respond to it. You can't offer that grace to the killers you profile and deny it to yourself. I will not sit here and listen to you put yourself in the same box as Vanessa.' Her fierceness was hard to deny. To have provoked that in her, there must be something worth defending about himself. He couldn't refuse to accept that.

He sighed. 'So what's Vanessa's version of the story behind the story?' He prodded the cutting with one finger.

Carol called on her most unusual gift, an eidetic memory for the spoken word. She had total recall of conversations, interviews and interrogations. It was an ability that had led her into some of the most dangerous places a police officer could be sent, and these days she regarded it as an extremely mixed blessing. Now, she closed her eyes and took Tony through the entire conversation. It was a depressing recitation, he thought, given all the more validity by the confirmation in Arthur's letter that Vanessa hadn't told him she was pregnant. If she was telling the truth about that, which hardly showed her in the best of lights, she was probably telling the truth about the rest of it. Carol was right. He hadn't learned anything about the real Edmund Arthur Blythe by sitting in his chair and sleeping in his bed.

'Thanks,' he said when she reached the end. It occurred

to him that Carol had answered one question whose existence she knew nothing of. No, he didn't need to listen to whatever self-serving tale Arthur had concocted for the record. He knew now what had happened. It wasn't pretty, but then most of life wasn't. He'd kidded himself for a day and a night that he was descended from someone decent, kind and smart. *No, be honest. You kidded yourself about that for years. You always had fantasy dads that were all of those things and more.* He dredged a smile from somewhere. 'You got time for coffee?'

Carol smiled. 'Of course.' Then she undercut everything he'd just told himself. 'And Tony – remember, Vanessa's always looking out for herself. She might have sounded like she was telling the truth, but don't forget what a good liar she is. The truth might be a long way from her version.'

CHAPTER 29

Niall slouched his way across the estate to the bus stop, shoulders spread, legs wide, making himself look as big and unattractive a target as he could. You never knew round here where the agg was going to come from. Too many fuckwits on too many drugs to be reliably bad. Some guy you'd been nodding mutual respect to for weeks could just turn on you like that and next thing you know, it's all gone off.

There were already a couple of Asian lads lounging in the bus shelter. He'd seen one of them from time to time hanging around in the school yard at break. He cut his eyes at Niall, looking away before they could make proper contact. 'Where you going, then?' the boy asked.

Niall knew it would be suicide to say, 'I'm meeting up with someone who's going to give me a Russian lesson. How exciting is that?' He shrugged and said, 'Into town, innit? Hang with my crew.'

The Asian lad's lip curled. 'I never seen you with no crew. You don't got no crew, you Billy No-Mates.'

'What you know?' Niall said, trying to sound like he couldn't be bothered with this. Which he couldn't, really. He had more going on.

Before they could really get into it, a car drew up at the bus stop. All three of them acted as if it was nothing to do with them. The window rolled down and the driver leaned across. 'It's Niall, isn't it?'

He frowned. This was a stranger, OK. But a stranger who knew his name. 'Who wants to know?' he said.

'I'm so glad I caught you. DD asked me to come and pick you up. He tripped on the stairs last night and broke his ankle – can you believe it? Three hours we were stuck in Casualty at Bradfield Cross. Anyway. Obviously he couldn't meet you in town, but he still wanted to get together, so he asked me to come and pick you up.'

It made sense, but Niall wasn't entirely won over. 'How did you know I was going to be here?'

'DD knew what bus you were getting off, so I've just been working forwards from the end of the route. He printed me off your Rig page with your photo, see?' The driver brandished a print-out with Niall's moody scowl in one corner. 'Jump in, DD's really looking forward to seeing somebody more interesting than me.' A winning smile, hard to resist.

Niall opened the door and climbed in. 'See ya, losers,' was his parting shot. The Asian boys were working so hard at being unconcerned that they were almost no use to the police when it came to describing either car or driver. But that was later. Much later.

*

Carol rubbed her eyes. They were so gritty and tired, she wondered whether she should be thinking about a visit to the optician. Last time she'd seen the doctor, complaining about back pain, he'd cheerfully informed her that she'd reached the age where things started falling apart. It felt unfair. She hadn't done half the things with her body that she'd intended and she really wasn't ready to say goodbye to all those wild ambitions and vague longings. She remembered Tony turning forty and pretending to complain that he'd never lead Bradfield Victoria out in a cup final. She suspected there were similar impossible dreams she should be saying goodbye to.

Her office blinds were open now and she looked through her glass wall at her team. She could see a thin wedge of Stacey's hair and arm. Every now and again she'd tuck her hair behind her ear. It was a habitual gesture, a pause for thought, a moment while a screen refreshed. Carol wasn't sure what exactly Stacey was working on right now, but knew that whatever arcane avenue she was pursuing, there was a good chance it would produce something useful.

Kevin was on the phone, leaning back and swinging round in his swivel chair, twirling a pen in his fingers. He was good at liaising between the different divisions, easy with the laddish camaraderie that Carol was inevitably excluded from. He managed to walk the line between siding with the lads and never forgetting he was on her team. She kept thinking she would lose him to promotion, but she thought he'd stopped applying for it. She wondered if that was because he had lost his former ambition or simply that he enjoyed what he was doing.

He'd rediscovered his attachment to his wife and kids over the past couple of years; maybe that had something to do with it. He was the only one of them who was a parent. His son was only a year or so younger than Seth and Daniel. Carol made a mental note to touch base with him, make sure these deaths weren't becoming too personal.

Paula was revisiting Kathy and Julia, her visit a mixture of demonstrating that she was aware of their grief, and trying to see if there was anything else of use that they might remember. Carol wasn't hopeful on either count.

Sam, too, was out of the office. When he'd come back from sorting out Tim Parker, she'd sent him to Worksop, to the head offices of RigMarole. The owners hadn't been thrilled about going in on a Saturday, but Sam had a warrant. They were supposed to hand over the keys to the kingdom – the codes that would allow Stacey official access to the back end of their system, to see if there was anything at all on their server that might point to the identity of the killer. Sam would also be checking their physical files, to see what sort of a paper trail might exist. Getting the warrant hadn't been easy – data protection had become such a totem. These days it was almost easier to get into a Swiss bank account than some data sources.

She hoped one of them was going to come up with a lead that would give them somewhere to go on these murders, and soon. This was supposed to be the age of total surveillance. But this killer seemed able to elude the ever-watching eyes in the sky. He covered his back. And his keystrokes. She was horribly afraid that he was already planning to add to his tally of victims.

Carol turned back to her own screen and called up the postmortem reports. Maybe Grisha had some results for them. Absorbed in her reading, she didn't notice Tim Parker's approach until he was in her doorway. 'Hi,' he said, inappropriately bright and breezy. 'Just thought I'd bring you a hard copy of my profile. I've emailed it to you, but, you know, belt and braces.'

'That was quick work.' *Probably too quick.*

He put it down on the desk. 'So, I'll head down to the canteen for a coffee. Maybe you could call me when you're ready to talk it through?'

'That would be good,' Carol said. A couple of pages, by the looks of it. Barely time for him to drink a coffee, she reckoned. He looked expectantly at his work, then at her. She smiled. 'Off you go, then.'

Carol waited till he'd left the main office before she picked up his profile. She read it slowly and carefully, not wanting to be accused of unfairly dismissing him. But her most strenuous attempts at fairness couldn't tamp down the rising burn of anger. There was nothing here that her own team couldn't have generated. They'd all picked up enough of the basics from working with Tony over the years. They could have told her all the obvious stuff that Tim Parker had dressed up with fancy prose. Organised killer. White male, 25–40. Uncomfortable with his homosexuality. Incompetent in relationships. Living alone or with mother. Likely to live in Bradfield. Criminal record may include arson, animal cruelty, minor sexual offences such as indecent exposure. Spotty employment record.

It was all straight out of the textbook. There was nothing here to carry them forward an inch. 'Jesus Christ,'

Carol said. She picked up the two sheets of paper and headed for the door, face grim. She caught Kevin's eye as she marched past and shook her head.

'Flak-jacket time for the boy wonder, then,' Kevin said to her retreating back.

'I'm doing it in the canteen so I won't be tempted,' Carol said without pausing.

She found Tim on a sofa in the far corner of the canteen, nursing a cappuccino and reading the *Guardian*. He looked up at her approach, his smile fading as he took in her expression. Carol dropped the profile in front of him. 'Is that it, then? Is that the product of your expensive training at the faculty?'

He looked as shocked as if she'd slapped him. 'What do you mean?'

'I mean that this is facile. It's superficial. It reads like it's been copied from the FBI's *Sexual Homicide* textbook. It gives me no sense of this killer at all. I don't know what he's getting from these crimes—'

'Well, sexual satisfaction, obviously,' Tim said. He sounded put out. She'd thought he was flushed with shame but realised now it was umbrage. 'That's what sexual homicide's about.'

'You think I don't know that? I need specifics. Why this process and not something else? What does it mean to him? Why the peaceful death and then the hideous mutilation? What's going on there?' She had her hands on her hips, standing over him, knowing she looked like a bully but not caring. He'd committed one of the worst crimes in her book – wasting time and resources in a murder inquiry.

'It's impossible to theorise with so little data,' he said pompously. 'Technically he's not a serial killer yet. That's three plus one, if you take Ressler's definition.'

'You think I don't know that either? You were still at school when I started working homicide. I've worked with one of the best profilers in the business for years. I've learned the basics. I could have written this. This is the sloppiest piece of work I've seen in a long time.'

Tim got to his feet. 'Nobody could have done any more with the limited information you gave me. If your detectives had come up with more evidence, it would be easier to write a meaningful profile.'

'How dare you blame my team? Let me tell you, on this showing, there would be no place for you on it. Where's the insight? There's nothing here we don't already know. Why these victims? You don't even discuss whether the victims are high or low risk. How he acquires the victims. Where he's killing them. None of that.'

'You're asking me to speculate without data. That's not what the job's about.'

'No, I'm asking you to make something of what you've been given. If this is the best you can do, you've no right to call yourself a profiler. And you're no use to me.'

His face took on a stubborn set. 'You're wrong,' he said. 'I got some of the highest marks for my course work. I know what I'm doing.'

'No, Sergeant. You don't know what you're doing. Classroom is not incident room. Now, take this back and do some work. I don't want another shallow pass at this killer. Think. Empathise. Get under his skin. Then tell me something useful. You've got till tomorrow morning before I have to tell my boss that you're a complete waste of space and budget.' She didn't wait for his response. He hadn't earned the right of reply.

She thought she'd never missed Tony more than she did right then.

The team at RigMarole had made Sam's afternoon a misery. He'd finally had to lose his temper to get them to behave. He didn't understand how anyone could weigh their business against the lives of innocent teenagers and hesitate for a nanosecond about opening their files. Once he'd pointed out to them how closely the victims overlapped their primary source of income, and how quickly that income stream could disappear once the media got hold of RigMarole's reluctance, they'd finally seen the light and agreed to hand over the access codes to Stacey and open their hard copy files to him. The contents of those files had turned out to be minimal and a complete waste of time. It was infuriating when he was so close to being ready to confront Nigel Barnes.

The tedious drive back from Worksop gave Sam plenty of time to plan his tactics, against both Carol and Barnes. He had to get the DCI on side. This was the sort of case break that would make him hard to ignore in the upper echelons of Bradfield Police, but it was also in the interests of Carol herself and the MIT. That gave him a better than even chance of getting her to agree that he could arrest Barnes on suspicion of something.

It was a pity he couldn't haul Tony in on his side of the argument. But he knew better than to show Carol he'd gone behind her back. The last time one of the team had played away with Tony, she'd just about lost her mind. And that had been her blue-eyed girl Paula. He'd just have to persuade her they had enough to make it worthwhile.

He looked at the dashboard display as he left the M1. With luck, he'd be back in Bradfield by eight. Carol would still be at her desk. After all, what else would she be doing on a Saturday night in the middle of a double murder inquiry? It wasn't as if she had a life.

CHAPTER 30

The digital recorder on the kitchen table was the first thing Tony noticed when he came down for breakfast. 'Not yet,' he said aloud as he filled the coffee machine. He needed time to work out the implications of what Carol had told him the day before. He had to figure out the meaning of Vanessa's story before he could listen to Arthur and weigh his version against hers. If indeed there was any significant difference between the two.

But Carol, who generally had good instincts about these things, had reminded him that Vanessa was not to be trusted. A woman who tried to cheat her only child out of an inheritance would have few scruples when it came to rewriting history.

All the same . . .

To keep himself from temptation, he fetched his laptop and logged on to the website of the *Bradfield Evening Sentinel Telegraph*. It wasn't the *Guardian*, but the *BEST* was one of the better provincial newspapers around. And of course it would have the most detailed coverage of Carol's murders.

It was the main story on the paper's home page. Tony clicked on the link and read their account. There was a fair amount of padding, but the heart of the story was pretty scant. Two fourteen-year-old boys who had no connection to each other had gone missing without explanation. They seemed to have vanished into thin air. Their murdered and mutilated bodies had been found in remote locations outside the city. Police believed they might have been lured to meet their killer via internet social-networking sites.

He couldn't help thinking of Jennifer Maidment. A hundred miles and a different gender. But a lot of similarities. He shook his head vigorously. 'You're reaching,' he said. 'You want to find a connection so you can get your foot in the door with Carol's cases. Get a grip, man.'

He clicked on the thumbnail pictures of the two boys. First Daniel, then Seth. He cut back and forth between them, wondering if he was imagining things. He picked up the laptop and went through to his study. He plugged it into the printer and printed out both photographs, in black and white to make comparison easier. As an afterthought, and in spite of the critical voice gibbering in his ear, he also printed out a photograph of Jennifer.

Tony took the three shots back to the kitchen and laid them across the table. He poured himself a coffee and stared at them, frowning. He wasn't making this up. There was a distinct resemblance between the three teenagers. A disturbing thought was worming its way to the front of his mind, refusing to be ignored. It was a given that serial killers often had a physical type. If gender wasn't relevant to this killer but physical type was, then maybe Tony wasn't so crazy to link Jennifer to the two boys.

He needed more information. And Carol certainly wasn't going to give it to him. Not after her lecture about refusing to exploit him.

But there was someone who might. Tony reached for his phone and dialled. At the third ring, a wary voice said, 'Tony? Is that you?'

'It is, Paula.' Then, remembering how it went between people who liked each other, he said, 'How are you doing?'

'We've got two murders on the go, Tony. How do you think I'm doing?'

'I take your point. Listen, Paula. I've got something to ask you.'

'If it's to do with the case, the answer's no. Last time you asked for my help, the chief tore me a new one for going behind her back.'

'But we were right,' he said. 'Who knows how many other people might have died if you hadn't done what I asked you to? And I only asked you because I couldn't do it myself.' *And you still owe me because I saved you from your despair.*

'Yeah, well, you're better now. Your leg's not in a splint any more. You can do your own running around.'

'You are one tough woman, Paula,' he said, the admiration genuine.

'I need to be, around the likes of you.'

'Listen, I'm not asking you to do anything for me, not as such. I just need you to answer one question, that's all. One simple question. Surely you can do that for me? After all we've been through together?'

A snort of something that might have been laughter or disgust. 'Christ, Tony, you don't give up, do you?'

'No, I don't. And neither do you. So you should sympathise.'

A long pause. A sigh. 'Tell me the question. No promises, mind.'

'Your two victims. It says in the paper their bodies were mutilated. Were they both completely castrated? Penis and testes?'

Another sigh. 'I know you won't tell anyone, right?'

'Right.'

'Yes. Completely. I'm going now, Tony. We never had this conversation.'

But he wasn't listening. His mind was already racing, wondering how he was going to explain to Carol that her two bodies were not the first victims of this killer.

Kevin looked across his desk at Paula. 'Tony? Would that be our Tony?' He spoke quietly, for which she was grateful.

'The one and only,' she said. 'The chief's obviously keeping him right out of the loop.'

'And he doesn't like it, am I right?'

Paula flashed a glance at Carol, who was in her office, intent on a phone call. 'You could say that. Don't let on I've been speaking to him, OK?'

Kevin chuckled. 'My name's not Sam. Your secret's safe

340

with me.' Before either of them could say more, his phone rang. 'MIT, DS Matthews,' he said.

'This is DS Jed Turner at Southern CID.' A strong Scottish accent, an unfamiliar name.

'How can I help you, Jed?'

'Is it you guys that are dealing with the dead teenagers? Morrison and Viner?' His tone was offhand, uncaring. Kevin didn't care for it.

'That's us,' he said.

'And they started off on the missing list, right?'

'That's right. Have you got something for us?'

'I tell you, I'd be happy enough for you to take it off my plate.' A bark of almost-laughter.

'That wasn't quite what I meant.'

'I appreciate that, pal. I'm under no illusions about that. What it is, we've got what looks like it might be another one for your merry band.'

'You've got a body?'

'Not yet. We've got a missing fourteen-year-old. Niall Quantick. His mammy's been giving us grief since early doors. It took the numpties on the front desk a wee while to process that he might fit in with the MO youse are looking at. They only passed it on to us this past half-hour. So, are you interested, or what?'

Kevin sat up in his chair and reached for a pen. 'What's the score?'

'Kid's a schemie. Lives with his mother in the Brucehill flats. She says he went into town yesterday afternoon. No word about where he was going or who he was meeting. He never came home. She tried ringing his mobile but it was turned off. Typical scummy mummy, doesn't know who he hangs about with or what he gets up to when he's out the door. So here we are, middle of Sunday morning and no trace of the kid. You want it?'

Probably even more than you want to offload it. 'Let's see what you've got. It sounds like it might be one for us. But I need to look it over then run it past my guv'nor. You know how it is.'

'Sure do, pal. OK, it's on its way to you as we speak. Missing-person report and a photo. Let me know what you decide, eh?'

Kevin replaced the phone, looking glum. Paula caught his eye and raised her eyebrows. Kevin gave her a thumbs-down. 'Looks like we've got another missing kid,' he said, heart heavy, thinking of his own boy and wanting to drive home and lock the kid in his room till all this was over.

'Oh no,' Paula groaned. 'His poor parents.'

Kevin tried not to think about that. 'I need to go and talk to the boss.'

The sense of déjà vu was never a pleasant one on a murder squad. It rammed Carol's failure home to her. They hadn't caught the killer, her brilliant team with their top-drawer skills. He was still out there, another victim taken and who knew how many more to come? Under strength, under pressure and understanding what was at stake, the MIT had never faced a tougher challenge.

Carol looked round her team, knowing in her heart they were already too late for Niall Quantick. If Grisha was right about the times of death – and there was no reason to doubt him – this killer didn't keep his victims

342

alive for long. He didn't take the risk of holding them prisoner while he satisfied his appetites. Which was unusual in itself, she thought. Usually they wanted maximum gratification from the experience. That was the sort of thing Tim Parker should have picked up on. He'd just delivered his second attempt at a profile and it was no better than before, in the sense that there was no significant insight and nothing that moved the inquiry forward. She'd not had the chance to talk to him about it yet, and he was hovering at the back of the room, like a small child anticipating parental praise. He wasn't going to get it from her, that was for sure.

'Right,' she said, trying not to let the weariness show. 'As I'm sure you all know by now, we have another report of a missing teenage boy. It's possible that it's an overreaction from the mother. Apparently we had three or four similar reports last night that turned out to be false alarms. But this looks like a stronger contender for being taken seriously, so for the time being we treat it as if it's the third in a series.' There was a general mutter of agreement.

'Southern Division are conducting the witness interviews and the search. Kevin, I want you to liaise with them. Paula, you go with Kevin. Any positive leads, I want you right in there reinterviewing the witnesses. I don't want anything missed because the officer who talks to somebody crucial doesn't have your skills. Sam, we're going to have to put Nigel Barnes on the back burner for the moment. You're with the mother. Anything you can find out from her, feed it back to us, but make sure Southern get copied in too. And Stacey – I'm sorry about this, I know you've got data up to the eyeballs, but you're going to have to go along with Sam and see what you can get from Niall Quantick's computer.'

'It's no problem,' Stacey said. 'Most of what I've got running is on autopilot. Anything that comes up will sit patiently in a queue till I get back to it.'

'Shame you can't program women to be like that,' Sam said.

'Not funny,' Paula said.

'Who said he was joking?' Kevin said. 'OK, I'm on it.' He shrugged into his jacket and grabbed his keys.

'He's dead already, isn't he?' Paula said, turning back to her desk to do the same.

From the doorway, a new voice joined the conversation. 'Almost certainly,' Tony said. 'But you still have to conduct yourselves as if you're looking for a live boy.'

Carol rolled her eyes. 'Dr Hill,' she groaned. 'Perfect timing, as usual.'

He advanced into the room. She couldn't remember ever seeing him so well groomed and smartly dressed. It was as if he was trying to impress, something which never normally penetrated his consciousness. 'As it happens, you're absolutely right,' he said. He passed Tim Parker and nodded. 'Tim. It's a bit different when you're doing it for real, isn't it?'

Kevin clapped him on the shoulder as he passed. The rest of them followed his example, touching Tony as if he were a talisman. Even Stacey brushed her fingers against his sleeve. 'Welcome back, Dr Hill,' she said, formal as ever.

'Don't get ahead of yourself, Stacey,' Tony said. He

carried on into Carol's office, leaving her the choice of following or abandoning her office to him. And she knew only too well that he would have no respect for her professional privacy. The case would be at his mercy if she left him to it. So she went after him, slamming the door shut behind her.

'What are you doing here?' she demanded, back to the door so Tim Parker couldn't see her face, arms folded across her chest.

'I've come to help,' Tony said. 'And before you repeat everything you said yesterday, please hear me out.'

Carol ran a hand through her hair and stepped away from the door. She pulled the blinds then crossed to her desk. 'This better be good, Tony. I don't know how much you overheard, but there's another missing boy out there and I should be focusing on helping my team bring him home.'

Tony sighed. 'That's very laudable, Carol. But we both know there's no rush here. This lad's already dead.'

Carol felt the fight go out of her. Sometimes it was infuriating to be around Tony. He had the ability to articulate what you already knew in such a way that you felt let off the hook. And right now, she didn't want to be let off the hook. She wanted to be cross with him for not listening to what she'd said yesterday. 'Why are you here?'

'Well, in an indirect kind of way, I sort of have jurisdiction. By virtue of the fact that I'm already working for the force that appears to have the first victim of this particular killer.'

'What?' Carol struggled to divine his meaning.

'Daniel Morrison isn't the first victim.'

Every SIO carried a fear in their heart. Because there was no joined-up reporting between the different police forces in the UK, every non-domestic murder threw up the possibility that it wasn't the killer's first outing. Some years before, a couple of dozen forces had put their heads together over their unsolved murders going back a decade or so. Working with Tony and other profilers, they'd examined them to see if they could draw common threads. The conclusion they'd come to was that there were at least three serial killers operating in the UK. Three previously unsuspected serial killers. It was a result that had chilled everyone working in homicide. As Tony had said to her at the time, 'The first killing is potentially the most informative, because he's trying out what works for him. By the next time, he'll have refined his method. He'll be better at it.'

And now he was telling her that she didn't even have that advantage. She wanted to challenge him. And she might still. But for now, Carol needed some answers. 'Who's the first? Where is he? When did you work on it?'

'I'm working on it now, Carol. It's Jennifer Maidment.'

She stared at him in stunned silence for a long moment. 'I don't believe you,' she said at last. 'Do you really need this so badly? Is this about Tim Parker? I never had you pegged as a man who needed constant professional validation.'

Tony covered his face with his hands and rubbed his eyes. 'I was afraid you were going to be like this,' he said. He thrust his hand into the inside pocket of his jacket, drawing out a folded sheaf of paper. 'This is not about me. If you still don't want me involved, fine. I can live with that, believe me. But it's important that you hear me out. Please?'

Carol felt torn between her respect and affection for him and her irritation at the way he was muscling in on her investigation. Whatever he said, she was sure it all came down to Tim Parker's presence. God, how she wanted a drink. 'Fine,' she said, her voice clipped. 'I'm listening.'

He unfolded his papers and laid out the three photographs he'd printed out earlier. 'Let's forget about gender for now. Because actually it's completely irrelevant to this case. I don't know why yet, but it is. Just look at the three of them. There's a definite resemblance. He has a type. Would you agree?'

She couldn't argue with the evidence of her eyes. 'OK, they look a bit like each other. Coincidence covers Jennifer on that one.'

'Fair enough. Though you do have to bear in mind that serial killers often have a very specific physical type. Remember Jacko Vance?'

Carol shuddered. As if she was likely to forget. 'He went for girls who looked like his ex.'

'Exactly. Killers who are fixated like that, they'll pass over victims of opportunity because they don't conform. And they'll take time and trouble to cultivate the ones they're truly drawn to. Now, remember I know nothing more about your cases than anybody who has read the papers and listened to the radio. You accept that?'

'Unless you've been going behind my back with my team like you did with Paula on the Robbie Bishop case,' she said drily.

'I have not been quizzing your detectives, Carol. But I'm going to tell you some things about your two murders which I know only because they were committed by the same person who killed Jennifer Maidment. I know the signature behaviour, Carol. I know what this guy does.' He enumerated the points on his fingers. 'One: they went missing in the late afternoon without an explanation. They didn't confide in anybody – not friends, not family, not sweethearts. Two: they'd been interacting with someone on RigMarole, someone outside their circle of friends. Someone who seemed to offer something they couldn't find anywhere else. Possibly someone using a pair of initials – BB, CC, DD, whatever. That last bit's a guess, but if I'm right, it might have some significance I haven't worked out yet. Three: the cause of death was asphyxiation by having a heavy-duty polythene bag taped over their heads. Four: there was no evidence of a struggle, indicating they were most likely drugged. Probably GHB, though that will have been harder to establish in your cases because of the time that elapsed before you found the bodies. They'd been dead for a while, hadn't they? They weren't fresh kills. Because, five: they were killed very soon after they were taken. How am I doing so far?'

Carol hoped her face wasn't betraying her astonishment. How could he have known? 'Go on,' she said calmly.

'Six: they were dumped out of town, in an area not covered by traffic cameras or CCTV or Street View. There was no serious attempt at hiding the bodies. Seven: their bodies were mutilated postmortem. Eight: they were castrated. Nine: no evidence of any sexual assault. Oh, and

348

ten: nobody seems to have noticed them being grabbed off the street, so chances are they had a perfectly amicable, non-violent initial encounter with their killer. So, Carol – do I know what I'm talking about? This is way more than coincidence, isn't it?'

He met her eyes with a level gaze. 'How did you know this stuff?' she said.

'I know it because it matches what happened to Jennifer Maidment. Except in her case, it was her vagina that was excised. Her vagina, please note. Not her clitoris. And this is what I mean about gender being immaterial. Because this is not sexual homicide.'

Carol felt herself floundering. Everything she knew about serial murder pointed to these killings having a sexual basis. It was the very assumption he'd taught her. Even if she couldn't fathom what the sexual kick was, it was there. 'How can you say that? Genital mutilation – isn't that always sexual in some respect?'

Tony scratched his head. 'Ninety-nine times out of a hundred, you'd be right. But I think this is the weird one. The one that blows all the profiling out of the water because it doesn't follow the probabilities.' He jumped to his feet and started pacing. 'There's three reasons why I'm saying this, Carol. He doesn't spend long enough with them—'

'I noticed that,' she said. 'It didn't make sense to me either. Why go to all the trouble to groom them, then kill them almost at once?'

'Exactly!' He pounced on the idea, turning on his heel and slamming the flat of his hand on her desk. 'Where's the pleasure in that? The second thing is that there's no

349

evidence of any sort of sexual assault. No sperm, no anal trauma. I take it that's the same with Seth and Daniel?'

Carol nodded. 'Nothing.' It dawned on her that she had been seduced by his argument in spite of her best intentions. Because, in a horrible way, it made sense. 'You said there were three reasons.'

'He's saying, it ends here. You're not just dead. You're the end of the line. Whoever it is they remind him of, he wants to wipe that person off the face of the planet.'

His words sent a shiver through her. 'That is harsh,' she said. 'So cold.'

'I know. But it makes sense in a way that nothing else does.'

In spite of everything, Carol felt a fizz of delight. These were the moments she lived for in this job. Those dazzling moments when the tumblers of the lock lined up and the door to understanding swung open. How could you not love that feeling, when the impenetrable suddenly yielded? She smiled at him, grateful for his insight and for the patient endurance he brought to their work. 'I'm sorry,' she said. 'I owe you an apology. I've never known you to be petty, I don't know why I imagined Tim Parker could have provoked it in you.'

Tony smiled back at her. 'Parker's history. Whatever Blake says, this is my case now. Worcester has precedence.' He took Stuart Patterson's card from his jacket pocket. 'This is the guy you need to speak to.'

Carol took the card. 'There's someone else I need to speak to first.' Her smile took on a grim edge. 'And believe me, I'm going to enjoy it.'

CHAPTER 31

Among the tight-knit fraternity of illegal egg collectors, Derek Barton had a reputation for always delivering what he had promised. It allowed him to charge top dollar, since his customers knew they could rely on the quality of his wares. That Sunday, he was looking forward to a good harvest. He'd been staking out the nest on the Forestry Commission land for a while now and he reckoned this Sunday was the time to strike. Peregrine falcon eggs were always in demand and they commanded a good price. It was always a challenge to get to the nests, but more than worth it.

Barton packed his rucksack carefully. Spikes to hammer into the trunk of the tall pine so he could climb it easily. Rubber hammer to deaden the sound. Helmet and safety goggles to protect him from the birds themselves. And the plastic boxes filled with cotton wool for his prizes.

He took his time driving out of Manchester, choosing a

sequence of back roads to make sure he wasn't being followed. Ever since he'd been nicked a couple of years back, he'd been cautious when he went out on the hunt. That time, he'd been followed by an RSPB warden and they'd caught him red-handed with a pair of red kite eggs. The fine had been bad enough, but what galled him was having a criminal record. All for doing what men had been doing for hundreds of years. Where did they think all those birds' eggs in museums came from? They weren't plastic replicas. They were the real thing, eggs collected by devotees like him.

Once he was sure he wasn't being followed, he turned on to the road that curled round the Stonegait reservoir. As usual, there wasn't another vehicle to be seen. Now the new valley road had been built, there was no reason to come this way unless you were planning to hike one of the forestry roads. Given how many spectacular paths there were around here, hardly anyone chose a walk through tall dense stands of pine with no view and nothing much in the way of interesting flora or fauna. Barton was pretty sure he'd have the place to himself.

It was a grand day for it, the sun dancing on the water like a mirrorball. Barely a breath of wind, which was a distinct advantage if you were planning to climb a bloody big pine tree. Barton slowed as he rounded the last bend, checking there was nobody else about. Convinced he was in the clear, he pulled off the road a couple of hundred yards from the start of the forestry road. He backed up a little so that the vegetation on the verge obscured his number plate. It wouldn't stop anyone who was serious about checking him out, but it kept him safe from casual passers-by. Then he grabbed his backpack and set off at a brisk walk.

As Barton turned into the forestry track, he looked back over his shoulder to check again that he was alone. Taking his eyes off where he was going turned out to have been a bad mistake. He tripped over something, stumbling into a half crouch. He collected himself and looked down at what had caught his foot.

Derek Barton prided himself on being tough. But this was well outside what he was capable of taking in his stride. He cried out, staggering backwards. The hideous image seemed to sear itself in his brain, still as vivid even after he covered his eyes with his hands.

He pivoted on the balls of his feet and sprinted for the safety of his car. His tyres screamed as he dragged his car through a five-point U-turn. He was five miles down the road when it dawned on him that he couldn't just ignore what he'd seen. He pulled into the next lay-by and sat with his head on the steering wheel, his breathing shallow and his hands shaking. He daren't use his mobile, he was sure the police would be able to trace it. Then he'd be in the frame for . . . that. He shuddered. The image flashed behind his eyes again. He barely got out of the car in time before his stomach emptied in a long hot spew that splattered his boots and trousers.

'Get a fucking grip,' he told himself in a shaky voice. He'd have to find a payphone. A payphone a long way away from where he lived. Barton wiped his mouth and collapsed back into the car. A payphone and then a very big drink.

For once, Derek Barton was quite happy to let a customer down.

It hadn't been easy, but Tony had persuaded Carol to leave Tim Parker to him. Tony left her in her office and crossed the squad room to where Tim sat, face set stubborn as a jammed door. As soon as Tony was close enough, Tim spoke savagely but quietly. 'You're got no right to barge in here. This is my case. You've got no standing here. You're not a police officer, you're not an official consultant. You shouldn't even be in this room.'

'Are you done?' Tony said, his tone somewhere between condescension and sympathy. He pulled up a chair and set Tim's profile down ostentatiously on the desk between them.

Tim snatched the profile. 'How dare . . . That's confidential. It's a breach of official protocol, showing that to someone who's not an accredited member of the investigative team. And you're not. If I report this, you and DCI Jordan are going to be in deep shit.'

Tony's smile was pitying, the shake of his head sorrowful. 'Tim, Tim, Tim,' he said sweetly. 'You don't get it, do you? The only person round here heading for deep shit is you.' He leaned over and patted Tim's arm. 'I understand how scary your first live case is. The knowledge that more people are going to die if you and your team don't get it right. So you play safe. You stick to what you think you know and don't take chances. I get that.'

'I stand by my profile,' he said, his jaw jutting but his eyes frightened.

'That would be a very silly thing to do,' Tony said.

'Given that it's wrong in pretty much every respect except the probable age range.'

'You can't know that unless Carol Jordan has given you confidential information,' Tim said. 'She's not God around here, you know. There are people she has to answer to and I'll make sure they know how she's tried to undermine me.'

He couldn't have known he was sticking his head into the lion's jaws by threatening Carol so directly. Tony's mood shifted from amused willingness to help to cold anger. 'Don't be a prat. The reason I know you're wrong is not because DCI Jordan shared information with me. The reason I know is because Daniel Morrison isn't the first victim.' He didn't like himself for it, but he enjoyed the look of shock on Tim's face.

'What do you mean?' Now he looked scared. Wondering, Tony thought, what he'd missed and how he'd missed it.

Tony fished around in the plastic carrier bag he'd brought with him. He pulled out a copy of his Jennifer Maidment profile. 'I'm not trying to screw you over, Tim. At least, not unless you think it's clever to go after Carol Jordan.' He gave him a long, level stare. 'You do that, and I will make sure you spend the rest of your career regretting it.' He stopped abruptly, frowned and shook his head. 'No, that won't be nearly long enough for you to suffer . . .' He placed the papers in front of Tim. 'This is my profile of a case I've been working down in Worcester. If you look at the last page, you'll see ten key points. Compare them to what you've got here, revise your profile to include some of them. Submit it to DCI Jordan and bugger off back to the faculty before anybody asks you any hard questions.'

Tim looked suspicious. 'Why are you doing this?'

'Why am I not routinely shafting you, do you mean?'

A long pause. 'Something like that.'

'Because you're the future. I can't stop James Blake and his kind choosing cheap over good. What I can do is try to make cheap better. So go back to the faculty and think about this case and learn something from it.' Tony stood up. 'You've got a long way to go, Tim, but you're not completely useless. Go away and get better. Because next time, chances are I won't be here to hold your hand. And you don't want to have to live with the knowledge that people have died because you couldn't be arsed to learn how to do a proper job.' Tony's eyes narrowed in remembered pain. 'Believe me, you don't want to do that.'

According to Kevin, who was always plugged into gossip central, Blake hadn't moved his family up from Devon yet. Both of his teenage daughters were on the verge of key exams and his wife had categorically refused to allow them to move schools before the end of the academic year. 'We're paying his rent till they come up here in the summer,' Kevin had said when Carol called her.

'I bet it's not a bedsit in Temple Fields,' Carol said drily.

'It's one of those converted warehouse jobs that over-looks the canal.'

A moment of nostalgia grabbed Carol. She'd shared one of those lofts with her brother when she'd first moved to Bradfield. It felt like a past-life experience now. She wondered what it would be like to live somewhere like that again. She had tenants in her Barbican flat in London, but their lease would be up soon. She could sell that at a tidy profit, even with the state of the housing market right now. That would give her more than enough to afford a warehouse flat by herself. 'I don't suppose you've got an address?'

It had taken Kevin seven minutes to get back to her with Blake's address. Carol had his mobile number, but this was one conversation she wanted to have face to face. She grabbed her bag and headed for the door, noting that Tony had left but Tim Parker was still there, looking faintly flushed. She wondered what had passed between them. 'Ma'am,' he called out plaintively. 'We need to talk about my profile.'

His self-confidence was unshakeable, she thought. He'd seen Tony arrive, he'd seen them closeted together, and he'd had to listen to whatever piece of his mind Tony had chosen to give him. At no point had they asked him to contribute to their discussion. And still he didn't get it. 'No, we don't,' Carol said as she opened the door. 'They've got the football on in the canteen.'

Blake's flat wasn't far. She'd be quicker walking, Carol decided, enjoying the afternoon sun warming the brick of the tall mills and warehouses that lined the old Duke of Waterford canal. It reflected off the high windows, making them look like black panels set against the weathered red and ox-blood bricks. She turned into his building, running up worn stone steps that led into an ornate Victorian lobby. Anyone would think this had been a merchant bank or a town hall rather than a warehouse for woven woollen fabrics, she thought, taking in the marble and elaborate tilework.

Unlike most of the flat conversions, this building actually had a doorman in a discreet dark suit rather than an intercom. 'How can I help you?' he said as she approached.

'I'm here to see James Blake.'

'Is he expecting you?' He ran a finger down a ledger open in front of him.

'No, but I'm sure he'll be delighted to see me.' Carol gave him a challenging stare. It had defeated stronger men than him.

'I'll just call him,' he said. 'Who shall I say it is?'

'Carol Jordan. Detective Chief Inspector Carol Jordan.' Now she could afford the charming smile.

'Mr Blake? I have Carol Jordan here to see you . . . Yes . . . Fine, I'll send her up.' He put the phone down and ushered her towards the lifts. When the door opened, he reached past her and pressed the button for the top floor. Before she could enter, her phone rang.

She held up one finger. 'Sorry. I have to take this.' She stepped away from him and answered the call. 'Kevin,' she said. 'What's happening?'

'Looks like we've found Niall.' The heaviness of his voice told her the lad hadn't shown up at his mother's flat with an unrepentant grin.

'Where?'

'Between Bradfield and Manchester, on a forestry road by the big Stonegait reservoir.'

'Who found him?'

'We don't know. It was an anonymous tip on the triple

niner. From a phone box in Rochdale. I went over with a team from Southern. We found him right away. Looks like he's been there a few hours. The wildlife's been snacking. It's not pretty.'

'Same MO?'

'Identical. This is number three, no doubt in my mind.'

Carol massaged her scalp, feeling a dull headache beginning at the base of her skull. 'OK. Stay with it. I'm about to talk to Blake. Tony had some interesting stuff to say. Is Sam still at the mother's?'

'I think so. Stacey too. Not that she's the one you'd choose for the death knock.'

'Get an FLO round there from Southern to liaise with Sam. I'll be back at the office once I've talked to Blake. This is a nightmare,' she sighed. 'Those poor bloody kids.'

'He's on a tear,' Kevin said. 'He's hardly pausing for breath now. Just culling them.' His voice cracked. 'How's he doing it? What kind of animal is he?'

'He's managing to do it so fast because he's got them groomed and prepped already,' Carol said. 'And because he doesn't spend time with them once he's taken them. We're going to get him, Kevin. We can do this.' She tried to project a confidence she didn't feel.

'If you say so.' His voice dragged. 'Talk to you later.'

Carol closed her phone and leaned her forehead against a marble pillar for a moment before she gathered herself together and headed back to the patient doorman and the lift.

Blake was waiting by the doors when she emerged. She suspected he was wearing what passed for casual in his wardrobe – an open-necked Tattersall check shirt tucked into fawn twill slacks, leather slippers on his feet. She wondered what the other tenants made of someone so lacking in what passed for cool in these parts. 'DCI Jordan,' he said, his voice and expression equally sour. *Not delighted, then.*

'They've just found Niall Quantick,' she said.

He jumped on her words with hope. 'Alive?'

'No. It looks like the same killer.'

Blake shook his head gravely. 'You'd better come in. My wife's here, by the way.' He turned and made for one of the four doors on the landing.

Carol hung back. 'I didn't come here to tell you about Niall. I've only just heard about that. Sir, we've got a complicated situation here and I need you to sit down and listen to me with an open mind. Talking about it in front of your wife is probably not an option.'

He glared at her over his shoulder. 'You want me to come into the office?'

Before she could reply, the door ahead of him opened to reveal a trim woman in a uniform Carol recognised. Caramel cashmere sweater, single strand of pearls, tailored trousers, kitten heels and immaculately waved hair. Her mother had friends who looked like this, who read the *Telegraph* and had thought Tony Blair a jolly nice young man at the outset of his premiership. 'James?' she said. 'Is everything all right?'

Blake introduced them, the veneer of politeness kicking in automatically. Carol was aware of Moira Blake's scrutiny and classification as her husband spoke. 'I'm afraid DCI Jordan has something that won't wait till tomorrow, my dear.'

Moira inclined her head slightly. 'I imagine she'd rather talk to you alone, James.' She stepped to one side and waved Carol into the apartment. 'If you'll give me a moment to get my coat, I'll take myself off for an exploration of the neighbourhood. I'm sure there are many little gems my husband hasn't discovered yet.' She disappeared behind a Japanese screen that separated the sleeping area from the main living space, leaving Blake and Carol to exchange awkward, hangdog looks. Moira returned with the inevitable camel coat over her arm and kissed her husband on the cheek. 'Call me when you're free,' she said.

Carol noticed Blake's eyes followed Moira from the room with a look of fond appraisal that made her like him more. When the door closed behind her he gave a brittle cough and led the way over to a pair of sofas at right angles to each other. The coffee table between them was swamped with the Sunday papers. 'We don't often get a Sunday without the girls,' he said, vaguely waving at the sea of newsprint. 'Their grandmother's holding the fort this weekend.'

'You can never call your time your own in this job. But I wouldn't be here if it wasn't vitally important.'

Blake nodded. 'Fire away, then.'

'Dr Hill came to see us today,' Carol began.

'I thought I'd made myself clear on that subject?' Blake interrupted her, his cheeks growing even pinker than usual.

'Abundantly. But I didn't ask him to come in. I've deliberately told him nothing about our cases that he couldn't have read in the papers. He came in because he believes the two murders – three now – that we're working on have been committed by the same killer he's been profiling in another jurisdiction.'

'Oh, for God's sake, that's pitiful. Is he so desperate for work that he has to thrust himself upon us with flimsy excuses like that? What's his problem? Is he jealous of young DS Parker?'

Carol waited till he'd subsided, then said, 'Sir, I've known Tony Hill for a long time and I've worked closely with him on several key cases. He just doesn't have that kind of ego. I admit I was sceptical about his analysis at first. But there's substance to what he has to say.' She worked her way through the list Tony had laid out for her, thanking her eidetic memory for the power to repeat them verbatim. 'I know it sounds far-fetched, but there are too many elements in common for coincidence to be an acceptable explanation.'

Blake had looked increasingly gobsmacked as Carol's recital had unfolded. 'You're sure he had no access to your team's information?'

'I believe him,' she said. 'He's a lot more interested in closing down a killer than he is in his own self-image.'

'What does Parker think of all this?'

Carol tried not to scream. 'I've no idea. I haven't discussed it with him.'

'You don't think he's the person you should have consulted before you came to me? He is the profiler assigned to this case.'

Carol blinked hard. 'He's an idiot. His so-called profile is a joke. Any one of my team could have come up with something more useful than his first attempt. And the second version was only marginally better. I know you set great store by the training they're doing at the faculty, but DS Parker is not going to make any converts. His work is callow and superficial.' She shrugged. 'There's no other word for it. I can't work with him. I'd rather do without a profiler than have one with so little insight.' Carol stopped for breath. She could almost smell her boats burning. Blake looked thunderous.

'You're crossing a line here, Chief Inspector.'

'I don't think I am, sir. My job is to bring serious criminals to justice. Every member of my team has been hand-picked because of the unique contribution they make to that goal. I'd have thought you would have supported my drive towards excellence. I'd have thought you would be glad that I'm willing to nail my colours to the mast and say, "This is not good enough for Bradfield Metropolitan Police."' She shook her head. 'If we're not on the same page on that aspiration, I don't know that I have a long-term future in this force.' The words were out before she'd had time to consider whether she wanted to say them out loud.

'This isn't the time or the place for that conversation, Chief Inspector. You've got three murders to solve.' He pushed himself to his feet, his struggle with the sofa revealing a man less fit than he looked. He walked over to the tall windows that overlooked the canal and stared out. 'Dr Hill makes a strong case for this West Mercia murder being part of our series. He may be overstating the case, you understand?' He turned and gave her a questioning look.

'If you say so, sir.'

'What I'd like you to do is to talk to the SIO in Worcester and see what he has to say. Once you've spoken to him, you'll have to decide whether Dr Hill is right. And if, on balance, it seems that he is, you're going to have to bring West Mercia on board with us. They may have the first in the series, but we've got more victims and he's still active on our patch. I want you heading up the task force to deal with this. Is that clear? This will be our investigation.'

'I understand.' Now she understood. Blake thought Tony's actions were about ego because that was his own guiding principle. 'Does that mean I can bring Dr Hill fully on board with our cases?'

Blake rubbed his chin between fingers and thumb. 'I don't see why not. It's West Mercia's tab, though. They brought him in. They can pay for him.' He gave the first genuine smile she'd seen all afternoon. 'You can tell them that's the price of admission to the party.'

CHAPTER 32

The team of officers on the knocker in the Brucehill flats didn't take long to turn up the two Asian lads who'd stood at the bus stop with Niall the previous afternoon. It was clear from the get-go that this murder was not connected to the quotidian villainies of the estate, so for once there was no threat to anyone local in talking to the police. The normal rules of grassing did not apply. True, some refused to talk to the cops on principle, but there were plenty who still thought the murder of a fourteen-year-old who wasn't connected to any of the estate's gangs should not go unavenged. There had been enough people more than happy to give up the witnesses.

So within a couple of hours of the discovery of Niall's body, Sadiq Ahmed and Ibrahim Mussawi had been huck-led into Southern Divisional HQ for questioning. Sam, who had left Stacey and the FLO with Niall's mother, had a brief discussion with Paula on how to play it. Neither wanted to work with an unfamiliar partner, but the alternative was for them to take one witness and to leave the other to a pair of detectives from Southern about whose abilities they knew nothing. 'What do you think?' Sam said.

'Look at their sheets. Mussawi's got half a dozen arrests for minor stuff, he's been in court. He knows the system. He's not going to go out of his way to help us. But Ahmed, he's a virgin. Never been arrested, never mind charged. He's going to want to keep it that way, I think. We should take him, you and me. Leave Mussawi to the local boys and hope they get lucky,' Paula said.

They found Ahmed in an interview room, lanky limbs in a hoodie and low-slung designer jeans, gold chain at his neck, feet in outsized designer trainers, laces undone. A couple of hundred quid's worth of gear on a fifteen-year-old kid. Well, there's a surprise, Paula thought. Dad works in a local restaurant, Mum's at home with five other kids. She didn't think Ahmed was getting his spending money from a paper round. She sat back while Sam did the introductions.

'I want a lawyer, innit.'

Paula shook her head, doing the 'more in sorrow than in anger' look. 'See, there you go. Making yourself look like you're guilty of something before I've even asked your name and address.'

'I haven't done nothing, I want a lawyer. I know my rights. And I'm a minor, you need to get me an appropriate adult.' His narrow face was aggressive, all sharp angles and twitchy little muscles round the mouth.

'Sadiq, my man, you need to chill,' Sam said. 'Nobody thinks you did anything bad to Niall. But we know you were at the bus stop with him, and we need you to tell us what went down.'

Ahmed rolled his shoulders inside his hoodie, trying for nonchalant. 'I don't got to tell you nothing.'

Paula half turned to Sam. 'He's right. He doesn't have to tell us anything. How lovely do you think his life is going to be in these parts when we let it be known that he could have helped us catch a stone killer, only he didn't want to?'

Sam smiled. 'Exactly as lovely as he deserves.'

'So there you have it, Sadiq. This is probably the one and only time in your life that you're going to have the chance to do yourself a favour with us without it coming back to bite you in the arse.' Paula's voice was at the opposite end of the kindness scale from her words. 'We don't have time to fuck around on this one, because this guy will kill again. And next time, it might be you or one of your cousins.'

Ahmed looked at her, calculation obvious in his face. 'I do this, I get a free pass off you twats?'

Sam lunged forward and grabbed the front of his hoodie, almost yanking him off the chair. 'You call me a twat one more time and the only free pass you'll be getting is to Casualty. Capisce?'

Ahmed's eyes opened wide and his feet scrabbled on the floor for purchase. Sam shoved him away and he teetered backwards before his chair settled on all four legs. 'Fu-u-uck,' he complained.

Paula shook her head slowly. 'See, Sadiq? You'd have been better off paying attention to me. You need to start talking politely to us or the next thing you know you will need a lawyer because DC Evans here will be charging you with police obstruction. So, what time was it when you and Ibrahim arrived at the bus stop?'

Ahmed fidgeted for a moment, then caught her eye. 'About half three, twenty to four,' he said.

'Where were you going?'

'Into town. Just to hang about, right? Nothing special.'

A little light larceny. 'And how long were you there before Niall showed up?'

'We'd only just got there, like.' He leaned back in the chair, feigning cockiness again.

'Did you know Niall?' Sam asked.

A shrug. 'I knew who he was. We didn't hang about, nothing like that.'

'Did you speak to him at all?' Paula said.

Another shrug. 'Might have.'

'Never mind "might have". Did you?'

'Ibrahim goes, "Where you going, brah?" And he goes, like, he's going into town to hang with his crew. Only, we know he don't have a crew so it's bullshit, right? So Ibrahim calls him Billy No-Mates.'

'The discreet charm of the bourgeoisie,' Sam said wryly.

'Do what?'

'Nothing. So what did he say when you called him Billy No-Mates?'

Ahmed ran a finger round the inside curve of his ear then inspected it. 'Fuck all he could say, was there? Cuz that's when the car turned up, right?'

'Tell me about the car,' Paula said.

'It was silver.'

Paula waited but nothing more was forthcoming. 'And? You must have noticed more than that.'

'Why the fuck would I? It was, like, a pile of crap. It was this silver hatchback thing. Medium sort of size. Total fucking nothing car. Something, like, of no interest.'

Of course it was. 'So what happened then?'

'The window comes down and the driver says something like, "You're Niall, right?"'

'He definitely used Niall's name?' If Ahmed was right, it proved this was a premeditated set-up.

He gave her the, 'Well, duh,' eye-roll. 'I said so, innit?' he drawled. 'He definitely said the name Niall.'

'What happened then?' Sam was back in the act. Paula wished he'd shut up, almost wished she was with a Southern Division detective she could have intimidated into silence.

'Niall stuck his head in the window, so I didn't catch what was going on between them. Niall said something like, how did the geezer know he was going to be there. But I couldn't make out what the driver was saying.'

Why was it always like this? Paula wondered. One step forward, one step sideways then one back. 'What did he sound like, the driver?'

Ahmed pulled a face. 'What you mean, what did he sound like?'

'Accent? High voice, low voice? Educated, not?'

She could see Ahmed struggling to recall. Which meant what he said would probably be worthless. 'It wasn't, like, deep. It was kind of ordinary. Like everybody round here speak. But like old people like my parents speak, you know? Not like one of us.'

'Did you get a look at him?'

'Not really. He was wearing a ball cap. He had long hair, brown, like down to his collar.'

Probably a wig. 'What did the cap look like? What colour? Any slogan?'

'It was grey and blue. I didn't pay attention, you know? Why would I be interested? Some geezer stops and talks to somebody I hardly know, why would I be paying them any of my attention?' He leaned back again and sighed. 'This is so bullshit, me being here like this.'

'So what happened next?' Paula said.

'Niall gets in the car and they drive off. End of.'

And that was also the end of Sadiq Ahmed's useful testimony. They hung on to him while they compared notes with the other interview team, who had even less to show for their chat. But they had no cause to hold either Ahmed or Mussawi any longer so they cut them loose. Paula watched them swagger down the street, jeans at half mast, hoodies over their heads. 'Sometimes I feel like counting the days to retirement,' she said wearily.

'Not a good move,' Sam said. 'It's always going to be too many. Even when it gets down to one.'

For Tony, there were no longer enough hours in the day. Carol had called him as soon as she'd left Blake. Her next call would be to Stacey, to instruct her to open the case files to Tony. She told him about Blake's parting shot, but he didn't care. Who paid the piper had never been his issue. All that mattered was having access to the information he needed to build his portrait of the killer.

Information on this scale, however, could be a curse as

much as a blessing. Stacey had emailed him the codes so that he could directly access all their files. But the amount of raw data generated by three missing-person inquiries that had turned to murders was vast. Just reading through it would take days. But thankfully, there were digests of the reports that had been prepared so that Carol's team could have a more accessible overview of the cases. The downside of this was that important details could have been lost in the sifting. So every time Tony came across something that piqued his curiosity, he had to backtrack to the original report to see what had been said or done in the first instance.

The worst of it was that he didn't know exactly what he was looking for. His conclusion that these killings did not have their roots in a sexual motive meant he had to reconsider evidence from anyone close to the victims. Because he didn't know what linked the victims, anything could be significant.

There was no way round it. He had to go back to square one and start looking in the dark corners of the victim's lives. The victims were always the key to cracking a series. But in all his years of profiling serial offenders, Tony had never known a case where they were as crucial as they were here. He settled down to work, completely oblivious to the digital recorder that was now buried under a drift of paper.

To Carol's surprise, DI Stuart Patterson couldn't have been less territorial about his inquiry. In her experience, SIOs jealously hugged their murders close to their chests. You generally had to drag information out of them piecemeal.

But it soon became clear that he genuinely believed two heads were better than one. Even if it was also obvious that he wasn't at all sure that the addition of Tony Hill's was an unmixed blessing.

'He's not your usual sort of expert witness,' he said cagily when Carol commented on Tony's brilliant linkage of the cases.

'He's one of a kind,' she agreed.

'Probably just as well. You do know he nearly got himself arrested down here? My bagman had to pull him out of the mire.'

Carol stifled a giggle. 'He did mention there had been a spot of bother, yes. I'd just put it down to the price you have to pay for having him on the team.'

'So what's the easiest way for us to proceed?'

They ran through the rules of engagement, working out how they could link the two investigations in practical terms. Stacey featured large in the conversation, and Carol couldn't help noting a certain wistfulness in Patterson's voice on the subject of resident geeks. 'We don't have anyone with that level of skill,' he said. 'I have to buy in that kind of expertise. You take what you can get, and it's not always what you might hope for. Not to mention you're always having to butter them up just to keep them on side.'

'You're welcome to use Stacey on this if there's anything you've got that might benefit from a more thorough analysis.'

'Thanks, Carol. I think we're covered, but I will bear it in mind. We have actually already got an intel-based joint op going on with GMP on this case.'

'Really? One of our bodies was dumped on the border between us and them. What's the connection?'

'It came from Tony Hill. We'd got a series of locations for public-access computers the killer used to communicate with Jennifer Maidment. He asked a colleague to run them through a geographic profiling program and it spat out a hot spot in South Manchester. So we took the product from our number-plate recognition system to DVLA and asked for details of all the Manchester-registered vehicles that came into town around the day Jennifer was abducted.'

Carol was impressed. It was the kind of lateral thinking she looked for from her own team. 'Great idea. So what was the pay-off?'

'Fifty-three possibles. I've sent my sergeant up there to work alongside the GMP officers. They're going round the addresses, checking alibis and looking for people with connections to the ICT industry. That's where Tony Hill reckons our perp works.'

'Sounds like that might just break something open. I'll be very interested to hear how it pans out.'

Patterson sighed. 'Me too. Because, frankly, it's the only lead we've got right now.'

Paula's phone vibrated against her hip. She pulled it from her pocket and got a quick hit of pleasure when she saw her caller was Elinor Blessing. She walked away from the knot of Brucehill teenagers she and Sam were pointlessly engaging with, phone to her ear.

'I saw the news,' Elinor said. 'I imagine you're having a rough day.'

'I've had easier,' Paula admitted, fishing a cigarette from her pack and wrestling her lighter free of her pocket. 'It's nice to hear a friendly voice.'

'I won't keep you. I realise you're busy. But I wondered if there was any chance of you having time for a late supper?'

It was a thought so beautiful that Paula could have cried. 'I would love to,' she sighed. 'If by late, you mean something like half past nine, I could probably make it. Unless there's something specific that needs a late-night posse, we're usually through by then. Well, I say through. What I really mean is that we're usually out of the office.'

'Good. Do you know Rafaello's? It's just off the Woolmarket.'

'I've seen it, yes.'

'I'll book a table. Nine thirty, unless you hear from me.'

'See you then.' Paula ended the call. She felt five years lighter, the weight of her recent past slipping from her. Restoration, that's what it felt like. Being restored to a person for whom a relationship was a possibility. She turned back, enjoying the look of shock on Sam Evans's face when he saw her transformed from leadenness to buoyancy. Oh, but it was going to be a fine evening.

Meanwhile, there was the small matter of the Brucehill boys to deal with. The way she felt now, they better watch out.

It had taken all Alvin Ambrose's powers of persuasion for Patterson to assign him to the Manchester trawl. The DCI thought this was donkey work for the lowly, but Ambrose wanted to be there with his hand on whatever transpired.

He'd pointed out that a good lead would be something for him to follow up on anyway, so he might as well be one of the bodies already on the ground. 'It's less than a hundred miles,' he'd said. 'If something breaks down here, I can be back on the motorway, blues and twos, in not much more than an hour.' Finally, Patterson had given in.

Now he was in the thick of it, Ambrose was less than excited about his assignment. But that was OK. He didn't have a problem with the fact that so much police work was pure drudgery. He'd arrived in Manchester with a list of fifty-three vehicles registered locally that had been in Worcester on the day of Jennifer Maidment's murder and abduction. DCI Andy Millwood had been welcoming, setting him up with a desk in the main Serious Crimes Unit. He'd given Ambrose a CID aide – a uniformed officer on assignment to the plain clothes branch to see if the work suited her – who would drive Ambrose round the unfamiliar territory and sit in on his interviews. Millwood made it sound like he was offering unparalleled assistance, but Ambrose knew the rookie was the lowest form of life available to be loaned out. And that she was there as much to keep an eye on the out-of-town guy as to help him. Still, it was a lot better than nothing.

'We think our perp's job is something to do with computers or ICT,' Ambrose said. 'But that's a suggestion, not a definite, so we want to keep an open mind on that one. What we're looking for is an alibi for the time they were in Worcester. What they did. Where they went. Who they were with.'

'OK, skip,' the aide said. She was a short block of a woman with legs like cricket stumps, her plain face redeemed by a luxuriant shock of blue-black hair and luminous dark blue eyes. Ambrose felt she was wary of him. He wasn't sure whether that was because he was an outsider or because of the colour of his skin. 'It's quite a compact area. Mostly Victorian terraces and big semis, a lot of them turned into student flats.'

'Let's make a start, then.'

Four hours in, they'd followed up ten leads and run the gauntlet of middle-class citizens who knew their rights and wanted to deliver a lecture on how the government was eroding civil liberties. It was a common theme right across the age spectrum, from students to legal aid lawyers. Ambrose, accustomed to a smaller city whose political ghettos ran to single streets rather than whole suburbs, felt stunned by the onslaught.

But once they'd expressed their trenchant views, it turned out that these were also the law-abiding types. Eight had given chapter and verse on where they'd been and who they'd met, information that could easily be checked by a phone call or a visit by the troops back in Worcester. One had only come off the motorway to try the food at a newly refurbished gastropub. He had a timed receipt from the pub, and another from a petrol station on the outskirts of Taunton which seemed to make it clear he couldn't have killed Jennifer. The tenth had set Ambrose's antennae twitching, but the longer they talked to him, the clearer it became that the reasons were nothing to do with murder. The guy, a market trader, was obviously hiding something. But not what they were after. As they walked away, the aide scampering to keep up, Ambrose said, 'You might want to get the local boys to turn over his lock-up. I bet they find it stacked to the rafters with pirate DVDs, counterfeit perfumes and fake watches.'

Six other vehicle owners hadn't been home. They'd stopped at a café for lunch when Patterson rang with the gobsmacking news that Jennifer's murder was now officially tied in to three others in Bradfield, thanks to that clever bugger Tony Hill. Even more surprising was that the victims were male. Now they had three other abduction dates to use as disqualifying alibis for their potential suspects. Ambrose ended the call and gave a grim smile. 'We've just been upgraded.'

'How do you mean?' she said through a mouthful of steak pie.

'This is now officially a serial-killer investigation,' Ambrose said. He pushed his plate of fish fingers and chips away. His appetite had disappeared with Patterson's news. Jennifer's death had been hard enough to bear. But add three other teenagers to the mix and the weight pressed down like a physical encumbrance. When he worked murders, Ambrose always got to the end of the day feeling like he'd literally been carrying an extra burden around. His muscles ached and his joints felt stiff, as if his body was taking on the psychological load. Tonight, he knew he'd lower himself gingerly into bed, hurting like he'd gone half a dozen rounds in the ring. 'We need to get back on the job,' he said, nodding at the aide's half-eaten food. 'Five minutes. I'll see you back at the car.'

They dealt with the next two hits swiftly enough. The first, a computer salesman, seemed promising. But they soon realised he knew next to nothing about the details of what went on inside what he sold. And he'd been on a three-day break to Prague with his wife which covered the abduction and murder of Daniel Morrison. The next was a woman whose entire time in Worcester was accounted for by meetings with the cathedral clergy to discuss designs for new vestments.

And then they arrived at the address where Warren Davy's Toyota Verso was registered.

CHAPTER 33

It wasn't a house or an office. It was a back-street garage tucked away at the end of a cul-de-sac which was also home to a craft bakery and a vegan café. Even though it was Sunday, a compact, muscular man with blond cropped hair and oil-stained overalls was respraying the wing of an elderly Ford Fiesta. He didn't stop what he was doing till the unmarked car came to a halt a few feet from him. Then he turned off his spray gun and gave them a challenging look. 'What is it, then? A hit and run?'

'Are you Warren Davy?' Ambrose asked.

The man tilted his head back and laughed. 'That's a good one. No, mate. I'm not Warren. What do you want with him?'

'That's between us and Mr Davy,' Ambrose said. 'And you are?'

'I'm Bill Carr.' A smile lit up his blunt features. 'Carr by name, car by trade. Get it?'

'And what's your connection to Warren Davy?'

'Who says there's a connection?'

'DVLA. Warren Davy's Toyota Verso is registered to this address.'

Carr's face cleared. 'Right. Now I get it. Well, sorry to disappoint you, but you won't find Warren here.'

'You're going to have to give me a bit more than that,' Ambrose said. 'We're here on a serious matter. It's not the sort of thing where you want to be caught out obstructing the police, believe me.'

Carr looked startled. 'OK, OK.' He put the spray gun down and stuck his hands in his pockets. 'I've got nothing to hide. I'm his cousin. Warren uses this place as an address for deliveries and stuff. That's all.'

'Why would he do that?' Ambrose didn't have time for finesse. He wanted answers and he was determined not to let this bodyshop monkey play games with him. Almost without thinking he moved a step forward, right on the edge of Carr's personal space.

Carr seemed unaffected by the move. 'Simple, mate. His place is out in the middle of nowhere. He got fed up with missing deliveries when him and Diane were out in the data-storage building, so he started using this place as a mailing address. I'm always here, see? And I've got plenty of space to store stuff. When something gets dropped off, I phone them and one of them comes into town to collect it.'

'Fair enough.' Ambrose was inclined to believe him. 'When was the last time you saw him?'

'Warren? A couple of weeks ago. But Diane's been in two or three times in the past week. She said he'd been out of town. Nothing unusual in that, you understand. They've got clients all over the place.'

'Clients for what?'

'They do internet security, data storage – whatever that involves. It's all double Dutch to me.'

The hair on Ambrose's arms twitched erect. This was starting to sound like a serious prospect. 'So where can I find your cousin Warren?' he asked, casual as he could manage.

Carr wheeled around and made for an office cubicle carved out of a corner of the workshop. 'They're out on the edge of the moors,' he said over his shoulder. 'I'll give you the address, but you'll need directions as well.'

Ambrose stepped smartly after him. 'If it's all the same to you, Mr Carr, I'd prefer it if you came with us, to show us the way.'

Carr gave him a baffled look. 'Like I said, I'll give you directions.'

Ambrose shook his head, a gentle smile on his face. 'You see, Mr Carr, this is a bit complicated. Like I said, this is a serious business. What I don't want to happen is for you to call your cousin the minute we walk out of here. I don't want you to tell him there's a couple of police officers coming out to his place to talk to him about his car. Because, you see, Mr Carr, I don't want your cousin Warren deciding to leg it before I have the chance of a chat with him.'

There was a hard edge to Ambrose's voice that only a fool would have chosen to ignore. It dawned on Carr that his best option was to give in with good grace. He spread his hands. 'I can see how you might feel like that. And I appreciate you not threatening me. I tell you what: why don't you come with me in my car and your lass here can drive behind us in your car? That way, I can shoot off when we get there and Warren doesn't have to know it was me that dobbed him in.'

'Are you frightened of your cousin, Mr Carr?'

Carr did the head tilt and laugh again. 'Are you kidding? I'm not scared. Don't you get it? I like Warren. He's a good bloke. I don't want him to feel like I let him down, you berk.' For the first time, Carr sounded annoyed. 'I know I'd feel pissed off if someone brought the cops to my door.'

Ambrose examined the suggestion and could find no fault with it. Carr seemed both co-operative and harmless. Apart from his discomfort at the notion of someone bringing the cops to his door, which wasn't necessarily a sign of guilt. 'Fair enough,' he said. 'Lead the way, Mr Carr.'

It had started as an experiment years ago, but now it had become part of the armoury Tony used to crawl inside the labyrinth of a killer's mind. He set up two chairs opposite each other, each illuminated by a single cone of light. He would sit in one chair as himself and pose the question. Then he'd physically get up and sit in the other chair to grope for a possible answer. Now, having assimilated as much as he could from the files, this was where he had to go.

Elbows on knees, chin on his fists, he sat staring at the empty chair facing him. 'This isn't about pleasure, is it?'

Then he got up and crossed to the other chair, where he sprawled, legs apart, arms draped over the sides of the armchair. A long pause, then in a different tone, much darker than his usual light tenor, he said, 'No. It's a mission.'

Back to the first chair. 'A mission to achieve what?'

'The end of the line.'

'The end of whose line? It's not random, is it?'

'No, it's not random. You just don't know the link yet.'

'I don't, but you do. And there's no room for doubt, is there?'

'No. I take my time, I make sure they're the right one.'

Back in his own chair, Tony folded his arms. 'Why do you care?'

This time, the pause in what he thought of as the killer's chair was longer. He tried to let the dark draw him into a place where these killings made sense. 'I don't want them to breed.'

'So you're killing them before they can get round to having kids of their own?'

'That's part of it.'

'It's all about them being the last in their line? That's why they're all only children?'

'That's right.'

Tony returned to his own chair, at a loss where to go next with this. He felt he was on the edge of grasping something, but it kept slipping from his reach. He went back to the victims, summoning their images up before his eyes, struck again by the underlying resemblance. 'They all look like you did,' he said softly. 'That's why you choose them. You've made your victims in your own image.'

Into the other chair. 'So what if I have?'

383

'You're killing your own image.' He shook his own head, not getting it. 'But most serial killers want immortality. They want reputation. You're doing the opposite. You want to obliterate yourself but for some reason, you're getting rid of kids who look like you rather than killing yourself.' It was baffling. And yet he felt he'd made some sort of a breakthrough. It was often the way with these dialogues. He didn't know how he did it or why it worked, but it seemed to free up some subconscious understanding.

Tony couldn't see how this latest insight would help them find the killer. But he knew that, when they did, it might be the key to breaking him. And for Tony, finding out why was at least as important as finding out who.

It was late in the afternoon when Bill Carr drew up in the middle of nowhere. Ambrose was taken aback by the emptiness of the landscape. It had only been ten minutes since they'd left the margins of the city behind, but out here on the edge of the rolling moors, it was as if Manchester didn't exist. Drystone walls bordered the narrow road. Behind them were slopes of rough pasture where sheep browsed uncuriously. The fields were broken up by dense stands of Forestry Commission conifers. They hadn't passed another vehicle since they'd turned off the minor road before this one. 'I don't get it,' Ambrose said. 'Where's the house?'

Carr pointed ahead, where the road disappeared almost immediately round a tight bend. 'It's a mile up the road. As soon as you come round the bend, their security cameras pick you up. There's no CCTV for miles on these roads, but Warren and Diane have their own set-up. They're paranoid about security. It's what their clients are paying for, I suppose. So this is where I leave you to it. Just head on up the road. You'll see the fence. There's a pull-in by the gate. You have to use the intercom.'

Ambrose checked the wing mirror to make sure his escort was behind them, then got out. He leaned back into the van. 'Thanks for your help.'

'Just don't mention it to Warren, OK?' Carr looked momentarily anxious but the cloud passed.

Ambrose wondered if his cousin paid Carr for his mailbox service. If he did, that might go a long way to explaining why he was so nervous about bringing them out here. 'I'll keep you out of it,' he said. He'd barely closed the door when Carr threw the car into a sharp turn and headed back towards Manchester. Ambrose watched him go then got into the car.

'Straight on,' he said. 'There's a gate up ahead on the left.'

It was just as Carr had described. The road swung round the corner and a line of trees gave way to a two-metre-high chain-link fence behind the wall. A camera was mounted on its corner, with others visible along the perimeter. Behind the fence there was more coarse moorland grass which grew right up to a cluster of traditional grey stone buildings. As they grew closer, Ambrose identified the farmhouse and two big barns. Even from the road, he could see that one barn had steel doors and extractor units on the roof. They pulled off in the gateway where a sign simply said, 'DPS' and identified themselves over the intercom.

'Hold your ID out of the window so the camera can pick them up,' a crackly voice said. Ambrose handed over his warrant card and the aide brandished them at the lens. One gate swung open and they drove inside. A woman emerged from the steel doors, which swished shut behind her. She waved them over to the farmhouse and joined them as they got out of the car.

Ambrose sized her up as he introduced them. Somewhere around forty, five five or six, slim and wiry. The kind of sallow skin that would tan well. Dark hair brushing her shoulders. Brown eyes, button nose, thin-lipped mouth, dimples that were starting to turn into deep lines. Black jeans, tight black hoodie, black cowboy boots. A pair of glasses hanging round her neck on a fine silver chain. Right from the off, she seemed to be buzzing with energy. 'I'm Diane Patrick,' she said. 'Half of DPS. Which stands for Davy Patrick Security or Data Protection Services, depending on how I'm planning to pitch you.' She smiled. 'How can I help you, officers?'

'You take your security pretty seriously,' Ambrose said, wanting to play for a little bit of time. Sometimes his gut instinct told him to ease into things, not go straight to the point.

'We wouldn't be a very effective data-storage facility if we didn't,' she said. 'Is this to do with one of our clients? Because I should warn you, we take the Data Protection Act very seriously here.'

'Can we talk inside?'

She shrugged. 'Sure, come on in.' She unlocked the door and led the way into a typical farmhouse kitchen. An Aga, scrubbed pine worktops, a big table in the middle of the room with half a dozen matching chairs. Money had been spent here, but not recently. It had the comfortable, lived-in feel of a home rather than a showpiece. The table was littered with magazines and newspapers. A webbook sat open in front of one of the chairs, an open packet of chocolate digestives next to it. Diane Patrick's boot-heels rang out on the quarry-tiled floor as she made for the kettle sitting on the range. She put the kettle on to boil and turned to face them, her arms folded over her small breasts.

'We're looking for Warren Davy,' Ambrose said, scanning the room and taking in every detail.

'He's not here,' she said.

'Do you know when he'll be back?'

'I don't. He's in Malta, setting up a new system for a client. He'll be there as long as it takes.'

Ambrose was disappointed. 'When did he leave?'

'He flew out of Manchester a week last Friday,' she said, puzzlement drawing a pair of lines between her brows. 'Why are you looking for him? Is there a problem with one of our clients? Because if it is, I can maybe help.'

'It's to do with his car,' he said.

'What about his car? Has it been stolen? He always leaves it in the long-term parking at the airport.'

'We just need to ask him some questions about his whereabouts a couple of weeks ago.'

'Why? Was he involved in an accident? He never said anything to me.'

'If you don't mind, I'd rather wait till I can discuss it with Mr Davy.' It was clear from his tone that there was no room for discussion.

She shrugged. 'Since you've come all the way out here, the least I can do is offer you something to drink.'

Both officers opted for tea. While she brewed, Ambrose took the opportunity to ask her about the business.

'There's two parts to it, really,' she said absently, as if she'd gone through it so many times she could do it on autopilot. 'We set up on-site security systems for our customers. Sometimes, like Warren's doing in Malta, we literally build the kit for them. But most of what we do is about providing secure off-site data storage. Companies can either upload their data to our secure servers at preset times every day or every week, depending on their needs. Or they can opt for the Rolls-Royce option, which is a real-time back-up of every keystroke on the system. That way, if their building burns down, they don't lose a thing.' She poured boiling water into the pot and replaced the lid.

'Is that what's out in the barn?' Ambrose asked.

She nodded. 'That's our storage facility. The walls are two feet thick. No windows, steel doors. The actual servers and the data blades in their chassis are held inside a climate-controlled inner room with reinforced glass walls. Only Warren and I can gain entry.'

'You're really not kidding, are you?'

'Absolutely not.' She handed them each a mug of tea and sipped from her own.

'Can we see it?'

Diane bit her lip. 'We generally don't let people in. Even clients only see it when they first sign up for the service.'

Ambrose gave her his best smile. 'We're not going to

misbehave. We're the police, after all. It's just that I've never seen anything like that before.'

'I don't know. Warren's pretty strict about it.'

Ambrose spread his hands. 'Warren's not here, though. Go on, satisfy my curiosity. I'm just a big kid, really.' He wasn't sure why he was so keen to see inside the data-storage barn. But her reluctance only sharpened his curiosity.

She sighed and dumped her mug on the table. 'Oh, all right. But you have to leave your tea here. No liquids in the control area.' Having decided, she didn't hang about, bustling out of the house and across the yard.

Ambrose watched keenly as Diane placed her finger on a glass plate in the lee of the doorway. 'How does it work?' he said. 'Is it fingerprints?'

'No, it's vein pattern analysis. Apparently, it's as unique as a fingerprint but the beauty of it is that it only works if it's still attached to a blood supply. In other words, you can't just chop off my finger and use that to get in, the way you can with fingerprints.' The door slid open and they followed her into a mantrap that was barely big enough for all three of them. They emerged in a small control room where half a dozen monitors continuously scrolled data past their eyes. Lights blinked and twinkled around them.

Beyond the monitors, a glass wall separated them from twenty metal towers, each of which had between a dozen and twenty dark red plastic handles protruding from them. 'Every one of those data blades holds more than a terabyte of data. Which is bigger than I can readily explain to you,' Diane said.

Ambrose was taken aback. 'It's amazing.'

'Especially if your only experience of computers is desktop and laptop systems,' Diane agreed, her voice softening. 'It's a bit like something out of Dr Who or James Bond – a fantasy come to life.'

Ambrose gave a little laugh. 'I don't even know what questions to ask.'

'Most people don't. Come on, let's go and finish our tea while it's still hot.'

Back in the kitchen, Ambrose asked for details of the client in Malta.

For the first time since they'd arrived, Diane Patrick looked discomfited. 'I don't actually know.'

'That seems kind of strange to me,' Ambrose said.

'I can see why you might think that. But mostly we each have our own clients. We only bother with the details of the other's accounts when for some reason we have to deal with them. Like this last week. I've had to make a couple of site visits to one of Warren's clients because he's out of the country and they've needed something physical taken care of. So Warren asked me to step into the breach, the same way I'd ask him if I was off the grid.'

'So you've been in touch with Warren?'

She looked as if she was puzzled by the question. 'Of course I have. He's my partner. I mean, he's my partner partner as well as my business partner. We email several times a day, and we skype.'

Now it was Ambrose's turn to look puzzled.

'It's a way of making phone calls via the internet,' she said. 'It's cheaper than using your mobile to make international calls.'

'Are you expecting to hear from him later today?' Ambrose said.

'I would think so.' She seemed to brighten at the thought. 'Do you want me to get him to call you?'

Ambrose took a card from the inside pocket of his jacket and handed it to her. 'My mobile's on there.'

'West Mercia Police,' she said. 'I didn't register that before. You're a long way from home. It must be serious if you've come all the way up here.'

It didn't surprise him that she was on the ball. You didn't get to own an operation like this without an eye for detail. 'It's just routine,' he said, not expecting to fool her for a moment. 'We take all crimes seriously.'

'I'm sure you do,' she said drily. 'Well, I'll pass your details on to Warren and tell him to get in touch.'

It was clearly a dismissal. They put down their mugs and headed back to the car. 'What do you think?' his driver asked as they drew out of the gate.

'I think it's very interesting that Warren Davy's out there in the wind somewhere. Right off his usual patch. And with all the cyber-capability he's got at his finger-tips . . .' He turned to look at the farm receding in the distance. 'Frankly, I'm wondering if he ever went to Malta.'

CHAPTER 34

Sam rang the doorbell and took a step back, taking in the expansive double front of Nigel Barnes's house. 'Doesn't look like the recession's hit Nigel yet.'

'Is he still in banking?' Carol asked.

'No, he moved into insurance five years ago. I've no idea what that means. Who knows what those bastards actually do?'

Carol grunted. She didn't want to be here. When Sam had walked into her office and proposed they deal with Nigel Barnes here and now, she'd protested. 'It's nine o'clock on a Sunday night.'

'Exactly. He'll be off his guard. And besides, we've hit the quiet before the storm in the murder investigation. We're waiting for the guys on the ground to come up with actionable information. We're waiting for Stacey to find something to move us forward. We're just sitting around fretting because we can't do anything to stop this bastard in his tracks. We might as well be out there doing something useful.' He gave her a sidelong grin. It might have been sexy if she'd been remotely interested in Sam. As it was, she read it as his attempt to get under her guard. 'Think how nice it would be to hand it to Blake all tied up in a bow, totally out of the blue.'

It had been the perfect line and so here she was. Instead of catching up on her sleep or reading the reports coming in from the divisions, she had Sam's back on a doorstep on a fourteen-year-old case where they had next to no evidence. 'He's not in,' she grumbled.

Just then a light turned on in the hallway. Sam gave her a triumphant smile before rearranging his face for the man who opened the door.

Judging from the photos in the file, the years had been kind to Nigel Barnes. Forty-three years old and still no trace of grey in the heavy shock of blond hair whose style was reminiscent of Michael Heseltine at the height of his Tarzan reputation. Smooth skin, no bags under his light blue eyes, his jawline still taut. His mouth and chin were too weak, his nose too fleshy, but he'd made the most of what he had. Carol thought he looked as if he'd spent more time in a facial spa than anyone should. He looked politely baffled at the sight of them. 'Yes?'

Carol introduced them. 'I'm afraid we have some bad news for you, Mr Barnes. I think it might be better all round if we were to come inside.'

His face seemed to harden. His lips barely moved as he said, 'You've found them.'

Carol dipped her head. 'Yes. We have.'

'Where?' He shook his head, as if he couldn't take it in.

'Where you put them,' Sam said, his voice cold and clipped.

Barnes took a step backwards, instinctively trying to put the door between them. 'I don't understand,' he said. 'What are you talking about?'

Sam stepped forward and put his foot in the doorway. 'We'd like you to come down to the station with us and answer some questions.'

Barnes shook his head. 'Are you out of your mind? You tell me you've discovered the bodies of my wife and child. And you want me to come to the police station? As if I was a suspect?'

'I never said anything about bodies,' Carol pointed out. 'I just agreed that we'd found them.'

Barnes's eyes narrowed. 'You said you had bad news. That's hardly what you'd say if they were alive and well and living in Brighton.'

'There's more than one kind of bad news. You're the one who jumped to the conclusion I was talking about your wife and child. Please get your coat, Mr Barnes. This will all be much easier in the police station than on your doorstep.'

'I'm not coming anywhere with you.' He tried to close the door but Sam leaned into it. His muscles were more than a match for Barnes, who had gym bulk but no real strength.

'You can come voluntarily or I'll arrest you,' Carol said.

'Arrest me?' He sounded incredulous. 'I'm the victim here.' He was still pushing against the door.

Carol rolled her eyes. 'Nigel Barnes, I am arresting you on suspicion of perverting the course of justice. You do not have to say anything. But it may harm your defence if you do not mention when questioned something which you later rely on in court. Anything you do say may be given in evidence. Sam, cuff Mr Barnes.'

Barnes suddenly stepped back from the door, catching Sam off-balance. Only a desperate grab at the door jamb saved him from sprawling on the floor. 'There's no need for that,' Barnes said, his voice tight. 'I'll get my coat.'

'Sam, go with him. You are under arrest, Mr Barnes,' Carol called after him.

It took twenty minutes to get him back to the station and another hour for his solicitor to show up. Carol was so tired she wanted to lay her head on the desk and cry, but at least Sam would be leading the interview. He thought she was doing him a favour because of the work he'd done on the case; the truth was she didn't think she had the energy to question Barnes properly. The one pleasant surprise while they'd been hanging around was finding Tim Parker's third attempt at a profile on her desk. As she read it, her smile grew. So that's what Tony had decided to do with him. She supposed training him to be better was a preferable option to ripping his arm off and hitting him with the wet end, which was what she'd felt like earlier. Trust Tony to find a way through the mess.

And now she had to pray Sam could do the same.

The waiter offered coffee; both women ordered espressos. Elinor caught Paula's eyes and burst out laughing. 'Docs and cops – the only people who can drink espresso after dinner and know it's not going to keep them awake.'

Paula smiled, a lazy smile that spread across her face like jam on a toddler. 'I don't usually have something this entertaining to stay awake for, though.'

'Me neither.' Elinor drained the last of her red wine and sighed with pleasure. Tonight she appeared to have cast off the weariness of work. Somehow she'd found the time to put her hair up in some complicated pleat and change into an aquamarine silk shirt that made her eyes look like jewels. She was radiant, apparently illuminated from within. Paula thought her skin actually glowed. She felt amazingly lucky. 'Thank you for making time for this,' Elinor said.

'Like you said, we both have to eat. And there's nothing else I can do tonight except go over my witness statements again till I'm cross-eyed. I'm just glad you were free.'

'Even Mr Denby has to set the slaves free sometimes.' The coffee arrived, hot and strong, and they appreciated it in a moment of quiet.

Paula couldn't remember the last time she'd had such a relaxed evening. It was what she'd longed for, but she couldn't quite let go of the old cop's maxim: hope for the best, expect the worst. But this time, she seemed to have beaten the house. The conversation had flowed easily between them. They liked the same music, their reading overlapped enough for them to share opinions, they had similar taste in films. They both loved red wine and red meat. Elinor even confessed that she enjoyed the occasional cigarette. 'One or two a week,' she said. 'Last thing at night, with a whisky.'

'If I could smoke like that, I'd be happy,' Paula admitted.

'With me, it's all or nothing. I want to quit again, but I know I have to work up to it.'

'You stopped before?'

'Yeah. I was doing really well until . . . Oh, it's a long story.' *And I don't want to tell it unless this starts to go somewhere.* 'The five-second version? A friend of mine – a colleague, actually, but he was my friend too – he got killed.' *And I nearly died too, but that's where I don't want to go tonight.*

'I'm sorry,' Elinor said. 'That must have been difficult. It's strange how often the death of people we love brings out the self-destructive behaviour in all of us.' And she'd left it at that, which Paula had been grateful for and impressed by.

Now, as they finished their coffee and split the bill, there was an unmistakable frisson between them. Paula wanted to touch Elinor's skin, to feel the electricity flow from fingertip to fingertip. Not that she wanted to rush into anything. She had too many reservations. About herself, not about Elinor.

They stepped out of the restaurant into a vicious swirl of wind. 'God, it's Baltic,' Elinor exclaimed. 'When did that happen? It was really mild when we went in.'

'Time flies when you're having fun. It's actually Wednesday now.'

Elinor laughed and tucked her arm through Paula's. 'You know what I'd really like?'

Paula's chest constricted. She felt delight, desire and dread combine inside. 'I'm far too well brought up to guess,' she said.

Elinor squeezed her arm. 'I like that you're not presumptuous. And I'd like for us to get to know each other a great deal better.'

'Yes,' Paula said cautiously, wondering where this was going.

'And I don't want this evening to end just yet. I know it's late, but do you want to come back to mine? For a coffee? More conversation?'

They paused for a moment under the canopy of a shop. 'I'd like that,' Paula said. 'I'd really, really like that. But please don't take this the wrong way. When you say coffee, it would have to be just that. I have to be in the office first thing, showered and alert and in fresh clothes.'

Elinor chuckled. 'In that case, we'd better go to yours, don't you think?' Before Paula could reply, Elinor had pulled her into an embrace. It was an electric moment for Paula. Her body tingled and her ears rang. She heard a soft moan and realised it had come from deep inside her. She wanted the kiss to go on for ever.

When they finally parted, they were both breathing heavily. 'Oh my,' Elinor said.

'Shall we go?' Paula said, her voice a squawk. She cleared her throat, patting her pockets. 'We can get a cab.' She stopped short. 'Hang on a minute.' She opened her bag and raked through the contents. 'I don't believe it. I've left my bloody keys in the office. I was in such a rush not to be late for meeting you . . . I can picture it. They're sitting on my desk, in front of my computer.'

Elinor shrugged. 'No problem. It's no distance to your office. We can walk over and pick them up then get a cab from there.'

'You don't mind?'

'No. And this way I get to see where you work.'

Ten minutes later, they were stepping out of the lift on

the third floor of Bradfield Police HQ. The night duty officer hadn't batted an eyelid when Paula signed Elinor in. It made her wonder just how many of her colleagues used the office for their out-of-hours trysts. 'We're down here,' she said, leading the way but not letting go of Elinor's hand.

There was a light on in one corner of the office, a desk lamp augmented by the eerie light of Stacey's monitors. 'Stacey? Are you still here?' Paula called in surprise.

'I'm working that Central Station CCTV footage,' Stacey replied. 'You shouldn't kiss your girlfriend in the lift, it's on the internal cameras.'

'Oh shit,' Paula said. 'It'll be all over the intranet tomorrow.'

'No, it won't,' Stacey said absently. 'I've already wiped it.' She stood up, her head barely appearing over the screens. 'I'm Stacey,' she said. 'It's nice to see Paula getting a life. That'll make three of us.'

Paula couldn't remember the last time she'd heard Stacey make such a long speech that wasn't about ICT. 'This is Elinor,' she said.

'I remember you from the Robbie Bishop investigation,' Stacey said. 'You're the one who spotted the poisons. Very impressive.'

Paula was gobsmacked by this exchange. Did Elinor have this effect on everyone?

'Thanks,' Elinor said. She was wandering round the room, checking out the whiteboards, getting the feel of the place. 'This place has a good vibe. Very grounded.'

Paula laughed. 'You wouldn't say that if you were here at nine in the morning.'

Stacey had sat down again behind her screens. 'Since you're here, Paula, come and have a look at this. I've been working on it for a bit, I think I've got something.'

Paula looked at Elinor, checking whether this was OK. Elinor smiled and waved her away with her hand. 'On you go,' she said. 'I'm fine.'

Stacey blanked four of her screens, leaving two live. 'This one here is the enhanced footage. See, the time here: four thirty-three. Plenty of time for Seth to have got here from school.' She clicked her mouse and one of the figures moving through the station entrance was highlighted. The others faded into grey background. Another click and everything about the image sharpened and clarified. 'I think this is Seth.'

'I think you're right. Kathy showed me some video of him this afternoon. I'd say that's definitely him. So where does he go?'

More mouse clicks. Stacey had stitched together shots from several cameras that showed Seth moving across the concourse. He passed the Costa Coffee outlet and then disappeared. 'Where did he go?' Paula asked.

'There's a blind spot between Costa Coffee and Simply Food. There's a passage that leads to the car park. I think he met someone and they left together.'

Paula groaned. 'That is the shittiest luck.'

'You think?'

'Well, what else?'

'Somebody who knows exactly where the cameras are and what they cover.'

A long silence. Then Paula said, 'That's a very interesting idea.'

'I know. The nice thing is that he's not quite as clever as he thinks he is.' Stacey tapped some keys and the other monitor sprang into life. A fragment of monochrome video played for a few seconds. Stacey paused it and clicked the mouse. A figure that might have been Seth leapt into relief. 'I think that's Seth again.'

'Could be.'

'It's the right area and the right time. OK, it could be practically anybody. But for the sake of argument and right time and right place, let's say it is Seth. Now look at this.' Another tap on the mouse button. A second figure was highlighted. Only half of him was visible because he was cut off by the Simply Food storefront. And the shot was from behind him so nothing of his face could be seen. But he definitely had his hand on the might-have-been-Seth's arm.

'That's him,' Paula said, the heat of the chase suddenly in her head.

'For all the good it does us. We can probably tell his height and that he has collar-length dark hair, which might be a wig. But that's all.'

'Have you looked for him on the rest of the footage?'

Stacey sighed. 'I know you all think I can do magic, but there are limits to my powers. This is needle-in-a-haystack time. I've had a try, but there are just too many possibilities.'

'Still, at least we can put out an appeal. We can be very specific about where and when. We might get something to go on.' Paula put an arm round Stacey and hugged her. 'You are truly brilliant.' She looked over at Elinor, who was browsing some papers on Kevin's desk. 'This woman is a genius.'

'Someone has to be. It's always good when they're on your team. Well done, Stacey.' Elinor seemed distracted and looked up, a thin frown line between her eyebrows. 'Is there a reason why you haven't released the fact that the victims are related?'

For a moment, Paula couldn't make sense of what Elinor had said. 'Well, we know the cases are related because of the MO. We've said we believe it's the work of the same killer.'

Elinor shook her head impatiently. 'No, I don't mean that. I mean literally related. As in, relatives.'

'What are you talking about? They're not related. Why do you say that?'

Elinor held up two pieces of paper. 'These are their DNA profiles?'

'If it says so on the lab reports. It's routine. We DNA-profile all murder victims.' Paula was halfway across the room, followed by Stacey.

Elinor kept looking from one piece of paper to the other. 'Well, unless there's been a cock-up at the lab, these two people are close blood relatives. I'm not an expert, you understand? But I'd say they're either cousins or half-siblings.'

CHAPTER 35

Nigel Barnes sat at the table, hands folded in front of him, looking less than thrilled. According to the custody sergeant, he'd been deeply pissed off that the criminal partner in the law firm he patronised wasn't prepared to turn out at half past ten at night and had sent his recently qualified junior instead. The lawyer had the air of a man whose feet keep scrabbling for bottom and not quite finding it.

Sam and Carol had barely sat down when the lawyer was twittering at them. 'I fail to see why my client is here at all, never mind under arrest. As I understand it, you have discovered the whereabouts of his wife and child, who disappeared fourteen years ago. Instead of allowing my client to grieve, you have dragged him down here on a trumped-up charge . . .'

'We haven't charged your client with anything,' Sam said, setting up the recording equipment. When it beeped, he recited the names of those present. 'Earlier this week—'

'For the record, I wish to protest at the treatment meted out to my client, who should have been given time to absorb this terrible news, not treated like a criminal.'

'Duly noted,' Carol said in a bored voice.

Sam started again. 'Earlier this week, three sets of human remains were removed from Wastwater in the Lake District. The remains proved to be those of a man, a woman and an infant. The bodies were discovered as a result of information obtained from a computer that had been hidden behind a false wall in a house that used to belong to you, Mr Barnes. A house where you lived with your wife Danuta and your baby daughter Lynette.'

Barnes shook his head. 'I have no idea what you are talking about.'

'Dental records prove the woman's body was that of your wife. DNA establishes that the infant was her daughter Lynette. And other physical evidence indicates that the third body was that of a man called Harry Sim. A man who used to work for you and your wife at Corton's bank.'

Barnes's face showed no emotion.

'You don't seem very upset, Mr Barnes,' Carol said gently. 'This is your wife and child we're talking about. So far, the only emotion I've seen from you is a burning desire not to come to the police station.'

'It was a long time ago, Inspector,' Barnes said courteously. 'I've come to terms with my loss.'

'You don't seem very curious about how your wife and daughter ended up at the bottom of Wastwater with another man,' Sam said.

Barnes looked down at his hands. 'Like I told your

colleagues at the time, Danuta had left me. She wrote me a note saying it was over, that she was in love with someone else. I had no idea who her lover was or where she'd gone. It's clear now that Harry Sim was the man in question.' He briefly met Sam's eyes. 'I was very hurt at the time. Very hurt indeed. But I had to get over it and move on.'

'You had no idea they were dead?'

Barnes's face twisted in what Sam thought was meant to be a spasm of pain. It wasn't convincing. 'No,' he said.

'Angela Forsythe did.' Sam let the words hang in the air.

Barnes couldn't hide the tightening of his hands' grip on each other. He gave a deep sigh. 'Angela is not the most balanced of women. She never liked me. I always wondered if she was in love with Danuta herself.'

'Turns out she was right, though. And maybe she was right about the other half of her theory.'

The lawyer leaned forward, as if suddenly remembering he was supposed to be doing a job. 'Is that a question, Sergeant?'

Sam smiled. 'I'm working up to it, sir. Angela believes Danuta didn't leave you. She believes you killed her. And Lynette.'

Barnes made a noise that almost resembled a laugh. 'That's insane. Harry Sim being in the lake proves she left me.'

'No,' Carol said, her voice lazy. 'It just proves that Harry Sim's body was disposed of at the same time as Danuta and Lynette.'

'And that's kind of a problem,' Sam said. 'And before

you try to tell us it must have been some bizarre suicide pact, or mad stalker Harry kidnapped Danuta and Lynette and killed them before topping himself, let me explain to you that the evidence is perfectly clear on one point. However the three of them got into the lake, it wasn't under their own steam. Somebody wrapped their bodies, tied a bundle of rocks to the package and dropped them into the lake. That was you, wasn't it, Nigel?'

'This is preposterous,' the lawyer protested. 'Are you going to produce any evidence at any point? Or have you brought us here for some sadistic purpose?'

Sam opened the folder in front of him. 'I mentioned a computer earlier. In spite of efforts to purge the hard disk, our experts were able to extract quite a lot of data. There's a whole section here—' he pointed to the page '—about the possibilities of carbon monoxide poisoning. And in another file, directions to Wastwater and information about its isolation and depth. Like I said, this computer was found hidden in your old house.'

'Anyone could have put that there.' Barnes was clinging on to his composure.

'Why would they do that?' Carol asked the question kindly, as if she really wanted to know.

Barnes unfastened his hands and ran his fingers through his thick hair. 'To frame me, of course.'

'What I don't understand is why, if someone wanted to frame you, they would go to all the trouble of planting the evidence and then not telling anyone about it,' Carol said. 'That seems a little pointless.'

'We'll find your DNA on it,' Sam said. 'We're checking back in the computer company records. It's going to show up as your computer, Nigel. You can't wriggle off that particular hook.'

There was a long silence. Then Barnes said, 'It could have been Danuta herself. She wasn't herself after the baby.' He shrugged one shoulder. 'Women and their hormones. They do bizarre things.'

'I'm going to tell you what I think happened,' Sam said.

The lawyer shook his head. 'No, I don't think so, Sergeant. You've got nothing. This is a fishing expedition. We've had enough of this. Either charge my client or we're walking out of here.'

'No,' Barnes said, laying a hand on his lawyer's arm. 'Let the man speak. I want to know what this fantasy is that he's constructed. Forewarned is forearmed, after all.'

Sam gathered himself together, remembering Tony's advice. *One chance.* And this was it. 'I think you killed all three of them. Sleeping pills to knock them out and carbon monoxide poisoning, is my guess. Then you dumped the bodies. Harry was your get-out-of-jail-free card. If the bodies turned up, there was the evidence that Danuta had had a lover. You were vindicated.'

'If I was that clever, wouldn't I have made it look like a murder and suicide?' Barnes demanded.

Sam nodded. 'That puzzled me to begin with. Then when I talked to Angela I realised that even us stupid plods might have thought twice about that scenario once we found out what a total loser Harry was. Danuta would never have run off with him, not in a million years. Not even under the influence of postnatal hormones. So I fell back on Plan B.'

'Fascinating,' Barnes said. 'And what's this Plan B?'

Sam grinned. 'You're going to confess to disposing of the bodies, aren't you? You're going to tell us how you suspected Harry might have abducted your wife and daughter, so you went to his caravan where you found they'd died of carbon monoxide poisoning from a faulty heater. You're going to tell us how you were in a quandary then. Because you'd no evidence of abduction. You'd already told the police that she'd left you. We might have thought you'd gone there in a fit of jealous rage, killed them all, then made it look like a terrible accident. And you're going to tell us that the only thing you could think of was to dump the bodies.'

Barnes laughed, a loud artificial sound. 'That is the most absurd thing I've ever heard.'

The lawyer pushed back his chair. 'Right. That's it. This is egregious. We're not entertaining these speculations a minute longer.'

Carol leaned across. 'Interview terminated at 10.57 p.m.' She switched off the tapes.

'It's not speculation,' Sam said, all geniality gone. 'It's cold, hard fact. We're going to be looking, Nigel. We're going to be turning over stones. Your life is going under the microscope. We're going to be announcing our discovery tomorrow and Angela's going to be talking to the press. She's already lining up a whole team of former colleagues from Corton's to talk about how pathetic Harry was. Virtually autistic, I hear. They'll all be talking about how truly terrible Danuta's life with you must have been if she preferred shacking up in a caravan park with Harry Sim to staying with you. Imagine. How shit must it have been for Harry to be the answer? And then there will be the speculation – did she really run off with Harry? Who could have put the bodies in the lake?'

Barnes stood up, his hands clenched by his side, his composure slipping like greasepaint under klieg lights. 'You can't do that.'

'We won't be doing it. What we'll be doing is going round every single person in your life asking about you and Danuta. Your friends, your colleagues, your clients. Because you're not that clever, Nigel. You've made this way too complicated. You should just have left them in the caravan with a dodgy heater. But no. You had to be Mr Clever Clogs,' Sam said sarcastically.

Barnes made a lunge for Sam, but his lawyer bumped his side, setting him off balance. 'You've got nothing on me,' he shouted.

'We will have,' Sam said. 'Because you're really not that clever. And when stupid people try to be clever, they make mistakes.' Hs turned to Carol. 'Fourteen years ago, what was he driving? Something nice, I bet. BMW, Mercedes, that sort of thing. There's got to be a good chance it's still around. Those quality motors last.'

Carol pretended to think. 'Credit-card receipts, Sam. He'll have had to buy petrol somewhere. Chances are we'll be able to track that down.'

'Or we could just issue a statement to the press saying we've interviewed her husband and we're not looking for anyone else in connection with the suspicious deaths of Danuta Barnes, Lynette Barnes and Harry Sim. I mean, if we're not going to get a conviction, we might as well not bother wasting our time.'

'Are you threatening my client?' the lawyer said, too timid to give either Sam or Carol cause for concern.

'How can telling the truth constitute a threat?' Carol assumed her most innocent face. 'Sam's right. That's the most efficient way to go. We've interviewed the husband – that's you, Nigel, in case you've forgotten, with all these years intervening – and we're not looking for anyone else.' She shook Sam's hand. 'Sorted. Sometimes the court of public opinion is all you need.'

Barnes looked wildly at his lawyer. 'You've got to stop this. It's an outrage. It's persecution.'

Sam knew there wasn't much the lawyer could do or say. He and Carol had been careful not to overstep the mark. He let the silence hang heavy while Barnes ran his hands through his hair. Then, very quietly, he said, 'Of course, if you were to admit to Plan B, none of this would have to happen.'

'I think this is bordering on the inappropriate,' the lawyer said weakly.

'Why don't DC Evans and I go have a cup of coffee so you can consider your options?' Carol said, setting off for the door with Sam at her heels.

They said nothing till they were clear of the custody suite. Then Sam sank into a squat, his head in his hands. 'I so wanted to nail him,' he said, his voice muffled. 'He's a stone killer.'

'I know. But I think he'll go for disposal of the bodies and perverting the course of justice. Better to face the certainty of that than endure the knowledge that everywhere you go people are pointing the finger.' Carol crouched beside him and put a comforting hand on his shoulder. 'It's a result, Sam.'

'No, it's not. It's about a quarter of a result.'

'I hate it as much as you do. Always have. But sometimes you have to settle for less. It's a closed case, Sam.'

He tilted his head back and sighed. 'You're always talking about how we speak for the dead. But sometimes we just don't shout loud enough.'

CHAPTER 36

Carol recognised the buzz in the MIT squad room that morning. It was always like this when the team was teetering on the edge of a breakthrough. The phone call she'd taken from Paula late the night before had signalled a new phase in their investigation and she'd called them together for this seven o'clock briefing because nobody wanted to wait to get cracking. That Nigel Barnes had chosen to confess to the disposal of the bodies in Wastwater was just a bonus.

They assembled round the table, coffees in hand. At the very last minute, Tony walked in. 'No show without Punch,' he said cheerily, grabbing the nearest chair and dumping his papers in front of it. He looked around, feigning surprise. 'I thought there was a new kid on the team?'

'DS Parker has been unavoidably called back to the faculty,' Carol said, glaring repressively at him. 'So we're stuck with you.'

'Welcome back, Doc,' Kevin said.

Carol cut across the general greeting. 'If we can get down to business?' They came to order and she began. 'We have some movement to report. Paula, would you like to explain how that's come about?' Carol raised her eyebrows at Paula. She'd already made it clear that, while she welcomed the breakthrough, she didn't appreciate Paula bringing an outsider into the middle of their confidential investigation.

Paula sounded as if she'd been rehearsing how to play this. 'I came into the office late last night with Dr Elinor Blessing—'

Her best-laid plans went up in smoke as her colleagues whooped and whistled. Carol knew they needed release from the tension of the case, so she let them have their head. Besides, Paula had asked for it. 'Couldn't you just get a room?' Kevin said innocently.

'Very funny. You're all very bloody comic,' Paula said, taking it in good part. Elinor's discovery might have brought an end to romance for the evening, but Paula was still on a lingering high from their encounter. And possibly also from lack of sleep. 'Some of you may remember Dr Blessing from the Robbie Bishop case, and how helpful she was then.' More whooping and nudging. 'Well, she's come to our rescue again.' Paula nodded to Stacey, who tapped a few keys on the webbook in front of her. The familiar strips of DNA analysis came up on the whiteboard. 'On the left, you have Daniel's DNA. On the right, Seth's. If we look more closely, we can see strong similarities.' Areas of the DNA strips were highlighted. 'According to Dr Blessing, this indicates that Daniel and Seth are blood relatives.'

Stacey tapped some more keys and another two DNA profiles appeared. 'Jennifer and Niall,' Paula said. 'And the same phenomenon.' Again, areas were highlighted. 'I got Dr Shatalov out of bed at two o'clock this morning to double-check that Elinor was right. And he agrees. He called in someone at the university who's more of an expert in DNA analysis than Dr Shatalov himself. Her view is that they are all half-siblings.'

'Are you saying all these women had affairs with the same man and got pregnant by him? In the same year?' Kevin sounded incredulous. 'That's mad.'

'Of course that's not what I'm saying. It's obvious. At least, it is to a lesbian. Donor insemination. It's got to be. Nothing else makes sense. And we already know Seth was a donor baby.'

There was a moment of stunned silence. Then Tony leaned forward. 'The bad seed,' he said. 'The end of the line. That's what he's doing. He's not killing them because they look like him. He's killing them because they are him.'

For DI Stuart Patterson, this was an interview that couldn't be delegated. Just as the Maidments had deserved a senior officer when they had to be told their daughter was dead, they were entitled to the same courtesy for the deeply personal question that had to be asked this morning. With luck, both of them would be home this early in the day.

Paul Maidment opened the door. He was suited up and freshly shaved. He looked exactly like any other successful businessman girded up for the start of the working week except that his eyes held no light. He nodded and sighed at the sight of the policeman. 'Come in,' he said lifelessly.

Patterson followed him to the kitchen. Tania Maidment sat at the kitchen table in her dressing gown. Her hair was uncombed, matted and asymmetrical from sleep. Dark shadows surrounded her eyes and she was smoking what was clearly not the first cigarette of the day. 'Have you arrested him yet?' she demanded as soon as she caught sight of Patterson.

'I'm afraid not,' he said, standing near the doorway. No one invited him to sit down. 'We are making progress.'

'Progress?' Maidment said explosively. 'What does that mean?'

Patterson didn't know what to say to that. He wished Ambrose was with him. He could have used that stolid certainty standing alongside. 'I need to ask you a question about Jennifer,' he said. 'I appreciate the sensitive nature of this, but we need to know the answer.'

Tania snorted. 'I didn't think we had any sensitivities left that hadn't been trampled all over. Do you have any idea how hard it is to cling on to your memories when the police and the media trample all over your daughter's life?'

'I'm sorry,' Patterson said. 'But I do need you to help me with this.' His collar felt tight. 'Was Jennifer conceived using artificial insemination?'

Tania pushed her chair back, the legs scraping harshly against the floor tiles. She jumped to her feet, her face an angry mask. 'What the hell has that to do with anything? Christ, have we no privacy left?'

Maidment hurried to her side and put his arm round

415

her. She turned to him, clutching his shirt tight in her fist and beating it against his chest. 'Yes,' he said, holding her close, his eyes glistening. 'We longed for a child of our own. We tried.' He sighed. 'We tried for a long time. Then we had tests. It turned out I was firing blanks. So we went to a fertility clinic in Birmingham. Tania got pregnant the second time we inseminated.'

She turned a tear-stained face to Patterson. 'Paul always treated her as if she was his own daughter.'

'She was my own daughter,' he insisted. 'I never thought about it from one year's end to the next.'

'Did Jennifer know?' Patterson asked.

Maidment looked away. 'We never told her. When she was little, we planned to tell her the truth one day. But . . .'

'I decided we wouldn't tell her,' Tania said. 'There was no need. We matched the donor to Paul, so she looked a bit like him. Nobody knew but us, so it wasn't like anybody else in the family could let something slip.'

Which answered Patterson's next question. 'Thanks for being so frank,' he said.

'Why are you asking this now?' Maidment asked.

'It might have some bearing on a line of inquiry we're pursuing.'

'Christ. Could you say anything more meaningless?' Tania said. 'Go away. Please.'

Maidment followed him down the hall. 'Sorry,' he said.

'No need.'

'She's not doing well.'

'I can see that. We are doing our best, you know.'

Maidment opened the door. 'I know. What bothers her is that it might not be enough.'

Patterson nodded. 'It bothers me too. But we're not giving up, Mr Maidment. And we really are making progress.' He walked back to the car, feeling the bereaved father's eyes on him, knowing that, whatever the outcome, for Tania Maidment it would never be good enough. Patterson was sufficiently selfish to be grateful that he didn't have to live with that particular hell.

Paula was about to give up on Mike Morrison when the door finally opened. He was wearing a T-shirt and boxers and reeked of alcohol. He peered blearily at her. 'Oh, it's you,' he grunted, turning on his heel and walking back into the house.

Paula took that as an invitation and followed him into the wreckage of the living room. Empty whisky bottles were lined up along the side of one sofa. On the coffee table, seven malt whisky bottles stood in a row, the levels varying from almost full to almost empty. A smeared tumbler sat next to them. Morrison reached for the tumbler as he sat down heavily on the sofa. There was a duvet next to him and he wrapped it round his legs. The room was cold but still it smelled of stale booze and stale man. Paula tried to breathe discreetly through her mouth.

The TV screen caught her eye. In freeze-frame, Daniel and his mother were dressed in winter sports gear, mugging at the camera. In the background, snowy mountains. Morrison poured a slug of Scotch and noticed her eyeline. 'The wonders of modern technology. Brings them right back to life,' he slurred.

'This isn't a great idea, Mike,' she said gently.

He gave a cracked laugh. 'No? What else is there? I

loved my wife. I loved my boy. There's fuck all else in my life to love.'

It was hard to argue with that, Paula thought. She'd call his GP later. And she'd call his office. See if they knew who his friends were. This was pain she couldn't ignore. 'I need to ask you a question,' she said.

'What difference does it make? You can't bring them back.'

'No. But we can stop him doing this to another family.'

Morrison laughed again, the manic edge obvious. 'You think I've got it in me to care about anybody else any more?'

'Yeah, Mike. I think you do. You're a decent man, you don't want to put anybody else through this.'

Tears welled in his eyes and he dashed them away with the back of his hand. He took another drink and said, 'Fuck you, officer. Ask your question, then.'

Here goes. Time to run for cover. 'Did you and Jessica have fertility treatment when you had Daniel?'

He paused with his glass halfway to his mouth. 'How the fuck did you know that?'

'I didn't know it. That's why I'm asking you.'

He rubbed his stubbled chin. 'Jess kept having miscarriages. She was desperate for a kid. Me, I wasn't that bothered. But I could never say no to her.' He stared at the screen. 'They did tests.' His mouth curled. 'She was allergic to my sperm. Can you believe that? There was us, thinking we were perfectly suited, and all the time she couldn't tolerate me.' He swallowed more whisky. 'I'd have left it at that, but she wouldn't. So we went along to the fertility clinic at Bradfield Cross and got some other bugger's sperm.'

'That must have been hard for you.'

'You have no bloody idea. I felt like some other man had been there. Inside my wife.' He scratched his head. 'I knew in my head it wasn't like that, but in my heart it was a different story.'

'What was it like after Daniel was born?'

A tender smile lit his ravaged face. 'It was love at first sight. And I never wavered in that. But at the same time, I knew he was an alien. He wasn't flesh of my flesh. I never really knew what was going on in his head. I loved him to bits, but I never knew him.' He gestured at the TV. 'That's what I'm still trying to do. But I never will now, will I?'

There was nothing to say. Paula stood up and patted him on the shoulder. 'We'll be in touch.' She couldn't remember the last time she'd said anything emptier.

'That was the beginning of the end of my marriage,' Lara Quantick said bitterly. 'I thought a baby would bring us together. But he was like a bloody silverback gorilla. He hated Niall because he was another man's child in his eyes. Plus it was a constant reminder that he wasn't a real man. I bet he's not even sorry.'

Sam nodded, trying to look sympathetic. He'd got what he came for. Confirmation that Niall Quantick was a donor baby and that the sperm had come from Bradfield Cross Hospital. He couldn't see what else Lara Quantick might have that would be any use to him. Now he just had to get out of here before he got sucked into a complete rerun of her fucked-up marriage. He almost felt sorry for her ex. He wouldn't mind betting that every time they had a row, Lara threw his lack of manhood in his face. He stood up. He was a copper, not a counsellor, and while he was stuck in this crappy flat with her, the real action was elsewhere.

'We'll be in touch,' he said, already halfway to somewhere else in his head.

Ambrose had felt ambivalent about the government's anti-terrorist measures ever since they'd been introduced. The policeman applauded anything that gave them the powers to make the streets safer. But the black man was made uneasy by anything that made it easier to isolate and target minorities. This lot were supposed to be the left, but they were capable of some pretty repressive stuff. Who knew how the new rules might be applied under a regime that really didn't care much for civil liberties. Look how much damage had been done to the US in the Bush years. And they had way more checks and balances than the UK.

But he had to admit there were some aspects of the legislation that made his job a lot easier. OK, sometimes you had to stretch a point and make somebody out to be a lot more dangerous than they were, but you could get all sorts of information these days that used to take a lot of time and more evidence than was often readily available. Take air passenger lists. It used to be a nightmare getting airlines to give you access to the names of the people who had flown on any individual plane. Warrants had to be obtained from magistrates who didn't always agree that your need to know was stronger than the airline's right to customer confidentiality. Then you had to hope the passenger list still existed.

But now, it was easy. You flew, you were in the security services computer system. And the likes of Ambrose could generally find a friendly officer who totally understood that catching killers was a lot more important than some notional idea of personal privacy. Especially if you were the kind of copper who made a point of making friends rather than enemies.

So it was that Monday morning that Ambrose received a text from an unidentified caller which simply said, Ur pal misd his plane. Didn't make another flite.

Ambrose congratulated himself on his instincts. He'd covered a lot of ground the day before. There had been a couple of possibles on his list by the end of play. But he'd had a gut feeling about the computer security geek, especially when his girlfriend had shown them the extent of their equipment. If anyone could have performed the cyber stalking evident in this case, it was Warren Davy. And whatever his girlfriend believed, Warren Davy wasn't in Malta. He was out there somewhere, a serial killer on a roll.

Wherever he was, Ambrose bet he was grooming his next victim.

After the frustration of the past few days, Carol felt almost exhilarated at the way information was coming at her. Connections were starting to emerge, and she felt the thrill of the hunter who is finally getting the scent of their prey. The DNA breakthrough had turned everything on its head, confirming Tony's earlier conclusion that these were not sexual homicides.

Now they knew for certain that all four victims had

been born as a result of artificial insemination. Three of the mothers had been treated at Bradfield Cross Hospital's sub-fertility unit, the fourth at a private clinic in Birmingham. Her next stop should be the clinic here in Bradfield. She had no idea what they could tell her. Her knowledge of the law around donor sperm was scant, but she did know that back when these babies had been made, the donations had been anonymous.

She was about to call Paula to get her coat on and join her when the phone rang. 'Stuart Patterson here,' he said before she could even identify herself. 'I think Alvin's come up with a suspect.'

'That's your sergeant, right? The one that's over in Manchester?'

'That's right. He was on the knocker yesterday, trying to make something out of the car registrations we got. He had a couple of possibles, but one of them, his girlfriend, who is also his business partner, she said he's in Malta, but he's not. And he's perfect for it. They've got a company, DPS, that deals in computer security and data storage—'

'Slow down, Stuart.' Carol's head was spinning as she tried to process his garbled sentences. 'What's Malta got to do with it?'

'Sorry, sorry. I'm just . . . this feels like the first proper break, you know? Everything coming together – the profiling, the back-to-basics door-knocking coppering and the technology – and giving us what we need.' She could hear him take a deep breath. 'Right. One of the cars that came into Worcester the day Jennifer was killed was a Toyota Verso registered to a guy called Warren Davy. He's a partner in a computer security company, DPS. When Alvin went to his place, it turned out he's not been at home for over a week. According to his girlfriend, he flew out to Malta to set up a security system for a client. But when Alvin checked the passenger manifests, he found that Davy hadn't flown on the flight he was ticketed for. And he didn't take another flight instead. Davy went off the map after Jennifer was killed but before the three boys. He told his girlfriend the lie about Malta to buy himself freedom to commit the other murders.'

'What about the girlfriend? Does Alvin think she knows what's going on?'

'Clueless, he reckons. She's supposed to get Davy to call Alvin next time he checks in. But so far, he's not been in touch.'

'You think he will be?'

'Depends how clever he thinks he is. He might reckon he's smart enough to bluff us.' Patterson still sounded excited. She knew how he felt but was better at hiding it. A shadow fell across her doorway and she saw Stacey hovering. She held up two fingers, indicating she was almost done.

'You think we should go public with this?' Patterson was saying. 'Put out his photo, tell people to call him in? Should we hit the farm where he lives with the girlfriend? See what we can find there?'

That was one she wanted to run past Tony. Her instincts were to hold back, but without any clue as to when he planned to strike next, it was a high-risk strategy. 'Can I get back to you on that, Stuart? I don't want us to make a snap decision. I'll call you later. Tell Alvin that's brilliant work.'

Carol ran a hand through her hair and summoned Stacey in. 'Nothing for days, then it's mayhem on steroids,' she said. 'I need you to pull everything you can off the grid about a man called Warren Davy who runs a computer security firm called DPS. I want everything. Credit details, mobile phone records.'

Stacey's eyebrows rose. 'I know Warren Davy.'

Shocked, Carol said, 'You know him? How?'

'Well, when I say know, I mean cyber-know. He's a security expert. He's approached me a couple of times about software apps. We've chatted online. He's very good.' She looked worried. 'Is he our suspect?'

'Is that a problem for you?'

Stacey shook her head but still looked troubled. 'It's not a problem in the sense of a conflict of interest. He's not a friend, he's not someone I have a business relationship with . . . It's just that, if he doesn't want to be found, it'll be hard to find him.'

'Great. That's all I need,' Carol groaned.

Stacey's face cleared. 'I'll consider it a personal challenge. The one thing I have going for me is that he doesn't know me as a cop. He thinks I'm just another geek. If he thought he was going up against me, he'd be taking every precaution he could think of, but if he thinks he's just dealing with standard plod, he might be a bit careless. I'll get right on to it. But there's something else I wanted to run past you.'

It was always worth paying attention when Stacey took the time to talk. 'I'm listening.'

'I've been doing some tinkering,' she said. 'The codes that the RigMarole people very kindly handed over have let me in the back door of their system. It would be quite easy for me to set up a global C&A on Rig.'

'Can you translate that?' Carol said. 'I thought C&A was a chain of European department stores.'

'Capture and analyse. You tell the server to look for a particular combination of keystrokes and then set up elimination criteria. I could set it up to deliver me anyone whose username is a double letter. Then we could manually look at what they're saying. We might be able to identify the next targets that way and stake them out. Then we'd be able to catch the killer in the act.'

Carol looked dubious. 'Could that really work?'

'The computer end of it is perfectly feasible. I can't speak for what will happen once you go live into the field with it. It's a lot of work. But I think it's worth trying.'

Carol thought for a moment then made her decision. 'OK. Do it. But Warren Davy is a priority. If you can ping his mobile and locate him that way, that would be a huge bonus.'

'Abracadabra,' Stacey said as she left. Carol could have sworn there was irony there.

CHAPTER 37

Alvin Ambrose was late. Paula had been detailed to meet him and bring him up to speed, but he'd just called to say he had a flat tyre and would be another forty minutes at least. She'd got his message in the car park at Bradfield Cross, just as she and Carol were heading back from a frustrating meeting with the consultant in charge of fertility services. 'I'm going to talk to Blake,' Carol said. 'I need him to authorise the surveillance if Stacey comes up with a potential victim. Why don't you grab something to eat before you meet up with DS Ambrose? The way things are going today, it might be your last chance.'

Paula knew how to make that an even better idea. She texted Elinor's pager: In Strbks. Lattes r on me. She wasn't holding her breath, but it would be more fun if she didn't have to eat alone. She bought two coffees and a panini and sat by the window. Back to the hospital, though. She didn't want to look pitifully eager.

Eleven minutes later – not that she was counting – Elinor appeared in a flurry of white coat and black jeans. 'I've only got twenty minutes,' she said, leaning down to give Paula a warm kiss on the cheek.

'I've not got much more than that myself.' She pushed one of the lattes towards Elinor. 'I didn't know if you wanted anything to eat.'

'I'm OK. How's your day been?'

'Up and down. I was in the office till four, then back at seven. Your brainwave with the DNA has really given us a new angle. Thanks.' She grinned. 'Even if I did get the piss taken out of me mercilessly.'

'Just as well Stacey was there to alibi us,' Elinor said drily.

'In spite of the piss-taking, I did get to be the star of the morning briefing. Which was nice, because it's been downhill since then.' She told Elinor about her encounter with Mike Morrison.

'I can't imagine how distraught he must be,' Elinor said. 'How do you climb back from losing your son like that, then your wife too?'

Paula sighed. 'It's amazing what you can recover from.'

Elinor gave her a shrewd look. 'You can tell me about it one of these days.'

Paula smiled. 'It's a pity not all doctors are as accommodating as you.'

'Meaning what?' Elinor stirred her coffee and gave Paula a speculative look.

Paula chuckled. 'Not like that. We've just had an exasperating encounter with your Mrs Levinson.'

Elinor made a face of horror. 'Not *my* Mrs Levinson.

Thankfully I've managed to avoid her team. She makes Mr Denby look humble. You know what they say about fertility specialists?' Paula shook her head. 'All doctors like to think they're God, but fertility doctors know they're God. The rest of us only have power over death. Mrs Levinson and her cronies have the power to bestow life. And don't they know it.'

'I think that only explains part of why she was so unhelpful,' Paula said. 'I do actually think in this case she does have the law on her side.'

'What were you after?'

'Well, we established that all four of our victims are blood relatives. Half-siblings, probably. In three cases, the mothers were inseminated here at Bradfield Cross. We wanted to know how we could find out who the donor was.'

Elinor pursed her mouth into an O and drew her breath in sharply. 'You guys have no fear, do you?'

'We try to hide it.'

'And she told you there was no way you could find that out?'

'That's right. Jordan threatened her with a court order and she just laughed. I tell you, I've never seen anybody do that to Carol Jordan before.'

'She's right, though. A court order would be useless. Because even Mrs Levinson doesn't have access to that information. Back when everything was anonymous, a donation was given a unique identifying number. The only place where the number and the ID can be matched is on the database of the Human Fertilisation and Embryology Authority. It's kept on a standalone computer. Even if Stacey hacked the HFEA, she couldn't get at it. You'd have to be physically present. You'd actually have to hack the machine itself.'

'How do you know this stuff?' Paula asked. 'You just said you've never worked for Mrs Levinson.'

'I wrote a dissertation about medical information sharing in a digital age for my BSc,' Elinor said. 'I'm an ambitious junior doctor. I'm addicted to qualifications.'

'There must be a back-up,' Paula said. 'You wouldn't rely on just one computer for that.'

'I'm sure there must be. But I have no idea where it is and I don't imagine anyone outside the ICT team at the HFEA would know.' Elinor stirred her coffee thoughtfully.

'She could have told us all that, but she didn't,' Paula complained. 'She just sent us off with a flea in our ear. She wouldn't even tell us how the same sperm ended up in Birmingham.' Paula bit into her panini savagely.

'I can tell you that. It's no big secret. We've got guidelines that say we should avoid producing more than ten live births from the same donor. The reason being that you don't want to compromise the gene pool with hundreds of kids running around with the same gametes. But you don't necessarily want ten kids of approximately the same age and with the same father in the same town. Because the psychologists tell us we're more likely to fall in love with an unknown sibling than a stranger.'

'Really? That's wild.'

'Wild but true. So if you've got a particularly fertile donation, it's common after half a dozen successful pregnancies to swap sperm with a clinic in another city. I imagine that's what happened here.'

'That makes sense.' Paula gave Elinor a frank look. 'You're doing quite a job of making yourself indispensable.'

'What I live for.' She was still looking pensive. 'I know this might sound a little off the wall . . . But are you guys thinking that the sperm donor might be the killer?'

Wondering where she was going with this, Paula said, 'Our profiler thinks that's a possibility.'

'I don't know much about these things, but it seems to me that someone who's going around killing people might have come to your attention before,' Elinor said. 'If he has, wouldn't he be on the national DNA database?'

'I suppose so,' Paula said. 'But their DNA is different.'

'I know. But I vaguely remember reading about a cold case where they got the killer after twenty years because his nephew was convicted of something and the database flagged it up.' Elinor pulled out her iPhone and connected to the internet, turning the screen so they could both see it.

'So how do you know this? Another dissertation?' Paula teased as Elinor navigated to Google and typed dna murder relative cold case into the search terms box.

'Dustbin mind. I have a desperate accumulation of trivia in my head. I'm your girl on pub quiz night.' She scrolled through the results. 'There, that's it.'

'"Man convicted fourteen years after crime by relative's DNA sample,"' Paula read. As she read on, she grinned. 'Good to see you're not infallible.'

'So it was fourteen years, not twenty.'

'And rape, not murder,' Paula said. 'But I take your point.' She finished her coffee and stood up. 'Now I have to go and talk to Stacey.' She glanced at her watch. 'And meet a colleague from Worcester.'

Elinor walked her to the door. 'My twenty minutes are up too. Thank you.'

'What? For mercilessly picking your brains?'

'For getting me off the ward and reminding me there's life out here.' She leaned into Paula and kissed her, warm breath tickling her ear. 'Go and catch your killer. I have plans for you when this is all over.'

A delicious shiver unsettled Paula. 'There's an incentive, if I ever heard one.'

When Carol finally made it back to her squad room, she found Tony sitting in the visitor's chair in her office. He was leaning back, fingers interlocked behind his head and feet on the wastepaper bin, eyes closed. 'I'm glad someone's got time for a nap round here,' she said, shrugging off her coat and kicking off her shoes. She snapped the blinds closed, opened her desk drawer and took out a miniature of vodka.

Tony straightened up. 'I was thinking, not napping.' He watched her open the vodka, look at him, then screw the cap back on and throw it back in the drawer. She glared at him and he held his hands up in a gesture of appeasement. 'I didn't say a word,' he protested.

'You didn't have to. You can do sanctimonious without moving an eyebrow.'

'How did it go with Blake?'

'No secrets round here, are there?' Carol fell into her chair. 'This job sometimes offers moments of pure pleasure. It was a beautiful thing to watch him wrestle between his smouldering desire to save money and his burning desire to kick off his time here with a brilliant coup. Even more beautiful because he made the right decision. If we can identify the next victim, we get to go with full surveillance.'

'Well done. I also hear that DS Ambrose has found us a suspect.'

Carol had had more time to think about Patterson's phone call. 'Well, he's found a possibility. It's based on a lot of assumptions. First, that Fiona Cameron's geographic profile is on the money. Second, that the killer used his own vehicle. And third, that Warren Davy isn't just off having a jolly with his mistress.'

'Good points, all of them. But I still think Davy's a strong possible. If Stacey can identify the next victim, that's likely to be a more definite way to go. Do we know anything about Davy yet?'

Carol brought her monitor to life and clicked on her message queue. There was a brief from Stacey. 'He's got no form. He's got one credit card which he seems to use for business only. No store cards. No loyalty cards. She says it's a typical profile for someone in his field. He knows how easy it is to breach security so he keeps his presence to a minimum. His phone hasn't been switched on for days. The last time it was on was when Seth disappeared on Central Station. And it pinged the nearest tower to . . . Care to guess?'

'Central Station,' Tony said.

'Got it in one. So he's definitely elusive.'

'Has anyone spoken to the girlfriend about him?'

Carol shook her head. 'I don't want to spook her into

432

warning him off. He's perfectly placed to fake or steal an identity. If he chose to run now, we'd struggle to find him. He could go to ground anywhere. Here or abroad.'

Tony shook his head. 'He's not going to disappear. He's got a mission and he's not going to stop until he's finished. Unless we stop him, that is.'

'So what's his mission?'

Tony jumped out of the chair and began to pace in the confines of the office. 'He thinks he's the bad seed. Something's happened to fill him with fear and self-hatred. Something that he thinks is passed on through the blood. I don't think it's as straightforward as a medical condition, although that is possible. But he's determined to weed out the bad seed. To be the end of the line. He's going to kill all his biological children. And then he's going to kill himself.'

Carol stared at him, horrified. 'How many?'

'I don't know. Can we find out?'

'Apparently not. According to the extremely unhelpful consultant at Bradfield Cross, all information about anonymous donors is totally off limits. So bloody off limits that, frankly, you wonder why they keep it. If they're never going to use it, why not just destroy it? Then nobody could ever abuse it.' Carol took the vodka from her desk drawer again. She also took out a small can of tonic water. She poured them both into the empty water glass on her desk. 'You want a drink?' she said defiantly.

'Oh no, not me. I'm high enough with all that's buzzing in my brain right now. Because there's something not quite right with this picture,' he said.

'But it makes sense of everything we know. I can't

think of another theory that fits the facts.' She sipped her drink and felt some of the tension in her neck start to ease.

'Neither can I. But that doesn't mean I'm right.' He turned sharply and stopped by her desk. 'If this information's so hard to get hold of, how did he find it out? And what happened to set him off on this crusade? He's spent ages grooming his victims. How has he kept it all together?'

'Maybe he hasn't. Maybe his girlfriend's been covering his back at work.' She knocked back the rest of her drink and sighed in satisfaction. 'God, that's better.'

'I wish I could talk to her,' he muttered.

'I know. But we have to hang fire till we see what Stacey can do.'

'I appreciate that. But I've almost never come across a serial offender who's had a sustained emotional relationship. If we're right about Warren Davy, there are so many questions she could answer. So many insights she could give us.' He sighed.

'You'll get your chance.'

Tony grinned. 'I'll be like a kid in a sweet shop.'

Carol shook her head, amused. 'You're weird.'

'I don't know how you can say that when there are people like Warren Davy out there. Compared to him, I'm normality itself.'

She laughed out loud. 'I wouldn't bank on it, Tony.'

CHAPTER 38

Alvin Ambrose felt at home in the MIT squad room right from the start. These were the kind of cops he understood. Paula McIntyre had sorted him out with a desk, a phone, a computer and a coffee. Everyone who had passed through had stopped to introduce themselves, even the little Chinese woman in the corner who seemed to be hard-wired to her computer system.

He also relished the sense of being at the heart of the operation. The only problem was that there wasn't really much for him to do there. Everyone was working their way through piles of paper or screens of data, but he knew they were only keeping busy. Everyone was on pins, waiting for Stacey to emerge from behind her barricade of screens with the motherlode.

With nothing else to occupy him, he thought he might as well check his email. Humming under his breath, he waited for the screen to load. The music stopped halfway through a bar as he realised what he was looking at. The second item in his inbox was: davywar1@gmail.com: how can i help?

Ambrose swallowed hard. He wasn't sure what to do. He wanted to open the email, but Stacey and her ilk had warned him so thoroughly about the destructive potential of email that he didn't want to take any chances. Still, he had an expert on the spot. He walked over to Stacey's corner and waited while her fingers flew and clicked. After a minute or so, she looked up. 'Did you want something?'

'I think I've got an email from Warren Davy,' he said. 'It's on my computer.'

Stacey looked at him as if he was a little slow. 'Which account?'

'My police one. Aambrose@westmerciapolice.org.'

'Go and shut it down on your screen, please,' she said. 'Then come back and sign in here.'

By the time he came back, she had the sign-in screen in front of her. She stood up and looked away while he entered his password. He suspected it was just for show. She probably had a record of every keystroke on her system. Once he was in, he stepped back and let her at the screen. She cocked her head and looked at the subject line. 'Let's go for it,' she said. 'Don't worry, I've got every virus protection known to humankind and one or two alien ones running on this system.' He wasn't entirely convinced she was joking.

The email unfurled on the central screen on the lower level. On the screen above it, a stream of numbers and letters suddenly sprang into life. But Ambrose was only interested in the message.

Hi, Detective Sergeant Ambrose

My partner, Diane Patrick, said you wanted me to contact you. Something about my car? Sorry not to phone, I'm in Malta on business and it costs an arm and a leg, plus I'm working pretty much full on so email is easier for me. If you let me know what it's all about, I will get back to you asap.

Best

Warren Davy

DPS Systems: www.dps.com

'Interesting,' Stacey said.

'Looks pretty straightforward to me,' Ambrose said.

'Except that it's not been sent from Malta.' Stacey pointed at the upper screen, which had come to rest with a very straightforward message. 'It's come from a computer owned by Bradfield City Council libraries department. He's in town, Sarge. And either he doesn't care that we know it or he's an arrogant twat who thinks we're a lot less sophisticated than he is.'

'Either way, he's probably getting ready to roll. How are you getting on with your trap?'

Stacey shrugged. 'It'll be done when it's done. These things are hard to predict.' She began to tap the keys again, her eyes flitting between screens. As Ambrose watched, she suddenly froze. Seconds ticked by and still she didn't move. He thought she'd even stopped breathing.

Then her fingers were flying over the keys, almost too fast to register. 'Gotcha, gotcha, gotcha,' she said, her voice a crescendo from whisper to shout. 'We've got him,' she yelled.

Almost before her words had died away, they were all clustered round. Carol Jordan elbowed her way through. Ambrose made room for her at the front. 'What is it, Stacey? What have you got?'

'I've got two. BB and GG. BB is on top right, GG top left. Both scrolling down to the bottom screen.'

They stood there transfixed as text unrolled before their eyes. BB was chatting to someone calling himself DirtAngel. From the sound of it, BB was setting up a meeting so they could go dirt biking the following day. He was promising to teach him the secrets of the sport. 'He's on the move tomorrow,' Carol said.

GG and his chat-mate weren't online live, but Stacey had pulled up their last chat. 'He's pretending to be a girl. He's setting up 1dagal for a makeover. After school on Thursday. Look: "Tel no1. I'l show u t bigst secrt. U'l look gr8 when we're dun." Secrets again.'

'He's playing with them,' Tony said. 'He knows their biggest secret, the one they don't know about themselves. So he teases them with the idea of secrets.'

'Who are these kids, Stacey?'

'I'm working on it,' she said absently. 'Why don't you all bugger off and leave me in peace? I'll email you all I've

438

got from the C&A. Now I need to backdoor these accounts and the less you know, the better.'

They melted away. 'She's something else,' Ambrose said to Paula.

'She's the best. She only works here for fun, you know?'

'This is her idea of fun?'

Paula chuckled. 'Oh yeah. She gets to poke her fingers into all sorts of stuff and nobody's going to be coming after her for it. But when she's not here? She's busy making millions with her own software company. Talk about secrets. She thinks nobody knows about her other life, but one time she let the name of her company slip to Sam and that was a red rag to a bull. No way he was going to stop till he'd found out every last cough and spit.' She cast a speculative look at Sam. 'God help her if he ever realises she's in love with him.' Suddenly she stopped short, her face shocked and puzzled in equal measure. 'Why am I talking to you like this?'

Tony, who had been standing behind them unnoticed, suddenly spoke. 'Because he's like you, Paula. People talk to him. The same way they do to you.'

Ambrose's laugh was a low rumble in his chest. 'It's a scary gift.'

'Don't tell Carol,' Tony said. 'She'll be recruiting you before you know it.'

Ambrose looked around the room where he already felt so at home. 'A man could do a lot worse.'

Tony studied Carol, who was talking to Kevin, her head bent over her desk. 'He could. On the other hand, you could say she deserves better than any of us.' And he walked away, completely heedless of the small sensation his words left behind.

It was definitely Stacey's day for demonstrating her value to the MIT. She'd been delighted by Paula's suggestion of searching the national DNA database for familial connections to the murdered teenagers. 'We can do it with the boys,' she said. 'Don't ask me to explain, but it doesn't work with female relatives in the same way.'

Paula backed off in mock-horror. 'Oh please, Stace. Not the scientific explanation, I'm just a simple city girl.'

But Stacey was already sending an urgent request to the database, attaching the three sets of DNA. Unusually, she followed up her email with a phone call to one of the analysts that she'd worked with before. Paula, still hovering in the background, noticed there was no small talk. If the ICT staff had needed that to make things run smoothly, there wouldn't be a functioning system in the Western world, she thought.

'Stacey Chen here, Bry. I've just emailed you three sets of data that we need checked. I need you to prioritise it. We've got a serial killer working on a tight turnaround, and this might just break it before he takes his next victim . . . Now? . . . Thanks. I owe you.' She hung up her headset and without turning said to Paula, 'He's on it. You can go and get a coffee now.'

Dismissed, Paula went back to her desk and the mountain of paper that always came with a murder inquiry. Carol and Kevin were closeted with a team that had been put together from Traffic and Western Division, planning their surveillance of Ewan McAlpine, the dirt biker. There had been a big discussion about whether they should warn the boy and have him wired. Paula had been a strenuous advocate of that approach. She knew how wrong these set-ups could go, and she wanted maximum protection for the boy, even if it posed a different set of problems. But she'd been outnumbered and overruled. Her opponents argued that a fourteen-year-old boy wasn't going to be able to carry off the subterfuge and the killer would sense a trap and abort, leaving them with nothing. They were probably right, Paula conceded. But at least her way meant the kid would have a better chance of coming out of it alive.

She pulled up the transcript of his conversations with BB on her screen and read it again. Ewan sounded like a nice kid. He made cute jokes and he didn't pick on anybody. Stacey had managed to track him down via his email account. He lived with his mum and dad near the city centre in a small enclave of Georgian houses that had somehow survived the post-war developers. His dad was a consultant urologist at Bradfield Cross, his mother a GP in one of the inner-city health centres. That was one thing about dealing with victims who were here as a result of fertility treatment – they weren't exactly skint. A couple she knew had spent the best part of twenty grand on IVF and still had nothing to show for it except a series of miscarriages. The downside was that they were dealing with the articulate middle classes, the sort of people who would gut and fillet them if anything went wrong with this operation.

Another good thing was that, thanks to Stacey's infiltration of RigMarole, they knew where Ewan was meeting BB – presumably Warren Davy. Ewan was to take the Manchester bus to Barrowden, a small village about five miles outside the Bradfield city limits. BB had arranged to meet him at the bus stop so they could go to his farm, a couple of miles away. I'l com 4 u on t quad bike, he'd said. Another enticement to a lad gagging for a bit of wildness in his very civilised city life.

'Alvin?' Stacey called. 'You got a minute?'

Ambrose strolled across to Stacey's corner, Paula in his wake. 'What is it, Stacey?' he said.

'Warren Davy's cousin? The guy with the garage? What was his name again? For some reason, I can't find your report on the system.'

Ambrose cleared his throat, looking embarrassed. 'Sorry, I forgot. I filed it with Manchester but I didn't send it to you when I got here. His name was Bill Carr.'

Stacey pointed to one of her screens. 'That's from the NDNAD. There's only one hit on our DNA. William James Carr from Manchester comes up as having a familial relationship to all three boys. Probably cousins or nephews, according to Bry.'

'Are you saying Carr's our man?' Ambrose was clearly puzzled.

'Well, he's a possible, I suppose,' Stacey said sceptically. 'But it strengthens the case against Warren Davy. If they're cousins, then it means the three victims also have a blood relationship to Davy. So what was hypothetical and circumstantial becomes more evidentially based.'

'But he's still only a possible,' Paula said. 'And we still don't know where he is.'

'Which means we still have to do the surveillance,' Ambrose said.

Stacey shrugged. 'As everyone around here delights in telling me, it always comes back to old-fashioned coppering.' She turned back to her screens. 'I better email the boss. There's nothing she likes more than another brick in the wall.'

CHAPTER 39

Ewan McAlpine woke up with the fizzle of excitement racing through his veins. Today, it was today. He was finally going to get a chance at something he'd craved for so long. By tea-time, he'd be bouncing over rough terrain on a dirt bike, a cloud of dust enveloping him as he breathed through a kerchief, like a cowboy on the range.

He'd never been allowed to do anything his mum and dad regarded as dangerous. They'd wrapped him in cotton wool all his life, like he was going to break if he so much as fell over. He could still remember the total humiliation of his first overnight school trip. He'd been eight years old and his class were staying at an outdoor pursuits centre up in the Pennines. As well as the teachers, some parents had come along to make sure there was the right ratio of adults to children. And of course, his mum had been one of them. And every time he'd been about to join in one of the activities – abseiling, climbing, kayaking or riding the zip drive, she'd intervened, stopping him from doing anything interesting. He'd spent two days on the obstacle course and the archery range. It had been God's gift to his enemies.

His mum meant well, he knew. But over the years, she'd made him the butt of endless jokes and sometimes worse. Luckily for him, his primary school had been hot on stamping out bullying and teasing. When he'd moved up to his private grammar school, he'd worked hard at being invisible. The sporty guys didn't know he existed, so they didn't notice he wasn't allowed to do anything remotely dangerous.

But still, Ewan craved the chance to do something exciting. He loved watching the extreme sports channel, and he'd worked hard over the last couple of years to get fit and build some muscle. Even his mum couldn't object to him working out in the gym his dad had set up in the cellar. All he lacked was the opportunity to use his body for anything that would push it to the limits.

Until he'd met up with BB on Rig. Lucky bugger lived on a farm where he had his own quad bike and dirt bikes. Even better, he'd chosen Ewan to be pals with. And now, tonight, he was going to get his chance to experience what he'd only fantasised about.

His mum thought he was taking part in a debating competition over in Manchester. She wouldn't expect him home till nine, which would work out perfectly. BB said he would lend him something to wear and he could shower before he left on the half past eight bus. It was all going to be perfect.

Ewan had no idea how he was going to get through the day without bursting with excitement. But he'd manage it somehow. He was good at managing his life.

A mile away, in the nearest police station to the McAlpine home, Carol was giving the surveillance crews their final briefing. There were three cars, one motorbike and an assortment of pedestrians, supported by a van where they could alter their look by changing jackets, hats, wigs and facial hair. 'It's going to be a long day,' Carol said. 'We'll mostly be able to stand down when Ewan's actually in school, but we will need someone front and back to make sure he doesn't sneak out early. There's no reason why he should – we know what the arrangements are. But the excitement might be too much for him. So we need to be alert. Any questions?'

Paula raised a hand. 'We know this killer acts fast. Are we going to move in as soon as he takes Ewan?'

'I'm not making any decisions about the take-down till we're in the thick of it,' Carol said. 'There are too many variables. Ewan is our priority, obviously. But we need to make sure we actually have evidence of abduction. Now, if we're all ready, we need to move into position. Following him to school will give us the chance to fix his appearance in our minds, as well as being a useful rehearsal. So, let's do it. And good luck, everybody.'

The school run presented no problems. Ewan's mother's Audi was sandwiched between surveillance cars, with the van bringing up the rear. Mrs McAlpine dropped him on a corner about a quarter of a mile from the school and two of the walkers picked him up from there. They left three officers on watch – two on foot, one in a car – then went back to the station. Waiting around was always the hardest. Some played cards, some read, some put their heads on their arms and slept. By the time Tony turned up at half past three, they were all ready for some action.

'I wasn't expecting to see you,' Carol said.

'I like to keep you on your toes.'

'You're staying in the control van with me,' she said, steering him away from the rest of the team.

'Perfect. I'm not trying to make your life more difficult,' he said. 'I just thought I might be able to help. You know – if you have to make difficult choices of when to intervene and when to sit tight. I'm quite good at this psychology stuff.' He gave her the cute little-boy smile that always irritated and amused her in equal measure. 'You might as well take advantage of my presence. After all, the more use I am to you, the easier your argument with Blake the next time he wants you to work with Tim Parker.'

'Are they all as crap as him?' Carol asked.

Tony perched on a desk. 'No. A couple of them have got real talent. One or two others are reasonably competent. And then there's a few who learned all the prescriptive stuff, but they've got no insight, no empathy. And those are unteachable. You've either got it or you haven't. When you do this for real all the time, if you've got the empathy and the insight, you should become a clinician. If you haven't, you go down the academic route.' He shrugged. 'Tim's got room for improvement, but he's never going to be brilliant. You just got really unlucky. If Blake pulls this on you again, don't let anybody else do the choosing. I've got a couple of names I'll give you that'll do a decent job for you.'

'Not as good as you, though.'

'I won't argue with that. But I might not always be around, Carol.' He sounded serious and it frightened her. She didn't really know what had happened to him in Worcester, not on the inside. But he'd been in a strange frame of mind ever since he got back. Carol didn't like what she couldn't understand, and she didn't understand this.

So she made a joke out of it. 'Aren't you a bit young to be retiring? Or have you been lying about your age all these years?'

He chuckled. 'I'm not the sort who retires. I'll be tottering around on my walking frame going, "You're looking for a white male, twenty-five to forty, who had difficulty in forming relationships." And some bright young DCI will still think I'm the bee's knees.'

'Well, that'll be a novel experience for you,' she said tartly. She stepped away and raised her voice. 'Right, everybody. Time to get into position.' She turned back to Tony. 'Did you hear that we've tied Warren Davy in to the victims? The NDNAD came up with a familial hit on Bill Carr, the cousin who fronts up as Davy's mailing address.'

'That's good to know. It's always a relief when us profilers have sent you barking up the right tree. I definitely owe Fiona Cameron a big drink now.'

They walked towards the door together. 'You never thought of doing the geographic profiling? As an extra string to your bow?'

He shook his head. 'Number crunching? I'd be so bad at

it, Carol. I'd spend all my time arguing with the computer. It's bad enough that I talk to myself, without bringing inanimate objects into the equation.'

Ewan's journey to the bus stop was uneventful. He showed no sign of having noticed any of the watchers. Two of them boarded the bus with him – a middle-aged woman in a raincoat and a young man with a leather jacket and a scarlet baseball cap pulled low over his face. Carol made a phone call as the bus drew away. There were two detectives already in Barrowden. One would catch the bus there, the other would narrowly miss it and hang around studying the timetable in the shelter. They assured her they were both in place and there was no sign of life in the village apart from two old men playing dominoes in the pub.

'This isn't going to be easy,' Carol said to Tony. 'I took a recce out there last night and it's like a bloody ghost town. Four streets, a village shop that shuts at six o'clock and a pub that you wouldn't use if there was another option. We're going to have to hang well back.'

'Are you going to put more walkers on the ground?'

'No. We've got the two on the bus, they'll be getting off at Barrowden. She's going to the pub, he's going to stop and chat to the bus-misser. Any more than that and it starts to look suspicious. We've also put a camera in the ivy on the Wesleyan chapel.' She pointed behind him. He turned to see a monochrome monitor. It showed a plexiglass bus shelter from behind and the gable end of the pub. Apart from the man standing in the bus shelter there was no sign of life.

'Are you expecting Davy on a quad bike, like he said on Rig?'

'I think he'll be in a car. He'll want him enclosed.'

They didn't speak as the van negotiated the narrow lanes. They were out of sight of the bus but the three technicians in the van were in constant voice contact with the followers. At last, Johnny, the lead techie, turned to Carol and said, 'The bus is coming into Barrowden.' Carol and Tony peered at the monitor and saw the bus approach the stop.

They were on the outskirts of the village now and the driver pulled off the road into a private driveway. 'I arranged this yesterday,' Carol said. 'We're going to sit here and watch and listen.'

The bus came to a halt. Ewan politely let the woman descend, then he followed. The man in the baseball cap bent down to tie his shoelace; the man in the bus shelter boarded the bus. Ewan looked around, curious rather than anxious. He checked his watch and moved away from the bus stop, coming to a halt halfway between the shelter and the pub, where he couldn't be missed. The woman bustled into the pub and the bus pulled away. As it picked up speed, a man came running down from one of the two side streets. Seeing the bus disappear, he stopped, hands on knees, breathing heavily. The man in the baseball cap went over to him, clearly a friend. They stood chatting, then drifted back to the bus stop where they had an animated discussion focused on the bus timetable.

Less than a minute passed, then a dark-coloured Volvo estate car nosed into the village from the Manchester direction. It was driving slowly, crawling past the village green and the bus stop. It performed a U-turn outside the pub and pulled up alongside Ewan.

'It's him,' Carol said, her voice grim.

Johnny pulled one earpiece away from his head. 'It's a woman driving,' he said.

'What?'

'A woman.' He clamped the earpiece back in place.

Carol looked at Tony. 'A woman? You never said anything about a woman.'

He spread his hands, as mystified as she was. On the screen, Ewan had moved forward and was leaning into the open passenger window of the car.

Johnny spoke again. 'She's saying something about BB's quad bike being broken . . . She's BB's mum, come to pick him up . . .'

'He's getting in,' Carol said. 'Phase two, Johnny, tell them.'

'Dark-coloured Volvo estate heading in Manchester direction from village. First letters of the reg are MM07. Can't get the rest yet. Walkers, to the van.'

And they were back on the road. Being stuck so far back was frustrating, but Johnny gave them regular updates. 'Heading steady towards Manc . . . Tango lima two behind . . . Motorbike coming up in rear, overtaking tango lima two, making it look dodgy . . . Motorbike in front now. Definitely a woman driving . . . The lad's drinking something out of a can . . . Junction coming up . . . Bike's gone straight on, Volvo's turned left without signalling. Tango lima two going right, tango lima three picking up . . . We're skirting the city, heading south . . . Bike's back in behind tango lima three.'

'It looks like we're going to Davy's farm,' Carol said. 'Where he's not supposed to have been since a week past Friday.'

'Maybe the girlfriend's a better liar than Ambrose realised,' Tony said. 'Presuming that's who's driving.'

'Tell tango lima two to overtake. He can lead us past Davy's farm and wait on the far side. Tango lima four to be in pole follow,' Carol ordered.

In twenty minutes, they were sure of the destination. The single-track road they were travelling on led to DPS's headquarters and not much else. 'I need tango lima three and the bike to hang back. Remember, Ambrose said the entire perimeter was camera covered. We want to stay out of range for now. Tango lima four to carry on past, join up with two a mile past the farm.'

They pulled up behind the motorbike as Johnny said, 'The Volvo's turned in to the gate . . . Tango lima three's out of range of their cameras he thinks. He's out of his vehicle, on the roof . . . He's got his binocs out. He can see the Volvo pulling up right by the farmhouse . . . The woman's out . . . Passenger door open, he thinks . . . Farmhouse door open. He can't see anyone, she must be dragging the kid inside . . . The woman's back outside, closing the passenger door, back in the car, moving it across the yard, blocking a barn door . . . She's walking back to the house . . . Inside. Door shut.' Johnny looked at Carol. 'Abductions R Us, I'd say.'

Carol opened the back door of the van and dropped to the ground, followed by Tony. 'All we've got is abduction,' she said. 'We don't know whether Warren's in there or if he's on his way.'

'He could have been there when Ambrose visited,' Tony said. 'He didn't search the place, did he?'

'No. And there was no point in putting the place under surveillance. With their security, we couldn't get close enough without being spotted. And there's miles of moor behind them. Someone who knew the terrain could easily come in under cover of darkness.' The more she spoke, the more unprepared Carol felt. 'But we do know he was in Bradfield yesterday morning because he sent Ambrose that email from the library.'

'You've got to go in, Carol. We know this killer doesn't hang about. The boy's already unconscious. If Warren is in there, he'll be wrapping his head in polythene right now. You can't afford to let this boy die. You won't forgive yourself. And Paula will probably kill you,' he added, not an atom of levity in his tone.

She nodded. 'You're right.' She leaned back in the van and shouted, 'Wagons roll, Johnny. Everybody to the gate now.' She jumped back into the nondescript white van, giving Tony a hand up. They pulled out ahead of the car and bike and made it to the gate first. Carol climbed out and went to the intercom. 'Police. Open up,' she shouted. 'I'm going to count to three . . . One . . . two . . .' The heavy gates slowly began to swing open. Carol jogged up the margin of the drive. The van, followed by the rest of the vehicles, drove slowly alongside her.

They abandoned their vehicles in the yard and swarmed towards the farmhouse. Carol led the way, throwing the door back. She stopped on the threshold, taking it all in. Ewan McAlpine lay on a plastic sheet in the middle of the tiled floor, unconscious but still breathing. On the table was a heavy-duty transparent polythene sack, a roll of packing tape and a scalpel. Head in her hands, a woman was sitting at the table, sobbing convulsively. 'I'm so, so sorry,' she wailed. 'So, so sorry.'

CHAPTER 40

Tony and Carol were both totally focused on the scene being played out on the other side of the two-way mirror. It had taken a while to get back from the DPS farm to Bradfield Police HQ. First they'd had to wait for the ambulance and the paramedics to confirm that Ewan McAlpine was well enough to be moved to Bradfield Cross under police guard. Then they'd had to wait for Diane Patrick's hysterics to subside. Once they'd booked her into custody, she recovered herself enough to ask for a solicitor. All of this had given Carol and Tony time to plan the interview.

'I think you should let Paula lead off,' Tony had said without waiting to be asked.

'It should be me, I'm the SIO. It gives status to the interview. Which unsettles people whether they're innocent or guilty as hell.' Carol opened her office door and shouted, 'Someone, anyone . . . We need coffee in here.'

Tony started pacing. 'It's precisely because you're the SIO that you should back off. Diane Patrick has clearly played a role in these crimes. She may have been coerced. But she may have been an active participant. If she was, then she's going to be pissed off at not being taken seriously enough to be interviewed by the boss. And pissed off is good. You know that. We like them pissed off. It makes them more likely to lose at least some of the plot.'

'Believe me, I can find other ways to piss her off,' Carol said.

'And if she's been coerced, she'll be much more likely to respond to someone she doesn't see as a threat. In other words, a junior officer. It's a win-win, letting Paula take first crack at her. I'm not saying you won't get your turn. But let Paula go first.'

'Will you sit down? You're making me crazy, storming up and down in this tiny space,' Carol fumed.

He dropped into the nearest chair. 'It helps me think.'

A knock on the door. 'Coffee,' Kevin said.

Carol opened the door, took the two mugs from him and used her hip to close it behind her. 'I'll put the earpiece in. You can keep me on track.'

'You know there's nobody better at this than Paula.' He knew he was playing with fire, but it had to be said.

'Are you saying she's a better interviewer than me?' She thrust the coffee at him. He thought she was inches away from having thrown it. He'd seldom seen her this wound up over an arrest. He assumed it was because Warren Davy was still out there in the wind.

'This isn't a pissing contest, and you know it,' he said. 'You've got no grounds for doubting your professional capability. Your leadership of this team made this result possible. It works because you let them do what they're good at, even when it's part of your skill set.'

'I don't understand,' she said, brows drawn down in a mulish stare.

'Take Sam,' he said. 'You know he's a maverick. You know he doesn't like to share because he thinks he can do whatever it is better than anyone else. He'll stab people in the back if he thinks it will further his career, but only when it doesn't jeopardise the investigation. A lot of SIOs would have canned Sam because he's not a team player. But you keep him close. You let him play to his strengths.' He paused, an 'Am I right?' expression on his face.

'Of course I do. He's got tremendous ability.'

'That's only part of the reason. The other part is that you see something of yourself in him. Something of the early Carol Jordan, the scrapper who hadn't risen to her natural level yet. You do it with all of them.' He pulled a face. 'Well, maybe not Stacey. But you know Paula's a great interviewer. You know it because the great interviewer in you recognises it in her. So let her do it, Carol.'

He saw the doubt on her face. 'Sometimes I feel I do all the graft round here and get none of the fun,' she complained.

He smiled. 'I love a good bit of self-pity. That's very generous of you. Besides, if it hadn't been for the new girlfriend being in the right place at the right time with the right knowledge, this might have taken us a lot longer to put together. Paula's earned her moment in the sun.'

Carol glared at him. 'I hate it when you make me behave well.'

'You'll respect yourself in the morning, though.' He drank some coffee and made a face. 'Come on, let's go and watch Paula do her thing.'

Paula kept Diane Patrick and her solicitor waiting for almost twenty minutes. She made the decision when she discovered the woman's lawyer was Bronwen Scott, the doyenne of Bradfield's criminal solicitors. Scott had earned her reputation by winning reprieves for the guilty as well as clearing the innocent so she was never going to be loved by the police. But she liked to rub their noses in her successes. Carol made no secret of her loathing for Scott, and her team cheerfully backed her to the hilt.

The disparity between the two women opposite Paula could hardly have been greater. Scott was immaculate in a suit whose cut and fabric screamed the opposite of state-funded legal aid. She'd always had a haughty expression, but these days her face hardly seemed to move at all. Paula suspected Botox or a face lift that had ended up a fraction too tight. Diane Patrick, by contrast, was dishevelled and ravaged by her earlier tears. Her hair was chaotic, her dark eyes puffy and bloodshot. She looked at Paula with piteous eyes, lower lip quivering. Paula remained unmoved by the pair of them.

She made sure Diane was cautioned on tape and then opened her folder. 'You abducted and drugged a fourteen-year-old boy this evening, Diane. When we walked into the house where you live with your partner Warren Davy, we found you alone with Ewan McAlpine. He was unconscious. On the table in front of you were a transparent polythene sack, a roll of packing tape and a scalpel—'

'Are we going to get to a question any time soon? We know all this. You have given us disclosure,' Scott interrupted.

Paula refused to let herself be needled. 'I'm just reminding your client of the seriousness of her position. As I was saying. The things on the table – they were identical to the paraphernalia of four murders committed against fourteen-year-olds in the past two weeks. It's hard not to draw the inference that you were about to murder Ewan McAlpine.'

Diane Patrick's eyes opened as wide as her swollen lids would allow. She looked horrified. 'I wasn't. No.' Her voice rose in panic. 'I never killed anybody. You've got to believe me. It was Warren. I was waiting for Warren. He made me do it.' She let out a terrible racking sob. 'I hate myself, I wish I was dead.' She buried her face in her hands.

Paula waited. Eventually Diane raised her head, tears streaking her cheeks. 'Is it your contention that Warren Davy murdered Jennifer Maidment, Daniel Morrison, Seth Viner and Niall Quantick? And that he planned to murder Ewan McAlpine.'

Diane gulped and hiccupped. Then she nodded. 'Yes. He killed them all. He made me help. He said he'd kill me if I didn't do what he told me.'

'And you believed him?' Paula deliberately sounded incredulous.

Diane looked at her as if she was mad. 'Of course I believed him. He already killed my baby. Why would I not believe him?'

'He killed your baby? When did this happen?'

Diane shuddered. 'Last year. She was just hours old.' A long sigh seemed to liberate her into words. 'He'd virtually kept me prisoner for the last few weeks of the pregnancy. I gave birth at home. He said there was no need for hospital, women had been doing it at home for generations. And he was right. It was OK. Jodie, I called her. It was the best thing that ever happened to me. It was all I'd ever wanted. And then he took her away and put his hand over her mouth and nose till she stopped breathing.' Her words began to jerk like a DJ scratching a record. She wrapped her arms round herself. 'He killed her. He killed her right in front of me.' She began rocking back and forth, her fingers clawing at her upper arms.

Again, Paula just sat out the storm. She knew Scott wanted this to end but she wanted the reason to be Paula. And Paula was determined to give the lawyer no excuse. 'Why would he do that?' she said once Diane was composed again.

'He did a bad thing. I don't know what it was. He couldn't tell me. It was something to do with a client's data. He did something and somebody died.' She seemed to be looking inward, as if reliving some scene in her memory. 'And something inside him seemed to come loose.' She met Paula's steady gaze. 'I know that sounds weird, but that's what it was like. He kept talking about carrying evil inside him like a virus. And he said my Jodie couldn't live to carry his virus to the next generation. He was crying when he did it.' She put her hand to her mouth and began rocking again.

Paula had been prepared for Diane to blame it all on her partner, particularly since he'd slipped through the net and wasn't there to present his version of events. She'd started from a position of scepticism, but as the interview proceeded her doubts were shrinking. There was something horribly convincing about Diane Patrick's narrative. And she was certainly in a state. It was hard to imagine how she could be faking this come-apart. 'I'm sorry for your loss,' she said. 'But here's where you're losing me. How did he go from killing his own child to murdering these teenagers?'

Diane Patrick's face registered naked astonishment. It was so blatant that it cast doubt over the rest of what Paula had seen. 'Because they were his children too. You didn't know?'

'How could we know?' Paula said. 'We knew they were connected by the same sperm donor, but we had no way of finding out it was Warren. Nobody gets access to that information. Not even police officers with a warrant.'

Diane stared at her, apparently lost for words.

Paula smiled. 'Which kind of begs the question. How did Warren find out who they were?'

There was a long silence. Paula would have bet Diane was weighing up whether a lie was going to be caught out. At last, she spoke. Slowly, as if feeling her way. 'He forced me into it. He threatened to kill me.'

'I got that, yes. He killed your baby then he threatened you. It didn't occur to you that you could escape?'

Diane gave a bitter little laugh. 'It's obvious you know nothing about the way the modern world works. When it comes to cyberspace, Warren is one of the masters of the universe. I could maybe run, but I could never hide. He'd have found a way to get me.'

461

'You're talking now,' Paula pointed out.

'Yes. But you're going to catch him and keep him away from me,' Diane said, completely calm for the first time in their interview.

'So where is he? Where are we going to find him?'

'I don't know. He hasn't spent the night at home since the first murder.'

'You told my colleague he was in Malta.'

Diane looked at her lawyer. 'I was afraid,' she said.

'You heard my client,' Scott said. 'She has been in fear of her life. Her actions have been the product of duress.'

'Duress isn't a defence to murder,' Paula said.

'And so far, nobody is suggesting my client has committed murder or attempted murder or treason, which are the only exceptions to the defence of duress,' Scott retorted, the steel of her tones matching her expression.

'I want to back up a little,' Paula said, looking directly at Diane, who had been apparently ignoring their exchange. 'How did Warren find out the names of the children he'd fathered?'

Diane couldn't hold Paula's stare. She picked at the edge of the table with her thumbnail and watched her hand intently. 'The HFEA employ a data security firm to hold their back-ups. We're a small community. Everybody knows everybody else. Warren found out who does the HFEA and basically bribed them. He said we'd do the back-up and hand it over to them and we'd pay them the same as the HFEA. So they'd get double their money for no work.'

'And they didn't wonder why you wanted to get your hands on the data? They weren't worried about compromising their security?'

'It's not compromising your security when you're dealing with one of your own.'

Paula thought that was bullshit and made a note to come back to it another time. 'So Warren went into the HFEA and backed up their database?'

She chewed the skin round her thumbnail. 'It was me. He thought they'd be less suspicious of a woman.'

'So you helped yourself to the data that would identify who got Warren's sperm?'

'I didn't have any choice,' she said, stubborn now.

'We all have a choice,' Paula said. 'You chose not to exercise yours and four children are dead.'

'Five,' Diane said. 'You think I don't know that?' Scott leaned over and whispered something in Diane's ear. She nodded.

'Did you know what Warren intended when you stole that data?' Paula asked.

'I wasn't thinking straight about anything at that point. I was half mad with grief.'

'We need to find Warren, Diane. Frankly, at this point you need to be thinking about yourself. Under the principle of joint enterprise, which I'm sure Ms Scott will be happy to explain to you, you're looking at four murder charges. I can't make any promises because we don't have the power to do deals like they do on the telly. But if you help us now, we'll help you down the line. Where is he, Diane?'

She blinked back more tears. 'I don't know. I swear to God. We've been together for seven years and he's never gone off anywhere like this. He's only ever away when it's business, and then I know what hotel he's in. He's never hidden from me before.'

'What was the plan tonight? Was he supposed to come over to kill Ewan?'

'He should have been there before I picked Ewan up. He told me he'd be back in plenty of time. When it came time to collect Ewan, I didn't know whether to go or not. But I was scared of what he'd do if I screwed up. So I went and got him.' She almost smiled. Paula detected triumph. 'He won't show up now you lot are there.'

'He won't see us,' Paula said.

'That's what you think. He'll be able to watch everything you did this afternoon. He's got remote access to all the cameras. He'll have known as soon as you drove up to the gate. He knew all about the big black cop who came on Sunday even before I emailed him. Wherever he is, he's one step ahead of you.'

'You sound pleased about that,' Paula said.

'If that's what you think then there's something wrong with your hearing.'

It was the first sign of combative spirit Diane had shown and it intrigued Paula. 'What about family? Parents, siblings? Friends?'

'We kept ourselves to ourselves,' she said. 'He doesn't get on with his parents. He's not in touch with them.'

'You're not doing yourself any favours here, Diane,' Paula said. 'We've got your computers now. You said Warren was a master of the universe with computers. Well, I've got a colleague who's even better than that. She'll be all over your contacts book by now.'

'I don't think so,' Diane said. 'We're security specialists. If she tries to get in, the data will all rewrite itself as gobbledygook.'

Paula chuckled. 'I wouldn't bet on that.' She pushed her chair back. 'If you're not in the mood to be helpful, I don't want to waste my time. We've got you bang to rights on abduction, false imprisonment and attempted murder.'

'Then charge my client or release her. You've got nothing. The boy went with her willingly. He passed out. My client cannot be held responsible for whatever her partner left lying around on their kitchen table.' Scott was working up a head of indignation but Paula cut her off.

'Tell it to the magistrates tomorrow morning. I'm done for now. We will have further questions later, so it would be helpful if you could keep yourself available, Ms Scott.'

CHAPTER 41

Tony took his hands out of his pockets and folded his arms. 'She's good. She's very good. She's only lying when she has to, so you don't really notice the lies. She doesn't have a tell either.'

He swung round as Paula walked in. She leaned against the wall, looking exhausted. 'She's a tough cookie,' she said.

'Well spotted,' Tony said. 'She's the best kind of liar. One of those who convinces themselves they're telling the truth.'

'What did you make of her?' Carol asked Paula.

'At first, I was completely with her. I bought it all. I thought she'd truly been terrorised. Then there was one moment – I think it was when I asked the question that made it seem like we didn't know that Warren was the father of the victims. Her reaction was so nakedly genuine that it reset the benchmark and I realised she wasn't nearly as candid as she wants us to think.' Paula pushed her hair back from her forehead. 'I got nothing from her. Nothing worth a damn.'

'I wouldn't say that,' Tony said. 'We know a lot more than we did before. The picture's starting to become clearer.'

'But we've got to find Warren,' Carol said. 'I've got Stacey covering his credit card, all his known email addresses, his driving licence and his passport. His photo is going out on the news tonight.'

'He'll be long gone,' Paula said.

'Tony thinks not. Tony thinks he's got a mission to finish, don't you?'

Lost in his own reverie, Tony frowned at her. 'What?'

'A mission. He's got a mission to complete.'

He scratched his head. 'That's what I said, yes. But you're not going to find him, Carol.' He grabbed his jacket from the chair where he'd tossed it. 'I need to go and talk to somebody.' He made for the door.

'Talk to who? About what?' Carol demanded. But she was talking to a closing door.

Stacey wasn't the only one who could take advantage of the information age. These days, once you'd got a warrant, things could move at amazing speed. Take the phone companies. As soon as they'd returned to the MIT squad room, Kevin had been detailed to acquire phone records for DPS and Diane Patrick. He'd managed to track down a magistrate to sign the warrant within the hour, then he'd scanned it and served it electronically. The mobile and landline companies had been just as quick off the mark for once.

He was surprised by how little phone traffic there had been from the numbers and said as much to Stacey. 'Do you think she's been using a phone we don't know about? A throwaway?'

'Maybe,' Stacey said. 'But most people in the ICT community prefer to use email or IMing. You can encrypt it much more easily. Phones are hideously insecure.' And then she'd given him access to a bit of software that acted as a reverse directory. At the touch of a key, the names and addresses associated with the numbers spooled out on the screen before him.

He looked down the list and saw it was mainly companies. He suspected they were probably all DPS clients, but he'd have to work his way through them and make sure. There were a couple of calls to Carr's Garage. Kevin thought that was the cousin who took in DPS's parcels, but he made a note to check with Ambrose.

One number stood out from the crowd – the direct line for the county council's environmental disposal unit. Diane Patrick had called them on Thursday morning. The call had lasted for eight minutes. On impulse, Kevin promoted it to number one on his call list and dialled it. It led to an inevitable automatic menu. It took three levels of options before he got a human being. He introduced himself and said, 'I'm interested in a call made to your unit on Thursday morning. It might involve evidence in a murder inquiry.' He'd found over the years that the word 'murder' provoked remarkable briskness among bureaucrats.

'Murder?' the woman on the other end of the phone exclaimed. 'We wouldn't know anything about murder.'

'I'm sure you wouldn't.' Kevin adopted his most placatory manner. 'I need you to consult your records. I believe a murder suspect called you on Thursday and arranged for something to be picked up from their home. I need to know if I'm right and if so, what it was.'

'I don't know if I'm allowed to do that,' she said dubiously. 'It's the Data Protection Act, you see.' Kevin almost groaned. The Data Protection Act had become the knee-jerk shield of every jobsworth in the country. 'Besides,' she continued, 'how do I know you're a policeman?'

'Why don't I give you the details and you can consult your supervisor and then you can call me back either way at Bradfield Police HQ? I really don't want to have to waste time getting a warrant for this, but if your manager insists, I will. How does that sound to you?'

'I suppose,' she said reluctantly. Kevin gave her Diane Patrick's details and the main switchboard number and repeated his name and rank. As he replaced the phone, he made a bet with himself that, since it was already almost half past four, he wouldn't hear another word from the council till the morning. He might as well start on the private sector.

He was on his second call to a DPS client when Sam waved at him. 'I've got someone from environmental disposal for you,' he called. 'Something about a freezer?'

Kevin ended his call and picked up the other line. 'DS Matthews. Thanks for getting back to me.'

'This is James Meldrum, head of section at environmental disposal,' a precise voice told him. 'You spoke to one of my staff earlier.'

'That's right. About a phone call from Diane Patrick or DPS.'

'I've consulted my guidelines and I believe I can provide you with the information you requested.' He paused, as if for applause.

'Thank you. I appreciate that,' Kevin said, belatedly realising something was expected of him.

'A Diane Patrick asked us to collect a chest freezer from her premises. We did so yesterday morning.'

'A chest freezer?' Kevin felt a burst of excitement. 'Was it empty?'

'If it had not been, our operatives would not have uplifted it.'

'Do you know where it is now?'

'We have a dedicated area for pre-disposal storage of fridges and freezers. We are obliged to take special disposal precautions according to the law. So this item will have been taken there.' Meldrum clearly took pleasure in the detail of his work. Not to mention his grammar.

'And it will still be there? It won't have been disposed of?'

'Regrettably, we do have something of a backlog in terms of actual disposal. So yes, it will be there. Along with many others, it should be said.'

'Can you identify which one came from Diane Patrick's house?' Kevin said, crossing his fingers.

'Not me personally, you understand. But it may be that

the operatives who removed it will be able to state with some certainty which appliance originated with Ms Patrick.'

'Will they still be at work, these operatives?'

Meldrum tittered. There was, Kevin thought, no other word for it. 'Good heavens, no. Not at this time of night. They begin work at seven in the morning. If you can be at our depot then, I'm sure they will be delighted to oblige you.'

Kevin wrote down the directions to the depot and the names of the 'operatives' he needed to speak to. He thanked Meldrum, then leaned back in his chair, a big grin on his freckled face.

'You look like the cat that got the canary,' Sam said.

'When a murderer gets rid of a chest freezer in the middle of their killing spree, I think it's safe to assume we're going to find some interesting evidence inside, don't you?'

Tony found Alvin Ambrose in the MIT squad room working his way down the client list DPS had posted on their website. 'I'm trying to find anybody who had any kind of social relationship with Warren Davy,' he explained when Tony asked what he was doing. 'So far, nothing.'

'I was wondering . . . Would you mind giving me a lift out to Davy's cousin's garage? What was his name again?'

Ambrose gave him an odd look. 'All right, all right. I should have submitted the report to you lot too. Bill Carr. That's his name.' He gave a rueful smile. 'Every unit has its little joke, right?'

Tony gave a weak smile. 'If you say so. Can you take me over there?'

Ambrose hauled his bulk upright. 'No problem. I don't think he knows where Davy is, though. I already spoke to him this afternoon.'

'I don't imagine he does know,' Tony said. 'That's not what I want to talk to him about, though. I'd go myself, but trust me, I'm the world's worst navigator. I'd be driving around South Manchester from now through till Sunday if I went by myself.'

'And you think I'll do better? I'm from Worcester, remember?'

'That still gives you a head start over me.'

As they drove, Tony got Ambrose talking about his life back in Worcester. What the West Mercia team was like. How he thought Worcester was a great little city, the perfect place to bring up kids. Small enough to know what was going on, big enough not to be claustrophobic. It passed the time, and he didn't need to think about what he was going to talk to Bill Carr about. He already knew that.

Ambrose turned into the cul-de-sac and pointed out the garage. It looked as if they'd just made it in time; Bill Carr had his back to them, pulling down the heavy door shutter. 'Don't take this the wrong way, Alvin, but I'll do this better on my own,' Tony said, getting out of the car and trotting down to catch Carr before he left.

'Bill?' Tony called.

Carr turned round and shook his head. 'Too late, mate. I'm done for the day.'

'No, it's OK, it's not work.' Tony stuck his hand out.

'I'm Tony Hill. I'm with Bradfield Police. I wondered if we could have a little chat?'

'Is this about that business with Warren's car the other day? Only, I told the other guy. I'm just helping a cousin out. I don't have nothing to do with their business or anything.' His eyes were casting about, looking for an escape beyond Tony. He turned up the collar of his denim jacket and shrugged his hands into the pockets of his jeans. Defensive as a guilty child.

'It's all right, I just want to have a bit of a chat about Warren and Diane,' Tony said, his voice warm and confiding. 'Maybe I could buy you a pint?'

'He's in trouble, isn't he? Our Warren?' Carr looked apprehensive but not surprised.

'I won't lie to you. It's looking that way.'

He puffed out his cheeks and expelled the air. 'He's been a different bloke lately. Like there was something bearing down on him. I just thought it was business, you know? There's a lot of folk on the skids these days. But he wouldn't have talked to me about it. We weren't close.'

'Come and have a pint anyway,' Tony said gently. 'Where's good round here?'

The two men walked in silence to a corner pub that had once been a working men's hostelry but had now been turned into a *Guardian* reader's haven. Tony imagined it had been gutted by a brewery in the seventies then recently restored to a faux version of its original scrubbed pine floors and uncomfortable bentwood chairs. 'Full of bloody students later, but it's all right this time of day,' Carr said as they leaned on the bar and sipped decent pints of some microbrewery bitter with a ridiculous name.

'Have they been together a while, Diane and Warren?'
he asked.

Carr thought for a moment, the tip of his tongue peeking from the corner of his mouth. 'Must be getting on for six or seven years now. They knew each other before, it was one of them slow-burn things, you know?'

Tony knew all about slow burns and smouldering fires. And how sometimes they never burst into flames. 'It must have helped, having the business in common,' was all he said.

'I don't think our Warren could have had a relationship with someone who wasn't knee-deep in computers. It was all he could ever talk about. He got his first computer when he was still at primary school and he never looked back.' He swallowed some beer and wiped the froth from his top lip with the back of his hand. 'I reckon he got the brains and I got the looks.'

'Did they get on all right, Diane and Warren?'

'Seemed to. Like I said, I didn't have a lot to do with them socially. We didn't have much in common, you know? Warren didn't even like the footie.' Carr sounded as if that were clinically abnormal.

'I'm a Bradfield Vic man myself,' Tony said. That led them into a lengthy diversion which included giving Manchester United, Chelsea, the Arsenal and Liverpool a good slagging. And by the end of it, Tony had turned Carr into a mate. As they supped their second pint, he said, 'They didn't have any kids, though.'

'You got kids?'

Tony shook his head.

'I've got two, with my ex. I see them every other

weekend. I miss them, you know? But there's no denying life's simpler without having to deal with them twenty-four seven. Warren could never have hacked it. He needed his space and that's one thing you don't get with kids.'

'Too many people have kids and then act like it's a big shock that you've actually got to interact with them.'

'Exactly,' Carr said, tapping his finger on the bar to emphasise the point. 'Warren was smart enough to realise that wasn't for him. He made bloody sure of it an' all.'

'How do you mean?' Tony's antennae were on full alert.

'He had a vasectomy, back when he was a student. We saw more of each other in those days. He always had a right clear idea about what he wanted his life to be, did Warren. He knew he was smart and he knew he had good genes. But because he knew he'd be a crap parent, he hit on the idea of being a sperm donor. He filled their little plastic cup and took the money and then he went and got himself snipped. What was it he said at the time? I remember it was right clever ... "Posterity without responsibility." That was it.'

'And he never regretted it?'

'Not as far as I know. He never dared tell Diane, though. She was mad for a baby, especially this last three or four years. Warren said she was doing his head in with it. On and on. The only thing that would do. And because he hadn't told her at the start about having the snip, it got so he couldn't admit to it. Especially since he'd told her right early on that he'd been a sperm donor. It was laughable, really. There they were, trotting off to the fertility clinic and he wasn't letting on about his vasectomy. In the end she tried using donor sperm, but it was too late by then. She's half a dozen years older than him, so she was already the wrong side of forty and her eggs were well and truly fried.'

'And she never found out?' Tony asked casually.

'Are you kidding? If she'd have found that out, she'd have fucking killed him.'

Tony stared into his pint. 'That's exactly what I was thinking,' he said.

CHAPTER 42

Carol stared at Tony, clearly astonished. 'A vasectomy? Are you serious?'

'As serious as I've ever been. Warren Davy had a vasectomy when he was in his early twenties.' He'd found Carol in the observation room with Paula, talking over strategies for the next interview with Diane Patrick.

'So how did she manage to have his child last year?' Paula asked.

'She didn't,' Tony said. 'It's the big fat lie that underpins all her other lies. Take that away and the whole story falls apart. No grounds to fear for her life. So why is she helping Warren to kill his children?' He looked eagerly at them both, flapping his hands upwards like a teacher encouraging an answer from his pupils.

The two women exchanged perplexed looks. 'She's not?' Paula ventured.

'Right answer,' Tony said.

'But she picked up Ewan McAlpine and drugged him,' Paula said. 'There's no getting away from that.'

Tony play-acted disappointment. 'Right answer, wrong reasoning. She's not helping Warren. She's doing it off her own bat.' He cocked his head and looked up at the corner of the ceiling. 'She probably killed Warren first, come to think of it.'

'You're going to have to back up a bit here,' Carol said. 'I'm struggling with this.'

'It's horrible, but simple. Her biological clock started ticking. She wants a baby, but not any old baby. She'd become obsessed with having Warren's baby. I mean, really obsessed. The kind of obsessed that wants to ram cars with a "baby on board" decal because they've got what she doesn't. She knows Warren was once capable of fathering children because he was a sperm donor, so he's got to be a prime candidate. They keep trying to have a baby, but the years are drifting by and it's not working. So they go to the fertility clinic and sooner or later they realise Warren's firing blanks. They try donor sperm, but that's not really what she wants. She wants Warren's baby. But they've left it too late, and her eggs are past their sell-by. She's devastated. Probably suicidal. With me so far?'

'I think I'm just about managing to keep up,' Carol said sarcastically.

'Now we get to the bit I'm not sure about. Somehow, Diane discovered Warren's dirty little secret – that after he'd done the sperm donor thing, he had the snip.'

'Maybe she wondered how he lost his fertility. Or maybe she just can't help herself. She's the queen of hacking, isn't she? All sorts of medical records are online now,' Paula said. 'Maybe she just likes to be the person who knows everything about everybody else in the room.'

'Maybe. The key thing is that somehow she does find out. And that uproots her anchor to reality. She completely flips out. This man that she loves so much she wanted to have his baby and nobody else's has betrayed her. Not only can he not give her a baby, he's effectively stopped her having a child by someone else because they spent so long trying. Trying pointlessly. And to add insult to injury, he's already fathered God knows how many little bastards.' Tony was almost shouting now. 'None of them deserve to live. Not that lying bastard Warren, not his brood of bastards.'

Carol clapped her hands in a mild mockery of applause. 'Lovely performance. And how do we prove any of it?'

Tony shrugged. 'Find Warren's body?'

'She's too good for that,' Carol said. 'If you're right, her long-term plan was probably to blame it all on Warren and either fake his suicide or pretend he'd gone underground. His body isn't going to be anywhere obvious.'

No one spoke for a couple of minutes while they contemplated their problem. Finally Paula said, 'You could always beat a confession out of her, chief.'

Carol managed a tired smile. 'This isn't *Life on Mars*, Paula. They don't like us doing that any more.'

Tony crossed the room and hugged Paula, who looked astonished. 'But she's right, Carol,' he said, stepping back. 'Not with fists but with words.'

'You're the only one who can do that,' Carol said. 'And

Diane Patrick's got Bronwen Scott. No way is she going to let you in the room.'

'She can't keep me out of your ear, though.'

Tony watched as Carol and Paula walked into the interview room. Bronwen Scott, who had been leaning over and talking to her client in a low voice, sat up straight. Carol sat down and slammed her file on the desk. 'When did you find out about Warren's vasectomy?' Carol demanded.

Diane Patrick's eyes widened.

'Beautiful,' Tony said into the mike. 'Hit her again.'

'Let me ask you again. When did you find out that Warren Davy had had a vasectomy?'

'I don't know what you're talking about.' Diane had opted for fearful and piteous. Tony didn't think that was going to work for long.

'Warren Davy had a vasectomy fifteen years ago. You do know what a vasectomy is, Diane?'

'Of course I do,' she said. 'But I don't believe you. I had his baby.'

Carol snorted. 'Oh yes. The mythical baby. It'll be interesting to see what your medical records say about that.'

'My client has already explained that Mr Davy kept her away from medical intervention when she was pregnant,' Scott interrupted. 'I see no need to go over this again.'

'Tell her there was no baby,' Tony said. 'Tell her, not ask her.'

'There was no baby. There couldn't have been a baby because Warren Davy had a vasectomy when he was twenty-one.'

'You're badgering my client,' Scott said. 'Ask the question and move on.'

'Ask her how,' Tony said in Carol's ear.

'How did you have a baby with Warren after he'd had the snip?'

'People do. I've read about it. People do have babies after that,' Diane said. 'If you're right, which I don't believe, that's what must have happened.'

'Ignore her answer, Carol. Move on to how she couldn't have a baby, how she'll never have a baby.'

'The truth is, you never had a baby with Warren. You've never had a baby. You can't have a baby now. Face it, Diane. You'll never have a baby. And if you can't have Warren's baby, nobody else is going to, either, are they?' Carol's tone was relentless, her eyes cold and unmoving. When Bronwen Scott spoke, Carol didn't even look at her.

'You're bullying my client, Detective Chief Inspector Jordan. I insist that you ask a question,' Scott said.

'I just did,' Carol said. 'I'll rephrase it, though. You don't want anyone else to have Warren's child, do you, Diane?'

'Those children are nothing to do with me,' Diane said in a low voice.

'Remind her that she'll never have his child,' Tony said. 'Because he didn't love her enough.'

'They're the children you'll never have. The children you dreamed of. The children he gave to other women. But not to you. Do you think he kept the truth from you because he didn't really love you?'

'He loved me,' Diane said. Tony thought he could see the beginnings of anger in her face.

481

'He didn't love you enough to tell you the truth. He didn't love you enough to have the vasectomy reversed. He didn't want to have children with you, did he? When it came to carrying his child, he thought a total stranger was a better bet than you, didn't he?'

'Inspector, if you don't stop this constant badgering, I am going to demand we end this interview now,' Scott interrupted, putting a hand on Diane's arm to shut her up.

Tony was momentarily distracted by Kevin, who stuck his head round the door. 'I think Carol might be able to use something I just dug up.'

'What's that?' Tony was trying to focus on two things at once.

'The council picked up a chest freezer for disposal from DPS yesterday. We'll have our hands on it tomorrow morning first thing.'

Tony grinned. 'You're a star, Kevin. Thanks.' He tuned back in to what was happening in the interview room. Carol and Scott were still skirmishing. He didn't think he'd missed much. He waited for a gap in the action then passed Kevin's information on to Carol.

Her smile was vicious. 'You want questions, Bronwen? OK. Let's have some questions. I'd like to ask your client why she asked the council to pick up a chest freezer from her place yesterday.'

This time, the shock on Diane Patrick's face was easy to read. 'Because . . . because it was broken. It doesn't work.'

'We're going to have our entire team of forensic technicians crawling over every square inch of that freezer,' Carol said. 'Will we find traces of Warren's blood?'

'I've told you.' Diane's voice was shrill now. 'I don't know where Warren is.'

'When did you kill him, Diane?'

'I don't know what you're talking about. Tell her, Ms Scott. I don't know where Warren is and I didn't kill him. I love him.'

'Ask her if she noticed how the kids look like Warren. What hers would have looked like,' Tony said.

'Did you notice how the kids all looked like Warren?'

'Of course they did. They were his children. His bad seeds, that's what he called them. He's the one who said they had to die, not me.' She was shouting now, in spite of Scott's hand on her shoulder.

'Did they make you wonder how your child would have looked? If he'd let you have his child?'

Scott pushed back her chair. 'That's it. I've had enough of this. My client is a victim of this evil man. Your bullying tactics are entirely unacceptable. When you have some evidence, come and talk to us.'

'Remind her that she failed,' Tony said. 'She's the last of the line but he'll go on.'

Carol ignored her and stared at Diane Patrick. 'You've failed, haven't you? You only got four of them. The rest of them, they're out there. Taunting you. The children you could never have. They'll grow up, Warren's children. They'll carry his bloodline. But when you die, they'll draw a line. The bad seed ends with you. You and your barren womb.'

Diane's teeth drew back in a snarl and she threw herself across the table at Carol. But Bronwen Scott was fast, and she grabbed her client. 'It's OK, Diane. Take it easy. Don't let her get to you. They've got nothing, that's why she's trying to provoke you.'

The tension of the moment was broken by a knock on the door. Stacey came in and identified herself for the benefit of the tape. 'I need to talk to you for a moment, ma'am,' she said formally.

Carol suspended the tapes and followed Stacey into the hallway. Tony rushed out of the observation room to join them. 'What is it, Stacey?' Carol said.

'Kevin's been talking to DPS clients,' she said. 'He was checking the calls from DPS's phones, making sure they were client calls and not something more sinister. Anyway, Kevin thought while he was on that he'd check the last time they'd seen Warren Davy. And he made a note of all the times. When I realised what he'd done, I ran a check against the times when we know the killer was on Rig, chatting to his victims. And the places he was sending his messages from. And a clear pattern emerges. Warren has solid alibis for at least twenty of the online sessions. He couldn't have been stalking the victims. He was with clients in completely different locations.' She handed Carol a sheaf of paper. 'That's where Warren was. And that's where the messages were being sent from at the same time.'

Carol tipped her head back. 'Halle-fucking-lujah.'

'So much for breaking her with psychology,' Tony said wryly.

Carol patted his shoulder. 'We softened her up. Now for the sucker punch. I'm going to enjoy this.'

CHAPTER 43

Tony pulled his tie off as he came through the front door, tossing it over the banister. He walked straight through to the kitchen and poured himself a tumbler of water, drinking it straight down. He stood leaning on the sink, staring at nothing. He'd left Carol and her team drinking in the back room of their favourite Thai restaurant. He understood their need to release the fearsome pressure of a multiple murder inquiry, but he couldn't join in their celebration.

For him, there was nothing to celebrate in the final disintegration of Diane Patrick. That screaming, gibbering wreck had once been a competent, successful woman with a career and a relationship. A single obsession had taken control of her, obliterating everything else. And when she had finally understood not only that it couldn't happen but that it had been taken from her by the one person she truly loved, something inside her had become unhinged. For most people in that state, it would have been enough to have killed Warren Davy. And if that had been all, she might have found a measure of forgiveness in the system, the balance of her mind having been well and truly disturbed by the appalling betrayal of her lover.

But Diane Patrick's obsession had been so overwhelming, so deep-seated a need that she had to obliterate him utterly. And that meant destroying the children who had been created with his genes. It was utterly unreasonable yet entirely comprehensible. But the system didn't have room to accommodate the complexities of human fixations, not when they included murdered children. Diane Patrick would never see freedom again. She'd end up somewhere like Bradfield Moor, if she was lucky, a maximum security prison if she wasn't.

It wasn't that he thought she should avoid some kind of retribution for her crimes. But he couldn't help feeling pity rather than hatred. He wondered how he would have coped with the hand she'd found herself looking at.

It didn't bear thinking about.

Tony pulled off his jacket and dumped it on the back of a kitchen chair. He took a beer from the fridge and sat down at the table. The downlighters under the kitchen cabinets glinted on something half-hidden in the drift of paper on the table. Unthinking, he reached for it and found the digital recorder Arthur had left for him. He stared at it long and hard. This whole case had been about fathers and children, he reminded himself. And at the heart of it had been ignorance.

There was nothing clever about avoiding knowledge. He'd known that all along. He just hadn't been ready for it. He picked up his beer and went through to his study, where there were comfortable padded headphones. Tony plugged them in to the tiny recorder and settled down in his favourite armchair. The other chair was still sitting opposite, left from his exercise with the mind of the killer the other night. He imagined Arthur sitting there, and pressed play.

'Hello, Tony. This is Arthur. Or Eddie, as I used to be known back when I was walking out with your mother in Halifax,' he began. His voice was light and musical, still threaded through with the Yorkshire accent of his youth. 'Thank you for being willing to listen to what I have to say.

'There's nothing I can say or do that will make up for not being part of your life. To begin with, I didn't know you existed. When I left Halifax, I cut off all ties. I'll explain why in a bit. So I knew nothing about your birth. Fourteen years later, I was on holiday in Rhodes when by sheer chance I ran into a couple who used to work in my factory in Halifax. Of course, they knew me straight away. There was no point in trying to deny who I was. They insisted on buying me a drink and bringing me up to date with all my old employees.

'They'd moved to Sheffield with the new company, but they had family back in Halifax so they'd kept in touch with things back there too. They remembered I'd been engaged to Vanessa, and they talked about what a polite young lad her boy had turned into. Not like most teenagers, they remarked. It didn't take much working out to realise that if Vanessa's lad was already a teenager, there was a good chance you were mine.

'But I've never been one to jump to conclusions. And so I didn't allow myself to hope, not really. When I got back from my holiday, I hired a private investigator to find out what he could about you. He tracked down your birth certificate and he took some photographs of you. The dates were right, and you looked a lot like I did at your age. I was amazed. I was overjoyed. There was no doubt in my mind that you were my son.' Arthur's voice trembled and Tony pressed pause. His eyes were damp and he could hardly swallow. He forced a mouthful of beer down and carried on listening.

'Then it dawned on me that there was nothing I could do about it. Vanessa had clearly decided we weren't to know about each other. I was afraid if I tried to come into your life, she would somehow take it out on you. And I knew she was capable of it.' He cleared his throat. 'Also, I was afraid of the effect it might have on you. You were doing well at school and I didn't want to interfere with that. Fourteen's an awkward age. You might not have welcomed me in your life. You'd have had good reason to be angry with the man who had abandoned you to Vanessa's care. So I kept my distance. I like to think it was for your sake, but probably some of it was to do with me being cowardly. And I'll explain why I had my reasons for that too.

'This is the hard bit for me. What I'm going to tell you, you might think I'm making it up. You might think I'm off my head. But this is the truth. I swear. You can believe it or not, it's your choice. You know your mother at least as well as I did. You can judge whether you think my story has the ring of truth or not.

'Back then, I was a bright young man who was going places. I've always had a flair for invention. Most of the ideas go nowhere, but a few of them have turned out well. My first company was successful because I'd come up with a unique process for electroplating precision surgical instruments. I was doing well, and there were a couple of big companies prepared to pay a lot of money for my patent. I was pretty pleased with myself. I knew I was on the road to becoming rich and successful, which was quite something for a working-class lad from Sowerby Bridge.

'I was walking out with your mother at the time. I was besotted with Vanessa. I'd never met a woman like her. She had star quality. She made every other lass in Halifax look colourless. I knew she was tough. Your grandmother was hard as nails and she'd brought Vanessa up in her own likeness. But when we got serious about each other, she seemed to soften. She was grand company. And she was beautiful.' His voice was passionate now, rich and strong. Tony had seen enough of his mother's charm with others to understand how she could have wrapped Arthur round her little finger.

'When I asked her to marry me, there was part of me was convinced she'd turn me down flat. But she accepted. I was on cloud nine. We talked about a spring wedding and Vanessa suggested we make wills in each other's favour. She was working in a solicitor's office at the time, so she could get it done for free. And of course, she would have been giving up work when we got wed, so it made sense to do it while we could still get it for free.' He gave a wry little chuckle. 'You'll be thinking I'm a typical

Yorkshireman. Owt for nowt, eh? Well, the will might have come for free, but there's other ways that it nearly cost me very dear indeed.

'We did the wills, both leaving everything to each other. Round about this time, a company from Sheffield came after me. They wanted to buy the business outright, and my patent too. They were offering a lot of cash plus a lifetime royalty on the process. It would have been a good deal for a man who didn't have ambitions to go a lot further. But I did. I had all sorts of dreams and hopes for the future and they included my business and my workforce. Vanessa thought I was crazy. She thought I should sell up and live high on the hog on the proceeds. "But what will we do when the money runs out?" I wanted to know. She said she knew me, I'd come up with some other clever idea and we'd do the same thing all over again. But I wasn't convinced. I'd read about too many other inventors who never come up with a second idea that works.

'Now, I reckon you probably know what your mother's like when she gets an idea in her head. It's like arguing with a steamroller. But I dug my heels in. It was my business and I wasn't going to give in to her. I told myself I had to stand firm or I'd spend the whole of my life giving in to what she wanted. So there we were, stalemate. Or so I thought.

'We were walking home one night through Savile Park. It was dark, it was late and there wasn't another living soul in sight. Vanessa was on at me again about selling. I remember saying, "Over my dead body," and the next thing I knew was this terrible searing pain in my chest. It was like everything went into slow motion. Vanessa was standing in front of me, and there was a knife in her hand, covered in blood. I looked down and my shirt front had a big red patch on it. I could feel myself falling and I swear I heard her say, "You said it, Eddie."

'The next thing I knew, I was in hospital, with the doctor saying it was a miracle I was alive. And there was Vanessa, holding my hand and smiling sweetly. I thought I was losing my mind. But when the doctor left us alone, she said, "I told the police we were mugged. If you try and tell them anything different, they'll think you're mad."

'I was supposed to die, you see. So she could have her way. But I didn't die. I ran away. After I recovered, I sold up and cleared out. I spent a year studying metallurgy in Canada, then I came back and settled in Worcester. It seemed like a nice place and I knew nobody who had any connections there. I never took up with anybody else, not seriously. Vanessa spoiled me for anything like that. It's hard to let yourself fall in love when the last person you loved tried to kill you.

'I made a good life for myself, though. And then I found out about you. Once I knew about you, I kept a discreet eye on you. I've watched your career with pride. I know I can't claim any of the credit, but I am proud of how you've turned out. I'd have liked to see you settled with a family of your own, but it's not too late. I'm told you're close to that detective you work with, Carol Jordan. If she's the one, don't let her go past you.

'Anyway. I've said what I wanted to. And I'm still sorry that I was never a father to you. I hope you understand now, even if you don't feel inclined to forgive me. And I hope you enjoy spending the money I've left you. Good luck with your life, son.' Then silence. The last word was the killer, of course.

Tony pulled the headphones from his ears and bit his lip. A weight of sorrow pressed down on him, making his chest and throat ache. He wasn't sure what was worse – hearing what he'd just heard, or not doubting its reliability. To hear such a shocking revelation about your mother would drive most men into a frenzy of rage. It wouldn't occur to them to believe it. Their first response would be that this was a vile fantasy. Because most men didn't have a mother like Vanessa.

For as long as he could remember, Tony had felt like the man Diane Patrick had described. The bad seed. The man who knew he carried the potential for evil inside him. One of the reasons he did what he did was his abiding conviction that he could so easily have become the sort of person he spent his life tracking down then trying to help. His empathy had to come from somewhere, and he had always believed it was rooted in his own potential for the road less travelled by.

And of course, Vanessa had never missed an opportunity to make him feel worthless. He had enough insight to understand how much she had undermined him, but even his professional training didn't allow him to blame upbringing and circumstances for everything. There had to be a genetic component too. A balance of nature and nurture, conditioning and circumstance. And now he knew just how much of the bad seed was in him.

But for the first time, he also knew that his own fantasy of his father was false. He'd always thought a man who could walk out on his child must have a fatal flaw. Tony had believed he was the product of two profoundly fucked-up people, a legacy that offered him little potential to rise above it in emotional terms. Now he had to reset his own expectations of himself. Because half of what had made him had been a decent man who knew how much he'd let him down. And who had been proud of him.

It was going to be a big adjustment. And even as he thought this, Tony realised that change needed its own environment. Somewhere in his life, he was going to have to find an outward symbol of this transformation.

CHAPTER 44

Carol woke much earlier than she had planned. These days, too much alcohol had that effect. When she'd been younger, going to bed pissed had been a guarantee of eight hours of unconsciousness. These days, if she'd had too much to drink, she slept fitfully and not for nearly long enough. Another reason to follow Tony's advice and cut it right back, she reminded herself. Her head felt muzzy and battered, her stomach bruised and tender. She vaguely remembered throwing up when she'd finally got back in the small hours.

But it had been worth it. It had been a night of great celebration for the team. Murders solved, lives saved, and Bronwen Scott stiffed. The icing on the cake had been the phone call Sam had taken from Brian Carson, the concierge of the Bayview Caravan Park. He'd been surprised to recognise the photograph of Nigel Barnes on the local TV news. He remembered him turning up at the caravan park one night with a puncture. Carson had insisted on helping him change his tyre, in spite of the man's insistence that he'd be fine. He particularly remembered the bale of clear polythene, the pack of black bin bags and rolls of duct tape in the back of the Volvo estate, because they'd had to move them to get at the spare tyre.

A woman couldn't ask for much more, really. Carol lay on her back and stretched like a starfish. There was a soft thud and then a smoochy tickle in her ear. 'Nelson,' she said affectionately, scratching her cat behind the ear. He purred and head-butted her. 'OK,' she grumbled. 'I'll feed you.'

Her two mobiles, personal and work, were lying on the worktop above the cutlery drawer. As she took out a spoon, she noticed there was a message on her own phone: Brkfst? Txt me whn u get ths. Im up. Tx

She checked the clock. She'd been right first time, it was only quarter past six. It wasn't like Tony to be up and about at this hour. Carol hadn't noticed him leave the restaurant but she knew it had been pretty early in the impromptu party. She'd looked for him around nine, when they'd been ordering some food. But he'd been nowhere to be seen. She'd asked Paula, the person most likely to notice his departure, but she'd been too wrapped up in Elinor Blessing. Which was a good thing, naturally, but inconvenient right then.

She dished up Nelson's food and texted back: Ur place or café?

Mine. I can haz sausages and eggs.

haf hour. She put the kettle on and headed for the shower.

Thirty-five minutes later, showered, dressed, Nurofen-ed and marginally caffeinated, she climbed the stairs from her basement flat to his house. The connecting door was already unlocked and she found him in the kitchen, pulling a tray of sausages from the oven and inspecting them suspiciously. 'I think they need another five minutes,' he said. 'Which is just long enough to do the eggs.' He waved at the coffee machine. 'That's ready to roll, do you want to help yourself?'

She did. While he whisked the eggs in the pan, she made lattes for them both and carried them to the table. 'I can't believe you're up at this time, and with the makings of a proper breakfast,' she added, noticing the plate of toasted crumpets dripping with butter.

'I've been up all night,' he said. 'I went for a walk and the supermarket was open and I needed to talk to you, so I thought, breakfast.'

Carol pounced on the key part of his reply. 'You need to talk to me? Don't tell me you think there's a problem with Diane Patrick?'

'No, no, nothing like that,' he said impatiently, plating the eggs and getting the sausages out. He put a plate of food in front of her with a flourish. Carol tried not to shudder. 'There you go. Free-range eggs and local sausages.'

'I can't remember the last time you cooked for me,' she said, gingerly trying the eggs. They were better than she expected.

'No,' he said, considering. 'Me neither.' He wolfed down a sausage and half his eggs. 'This is good,' he said, sounding surprised. 'I should do this more often.'

Carol was making slow but steady progress. 'So what do you need to talk to me about?'

'You have to listen to something. But let's finish eating first.'

'This is very intriguing,' she said.

'It'll blow your socks off,' he said, suddenly sombre. 'And not in a good way.'

Carol forced the rest of her food down and pushed her plate away. 'I'm done,' she said. 'Wedged.'

'Well done for a woman who walked in gripped by the hangover from the outskirts of hell,' Tony said drily, taking the plates away. He came back with the recorder and the headphones. 'This is what you need to listen to.'

'What is it?'

'It doesn't need an explanation,' he said, putting the cans on her ears and pressing play.

As it dawned on her what she was listening to, Carol's jaw dropped. 'Oh. My. God,' she breathed. Then looking at him with tears in her eyes, 'Oh, Tony . . .' And then, 'Unbe-fucking-lieveable. Jesus!' Tony said nothing, just sat impassively watching her reactions.

When she reached the end, she pulled the headphones off and reached for his hand. 'No wonder you were up all night,' she said. 'Talk about bombshells.'

'We both said we didn't trust Vanessa's version. That there must be a hidden agenda. Turns out we were right.' His voice was dull and hard.

'Yeah, but I never expected to be right like this,' Carol said. 'What are you going to do? Are you going to confront her with it?'

He sighed. 'I don't see the point. She'll just deny it. It won't have any effect on how she lives her life.'

'You can't just let her get away with it,' Carol protested. What he was suggesting ran counter to all her convictions about the importance of justice.

'She's got away with it. Nothing can change that now. Carol, I never want to see her again. All I want to do is to cut her out of my life the way she cut Arthur out of mine.'

'I don't know how you can be so calm about this,' Carol said.

'I've had all night to think about it,' he said. 'This case, it's not been my finest hour. The only real lead that came from the profiling process was where to look. And that was Fiona Cameron's work, not mine.'

'You worked out Warren was dead. And you knew to ask the questions that uncovered the vasectomy,' she protested.

'You'd have got there in the end. But I've had to face the fact that I'm maybe not as good at this as I like to think. The last couple of weeks have made me realise I need to completely reconsider who I am. I've made choices about my life based on incomplete data. I need a total rethink, Carol.'

There was an absolute quality about his seriousness that she knew she had no power to argue against. She fell back on the tactics she knew best. The ones that had made her such a formidable copper. When in doubt, attack. 'What does that mean, Tony? You sound like a politician. All words and nothing concrete.'

He gave a sad little smile. 'I can do concrete, Carol. I just wanted to explain myself first. I'm planning on handing in my notice at Bradfield Moor. I'm planning on selling the narrowboat because I don't like it. And I'm planning on moving into Arthur's house in Worcester because it's the only place I've ever slept that felt like home. Beyond that, I don't know.'

She understood all the words, but taken together they made no sense. It was as if she'd gone to bed in one world and woken in another. 'You're going to live in Worcester? In *Worcester*? You spent one night there and now you're going to move there? Have you lost your mind?'

He shook his head, misery on his face. 'I knew you'd be like this. I've not lost my mind, no. I'm just trying to figure out how I move forward in my life knowing the things I know now about where I came from. So much of what I thought I knew isn't the case. And I need to work out where that leaves me.'

She wanted to scream, 'What about me?' Not screaming it was a physical effort. She gripped the edge of the table and forced her lips tightly together.

'It's OK, Carol. You can say it. "What about me?" That's what you want to say, isn't it?'

'And that's why I want to say it,' she said, dismayed that she sounded so choked. 'Because you know without me telling you.'

'I can't make your choices for you,' he said. 'It's up to you. You've won this round against Blake, but he's not leaving any time soon. You've met Alvin Ambrose, you've spoken to Stuart Patterson. They're decent men who care about what they're doing. If you wanted a change, West Mercia would probably bite your hand off.' He made a small gesture with his hands, as if to suggest an offer.

Carol knew that for him to ask her to come with him was probably an impossibility. He'd never believed he deserved her. But she needed more than this. 'Why should I, Tony? What's in it for me?' She challenged him with the hundred-yard cop's stare.

He looked away. 'It's a big house, Carol. There's plenty of room for two.'

'Room for two like there's room for two here? Or a different kind of room for two?' She waited, watching for something in his face to give her hope.

Eventually Tony picked up the chrome recorder and weighed it in his hand. 'This morning,' he said slowly, 'anything seems possible.'

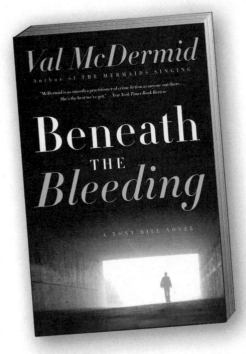

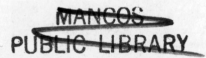